Acclaim for Suzanne Adair

Deadly Occupation
"Thick with intrigue and subplots to keep readers guessing."
—Caroline Clemmons, author of the "Kincaids" series

Regulated for Murder
"Best of 2011" from Suspense Magazine:

"This is mystery writing at its best."
—Great Historicals

A Hostage to Heritage
winner of the Indie Book of the Day Award:

"Suzanne Adair is on top of her game with this one."
—Jim Chambers, Amazon Hall of Fame Top 10 Reviewer

Books by Suzanne Adair

Michael Stoddard American Revolution Mysteries
Deadly Occupation
Regulated for Murder
A Hostage to Heritage
Killer Debt

Mysteries of the American Revolution
Paper Woman
The Blacksmith's Daughter
Camp Follower

Regulated for Murder

Suzanne Adair

A Michael Stoddard American Revolution Mystery

Acknowledgements

I receive help from some wonderful and unique people while conducting research for novels and editing my manuscripts. Here are a few who assisted me with *Regulated for Murder*:

The 33rd Light Company of Foot, especially Ernie and Linda Stewart

Mary Buckham

Dr. Jerry C. Cashion

Mike Everette

Almuth Heuner

Nolin and Neil Jones

Rhonda Lane

Tom Magnuson

Kris Neri

Susan Schreyer

Virginia Smith

Dr. Carole W. Troxler

John Truelove

Special thanks to Ava Barlow for cover photography; to Ava Barlow and Jenny Toney Quinlan for cover design; and to Karen Lowe for interior design.

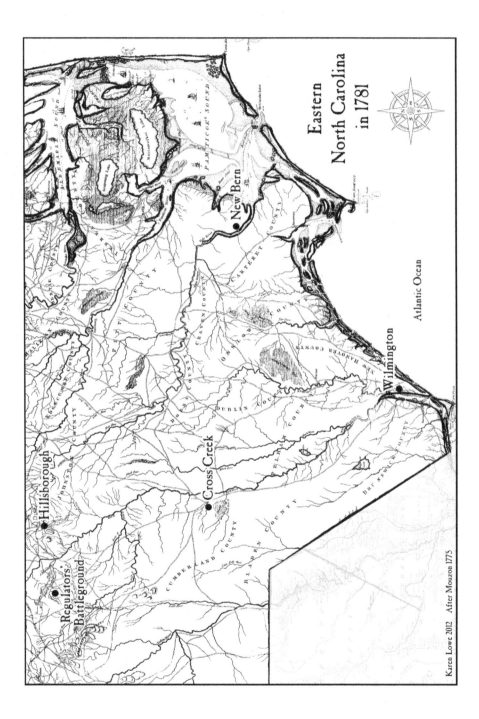

Eastern
North Carolina
in 1781

Atlantic Ocean

New Bern

Wilmington

Cross Creek

Hillsborough

Regulators'
Battleground

Karen Lowe 2012   After Mouzon 1775

Chapter One

A MESSAGE SCRIPTED on paper and tacked to the padlocked front door of the office on Second Street explained how the patriot had come to miss his own arrest:

Office closed due to Family Emergency.

Family emergency? Horse shit! Lieutenant Michael Stoddard hammered the door several times with his fist. No one answered. He moved to the nearest window and shoved the sash.

Two privates from the Eighty-Second Regiment on the porch with him pushed the other window sash. It was also latched from within. One man squinted at the note. "What does it say, sir?"

Michael peered between gaps in curtains. Nothing moved in the office. Breath hissed from him. "It says that the macaroni who conducted business here sold two clients the same piece of property and skipped town with their money under pretense of family emergency."

"A lout like that wants arresting." The other soldier's grin revealed a chipped front tooth.

"Indeed. Wait here, both of you." Michael pivoted. His boot heels tapped down the steps.

Afternoon overcast the hue of a saber blade released icy sprinkle on him. He ignored it. Ignored Wilmington's ubiquitous reek of fish, wood smoke, and tar, too, and trotted through the side yard. At the rear of the wooden building, two additional soldiers came to attention at the sight of him. The red wool of their uniform coats blazed like beacons in the winter-drab of the back yard.

He yanked on the back door and found it secured from the inside, rather than by padlock. The young privates had no luck opening a window. Michael looked inside, where curtains hadn't quite covered a pane, and confirmed the stillness of the building's interior.

A plume of white fog exited his mouth. He straightened. Ever since Horatio Bowater had grudgingly dropped assault charges against Michael and his assistant days earlier, Major Craig had bided his time and waited for the land agent to supply him with an excuse to take another rebel into custody. A disreputable business transaction presented the ideal pretext for arrest.

And when James Henry Craig ordered someone arrested, it had damn well better happen.

Michael squared his shoulders. By God, he'd nab that bugger, throw his dandy arse in the stockade, where the premium on real estate that past week had risen in direct proportion to the number of guests incarcerated.

Surely Bowater had left evidence in his office. Business records or a schedule. Without facing his men, Michael regarded the back door anew, attention drawn to the crack between door and jamb. "The men sent to Mr. Bowater's residence should be reporting shortly. However, I suspect our subject has departed town." He half-turned toward his soldiers. "Henshaw."

"Sir."

"Fetch a locksmith from the garrison, quickly. Tell him we've a padlock on the front door."

"Sir." Henshaw jogged for the dirt street, the clank of his musket and cartridge box fading.

The other soldier, Ferguson, remained quiet, awaiting orders. A wind gust buffeted them. Glacial sprinkle spattered Michael's cheek. Another gust sucked at his narrow-brimmed hat. He jammed it back atop his dark hair. He and the men would be drenched if they didn't complete their duties soon and seek shelter.

He shrugged off February's breach beneath his neck stock and ran fingertips along the door crack. The wood was warped enough to reveal the metal bolt of the interior lock. He wedged the blade of his knife into the crack and prodded the bolt with the tip. Wood groaned and squeaked. Splinters shaved from the jamb. In another second, he felt the bolt tremble. He coaxed it, one sixteenth of an inch at a time, from its keeper until he found the edge and retracted the bolt.

He jiggled the door by its handle and felt it quiver. At the edge of his senses, he registered an odd, soft groan from inside, somewhere above the door.

But the warmth of enthusiasm buoyed him past it. There was no bar across the door on the inside. The latch was free.

Satisfaction peeled his lips from his teeth. Horatio Bowater was such a careless fool. Had the agent replaced the door and jamb with fresh wood, an officer of His Majesty would never have been able to break in like a common thief.

He stepped back from his handiwork and sheathed his knife. Ferguson moved forward, enthusiastic. Michael's memory played that weird impression again, almost like the grate of metal upon metal. *Careless fool indeed*, whispered his battlefield instincts. He snagged Ferguson's upper arm. "Wait." He wiggled the latch again. Skin on the back of his neck shivered. Something was odd here. "Kick that door open first, lad."

Ferguson slammed the sole of his shoe against the door. Then he and Michael sprang back from a crashing cascade of scrap metal that clattered over the entrance and onto the floor and step.

When the dust settled and the cacophony dwindled, Michael lowered the arm he'd used to shield his face. Foot-long iron stalagmites protruded from the wood floor. Small cannonballs rolled to rest amidst scrap lumber.

The largest pile of debris teetered, shifted. Michael started, his pulse erratic as a cornered hare. With no difficulty, he imagined his crushed corpse at the bottom of the debris pile.

Bowater wasn't such a fool after all.

Ferguson toed an iron skillet aside. His foot trembled. "Thank you, sir," he whispered.

Words hung up in Michael's throat for a second, then emerged subdued. "Indeed. Don't mention it." With a curt nod, he signaled the private to proceed.

Ferguson rammed the barrel of his musket through the open doorway and waved it around, as if to spring triggers on more traps. Nothing else fell or pounced. Michael poked his head in the doorway and rotated his torso to look up.

A crude cage stretched toward the ceiling, a wooden web tangled in gloom, now clear of lethal debris spiders. Bowater hadn't cobbled together the device overnight. Perhaps he'd even demonstrated it for clientele interested in adding unique security features to homes or businesses.

Michael ordered the private on a search of the stable and kitchen building, then stepped around jagged metal and moved with stealth, alone, past the rear foyer. The rhythm of his breathing eased. He worked his way forward, alert, past an expensive walnut desk and dozens of books on shelves in the study. Past costly couches, chairs, tables, brandy in a crystal decanter, and a tea service in the parlor. He verified the chilly office vacant of people and overt traps, and he opened curtains as he went.

In the front reception area, he homed for the counter. The previous week, he'd seen the agent shove a voluminous book of records onto a lower shelf. No book awaited Michael that afternoon, hardly a surprise. Bowater was devious enough to hide it. And since the book was heavy and bulky, he'd likely left it behind in the building.

Wariness supplanted the self-satisfaction fueling Michael. A suspect conniving enough to assemble one trap as a threshold guardian could easily arm another to preside over business records. Michael advanced to the window beside the front door. When he unlatched it and slid it open, astonishment perked the expressions of the redcoats on the front porch. "I've sent for a locksmith to remove the padlock." He waved the men inside. "Assist me."

While they climbed through and closed the window, Michael's gaze swept the room and paused at the south window. Through it, the tobacco shop next door was visible. The owners of the shop kept their eyes on everything. In contrast to Bowater, Mr. and Mrs. Farrell hadn't griped about the Eighty-Second's occupation of Wilmington on the twenty-ninth of January, eight days earlier. *If* they'd happened to notice atypical activity in Bowater's office over the past day or so, he wagered they'd be forthcoming with information.

How he wished Private Nick Spry weren't fidgeting, restless and useless, in the infirmary, while his leg healed. But for the time, Michael must make do without his assistant. He signaled his men to the counter, where Ferguson joined them. "Lads, I think Mr. Bowater left his records book in this building.

I want the entire place searched for it."

Michael's hands sketched dimensions in the air. "The book is about yea high and wide. Medium brown leather. Heavy and large. Pick any room to begin your search." He checked the time on a watch drawn from his waistcoat pocket. "Going on three o'clock." He rapped the surface of the counter with his knuckles. "Help yourselves to candles here if you need some light." He replaced his watch and turned to Ferguson to receive the private's report.

"Sir. The stable was swept clean. From the looks of it, months ago. No straw, no dung, just reins and a broken old harness hanging on the side, gathering dust. Dust in the kitchen, too. I found an old broom and bucket and some cracked bowls. That's all."

Flesh along Michael's spine pricked. "My orders, lads. If you believe you've located the records book, don't touch it. Fetch me first."

***

The privates dispersed to search the office. Henshaw returned with the locksmith, a slight fellow about three inches shorter than Michael. Pick in hand, the civilian contractor squatted before the padlock. Michael directed Henshaw to the tobacconist's shop to learn whether the Farrells or their apprentices had witnessed recent unusual activity associated with Bowater.

As Henshaw clanked down the front steps, the locksmith stood and brandished the freed padlock like a severed head. Michael sent him to the back door to assess how to secure it. Then he lit a candle and strode to Bowater's study. One of the privates was already inspecting books and shelves, his examination meticulous, cautious.

Moments later, the scuff of shoes in the doorway interrupted Michael's scrutiny of bills and letters he'd spread open before him on Bowater's big desk. "Sir," he heard Ferguson say, "I believe I found the records book."

Michael swiveled and spotted the bleak press of Ferguson's lips. His tone snapped at the air. "You didn't touch it, did you?"

"No, sir, not after what happened out there. I did as you ordered. Told the others to stand back."

Thank God his men weren't rash. Michael relaxed his jaw. "Good." He caught the eye of the soldier in the study with him and jutted his jaw at the door. "Let's have a look."

In the parlor, soldiers and the locksmith had withdrawn a prudent distance from where a plush rug had been rolled away and three floorboards pulled up. Michael regarded the floor, then Ferguson. "However did you find this hidden compartment?"

"The floor sounded peculiar when I walked over it, so I pulled away the rug and realized that the boards weren't quite flush with the rest of the floor."

"Excellent work." Michael knelt beside the hole in the floor and gazed into gloom.

"Here you are, sir." One of the men handed him a lit candle.

The faint glow enabled him to resolve the shape of a book lying flat about three feet down in the hole. Something lay atop it: an open, dark circle that appeared to contain a smaller, closed circle in its center. Without sunlight, he doubted that even a torch would provide him with enough illumination to identify what lay atop the book.

The gap in the floor howled at him of the cage above the back door, loaded with projectiles. Foulness wafted up from the hole. Like feces. Like death.

No way in hell was he was sticking his arm down there. He rocked back on his heels, stood, and gave the candle back to the soldier. "Ferguson, fetch the broom from the kitchen."

"Sir." He sprinted out and returned with the broom in less than a minute.

Michael inverted the broom, handle first, straight into the hole. As soon as the end of the broom made contact below, he heard a loud clap. The broom vibrated, gained weight. His arm jerked, and he tightened his grip. Men in the room recoiled.

He brought the broom up. Metal clinked, a chain rattled. Affixed to the handle, approximately where a man's wrist would have been, was a metal leg trap used by hunters to snag wolves and bobcats. Its teeth, smeared with dried dung, had almost bisected the broom handle.

A murmur of shock frosted the air. "Damnation," someone whispered.

Revulsion transfixed Michael. His stomach burned when he thought of anyone catching his wrist in the trap. Almost certainly, the victim's hand would need amputation, and the filth on the metallic jaws would encourage the spread of general infection, resulting in slow, agonizing death.

The locksmith coughed. "Mr. Stoddard, sir, I've a question of you."

Michael blinked, broom and trap still in his grasp, and pivoted to the locksmith. The wiry man held a metal chunk that he must have pried off the floor while inspecting the rear door. Hair jumped along Michael's neck when he recognized the metal as a bayonet, its tip broken off.

A muscle leapt beneath the locksmith's eye. "Who designed that trap at the back door?"

"The owner, Mr. Bowater, I presume."

"Sir, with all the valuable property in this building, there's no reason Mr. Bowater shouldn't have secured the rear as well as he did the front, except that he . . ." The locksmith trailed off. His lips pinched, as if to seal in disgust.

Michael leaned into his hesitation. "Except that he *what*?"

"Inferior workmanship, warped wood on the door. I believe Mr. Bowater intended to lure someone in with the promise of an easy entrance, then kill him horribly in a rain of debris. You've a madman on your hands." The artisan glanced over the redcoats. His empty palm circled air twice, fingers open. "Battle places its own gruesome demands on you fellows. But outside of battle, have you tried to lure a man into a trap and kill him?" He caught Michael's eye.

Michael's expression and body stilled. He held the man's gaze. Winter crawled over his scalp and down his neck. The artisan didn't know, Michael told himself. How could he know?

"You see my meaning." The locksmith raised the bayonet for emphasis. "A decent man like yourself would never set up such a snare."

Chapter Two

THE BELL JINGLED above the front door. Shoes clomped the floor with a man's approach: Henshaw returning from the tobacconist's shop. He entered the parlor, stopped short, and gawped at the trap dangling from the broom in Michael's hand. By candlelight, raindrops beaded the shoulders of his coat like rubies.

Michael turned from Henshaw to the other soldiers. "Ferguson, haul the book out of there." He dropped the broom and trap. The clatter on the floor echoed through the parlor like a coffin of bones overturned. "All of you, keep searching the office. No telling what else Mr. Bowater has hidden, so I needn't remind you to use caution. Hop to it, now." The men went to work.

He stepped in the locksmith's direction, aware of Henshaw squirming, awaiting an opportunity to report. "Fetch a carpenter to help you if necessary," Michael told the civilian, his voice low. "We must have the rear door repaired well enough by nightfall to secure the building from Mr. Bowater's attempts to sneak back in." The locksmith bobbed his head and left.

Ferguson approached, brushed dried dung off the cover of the retrieved book, and handed it to Michael, who waved for Henshaw to accompany him. In the study, rain spattered the window glass. Michael stacked bills and letters, and made room for the book upon the desk.

Hands on his hips, he regarded the soldier, who stood about three feet from him. "Your report, Henshaw."

"Sir. Around seven o'clock yesterday morning, well before Mr. Bowater usually opens business for the day, Mrs. Farrell overheard a heated exchange between the agent and a man inside his office. She says she couldn't understand what they were saying, but then Mr. Bowater followed the man out onto the front porch, where they cursed and threatened each other."

Ah ha! Michael grinned. "Was this man someone that Mrs. Farrell recognized?"

"He was a stranger to her. Not someone from town, she said."

"What was his appearance?"

"White man, medium height, somewhere in his prime. It was barely day-light, so she couldn't discern more."

Not someone from town. The piece of news didn't weaken a theory Michael was developing about Bowater's "family emergency." "Did the men come to blows out there on the porch?"

The private wagged his head. "The visitor galloped on a horse toward Market Street. Mr. Bowater took the name of the Lord in vain, retreated into his office, and slammed the door."

"Interesting." Michael rubbed his chin. "Mrs. Farrell heard the men curse and threaten each other. What curses? What threats?"

Henshaw shifted his weight. His jaw quivered. He steadied it with the re-solve of a boy convincing himself he hadn't seen a ghost. "She says Mr. Bowater stood on his porch, shook his fist at the man, and yelled, 'You'll never prove a thing, you scoundrel.' The man hollered back something like, 'You'll hang, just like all of them, and be buried in ground just as unhallowed.'"

Intrigue shimmied over Michael's skin. He returned his hand to his hip. Mrs. Farrell's testimony might well imply that Horatio Bowater's recent visi-tor intended to expose the agent's criminal activities. But why was Henshaw unnerved?

"Unhallowed," the private murmured. The word seemed to lodge in his lar-ynx.

An odd choice of words from Bowater's visitor. A convicted swindler more often found his future to hold a lengthy sentence on a malaria-infested tropical island, rather than a quick step up to the gallows. Unhallowed ground was the final resting place reserved for those who'd committed murder or treason.

Mrs. Farrell must be questioned further. Michael was certain she'd noticed additional details about the encounter. Whether the stranger was armed, what type of hat he wore, and the quality of his English. Such was always the case with witnesses. "Did she see either man again?"

"No, sir. Later yesterday morning, one of the apprentices reported that the sign had been tacked to Mr. Bowater's office door."

"Hmm. What type of horse was Mr. Bowater's visitor riding?"

The private's gaze dipped a second. "Er, I forgot to ask her that, sir."

Michael's lips compressed, then released. No point in haranguing Henshaw. He'd performed his best. But it explained why Nick Spry was Michael's investi-gative assistant, not Henshaw. "What else did she contribute?"

Henshaw hesitated. "Mrs. Farrell insisted that I *must* tell you." Michael watched him manipulate his facial muscles into an expression so bland that, could it have been tasted, would have passed for one of those dull, white sauces the bloody French forever raved about. "The Wilmington ladies have planned a dinner party, for two weeks from this coming Saturday."

Michael cocked his head and frowned. How did this fluff figure into Bowater's disappearance?

"And you should receive your invitation today or on the morrow." Henshaw's cheeks pinked, and his gaze rolled to the side, like that of a lad seeking to evade barnyard shovel duty.

Michael was invited to their party? What on earth did it have to do with the land agent? He straightened his neck and wiggled a finger in one ear. Somewhere, somehow, he'd missed a link.

Henshaw blurted the rest. "You arrested those rebel weapons smugglers last week. You're the guest of honor at the party, sir. A hero." There was a faint, smug pinch to Henshaw's lips.

Realization rolled over Michael with all the appeal of a Wilmington fog. Hero, his arse. Mrs. Farrell had likely schemed to match him up with a town widow. His neck burned. "Thank you, Henshaw. That will be all." He jerked his thumb toward the door. "Assist in the search."

The private hastened from the study. Michael slouched in the cushioned chair before the desk and watched rivulets of rain channel down the panes. Growing up in Yorkshire had provided him with numerous opportunities to experience drenching rain. He saw no need to rush out that moment, brave the elements to question Mrs. Farrell further about Bowater.

Besides, he'd no guarantee that the hen next door would pair him with a lady his age, like the lovely Widow Duncan, instead of a grandmother. Irritation buzzed his ears. His participation in a civilian social event would first have to be approved by Major Craig. At Craig's desk, the motion would be bayoneted. The Eighty-Second was spread thinner than muslin, endeavoring to fortify and defend the town against rebel attack. Major Craig wouldn't spare him to attend a party.

"Bah." Michael scooted forward and opened the book that Bowater had gone through such lengths to protect. He rubbed his palms together and smiled, envisioning the agent swindling others over that piece of land, then being confronted by a victim in his office yesterday morning. Perhaps Bowater's absence meant he'd met with foul play at the hands of the man who'd threatened him. Michael imagined Bowater face up in a ditch outside Wilmington, brown water lapping at his white wig, dull eyes wide to the swollen, frigid sky. A genuine family emergency.

The bell over the door jingled again. A man's voice called, "Mr. Stoddard, sir?"

Michael shut the transactions book, secured letters and bills, and rose. Soldiers he'd sent earlier to Bowater's residence met him at the front counter. Both men dripped rainwater, and their shoes were caked with sandy mud. One private reported that the previous morning about seven-thirty, the agent came home unexpectedly from work and told his housekeeper that he'd received word of a family emergency. "Mr. Bowater bade her prepare one day of travel rations and departed in his gig with the food, a small valise, and a rifle. And, sir, he hasn't returned."

An image of the land agent thumbing his nose at the Eighty-Second from a warm tavern twenty miles away pounded Michael's imagination. A sour taste coated his tongue, like hasty pudding gone foul. Three murders he'd solved, and one case of arson. He'd tracked down burglars and livestock thieves. Yet Bowater, damn his eyes, had evaded him.

Hands knotted into fists, he crossed arms over his chest. "Where was he headed?"

"He didn't specify his destination. And the housekeeper doesn't know where to find his family. In the ten years that she's worked for him, she says he never mentioned a family. Or what he was doing before he began selling properties from this office."

Baffled, Michael allowed his gaze to drift past the privates, out the window to the street and the rain. Bundled in wool cloaks, four goodwives trudged from Market Street with full baskets. A wagon of turpentine kegs rolled past on the opposite side of the street, horses plodding, driver hunched against the weather, his shoulders projecting perseverance and desire to be done for the day so he could relax at his hearth.

How could a man have no family, no past, and vanish without a destination? Michael had a mother, father, sister, and nephews more than a thousand miles away, across an ocean. Home was where he'd been a boy who tumbled in summer grass with hound puppies, and later cleaned the mews for Lord Crump's falcons, and later still loosened the neckline of Lydia's fine silk shift— oh, bloody hell, why was he thinking about *her*?

Impatient, he hauled his attention back to the investigation and ordered events in his head. He uncrossed his arms and said to his men, "How long did Mr. Bowater expect to be gone?"

"He didn't specify that, either, sir."

"Very well, what did the housekeeper say he was wearing when he left his house?"

The privates glanced at each other. Shoulders bowed. "Er, we didn't ask her that."

Gods, if only Spry weren't stuck in the infirmary.

The men had nothing further to contribute. Michael instructed them to join the search, cautioned them about the traps, and dismissed them. They headed around the counter, and one added, "Oh, sir. The major wants to see you. Immediately."

Immediately. Knots formed in Michael's stomach. He stiffened, then lifted his chin.

***

At his headquarters in the house on Market Street, stocky Major Craig sat at a table near the fireplace, absorbed in writing, the bridge of his patrician Roman nose furrowed above the missive. Unnoticed, Michael held a salute. Rainwater dribbled down his left hand onto the rug below his wet boots. His feet itched, still icy from his sprint of several blocks. He clenched his jaw to quiet his teeth. Silently, he cursed Bowater.

Craig's adjutant strode into the study bearing a tray and silver tea service. He whizzed past Michael and set the tray on the major's table near a decanter of what was probably brandy—and not brandy of a mediocre grade, either. "Sir, Mr. Stoddard is here."

Absorbed in the document's content, Craig braced his forehead in his fist and rolled his quill between fingers and thumb. He muttered, "I said, send him in."

That was Michael's cue. "Sir!"

Craig dropped the quill and jerked upright in his chair. Stress commanded his expression. His scrutiny of Michael's sodden state was ruthless. After Craig acknowledged the salute, he barked the adjutant from the study and pointed out a solitary chair opposite the desk from him. "Sit."

Joints rigid with cold, Michael lurched forward to the proffered chair. Alas, the table blocked too much heat from the fireplace. Tremors in his muscles compounded beneath the sear of his commander's scrutiny. Michael's lungs felt as if they'd shrunk to half their size.

Craig's cheek twitched. He pushed aside missive and writing implements, angled forward in his chair, and planted fists on the tabletop. His stare hammered Michael. "Horatio Bowater has left town."

"Sir. He departed yesterday morning at approximately seven-thirty, the day before the two civilians filed a grievance with you." How cold Michael was ceased to matter. Of more relevance was how long he'd be buried in inventory, interment for junior officers who'd failed at crucial assignments. "A notice on his office door indicates his absence is due to a family emergency. He told his housekeeper he was leaving for the same reason."

His face like chiseled alabaster, Craig sat back, hands in his lap. The assessment extended what felt like hours. Michael restrained himself from flinching and tried to brace himself for being reassigned. But no man could adequately prepare for demotion.

"Mr. Stoddard, the surgeon informs me that your assistant has exhibited an excellent recovery from the pistol ball injury to his thigh. His infection was minimal, and his spirits have been high throughout his convalescence."

"Sir. Spry has been most fortunate." Peculiar shift of subject from his report about Bowater.

"The surgeon set Spry's release for the morrow, light duty for several days."

Concern for his assistant lifted off Michael. His shoulders rolled back. "Why, that's outstanding news, sir!"

"Indeed." Craig's eyebrows lowered, wrinkling the bridge of his nose. Curiosity crept into his voice. "How would you rate your assistant's investigative abilities?"

Thank God they'd switched topics without the issue of demotion coming up. A quick smile sneaked from Michael. "I couldn't be more fortunate. A few more cases solved, his methodology and logic tightened, and Spry will be able to handle investigations on his own."

The major grunted. "Excellent. What evidence have you on Mr. Bowater?"

The tension cramping Michael's shoulders subsided. He described the traps they'd found in the agent's office.

Craig frowned. "So, all you have on Mr. Bowater are these gruesome traps?"

Michael stopped himself from opening his mouth with, "I'm not certain." With Craig, that phrase went over like fresh dung afloat in a punchbowl. "Mr. Bowater's desk contains a number of letters and bills that I've yet to analyze, sir. Between the records book and the letters and bills, I should be able to corroborate the claims of the two civilians shortly."

"But it doesn't sound as though you've progressed very far in this investigation."

Michael's toes and fingers throbbed with cold. He fought the urge to writhe, to blurt out his own defense, like a criminal dragged to the gallows. Words rushed from him. "Sir. The wife of the tobacconist in the shop next door overheard the end of an argument between Mr. Bowater and a stranger early yesterday morning, just prior to Mr. Bowater's departure from town. Mr. Bowater was being threatened by the man."

"Threatened." Another grunt, more like a snort, issued from Craig. "What other witnesses have you interviewed?"

"None yet, sir. I believe that we've plenty of evidence against Mr. Bowater. I just need a little more time to sort through all of it."

Craig's hands lifted to the table. "Time, Mr. Stoddard, is something we have little of." His fingers steepled. "Therefore, I'm removing you from the Bowater investigation. You've confirmed your assistant as capable. I'm reassigning the investigation to him."

Disbelief and betrayal stabbed through Michael's heart like a pike. "But—"

"Give your notes to Spry," said Craig. "On the morrow, he'll pick up where you left off."

"Sir." Probably the most difficult word he'd ever forced past his lips.

His heart stung as if tunneled out with acid. Never before had he been yanked off an inquiry. By God, he was envious of Spry—as if the investigation were a mistress, and she'd abandoned him for his six-foot-tall, eighteen-year-old blond assistant with an easygoing personality. Disillusioned, he wondered what kind of man he'd become of late, wooing criminal investigations as if they were ladies.

He leaned forward and gripped his knees. "You cannot expect Spry to solve the matter any faster than I can. Sorting through records, letters, and bills and interviewing witnesses takes time. No one can circumvent that process, sir."

Again, the frown tensed Craig's visage. "I don't expect Spry to solve it overnight."

So that was the problem. The major wasn't just displeased with Michael's pace. He'd lost faith in his ability to perform investigations. Damnation.

Chapter Three

MICHAEL BLINKED SEVERAL times, closed his lips. As if his knees had become lumps of ice, he loosened his grip on them, let the chair brace him as he exhaled, sank against the wooden back of it. He realized that he knew another investigator who'd been yanked off a case.

More than half a year ago, Lieutenant Fairfax had been commanded to transfer information to Michael: Fairfax's notes on the investigation of a murder that he himself had committed, for sport. Since then, Fairfax had continued to murder for sport. Not just murder, but torture.

Fairfax would find the cage of death above Bowater's back door amusing, intriguing.

Acid rippled Michael's gut. If only he'd been able to consummate his desperate plot back in December to rid the colonies of that monster who wore the scarlet uniform of the Seventeenth Light Dragoons. Michael eased out a taut lungful of air and reminded himself that no one knew what he'd schemed. Only a disaffected scout named Adam Neville suspected.

"Let us leave the matter of Mr. Bowater." Elbows on the table, Craig interlaced his fingers. A knuckle cracked. "It's but a nuisance compared to other matters. Definitely not the reason you're sitting in that chair."

Ice gouged Michael's spine, pasted it to the ladder-back of the chair.

"In December, you successfully rode dispatches into the backcountry of South Carolina, to Camden, Ninety Six, and the British Legion." Piercing discernment in Craig's eyes immobilized Michael. "What was your motivation for volunteering for that assignment?"

Shit, no. Someone *had* figured it out and informed Craig. It had finally caught up with Michael. He wasn't being demoted to inventory after all.

His heart battered his ribcage. He pried his back off the chair and darted a look behind, expecting a detachment of the provost marshal's guards in the open doorway. But the door remained latched.

His throat resisted two attempts at a swallow.

"To—to serve king and country, sir." *To kill the fiend and make his death look accidental, because senior officers overlook the sport of an aristocratic junior officer who murders enemies of Britain.* How stupid could he have been?

"A pat response." The major's tone shot out at him. "A dispatch rider has one of the most hazardous jobs that exist. He's on his own. If rebels catch him, he's subject to torture and execution." Craig's nostrils widened. "Men accept these assignments for personal gain. Same reasons why they accept a forlorn hope." His fists planted upon the table's surface. His stare ground away at Michael. "A truthful answer this time. Why did you volunteer for that assignment?"

Michael's pulse knocked about and missed beats, but he resisted flinching from Craig's intensity. His swallow went down with all the ease of vinegar on a raw throat. "*Someone* has to run dispatches, sir."

Craig snorted and whipped about to the fireplace, his gaze directed into the coals, his authoritative chin and Roman nose in profile. "Mr. Stoddard, the Army teems with bum kissing lieutenants and captains desperate to distinguish themselves and play leapfrog up the ranks. I don't reward arse-kissers."

A slow breath streamed from Michael. He didn't comprehend the shift of subject, a perspective from which he couldn't envision Craig browbeating the truth from him about his motivation. "Sir, what actions of mine mark me as such a man?"

"Isn't that why men run dispatches?" Craig swiveled back to him. A smirk corroded the iron in his eyes. "To draw attention to themselves and hope the assignment earns the regard of a senior officer who will advance them?"

"Not this man. Sir." What a relief, to give an answer that was wholly true.

Craig's eyebrows dove downward at the simplicity of his response. Then he flung back his head and laughed, brief and caustic. "Don't tell me you cannot be bought. All men can be bought."

Michael didn't doubt that he had a price. Often during his early months in North America, he'd wondered what his own price was. But his price wasn't the issue here. Or was it?

"Sir, I ran those dispatches because they needed delivery. No one else volunteered." That was the story he'd stick with. He squared his shoulders and awaited the next round from the thorny commander of the Eighty-Second.

Craig pushed up from the table and motioned for him to remain seated. At the nearest window, he glared out, hands clasped behind him, thumbs batting each other. Michael suspected that he seldom stood during these meetings with officers in the study because it reinforced the fact that most of them, himself included, stood taller than the Eighty-Second's commander.

Michael's gaze tracked the fidgety fingers. Many men who'd crossed Craig's path must have impressed upon him the desire to arse-kiss their way to the top. From where he sat, the top didn't look so appealing. Power, yes, but pressure also, evinced in restless thumbs. With dull surprise, he realized that advancement appealed to him the most if it provided additional means for him to continue investigating criminal activity and seeing justice served.

None of that mattered if Craig had latched onto his true reason for running those dispatches. He'd be executed for plotting murder of a fellow officer. Yet the longer Craig stood at the window, his back to Michael, the more Michael sensed that he didn't know his motivation.

Craig spoke at last, in monotone, like a man who was thinking aloud. "The Eighty-Second has been sent to the Cape Fear to establish and defend a supply depot here. We are expected to support Lord Cornwallis's initiatives on the interior of North Carolina."

Puzzlement slowed Michael's pulse and banked the fire in his stomach. Craig surely didn't sound as though he were prepared to arrest him for conspiracy against another officer. But why else would Craig terminate his participation on the investigation and press him about his motivation for those trips into the South Carolina backcountry?

"Lord Cornwallis expects us to make an auxiliary supply depot available eighty miles to the northwest, in Cross Creek. Have you heard the reports from scouts?"

Michael cocked an eyebrow. "Sir. They say rebels patrol the area unchecked between Wilmington and Cross Creek and easily interfere with traffic upon the Cape Fear River."

"Indeed, and thus have I been unable to deposit supplies in Cross Creek without concern that my men will be attacked and our supplies confiscated by rebels."

Lord Cornwallis couldn't be aware of this crimp in strategy yet; he operated too far into the North Carolina backcountry to be quickly reached. Michael stared at Craig's back, and a draft polarized hairs on his neck. "Sir, if his Lordship executes a maneuver that depends upon his accessing those supplies from Cross Creek, it could result in disaster."

The major's hands stilled. "Yes, Mr. Stoddard. I've sent two riders in search of him. Their dispatches bear a summary of my findings about the unsuitability of using Cross Creek as a depot." He turned from the window, and Michael recognized the tension his commander had borne in his face during the entire meeting as his anxiety over the fate of Charles, Lord Cornwallis, should his army arrive in Cross Creek desperate for supplies and find none. "I fervently hope he receives my dispatches. In my opinion, two riders aren't enough to ensure that he does, but we're undermanned here in Wilmington. I can spare but one more man as courier." He took a step toward Michael. "Do you know where I can find that man?"

The rhetorical question dried up relief that had begun trickling into Michael's veins and plunged sleet beneath his neck stock. So this was the reason Craig had given the investigation to Spry. And why the major had interrogated Michael over motives.

Michael had lied himself into another perilous dispatch assignment. But this time, he'd catapulted himself into danger without the promise of a clear opportunity to track down Lieutenant Fairfax and shove a discreet dagger between his ribs.

"Sir," he said, his voice barely audible, personal choice in the matter irrelevant.

Craig strutted back to the table. "I'm not at leisure to err in judgment over a dispatch rider's character. In the nine years you've given the Army, your records indicate no motivation except a desire to serve His Majesty." He hovered above the tea service. "Your lips are still blue, Lieutenant. Would you care for tea or brandy?"

No amount of tea would diffuse Michael's disbelief. He may as well learn what quality brandy Craig served. "Brandy, thank you, sir."

After he handed him a glass one-third full of liquid amber, Craig retreated to his side of the table, poured an equal amount of brandy in a second glass, and sat. The glass between his palms, he studied Michael. "Intelligencers suggest that Lord Cornwallis's pursuit of General Nathanael Greene has moved by now into the northern tier of the colony, possibly as far north as Virginia. We've a dedicated agent near Virginia, in the town of Hillsborough. His name is Ezra Griggs. Make contact with him. He'll have the best idea of the Army's location."

Countering Michael's relief at not being required to crisscross all of North Carolina on horseback in search of Cornwallis was his apprehension over Hillsborough as a destination. From what he'd heard of the town, Ezra Griggs was probably one of a handful of true loyalists there. A sip of brandy cascaded a coating of mellow warmth through his stomach and veins. His brain acknowledged that it was the finest brandy he'd ever tasted, while his tongue refused to cooperate in savoring it. "And Mr. Griggs's appearance?"

"Mid-forties, medium height and weight, dark hair, native Englishman. If he's in a position to deliver the dispatch, allow him to do so. We know him to be a reliable courier. He'll shelter you for the night, before you ride back to Wilmington.

"Hillsborough residents are reportedly apathetic toward the war. A rebel Committee of Safety governs the town. The position of sheriff in those parts changes hands often, and it's said that no sheriff of Orange County has ever turned in an honest tax collection." Craig tasted his brandy and set down the glass. "Obviously, you won't be traveling in uniform. The quartermaster will issue you a rifle like those of residents in the backwoods. Inquire of him should you need additional clothing to complete the disguise of a civilian who is neither wealthy nor penniless."

A map unfurled beneath his hands, and atop it a paper scripted with a list of ten men's names. He rotated both to Michael. Michael swigged more brandy and slid the map and list closer.

The major said, "On the morrow at five-thirty, you'll depart Wilmington. Conceal your civilian clothing beneath a greatcoat. Spies don't wait for daylight. Take this road paralleling the Northwest Cape Fear River, toward Cross Creek." Craig's forefinger traced the angled line of a road and paused where a small "X" and a subscript numeral one was inked on the parchment. "Your first stop on the morrow, here, is a known residence of safety." His forefinger tapped a second "X" then moved to others between Wilmington and Hillsborough, one near Cross Creek. "Safe. Safe." He retrieved his brandy and pushed back to observe Michael.

The tenth "X" was the house of Ezra Griggs. Gloom gnawed at the edges of Michael's soul. He fended it back with more brandy, then set the glass upon the table. Craig tossed a leather pouch over to him. Michael rolled the list within the map and secured both in the pouch.

"How's the brandy, Mr. Stoddard?"

"Superb, sir." He wished he were of a mood to appreciate it.

"You've the better part of a week on the road. I can spare only the mare you rode last week. Treat her gently. The gods know how I've supplicated my superiors for more horses. More men, too." Craig glanced out the window, toward earthworks under construction, and soldiers who toiled in the cold rain. Then he pressed a small, sealed note on the table where the map had resided seconds earlier. "A cipher is hidden here between the lines of a love letter, penned by one Mr. Kirkleigh to a lady love he calls Peaches."

Peaches. Christ Jesus. And a cipher. Worse. Ciphers riled rebels, he knew. Something about being unable to immediately understand enemy secrets propelled them into a murderous haze. Misery made another charge for Michael. This time, he only half-heartedly repulsed it.

He knocked back more brandy before thrusting the note in his waistcoat pocket. "Sir, to protect my cover or that of Mr. Griggs, I may have to destroy your message. Is the information about Cross Creek's unsuitability the sole content of this note?"

"Yes." Craig stretched over and deposited a leather purse before Michael. Coins clinked within. "What the journey doesn't claim of this is yours."

Michael's lips shuddered for a smile and failed. He pocketed the purse without opening it. "Thank you, sir." To his ears, the words sounded like they came from a larynx constructed of oak, the voice a marionette soldier in bright paint would make if it could speak on its own.

Craig's gaze had marked the fact that Michael didn't count the money. The major nodded once. "The reserve with which you've accepted this assignment confirms that I've selected the correct man for the job." He lifted his glass in salute. "Here's to your success and good luck."

Michael could use some of both. "To success and luck, sir." He drained his glass and stood, hands at his sides.

Sudden humor cracked Craig's stoicism and trailed a smile across his lips. He lifted a piece of paper from the table. "By God, I'd almost forgotten this other matter of business. I received a petition signed by twenty-five ladies of Wilmington requesting your appearance as guest of honor at a social occasion two weeks from this coming Saturday."

Panic flared through Michael, tightened his tone. "Sir, I thank you in advance for being unable to spare me and declining the invitation."

"I shall do nothing of the sort." Craig tossed the paper to the table. "Last week, you apprehended men who menaced the community. The ladies regard this as their opportunity to thank you, to thank the Eighty-Second. And this is an event of great visibility. Your escort for the evening will be the Widow Duncan, owner of White's Tavern, one of the town's most *profitable* businesses." Craig scowled at him. "This is a party. Don't you like parties, Mr. Stoddard?"

What self-respecting officer didn't like parties? "Of course I like parties, sir." At attention, Michael fixed his gaze on the top of Craig's left ear.

"Good. I expect you'll have returned to town by then. I see no scheduling conflicts. You will accept the invitation."

Again, Craig wasn't giving him a choice. He'd just couched his mandate in a smile. More than anything, Michael wanted to sit somewhere quiet for a few moments and digest the reality that he'd just become firearm fodder on-the-hoof for the next two weeks. "Will that be all, sir?"

Craig resumed a critical appraisal of Michael's jaw and posture. Seconds passed. "No." Fatigue softened his voice. "I didn't attain this command without acquiring the ability to read what lies behind a man's eyes." He closed one fist on the table. "A clever man learns when to grasp an opportunity." The fist opened, relaxed. "A wise man discerns when to let one prospect go and make himself available for another."

The major's lips slid across his teeth in the grimace of a man who'd bitten off a mouthful of moldy cheese and didn't know where to spit it. "You aren't the only twenty-six-year-old junior officer who doesn't know when to let go. You've made apprehension of this petty rebel sympathizer an *intimate* goal. The mission to deliver this dispatch is critical. Live and breathe it!" Craig's fist became a judge's mallet upon the tabletop. "A courier who misses opportunities for success because his head is hundreds of miles away is useless to me." Paper rustled when he pushed back in his chair. By some trick of lighting, the breadth of his shoulders expanded. "Any further questions?"

"No, sir." Michael released the clench of his fingers. No amount of grasping would help him bring the "petty rebel sympathizer" to justice.

Shadows deepened beneath Craig's eyes. "Godspeed, Lieutenant."

Chapter Four

VITALITY BOOMED FROM all six feet of Nick Spry. When he strutted past Michael in the infirmary, Spry didn't even limp on his left leg. "Enid gets the credit, sir. She smuggled in a foul-smelling salve that I sneak onto my leg whenever the surgeon isn't looking." He pointed to his left thigh. "Keeps infection down. Those Welshwomen, they have medicines like that stuff she gave you." Spry nodded to Michael and stroked his own chin.

Michael ran fingertips over his chin, cluttered a week earlier with pimples. Twice daily, the housekeeper where he and Spry boarded made him apply a linen rectangle drenched in witch hazel and an herbal concoction. The pimples had vanished.

But pimples didn't present the predicament of gangrene. Although Spry was in good spirits, his left thigh was bandaged beneath his trousers. "So you're to be released on the morrow."

A mouthful of big, healthy teeth accompanied his assistant's grin. "Won't be soon enough, sir. I hate spending the day dressed just in my shirt. Sitting around on my arse staring at walls. Being poked and bandaged. Not feeling the wind on my face. And the food. God almighty. Being in an infirmary is like being bitten in the bum hourly."

To be sure. Three years earlier, malaria had sent Michael to an infirmary. After two weeks, he wished he'd been sent to the front line. His expression sobered at the thought. He hooked the back of one of two nearby chairs and planted it so he could sit facing the younger man. "Spry, last Thursday you took a pistol ball in the leg. Ignore the command of 'light duty' after you're released, and you could wind up right back in here." He pressed forward, elbows on knees, and captured Spry's full attention. "I don't want that to happen any more than you do."

The private's grin faded, and his larynx bobbed in a swallow. Then his eyes widened, and his grin resumed. "Wait a minute. That look on your face. Sir, Major Craig just gave us another investigation this afternoon, didn't he?" By candlelight, ruddiness permeated his expression.

Heartened by Spry's fervor, Michael straightened. "Have a seat." From his waistcoat pocket, he extracted the page of notes he'd scripted about the investigation as well as the key to the replacement padlock on Bowater's office door. The private pulled up the other chair, and Michael handed the notes and key to him. "Tell me what you make of this business."

Spry's gaze devoured the note's details. "Horatio Bowater, that bugger. I'm not surprised." He continued reading to the bottom of the page before extending it to Michael.

"No, that's—" Michael's voice faltered a second. "That's all yours."

Spry deposited the key in his pocket. "Thank you, sir." He folded the page but held onto it. "The gall of him, swindling his clients. Well, we'll catch him for sure."

Michael sat back and coughed to moisten a mouth dry of a sudden. "*You'll* catch him. Major Craig has taken me off the investigation. He wants you to solve it by yourself."

"Sir?" Spry stared at him, lips parted. "Why?"

Michael studied the perplexity on his assistant's face, seeking but not finding another emotion there. He lowered his voice. "We're unable to establish the depot in Cross Creek. Lord Cornwallis must be apprised of the changed plans so he avoids Cross Creek and doesn't depend upon those supplies. I leave in about twelve hours bearing a dispatch for his Lordship. I'm to meet a loyalist in Hillsborough named Ezra Griggs. Hand off the dispatch to him."

"You get to be a courier." From his whisper of awe, Spry had been smacked in the head with the fist of envy.

Michael almost laughed with irony. His assistant wanted to be the one to ride ten days and dodge musket balls for King and country. Ah, to be eighteen years old again, and immortal. "See here. Riding dispatches isn't the glorious task you fancy. It's frightening. Death always rides with you."

"And you'd rather conclude the Bowater investigation, wouldn't you, sir?" Spry slapped his right knee. "Hah!"

Then he skittered his gaze away, pressed his lips together, and rolled them inward a moment. "But to expect me to close this investigation without your guidance—"

"I do expect you to succeed, yes."

The private's shoulders curved, as if compensating for a load that Michael had dumped onto him. "Sir."

He looked lost. Ambivalence surged through Michael. Did his assistant lack confidence?

Spry cleared his throat, opened the note, and reexamined it. "The housekeeper might provide more details about Mr. Bowater's departure, sir. A description of his horse and gig. What he was wearing when he left." The private thought a moment. "At seven-thirty in the morning, surely someone in Wilmington noticed him in his gig and can recall which direction he took."

Tension emptied from Michael's nostrils, a silent flow of breath.

"Bah. That Henshaw must have been half-asleep when he questioned Mrs.

Farrell." Spry flicked the note with the backs of his fingers. "He didn't get a description of the stranger's horse. Was the man wearing a wig? Carrying a firearm?" Spry's brow puckered. "You know, sir, Mrs. Farrell might even have heard enough of his speech to identify where he was from."

Spry would nab Bowater, all right. Relief plucked a smile from Michael, and a nod for his assistant. "While you're searching the office, be certain to watch for more traps."

The private sat up straight. "Oh, yes, sir."

"Stay alert. Remember, Mr. Bowater took only one day's supply of food with him. If he was dressed the dandy, he may return for food, rather than soil his silk by hunting his supper."

Spry pocketed the note but stayed mute a moment. The track of his gaze searched Michael's face. In the silence that stretched between them, Michael wondered whether the Powers That Be had brought the private into his life to teach him about more than just humor. "Why did you join the Army, Spry?"

A brief laugh gusted from his assistant. "Oh, I thought I told you that story, sir. It was either join the Army or take up juggling and become a fool."

Michael chuckled politely, remembering the conversation. Spry was such a lame liar. Some sort of trauma back in Nova Scotia had pushed him into the Army. He knew how that was.

"And you, sir?" Keenness illuminated Spry's eyes.

"When I was younger than you are, I earned the appreciation of my employer by figuring out how his steward and gamekeeper were embezzling from him. My uncle, a wealthy blacksmith, later approached him about the two of them purchasing an ensign's commission for me. They wanted me to make something of my life. So I was commissioned."

Spry studied him, waiting for him to speak the rest of his story. But Michael had never told that part to anyone.

He stood, followed by the younger man. "Good luck with the investigation, Spry." It made an unsettling adieu, Spry lying to him, him lying to his assistant. But they both had their reasons.

"Thank you, sir. And a safe journey for you."

***

Next, Michael made his way to Front Street. The rain had converted to mist while he'd spoken with his assistant in the barracks. Ice rimmed puddles on the road. Cold burrowed into the earth's embrace, shooting javelins through his boot soles with every step.

At White's Tavern, he yanked open the door. The clamor of men in jollification and two fiddles sawing out a sailor's hornpipe leapt at him. He stepped inside and blew on his hands. Smoke from the fireplace, pipes, and lanterns surged over him, along with the smells of beer, bean and cabbage soup, and body odor. Ah, he really was going to miss White's.

Six busty barmaids wiggled between tables, taking drink orders and replacing pitchers of brew. To his right, a table of soldiers and civilians belted out the refrain to "The Black Jake." To his left, an entire long table was set aside for backgammon, checkers, and chess competitions. Men hovered above seated contestants, tankards in hand, viewing the moves. He wove through the crowd, acknowledging those who greeted him, and joined the backgammon spectators.

A barmaid leaned past him from behind to replace an empty pitcher in the middle of the table with one topped by beer foam. Her breasts massaged his back, no less subtle a reminder than the last time she'd let him know that she rated him worthy of sport. His ears heated.

Three men across the table ogled the contact, eyes sly slits when Michael pulled her in close so she could hear his drink order: claret. When he released her, she blew him a kiss and sashayed off, earning applause from men at the table.

He wandered away with the easy carriage of a swain who has barmaids vying for him every night—which he had until, dissatisfied, he'd braked all the shallow romping more than a year earlier. Nowhere did he catch so much as a glimpse of the tavern's owner, Kate Duncan. Usually she bustled in and out of the common room. But he hadn't seen her since Friday night. That was when he flirted with her with all the adroitness of a foal attempting to stand for the first time. And she'd rebuffed him with the cool finesse imparted by five years of committed widowhood.

So. Mrs. Farrell had paired him with the Ice Widow instead of a grand-mother for that blasted party. Discomfited, restless, he meandered.

His favorite table in the rear of the tavern was full. The barmaid tracked him down with his claret, all business until he paid her, then another kiss blown his way before she hurried off. He gulped wine, wandered into the back room where officers sometimes socialized, only to find it empty. He exited out into the common room again.

The tavern manager, Kevin Marsh, his apron, shirt, and blond hair rum-pled, wheeled past with a tray of empty tankards. Spotting Michael, he circled back in a clank of tankards. Jubilation galloped across his face. "Evening, Mr. Stoddard! Got your claret, I see. Can you believe this crowd? I don't think my sister and I have ever been this busy!"

The racket wasn't as intense where they stood, so Michael could hear him. "Evening, Mr. Marsh. Why the celebration? It's Tuesday night, not Saturday."

"It's confidence in the Eighty-Second. Major Craig isn't taking bullfeathers from anybody. Devil of a time for Kate to travel out of town, though. I could use her help, with all the extra business."

"Your sister's gone from Wilmington?" Like a slow moving gas bubble, an ache rose through Michael's gut.

"For a few weeks. She left Saturday." Marsh shifted the tray to his right shoulder. "We've one very stubborn Aunt Rachel. She needs to sell that tavern of hers, move here with us."

Michael's stomach, churning slowly since he'd entered the tavern, stilled. After Friday, he'd imagined that Mrs. Duncan was avoiding him, snickering be-hind his back, whispering to the Wilmington ladies about the Eighty-Second's Don Quixote who mistook himself for Don Juan.

A smile worth a month's pay stretched his lips. Yes, there was a god. God had deemed that he wouldn't have to negotiate truce with Marsh's sister that night over misguided matchmaking.

A grin scraped Marsh's mouth. "Got your invitation to the dinner party yet?"

Did Marsh know who'd been assigned to escort his sister? Michael doused his smile. Best to not appear cocky. After all, he was in the company of the lady's brother.

"Oh, it's coming, don't worry." Marsh's blue eyes glowed. "We haven't had any fun after the Committee of Safety ran Governor Martin out back in '75. No horseracing down Market Street. No cockfighting, balls, gambling, or theater productions. Nothing that gives life variety. And Kate, hah, I'd swear she took her cue from the Committee and turned Presbyterian on me. See here." He pulled a somber, long face. "Presbyterians aren't supposed to laugh, you know."

Marsh's apparent insensitivity baffled Michael. "Mr. Marsh, your sister told me her husband was killed five years ago during the battle at Moores Creek Bridge. Did you expect her to laugh after she was widowed?"

Resolve replaced the humor about Marsh's mouth. "Good riddance to Daniel Duncan. He wasn't the right man for Kate." He drew himself up to his full lanky height, two inches taller than Michael, almost as tall as Spry. "You know what?" The fingers of his free hand thumped Michael's chest once. "I'd have told him so to his face if I'd been a man instead of a boy when he married her."

For a second or two, Michael had nothing to say, fascinated by his first glimpse of a Kevin Marsh who wasn't a blithe twenty-two-year-old always deferring to his older sister, intrigued also by what Marsh *hadn't* said. Then, fifteen feet beyond the younger man, a barmaid with a tray laden with dirty crockery and tankards missed her step. Down both she and the tray went. The crash resounded through the building. A lull ensued in music and conversation.

Marsh winced. Without a glance of verification, he said low, "From the sound of it, that was at least nine soup bowls, six tankards, and one wench."

"Right you are, Mr. Marsh." Michael watched a patron give the barmaid a hand up and pass her a handkerchief to wipe bean soup off her arm.

Patrons' murmurs swelled back into the chatty din of good times. Marsh's mouth settled into a line of forbearance. "Enjoy your evening, sir." Then he strode over to assess the damages.

✱✱✱

At four thirty Wednesday morning, February seventh, Enid's rap at Michael's door signaled the availability of hot water just outside the door for his shave. He staggered from bed in a fog, having spent the entire night not quite asleep or awake, claiming benefits of neither state.

Fifteen minutes later, he deposited a bedroll, travel gear, greatcoat, and cocked hat just inside the dining room door. Then he wriggled about, irked with the snugness of his coat and waistcoat across his upper chest. He should have verified the fit of clothing he hadn't worn since the year he'd received his commission, then gotten Enid to let out the seams a bit.

Cold seeped in through the windows and flicked flames on two candles at the table. He uncovered a plate of fried eggs, ham, and toast. Alas, the coffee cup was empty. About the time he finished eating, he heard the back door squeak. In rushed Enid brandishing a pot of steamy, fragrant good morning, proven to shred sleep's ghosts within a quarter hour.

She filled his cup. While he mumbled gratitude, she set a canvas sack of travel rations on the table, then stepped back. Heat had flushed her plain face and imparted a demonic edge to her swarthy, Welsh features. Her black-eyed gaze jabbed the length of him, encompassed his clothing, and his dark hair drawn back at the nape of his neck with a ribbon, rather than in a military queue. Her glint softened. "You don't look like the same man."

He hoped not. Amused, he sipped more coffee. "And what man do I look like?"

"Like a man who owns a house and has four children and a wife, Mr. Honest Face."

Cynicism tinged his laughter. How fortunate that she hadn't thought he looked like a dispatch rider. He pushed away his plate and wiped his mouth with a napkin. "If I'm to own a house and support a family, hadn't I best find work that pays well?"

She sighed with sympathy. "Ain't it the truth? Give your life to fight for the King, and the Army doesn't award you but a pittance. What will you do when the war is over?"

The war. Yes, some day, it would be over. Then he'd be discharged.

He broke eye contact. Once he'd been Lord Crump's falcon handler. By the end of his first year in the Army, he could no longer see himself in such a position. With each passing year, he'd grown more disconcerted that he didn't know what to do with his life after his discharge.

Even with his connections, he didn't entertain the delusion that he'd see further promotion. When the war was over, he'd compete with hundreds of retired junior officers, all desperate for work, none able to support himself on his miniscule pension but eager to distinguish himself as more employable than the man before him, despite similar skills.

The mantle clock in the parlor announced the hour of five. Glad for the diversion, he pushed up from the table and snagged the sack of food. "I must be off. Feed Spry well." At the dining room door, he shrugged into the greatcoat, dropped the hat on his head, and shouldered his gear.

She raced ahead to the front door. "Two weeks you'll be gone, eh? My mistress might have returned home from South Carolina by the time you're back."

After what had happened to Enid's mistress in South Carolina, especially after her life had possibly been imperiled during Michael's collusion with that Janus-faced Adam Neville in attempt to kill Fairfax, Helen Chiswell might never want to see Lieutenant Stoddard again. But he had neither the time nor inclination to enter that discussion with Enid. "If necessary, have Spry claim my gear from the room."

Enid frowned. "I doubt my mistress will ask that you two board elsewhere. I shall speak well of you." She flapped her hand at the door. "Now get on with you and your secret mission."

Michael's head recoiled an inch. He hadn't told Enid anything about his mission. If she could guess so well, what would others figure out about him? He held up his forefinger. "Don't speak a word of this to anyone, not even to Spry."

"Not a word." She lifted the bar across the door and let him out into the raw predawn.

Chapter Five

TRAILING GOLD, THE sun stretched for the west horizon. Michael's mare, Cleopatra, splashed across the Eno River ford and clambered up the muddy north bank onto rust-colored Churton Street, Hillsborough's main road. The hamlet was tranquil, its businesses closed befitting a Sunday afternoon at five. Fragrant wood smoke arose from the chimneys of houses.

At King Street, tar splotched the roof of a crude courthouse. Just north of the courthouse, through cracks in a palisade surrounding a quiet jail, Michael glimpsed several horses hitched to a post. Hedgerows and low stone walls separated lots and gardens. Interspersed with the story-and-a-half-high dwellings that defined most residences were a few more grand, framed houses.

In the five days he'd sat in Cleopatra's saddle, Michael had ridden through sleet and outrun highwaymen. At the end of his third day on the road, he'd been forced to make camp in the brush, having discovered that his place of safety for the night was burned to the ground months earlier. Travel weary like his mare that Sunday afternoon, he envisioned Ezra Griggs knowing Cornwallis's exact location, Spry back in Wilmington throwing a local swindler into the stockade, and himself headed south on the morrow. With daylight fading, he pressed Cleopatra north to Queen Street.

Griggs's residence was last on the east end of the street. Hardwood forest and pines bordered the east and north edges of his property. Suppressing a yawn, Michael dismounted with his rifle before the little two-story, white wooden house and unlatched the gate. Griggs's neighbors to the west and south emerged from their houses and observed him in silence. He pushed the gate open, its hinges making a ghoulish grate upon the still air, and led Cleopatra into the yard, where he secured her reins, flung his greatcoat over the saddle, and closed the gate.

Movement in the dusk caught his eye. He blinked at a cloaked man who strode east across the back yard and vanished two seconds later among the trees. Curious, Michael stepped off the walkway toward the trees but was unable to spot more detail than the man's back and hat.

Stifling another yawn, he walked to the front door. By the third time he'd knocked and received no answer, dejection snared his weary body. Was it Griggs he'd spotted headed into the woods? Gods, he hoped not. He and Cleopatra were exhausted.

In the back yard, he walked past a garden and kitchen. At the stable door, he heard rustling from within. "Mr. Griggs? Ezra Griggs, are you in there?" But only a horse's snort responded.

Shoulders sagging, he faced the house, loath to seek an inn for the night when his host had probably stepped out for fresh air. His gaze landed on the back door. Ajar. He walked over and rapped on the doorframe. "Good evening, Mr. Griggs? Are you at home, sir? Mr. Griggs?"

Unnatural quiet issued from within. Hair prickled on his arms and neck. He pulled the door open, exposing a shadowy hall to feeble daylight. Air snagged in his throat. In the foyer, a table had been toppled, a vase lay smashed upon the floor, a bunched rug beneath both.

The image of the cloaked man in the yard jolted Michael's memory. His fingers clenched around his rifle. Had his arrival interrupted a burglary, an assault? "Mr. Griggs?"

He'd advanced four steps into the house when the metallic stench he knew too well from the battlefield assaulted his tongue. His gut tensed. He braked his hurry, slunk to the nearest open doorway, and peered around the frame into the study. Drawers were yanked from a desk and overturned. Ink, quills, and papers were strewn upon the wood floor, mixed with books heaved off shelves. Three ladder-back chairs lay upended, one splintered, as if slammed atop the others.

Michael's gaze skimmed the chaos but lingered on the broken chair. Rage. The intruder hadn't found what he was looking for. Rage, and possibly fear?

He dragged his focus to the front door, where he noted the bar lowered across it. Griggs hadn't let the intruder in through there. Heartbeat uneven with dread, Michael pressed onward. To his left, disorder in the dining room equaled what he'd seen in the study: chairs overturned, remnants of a china set tangled with table linen on the floor, cabinet doors open, shelves gaping.

At the front door, the source of the stench became clear. An automatic numbness that had served to blunt horror on battlefields permeated him. With powers of observation sharpened and instinct for survival honed, he rotated his head right, to the parlor.

By then, nothing in there came as a surprise. Not an overturned table beside a harpsichord. Not fireplace tools strewn about, a mantle clock shattered, a young lady's portrait above the fireplace slashed, or couch cushions scattered and ripped. Not even the man's body sprawled prostrate under the pile of debris. A dark, rank pool of lifeblood had emptied onto the rug beneath him. And from what Michael could see, he matched Major Craig's description of Ezra Griggs, his host for the night.

Men's voices in the front yard jerked his attention off the corpse. Griggs's murderer couldn't have been quiet in his search of the house. Neighbors must have reported the disturbance to the sheriff. Neighbors had also watched Michael arrive and walk around to the rear of the house.

A heavy fist pounded the front door, followed by a voice well over six feet tall and drenched in Prussian accent. "Mr. Griggs, you are at home? Georg Schmidt here, with my deputies."

Although Michael had lost his opportunity to escape unnoticed, he spun about and raced out the back door. Two men rounded the corner of the house and spotted him. In the second their surprise bought him, he knew how he must play it. He allowed shock to flood his expression and voice. "Are you men sent from the sheriff?" He pointed a shaky arm at the house. "There's a man murdered horribly in there, in the parlor!"

A dashing fellow with a dimpled chin and dark hair whipped a civilian pistol from his belt and leveled it at Michael. "Drop the rifle! And your dagger!" When Michael complied near the back step, the man motioned with his other hand. "Now step away from that door and your weapons, toward me. Good. Stand there, and don't move. Henry, grab his weapons and check the parlor." Irish brogue tangled his tongue.

Henry bypassed Michael, confiscated his weapons, and entered the house. The Irishman glared at Michael as if itching for him to attempt escape so he could plug him with a pistol ball.

Michael stood still and slumped his shoulders. His heart bounced off his ribs. Damn it all to hell. Here he was, on the scene of a murder in a town that bore no love for the Crown, carrying a coded message for Lord Cornwallis.

From inside the house, men's voices rose. Michael presumed that Henry had opened the front door. Ursine footsteps stomped for the back door. The voice of the man who'd named himself Georg Schmidt rumbled over Michael's right shoulder, "This one was in the house?"

Michael swiveled for a look at Schmidt, a man in his mid-thirties with red-blond hair, taller than Spry by several inches. The Prussian had crossed arms over his barrel chest and braced his legs apart on the back step. If the Norse god Thor threw his hammer at him, he looked capable of catching it and flinging it back with equal force.

"Aye, Mr. Schmidt."

"Mr. Griggs had his throat slit. I sent Henry to fetch the undertaker." Schmidt left the back step to walk a slow circle around Michael, eye him up and down. "I see no blood on him. Bring him front, where the light is better." Schmidt thumped into the house and banged the door shut.

"You heard him. Walk to the front yard. And don't try to escape."

Michael wondered, rattled, where he'd go, if he managed to escape. Not very far, even if he somehow gained access to his tired horse and galloped off. He had no shelter in Hillsborough.

When he rounded the front corner of the house, Cleopatra stood where he'd left her, his greatcoat still flung across the saddle. At least fifteen curious neighbors had gathered outside the fence. The reality that the incident had escalated to public spectacle ground panic in his gut.

His link to Cornwallis had been brutally slain. Thrust into the heart of the crime, Michael was no longer anonymous in Hillsborough. Even if he were cleared completely of Griggs's murder, his movements would be noticed. He wouldn't have the leisure of visiting local taverns and making discrete queries about the location of Cornwallis's army.

He used the seconds to steady his breathing and grope for the logic he channeled as an investigator. In his head, he stitched together a story, part truth, part lie, to clear himself of involvement in the murder. Never had he dreamed that he'd use that logic to save his own hide.

Two men he hadn't seen before exited the house and left the door open. Maybe they'd been with Schmidt when he knocked on the front door. Less than a minute later, Schmidt exited, Michael's rifle and dagger in his hands. Schmidt shut the door, inspected both weapons, and handed them to one of the men. He trudged out to where Michael waited. The men followed.

Teutonic blue eyes measured the Irishman hovering nearby. "O'Toole, you searched him?"

"No, sir." The man guarding Michael shoved his civilian-caliber courage into his belt.

A sigh of what sounded like forbearance hissed from Schmidt. "Search him."

Before he'd left Wilmington, Michael had committed to memory safe locations, bringing with him an unmarked map which he stored in a saddlebag. He submitted to the brief search, heard the clink of coins when O'Toole confiscated his purse and tossed it to Schmidt. When the Irishman relieved Michael of Craig's cipher, Michael willed himself to relax. O'Toole waved the dispatch in the air. "Hoo, see what I found in his waistcoat pocket. Shall I open it, Mr. Schmidt? He might be a loyalist spy!"

Michael's stomach became a flaming whirligig. That bloody cipher. He hoped Schmidt subscribed to the logic that a "spy" would conceal a dispatch in his boot or sleeve, rather than carrying it casually, in his waistcoat pocket, where ordinary men carried ordinary letters.

The redhead ignored O'Toole and tossed Michael's purse back to him. After replacing his purse, Michael reflected back to Schmidt the steady gaze of an innocent man.

Schmidt sucked his teeth about ten seconds. "What is your name?"

"Are you the county sheriff?"

Muscles around Schmidt's lips dragged one corner of his mouth up, then crooked the other. The smile spread his lips to a shape somewhat like that of North Carolina. "Schmidt, sheriff of Orange County. What is your name?"

From the smile and the sheer mass of the man's fists, Michael decided that being interrogated by him would not be a pleasant experience. "Compton."

"A very English name you have, Mr. Compton."

Eager O'Toole shifted from one foot to the other. "Sounds like he comes from the other side of the Atlantic, Mr. Schmidt."

Michael leaked a dry humor that he didn't feel into his voice. "So do half the people in this land, including both of you."

One of the two men behind Schmidt snickered. "He has a point there, sir."

Schmidt silenced him with a single look, directed his attention back to Michael, crossed his huge arms, and braced his feet apart again. The smile had faded from his face. "Mr. Compton, we come here in response to complaints of uproar. We find a murdered man inside. We find *you* inside. But if you are the killer, you are a mystery. You have no blood on you or your dagger."

More townsfolk had gathered beyond the fence. A wintry breeze rustled dried leaves. Michael repressed a shiver. "I didn't kill him, Mr. Schmidt."

The redhead uncrossed his arms and gave Michael's upper back a good-natured whump that jarred his teeth. "I am glad to hear you say that. Such an honest face. So we establish you are not a killer. Tell me how you know the victim, Mr. Griggs, when I have never seen you in town."

"I don't know Mr. Griggs. A neighbor of mine in Cross Creek was his friend years ago. When he learned I was headed this way to visit my aunt, he provided directions to Mr. Griggs's house and asked me to call on him, to see to his health."

"How many years ago did this neighbor of yours know Mr. Griggs?"

One of Michael's shoulders lifted in a shrug. "Oh, ten, maybe eleven, years ago."

Schmidt and his men drew in noisy breaths. A murmur swept the onlookers. Conscious that he'd said something volatile, Michael looked from face to face.

Schmidt's upper lip jerked. "A friendship from the time of the Regulators."

Regulators? Memory sputtered a reference to farmers who'd battled some ten years earlier with Royal Governor Tryon's militia. Ye gods. In his desire to knit together a plausible story, Michael hadn't factored in local history. "Mr. Griggs was a Regulator? Well, I can guarantee you that my neighbor in Cross Creek wasn't a Regulator."

Schmidt thrust out his chest. "Mr. Griggs was one of Henry McCullough's bookkeepers. He most certainly was not a Regulator. But Mr. McCullough and his land brokers made enemies by swindling farmers. The desire for revenge still runs deep in some."

Michael wondered if he'd just shifted suspicion for the murder onto the wrong party. In his peripheral vision, he saw O'Toole waving Craig's note around.

Without taking his gaze off Michael, Schmidt spat out, "*Ja*, O'Toole, what is it?"

"Suppose this friend of Mr. Griggs's in Cross Creek wrote something in his letter that tells us more about the killer? If a Regulator was responsible, maybe there are clues in here."

Michael wished he had about five minutes alone with O'Toole so he could rearrange his face. He chilled his tone. "Mr. O'Toole, you presume that letter was written for Mr. Griggs. It was not. The recipient is my widowed aunt."

His lunge for the letter came up short, a huge paw on his shoulder detaining him. "Who wrote the letter to your aunt?"

"An old beau in Cross Creek. He's now a widower. May I have her letter back, please?"

Schmidt released him and resumed his crossed-arms stance. This time, he pondered Michael with eyes like shillings: flat, metallic. "How did you come to call upon Mr. Griggs at this time?"

His confidence earlier that Michael hadn't been involved in Griggs's murder had been a ploy, an attempt to loosen up his witness enough to leak confession. Michael's pulse hopped about. So this was what it felt like to be on the receiving end of interrogation.

"See here. Two of Mr. Griggs's neighbors saw me arrive five minutes before you did." He dragged his tongue over dry lips. "Someone tore Mr. Griggs's house apart in a search." Michael stabbed a finger at Schmidt. "In five minutes, no one has time to murder, destroy evidence, and despoil a house." He straightened to his full height. "But I believe I saw the man who did so."

A gasp traveled the crowd. Schmidt's torso jerked as if Michael had struck him. His brows clashed in a burly reddish thunderstorm. "What do you mean you saw the murderer?"

Michael faced northeast and pointed to the trees, shrouded in the gloom of night. "Just after I arrived, I glimpsed him in the yard. Then he vanished among those trees. Mr. Griggs didn't answer my knock upon his door. I thought perhaps the man I saw was Mr. Griggs, so I walked to the back yard. That's when I noticed the door left ajar. I entered the house to investigate."

"You entered the house to investigate." His barrel of a chest shoved out, Schmidt lumbered around to face Michael. The sheriff's eyes were the temperature of the Matterhorn's summit. "Investigate? Who do you think you are, a criminal investigator?"

Again, Michael held his gaze, this time compressing his lips to lock in the truth of his occupation with the Eighty-Second Regiment. Schmidt was wasting time. He should have obtained a description from him and sent deputies into the woods after the cloaked man.

"Here is what *I* think, Mr. Compton. I think your family was cheated by Henry McCullough years ago. Since he is long gone from this area, you hired a henchman to kill his bookkeeper, then tear his house apart, make murder look like burglary. All of it to throw off suspicion from your Regulator past. You entered the house to make certain your man's work was thorough."

Tremors not from the cold gripped Michael's belly. He lowered his voice. "Mr. Schmidt, am I under arrest for this murder?"

"Who in this town can vouch for your identity, Mr. Compton? Mr. *Compton*. Is that your real name? Are you truly from Cross Creek?" The sheriff leered at the dispatch in O'Toole's hand. "Is your letter really for a widowed aunt?"

Sweat tickled Michael's back. "I see. You think it's some sort of secret message, and I'm a spy. Would a spy hide a secret message in his waistcoat where the local halfwit could steal it?"

"Hmm. Probably not."

Michael heard the scowl in O'Toole's voice. "Did you just call me a halfwit?"

"O'Toole never searched my boots. Isn't that where spies hide secret messages?"

People in the crowd laughed. Schmidt spread his hands and tilted his head a second to affect a posture of generous apology. "I do not know. I will not know until I have the opportunity to converse at length with you. Without the distractions of this audience."

Michael felt himself blanch. The sheriff planned to interrogate him tonight. He'd start by opening the letter, and he'd figure out the invisible ink, at which point it would become obvious that "Compton" hadn't couriered a love letter in his waistcoat pocket. From there, the night would degenerate.

"Come now." Schmidt pressed toward Michael one step. His leer creased chasms into his cheeks. "If *you* were investigating a murder, would you allow a stranger to go free when he has been apprehended on the site of the crime?"

Chapter Six

FEAR AND ANGER boiled through Michael. He dug in his heels against Schmidt's encroachment. "If I were a *competent* investigator, I'd obtain a description of the man a witness saw leaving the site of the crime, send my men into the woods after him. Before the undertaker arrived, I'd be inside that parlor listening to what Mr. Griggs can tell me about his last moments on this earth. From what I saw, it was clear to me that the man who killed him was enraged and desperate. How long will you let a man like that run loose on the streets of Hillsborough?"

A murmur of unease swelled from the spectators. Schmidt scowled and addressed the crowd in his heavy accent. "I give all of you my word that I will deal with the scoundrel who has taken the life of Mr. Griggs." He glowered at Michael. "And as for you—"

"Cousin Michael! What sort of trouble have you landed in this time?" A woman's voice rang out from the crowd, cutting off Schmidt.

Recognition slammed Michael. He swung around in incredulity. At the forefront of the crowd, just outside the fence, stood Kate Duncan, owner of White's Tavern in Wilmington, her hands on her hips beneath her cloak, annoyance rippling her face. In the next second, he read the flicker of fear that contracted her lips, the imploring in her eyes: *Play along!*

He exhaled disbelief and dragged the fakest grin he'd ever produced across his face. "Katie!"

Sincere indignation stamped out her annoyance. "You *know* I hate being called Katie." People made room for her to progress to the gate. "I've half a mind to let them haul you off to jail. But Aunt Rachel will have my head as well as yours if we're late for supper tonight."

"O'Toole," said Schmidt, "do you know this woman?"

"Widow White's niece, the Widow Duncan. Lives in Wilmington. Arrived

Friday to visit her aunt." A long, low growl of lust emptied from O'Toole.

That son of a dog. Michael lunged for and retrieved Major Craig's letter, in the process clipping the Irishman's groin with his knee and making it look quite accidental. "Oh, pardon me, sir." Leaving O'Toole gasping and doubled over his pistol, he strutted toward Kate Duncan, who had cleared the gate and stood beside Cleopatra.

Behind him, he heard O'Toole retch. A sick snake of satisfaction slithered through his blood. He had to play out his advantage. "How about a hug for your favorite cousin, eh?" He flung his arms wide, the letter still in his hand.

She grimaced. "You aren't my favorite, but I'll hug you anyway. It's been awhile."

La, he could grow fond of Kate Duncan's mercy. Aware of the scrutiny of spectators, he caught her up in his arms and swung her around a few times, the way he'd twirl his sister when he saw her again, after more than nine years of separation. Except that when he embraced his sister Miriam, he doubted the salty scent of a woman's throat or the roundness of her hip beneath his hand would rush heat from the soles of his feet to the crown of his head. And he doubted that Miriam would emerge from the hug with such high color in her cheeks.

He thrust Major Craig's note at her. "Here's another love letter to Aunt from Mr. Kirkleigh. Keep it safe, will you? I promised Cleopatra extra care before supper." He patted the mare's withers, dragged his greatcoat down, and draped it casually over his arm, hoping to divert spectator gazes off the flame in his face.

Blue eyes wide, she nodded. "A love letter, ah, yes." Her gaze flitted over his civilian clothing, hat to boots.

A spectator said, "Schmidt, looks like you barked up a wrong tree with this witness." Several people laughed in agreement. The crowd trickled away.

Michael faced the sheriff. Curiosity fueled Schmidt's regard as he approached him. Michael also read the score of potent hatred on O'Toole's handsome face as he straightened. No, he wouldn't be interrogated by Schmidt tonight. Yes, he'd best steer clear of the Irishman.

Schmidt's man Henry hustled into the yard through the gate. The somber fellow in his early twenties who accompanied him was dressed in a black wool coat and breeches and carried the leather valise of an undertaker. Schmidt's attention diverted to them. "Where is Mr. Pratt?"

"Abed and not well at all, Mr. Schmidt," said the younger man, his voice ethereally calm. "Had the parson praying over him this afternoon, reading scripture."

After a nod of acknowledgement, Schmidt gestured to the house. "Your client rests in the parlor. Mr. Henry will give you what help you need." Schmidt caught himself and glanced at Michael, as if mindful of his advice to "competent" investigators. "But I require a few moments with him first, so await me in the foyer." The undertaker's journeyman bowed and headed up the walkway for his realm, followed by Henry. Schmidt focused on Michael and assumed his signature stance.

Michael eyed him coolly. "I don't think much of your welcome to Hillsborough."

The Teutonic blue-eyed stare made a foray to Mrs. Duncan before pinning on Michael. "About this man you witnessed leaving the property as you arrived—"

"White man, medium height, dark gray or brown greatcoat, black cocked hat, neither very young nor very old. As the area was already in heavy shade, and his back was to me, I'm unable to provide more detail."

Schmidt's lower lip pushed upward. "Too dark in those woods now. We will find nothing in a search tonight. I shall set men on the task at first light." His gaze narrowed and scraped over Michael, up and down. "Also in the morning, I will have more questions for you. I will call upon you at Mrs. White's residence."

Well, that settled the question of where Michael would lay his head for the night. Terror had emptied from his blood, trailing behind a tremble in his fingers and a quick chatter of his teeth. He slung his greatcoat over his shoulders, making certain it covered his shaky hands from Schmidt's sight. "You do that. Excuse me. I've a dining engagement with two lovely ladies."

"A moment longer, Mr. Compton." A generous smile oozed from Schmidt's face. "You do not have my permission to leave town until Mr. Griggs's murder is solved."

"Eh?" Michael frowned at him. "I cannot wait on you. I own a business in Cross Creek."

"If you leave town without my permission, I will pursue and arrest you."

"But you may never find Mr. Griggs's killer!"

"Ah, but I will, and I will find him soon, because you will be helping me."

Panic smeared fire through Michael's blood. How was he to find Cornwallis and deliver the message in a timely manner if he were ensnared in an inquiry? "Absurd! I'm no investigator."

"Ha ha ha, what *Scheiße*." Schmidt's eyes glowed like an aurora borealis. "I know a logical man when I meet him. If you have never in your life participated in an investigation, I will eat Mr. Kirkleigh's love letter to your aunt."

He uncrossed his arms, seized Michael's right hand, and pumped it. "I hereby deputize you as my assistant. Congratulations!" He grabbed Michael's weapons from his man and presented them to Michael as if they were keys to unlock every door in town. "Welcome to Hillsborough, Mr. Compton."

***

In the dusk, Michael stomped away from Ezra Griggs's house with Cleopatra's reins in one hand and his rifle in the other. He'd made Schmidt, already suspicious of him, appear incompetent in front of townsfolk. That earned him the opportunity to work his tail off beneath the eye of a hostile investigator. Huzzah.

The petite blonde scurrying to keep pace at his side didn't wait for them to outdistance Schmidt's hearing. "Will you please tell me what's going on?"

"You've my eternal gratitude, Cousin Kate. You rescued me from spending a night in jail."

She didn't lower her voice. "I haven't rescued you. Don't expect to have a rollicking fun time here. You just got yourself deputized as Mr. Schmidt's assistant. You'd be better off spending a night in jail than investigating murder. That's dangerous."

Not *this* jail, with *this* lead investigator thrashing him for the truth. He leaned toward her, wiggled an eyebrow, and whispered, "And spending a night under your roof *isn't* dangerous?"

She gaped, then attempted a severe expression—spoiled when a snort of humor popped through. "Those aren't cousin-like thoughts," she murmured, evading his gaze.

How true. But many of his thoughts about Kate Duncan weren't very cousin-like. From the fresh color in her cheeks, he suspected the feeling was mutual to some extent. Cocky elation filled his stride. Ice Widow his arse.

The gravity of his circumstances returned and yanked his feet back to earth. "Er, Aunt Rachel's letter—"

"Yes, yes, I have it safe. Aunt reads all of Mr. Kirkleigh's letters to me. He has quite a way with his words. I look forward to this letter." She cocked an expectant eyebrow at him.

He hadn't determined how much of the black, bloody mess he could tell her, but instinct warned him to destroy that letter at the earliest opportunity. Aware that townsfolk might still be listening to their conversation, he said, "I don't recall exactly how to get to Aunt's house, so do lead the way, else we shall be wandering town after dark with a killer on the loose."

She fell silent and took the lead back south on Churton Street, allowing him time to ruminate over his predicament. For all of ten seconds, he considered his odds of succeeding if he sneaked from town. Not only could he envision Schmidt pursuing him like a game hunter, but he'd also encounter resistance from residents to divulging information about Cornwallis's army movements. An escape attempt was almost certain suicide. Alas, for the time, he saw assisting Schmidt in solving Griggs's murder with haste as his best route to extricating himself from the muddle in Hillsborough so he could complete his own mission.

On the opposite side of town from Griggs's house, Kate Duncan led him past the front of a tavern on west King Street—her aunt's, closed for the night— and onto property behind the tavern. He took his bearings in the darkness and, from several smaller buildings behind the tavern, including a two-story house, concluded that Mrs. White owned at least two adjacent lots.

A couple of mid-sized hounds barked at them from the back porch of the house and loped over to investigate, their tails wagging for the woman, but reserved around Michael until they'd sniffed him and his mare. When they'd satisfied their curiosity, he was free to pat their heads. They returned to the porch.

At the stable, Kate said, "Here we are, Mr. Stoddard. Plenty of fresh straw and hay for Cleopatra inside. I shall run over to the kitchen, fetch a light for you, and heat water so you can wash up behind the stable. And locate Aunt, let her know we've a guest."

He winced at the use of his surname, glanced about to reassure himself that they were alone. "You cannot use my true family name. I gave Mr. Schmidt the name of Compton."

"Oh, yes, you did. Hmm. You realize that you'll have to tell Aunt some of this." In the darkness, he saw the defiant tilt of her chin. "And me. Tell me why you're here in civilian clothing, and—and the letter. It's a dispatch, isn't it?

You're a courier, and—" In the silence of a few seconds, he heard wind murmur in the pines above them. Then she sighed, her tone flat. "You're carrying a message for the British Army. If you're revealed, you'll be executed."

He wondered that she hadn't puzzled out that much at Griggs's house or during the walk and studied the outline of her face, silent. She was an intelligent woman. She'd figure out the final piece with no prodding from him. Ultimately, she had a decision to make. How well did he know Kate Duncan? Not half as well as he wished he'd known her before the universe had seen fit to place his life in her hands. He waited, his mouth dry.

"If you're revealed, and Aunt and I have been sheltering you, sanctions will be imposed upon us and the tavern." She exhaled this time, the sound hard. "Blast war. It doesn't ask us to cleave to higher principles, character traits such as integrity. It commands us to choose between arbitrary divisions that may not even exist a year later.

"I saw how you handled that investigation in Wilmington two weeks ago. I heard how you helped Alice Farrell, too. I know what kind of person you are. If I can help it, no one will find out about you or that dispatch."

He bowed his head long enough to exhale relief. "Thank you." There was still Aunt Rachel to deal with, but he'd take support when and where he got it.

"You need your letter straight away so you can deliver it." She pulled one side of her cloak open, prepared to retrieve the dispatch from wherever she'd secured it.

"No. Keep it safe for now. Ezra Griggs was the intended recipient, the final courier who knew where to find the army. Someone killed him, so I must burn the evidence, locate the army myself, and verbally deliver the message."

Her cloak fell closed, and he felt her stare on him. "My God. How can you do that when Mr. Schmidt has you trapped here in Hillsborough?"

Dark humor escaped him in a brief laugh. "Yes, Mr. Schmidt 's terms present a bit of hurdle for me, don't they? It behooves me to close this inquiry as quickly as possible so I can be on my way. The longer I remain—"

"The less valuable your message, and the more your life is endangered." She turned from him, unlatched the stable door, and swung it open. From within, he smelled horse, heard a sleepy snort. "Heigh there, Charlie, good boy." The white blaze up a horse's nose emerged from night in the nearest stall and wandered toward Kate's extended hand, received her caresses.

"That's your horse? You didn't ride here all by yourself, did you?"

"Goodness, no. There are plenty of regular business travelers between Wilmington and Hillsborough. I know many and ride with them and their wives. And we all know the places to stop for the night." She peered at him. "I presume you found guest houses on the way up. No sleeping in the brush like a barbarian?"

He thought of Friday night, when he'd slept in the brush like a barbarian. "Of course I found guest houses."

"Good." She unhooked a lantern from a peg beside the door and regarded her horse again. "Charlie, here's a lady named Cleopatra to share the stable with you for a few days. And meet her master, Mr. Stoddard, er, Mr. Compton—hmm, this will take some getting used to."

"Mr. Schmidt has heard us use our Christian names. Cousin."

She held still, her face tilted from him, and he sensed her adjusting to the wrinkle in social convention. Then she scratched the horse between the ears. "Whew, Charlie, I don't know what Aunt will make of all this. But do say good evening to Cleopatra's master, my long-lost cousin, Michael."

Chapter Seven

BY LANTERN LIGHT, he removed greatcoat, coat, and waistcoat and donned a grimy, horsy apron hanging in the stable. He took off Cleopatra's tackle and picked burrs from her tail and mane and dirt from her hooves. The tri-colored hounds returned with a slobbery, twelve-inch-diameter canvas ball stuffed with the gods only knew what, insistent that he complete the welcome ritual by playing fetch with them for half an hour, and bumping him with cold, wet noses whenever they felt he spent too long on Cleopatra. By the time he brushed the mare down with a currycomb and dislodged dried mud from the trail, she nuzzled him like a mistress, well pleased at being kept in such comfort.

Exhaustion dragged at his arms and legs. With the mare settled in her stall munching hay, he removed the apron, collected the lantern, his clothing and gear, and secured the stable, hardly able to bear the smell of himself: a bracing blend of man-sweat, horse, dog, and trail that threatened to befoul the delectable aromas from the kitchen next door. A trudge behind the stable rewarded him with privacy and the warm water, soap, and towel that Kate had left him. He rid himself of resemblance to a barbarian, changed into clean clothes, just as snug fitting as the other set, and swapped boots for shoes for his first meeting with Rachel White.

Intercepted by Kate outside the kitchen, he deposited his soiled clothing in a basket she extended. She pronounced him presentable and marched him to the house.

Notions of what Mrs. White would look like, based on his brief chat with Kevin Marsh at the tavern Tuesday night, shattered as soon as he entered the parlor. Instead of a frail, tiny lady with snowy hair who was too befuddled to operate a tavern by herself, he found himself faced with a sturdy-boned matron with iron-gray hair caught up beneath a prim mobcap. She rose erect from her couch and presented a formal curtsy, her dark brows pinched downward.

When he straightened from his bow, Kate said in a firm tone, "This is my aunt, Mrs. White."

"I'm pleased to meet you, Mrs. White." His stomach didn't feel pleased at all.

Aunt Rachel's gaze sliced the length of him like a razor on a strop. She swept over and inspected him up close, less than an inch shorter than he. "I suppose I'm pleased to meet you, too, Mr. Stoddard." At his start upon hearing his name, she twitched her nose. "Oh, yes, I know all about you. My niece patched together a piece of your story, but I sniffed out the rest and now have the entire game of whist spread upon the table before me."

If women could wear the scarlet of His Majesty, Mrs. White's uniform would sport braid on both shoulders and buttons of gold. "Thank you for your hospitality, madam."

"An officer of the King, out of uniform, bearing a secret message."

He said nothing. Kevin Marsh wanted this woman to live with them in Wilmington—why?

"And a criminal investigator—how long do you expect to stay under my roof?"

Kate stepped forward, shoulders stiff. "Aunt Rachel, that's impolite of you!"

Jail and Georg Schmidt were looking better and better with each passing second. If Mrs. White insisted that he sleep in the stable, by God, he'd oblige. The horses and dogs liked him. "This isn't a forcible occupation, madam. I shall leave town as soon as I have assisted Mr. Schmidt in apprehending a most heinous criminal."

"Assisting Georg Schmidt, of all people—ye gods!" Color compressed from her lips. Then the Queen of the Olympians brushed past him, the heels of her shoes flogging the wooden steps in a tattoo of anger and frustration during her exit from the parlor. He thought he heard a stifled sob.

"I don't believe this!" Kate's teeth sounded clenched.

As she rushed past him, giving chase to her aunt and still in her shawl, Michael snagged her upper arm. "This arrangement isn't going to work. I shall sleep in the stable tonight, and on the morrow, concoct a plausible story for Mr. Schmidt that allows me to reside in an inn while I'm in Hillsborough."

"You'll do nothing of the sort." Kate shook his hand off her arm and jerked her head toward the couch. "Have a brandy. You could probably use one after finding Mr. Griggs murdered this afternoon. Wait on the couch. Aunt will come around. I suspect that Mr. Griggs's death has rekindled her grief over my cousin, Aaron."

A fog swept through Michael's reasoning. "Your cousin Aaron? Who the devil is he? What does he have to do with all this?"

"Aaron eloped with Mr. Griggs's daughter, Violet, almost ten years ago. We've never heard from either of them since then. It just about broke Aunt Rachel's heart." Kate stalked from the parlor after her aunt.

For a quarter minute, Michael stared at a parlor doorway empty of women but resonating with their anger and loss. "Shit," he muttered, and sought first the brandy decanter, then the fireplace, the only area in the house where he could expect to find warmth. An elopement. Almost as traumatic to a family as a suicide. Damned, fouled-up families. Blockheaded children and parents.

He sipped brandy and studied the visual play of flame upon wood. Tricked out of tension, his tired brain feinted at the question of who had killed Ezra Griggs. Had the murderer been an ex-Regulator exacting revenge on the employee of a man who'd cheated him? What man would harbor thoughts of vengeance for a decade? Might Griggs's downfall actually be rooted in more recent, less complex events? Griggs had couriered messages for Crown forces. North Carolina was loaded with rebels who'd slit the throats of such loyalists spies.

At length, grown too warm before the fire, Michael perched on a couch cushion and examined the one-eighth glass of brandy in his right hand. " 'Alas, poor Yorick,' you and I must seek another place to lay our heads for the morrow, then close this investigation quickly before we run out of money in Hillsborough."

The clock in the parlor struck eight. A leonine roar erupted from Michael's empty stomach. What lie about his lodgings could he tell Schmidt on the morrow that sounded believable? He held his brandy glass higher and rehearsed into it. "My aunt turned me out. My fault. I had a bit much wine, was an insufferable lout, made the mistake of mentioning that I'd once been infatuated with Miss Violet Griggs. And maybe if I'd pressed my suit more convincingly upon her, she might have married me and not eloped with Cousin Aaron."

Over the rim of his brandy glass, his gaze met Kate's. She squinted at him from the doorway. "What's that you say?"

He stood, the glass of brandy at his side. "The ravings of a weary traveler. How is Mrs. White?"

"I gave her laudanum. You and I shall dine alone tonight." She strolled forward to sit on the couch not far from him. "We've leftover beef stew. Aunt's servant, Martha, has Sunday off."

"Thank you." Michael realized that she'd removed not just her shawl but her tucker. A pale blue, boned jacket pushed up her breasts, exposing a plentiful expanse of creamy skin on her bosom, throat, and neck to the orange glow of the room. He gulped the remainder of his brandy, lowered the glass to the tray, and sat as close to her as propriety would allow. "Under the circumstances, I feel awkward imposing upon you and your aunt."

Her focus was directed across the room. "Under the circumstances, you have few options. Didn't Major Craig tell you that there are few loyalists in Hillsborough? Almost as few true rebels. It creates a political climate where there are few places an officer of the Eighty-Second can shelter without drawing attention to himself."

Michael made his words emerge lazily, as if he were bored and no longer cared. "So if Crown forces came through the area, they'd find their recruitment efforts wasted. The nearest regiments are probably deep in Virginia or South Carolina."

"Yes, who knows? Yesterday in Market, I overheard two men batting about a rumor that General Cornwallis's army wasn't but ten miles away."

The news, even wrapped in rumor, whisked the blaze of purpose along Michael's nerves. "If the army were that close, area residents would already have spotted advance forces, scouts and dragoons."

"Exactly. It must be a rumor. In the meantime, don't you worry about Aunt. That business will all straighten out on the morrow." Pensive, she leaned forward and grasped her knees.

The action deepened her cleavage, and her breasts seemed to be pressing against something within her shift. Fascinated, he craned his neck to get a better view. "Ah, tell me, why wouldn't the Whites and the Griggses allow Aaron and Violet to marry?"

"Oh, my aunt and uncle were fine with a wedding, but Aaron, he had a club foot, and all he stood to inherit was the tavern. Apparently Mr. Griggs entertained fantasies that he could arrange a match between Violet and someone a bit higher up socially."

"Because he worked for the land agents and Henry McCullough."

"Yes."

"A sordid mess that was, then, and one of the quickest recipes I know for reinforcing the desire to elope in young people." Michael twisted his torso and achieved visual identification at last on the object nestled in Kate's bosom. He slid his arm along the back of the couch behind her, jarring her from reflection. "I appreciate your keeping my letter safe." He darted a glance to her bosom.

She straightened, realized that his face hovered about ten inches from hers, and pulled back a bit, little spots of color on her face again. "You look *so* different in those clothes. I almost didn't recognize you in Mr. Griggs's yard."

"I'm grateful that you did."

"Do you want the letter back now?" He lifted his hand and flexed his fingers. Her brows lowered, and her upper lip pressed downward. "You're joking, of course." She reached into her bodice, worked the letter out herself inch by inch—a wrinkled, crumpled descendent of the letter he'd given her a few hours earlier—and slid it between his expectant fingers, warm and no longer smelling the slightest bit like Major James Henry Craig. Michael's groin tightened and delivered a rousing salute.

Hiding a secret message in a woman's bodice was every bit as hackneyed as hiding a secret message in a man's boot. Still, he was glad he'd lived to see the day. "Seems a shame to destroy it now."

"Don't be a lamebrain." She gave his chest a gentle shove backward.

He pushed up from the couch, walked to the fireplace, and, while the jollification in his breeches calmed down, broke the seal on the letter. A perusal of it had him thanking the Fates that Schmidt and O'Toole hadn't read it. Although Michael had never personally written a love letter, he'd "proofread" successful missives penned by ardent fellow officers. Craig's letter, trite and bland, read exactly like what it was, the cover letter for a hidden cipher.

He cast the letter in, where coals captured and inflamed it. After it appeared incinerated, he stirred coals with a poker, made sure no large chunks of paper remained to be sucked up the chimney, and added a split log to the glow. The right combination of air and dried surface for the log eluded the flame. He squatted and prodded the split log with the poker. "Kate, back at Mr. Griggs's house, Mr. Schmidt mentioned the Regulators. I admit to knowing their story in only a vague sense."

"What would you like to know about them?"

"I've heard they were settlers, mostly farmers. Back in the '60s, land agents for Lord Granville cheated them, yes?" Hearing her murmur of affirmation, he prodded the log again. "Governor Tryon wasn't as responsive on the issue as they'd have liked." Sarcasm pulled a snort from him. "No doubt he was friends with some of the agents. So these disgruntled farmers banded together, and Tryon assembled his militia, and they battled—when? Where?"

"May of 1771. In Alamance County, about twenty-five miles from here."

"Governor Tryon's militia prevailed?" He rotated his neck to study her.

"Yes, easily. The Regulators scattered. Over the next week or so, the militia rounded up leaders of the movement. In June, they were tried here in Hillsborough." Her lips puckered, as if she'd tasted something sour. "The trial didn't last very long. They say that Tryon had already received his appointment to the governorship of New York by then. He was eager to put the Regulators behind him, move along to a civilized colony. So he rushed through the trial, acquitted two men, condemned twelve to death, and pardoned six of those on execution day."

Thus demonstrating the mercy of the Crown. Acrimony sat in Michael's gut. In his experience, neither the Crown's clemency nor its cruelty had kept men and women from committing crimes. Not that rebel justice worked any better.

Kate continued, "The governor hanged the six men east of here, off the Halifax Road. Old Abijah Pratt the undertaker buried them in a common grave somewhere that night. Tryon and a number of local officials who had incurred his favor left town for New Berne the next day. I hear they sailed for New York together, a happy family." A sigh jerked from her. "Aaron and Violet had eloped sometime on execution day. Mr. Griggs staunchly proclaimed that they'd eloped the day before, arguing with Aunt for years about it, but she declares that Aaron swept the tavern floor the morning of the executions. They cannot both be right." She rubbed her eyelids with fingertips. "I do wish that Aunt hadn't feuded with Mr. Griggs all those years."

"What did you think of Mr. Griggs?"

"I didn't know him very well." She folded hands in her lap. "Not a very warm man."

"The sort who would make enemies?"

She smoothed a wrinkle in her petticoat. "I don't like to speak ill of the dead."

Dejection plucked at Michael's heart. He'd seen it before. Murder victims who'd been unfriendly in life never had just one suspect in death. No doubt a number of area residents still held sympathy for the Regulators and—because Griggs had worked indirectly against them—antipathy toward Griggs. "What can you tell me about Georg Schmidt?"

"He's been a deputy until recently. Supposedly he came from the Moravian community in Bethabara about seven years ago."

That confirmed Michael's hunch about Schmidt's accent. But Michael couldn't envision Schmidt leading the pacific life of a Moravian, herding cattle and praying. He jabbed the log into just the right spot, stood, and replaced the poker in its stand. "He doesn't strike me as a conflict-averse fellow. Was he expelled from the community?"

"Aunt would know better than I." Her voice sounded tense. "She and

Schmidt have never seen eye-to-eye, as long as he's been in Hillsborough."

"Where were you during that time?" He faced her, arms at his sides.

"In Wilmington." *Married*, said her eyes before she picked imaginary lint off her petticoat.

After what her brother had told him Tuesday night, after what she herself had implied the previous week, he knew that widowhood was both boon and convenience for her. To the courts, a married woman was property, powerless. But a widow was no longer legally under the control of a man.

Whenever undesirables came courting, Kate offered a brusque rejection, the shield that Daniel Duncan still claimed her heart. What Michael wondered was whether the Scotsman who'd died at the Battle of Moores Creek Bridge had ever claimed her heart. He'd certainly left a rotten taste in her mouth for the entire masculine gender.

And what did Kate do when she found herself the object of a handsome fellow's admiration? "What can you tell me about Schmidt's assistant, O'Toole?"

Face contorted, fists balled, she rose with a hiss. "I was hoping he'd be gone when I returned to Hillsborough on Friday. The way he tomcats around with the ladies, even the married women, is vile. Not a drop of integrity in that man."

Michael stood still, taken aback by her intensity. Then smugness rolled over him. O'Toole's free navigation among the ladies that night could be a bit hampered by the warning shot Michael had fired across his bow in Griggs's front yard earlier.

The next moment, he realized that Kate had used the word "integrity" again that night, in an unconscious contrast between him and O'Toole. If the Irishman had been the redcoat in civilian clothes carrying a ciphered message, and he'd been the one to stumble upon Griggs's body, Kate would never have stuck her neck out for him. She'd have let Schmidt haul him off to jail and toy with him all night. And she certainly wouldn't have sheltered him in her aunt's home.

The courts were mistaken to believe that women had no power. He laughed, understanding that sooner, rather than later, Aunt Rachel would accept a redcoat beneath her roof because Kate would make it so.

Kate's scowl deepened. "What's so amusing about O'Toole?"

"He won't lose his job for philandering."

"How unfortunate." She rushed past him for the foyer, wafting the scent of cinnamon his way. "Let's eat."

Poor O'Toole, dismissed in favor of day-old stew. One corner of Michael's mouth crooked, and he followed Kate to the cloak rack.

Chapter Eight

"SAMMY. LIZZIE. COME." Kate headed upstairs with her candle.

The hounds followed her halfway, then scampered back for the parlor, toe-nails clicking on wood, to curl up with groans of contentment at the head and foot of Michael's pallet near the fireplace. Squeaky stairs announced Kate's return to the parlor doorway. Michael rose up on an elbow. "Go on to bed. I don't mind it if the dogs want to sleep in here with me."

Dubiousness rippled her lips: the sort of pink, full, moist woman's lips that parted in a kiss with little persuasion. "Both of them snore."

He forced his gaze off her lips and onto the closest dog, giving him a scratching behind the ears. Sammy rewarded him with a hearty tail-thumping. "And soldiers don't snore?"

"I see your point. Very well, Sammy and Lizzie may keep you company to-night."

And off to bed Kate went, for the fourth time that night. Michael listened to the retreat of her footsteps and the dwindling creak of the stairs, lay back, and pulled the blanket over his shirt to his chin. Relief and disappointment emptied from him in a sigh. Most of him hoped she really had gone to bed that time. Integrity was a wonderful quality in a man, but surely it couldn't stand up to the creativity more than a year of abstinence had honed in him for the skill of seduction, not when a woman like Kate Duncan was involved.

Foolish idea, more than a year of abstinence.

But was continuing to lust after an unattainable woman a foolish idea? He had no money, no way to keep a mistress, no employment awaiting him in Yorkshire, no means to support a wife and family. All he could afford to lust after were dreams. He may as well indulge in those.

Schmidt wouldn't accept less than his best work on the morrow. Michael needed all of his brains lodged in his skull. He flung a forearm over his eyes and told himself to sleep.

***

If he'd been less exhausted, less turbulent, even in sleep, he'd have recognized the cruelty his mind worked on him and escaped the nightmare before it ran its course. In his eagerness to take advantage of a dreamtime foray Kate made beneath his blanket, he neglected to pay attention when they switched location from the pallet in her aunt's parlor in wintry Hillsborough to a straw pile in Lord Crump's mews, in summery Yorkshire. However, he didn't fail to take notice when the blonde straddling his sweaty, naked hips was no longer Kate, but Lydia.

He cursed and tried to buck her off him. After the way of nightmares, paralysis besieged him. Blue eyes soul-less, she slapped her palms to his shoulders and pinned him to the straw with the weight of her upper body. Dust motes lazed across his field of vision, swirled around her dangling, damp breasts. Horrified, fascinated, his gaze followed a bead of sweat as it rolled the curve of her breast and clung to the end of a nipple as taut as a ruddy, baby grape.

"My pet," she murmured, "you were too hasty last time. Where are your manners? You must allow the lady to go first." The droplet of sweat dislodged from her nipple.

When it plopped to his chest, it ignited. A scream ripped from Michael. He writhed against Lydia, his torso blistering, engulfed in flame like Major Craig's message to Lord Cornwallis. Finally he cast her off him, only to jettison himself onto the battleground at Brandywine, face down in the dirt. Just above him, the sergeant who'd knocked him down caught the cannonball. It sheared off the right side of his head, showering Ensign Stoddard with blood and brains. On hands and knees, he hauled himself from beneath body parts and, five feet away, puked up the reek of dirt, dung, and death.

***

Shaking, he crouched on the pallet in Rachel White's parlor. If damnation had a sound, it would be that of his own ragged breath in the middle of the night after careening through hell in his sleep. He rocked back on his heels and sat, pulled the blanket around him. Some soldiers were cursed with these nightmares every night. One he'd known had rid himself of the nightmares by jamming the barrel of a loaded pistol in his mouth and squeezing the trigger. Many were never able to divert the course of the hell-beasts they rode in their sleep. He imagined men who survived the war being shipped home and turned loose upon society to earn livings, raise families. An entire generation of young men, demon-ridden to eternity.

One of the hounds whined. Michael realized that both dogs had left his side and moved into the foyer, near the door. He pulled on his breeches and buttoned them. Middle of the night, devil of a time, but when a dog needed to piss—

A whisper of sound outside the parlor window made him stiffen, listening. Maybe just branches shaking in the breeze. Then both Sammy and Lizzie growled, low. Michael knelt, fumbled about for his stockings and drew them on. Unable to locate his garters in the dark, he stuffed his feet into his shoes.

The dogs' growls intensified. Something scratched at the window. A hound bounded over and emitted a deep, protective bark. Michael lunged forward and flung back the drape. On the other side of the glass, crouched in the low bushes, a man froze in the act of trying to force open the window, his facial features wrapped in the shadow of a hat with a huge feather in it. Michael's blood leapt from his veins before diving back in again. "God damn it!"

He sprang back, and both hounds launched at the window, barking and baying. Michael scooped his loaded rifle from where he'd propped it beside the fireplace and scrambled for the front door, hounds at his heels. Tempted to turn dogs loose on the would-be burglar, he acknowledged that the animals weren't his to command, so he forced them back into the foyer before unbarring the door.

Kate called downstairs, "Michael, what is it? What's wrong?"

Ignoring her, he cracked the door open enough to let himself out into the frigid night, all senses on alert. A cursory glance told him that no one crouched in the bushes beneath the parlor window. He stepped off the porch, away from the house to diminish some of the clamor of dogs, and recognized the crashing run of a retreat in progress. He squinted out, saw the rogue closing on trees bordering the property. He appeared to be limping. Maybe he'd twisted his ankle in his haste to escape. "You greasy rat." With the rifle cocked, he drew it to his shoulder, sighted despite the long odds of hitting a target at night, and squeezed the trigger.

With the boom of the fired rifle, he imagined he heard the man yelp, but when the echoes of the shot had faded and smoke had cleared, his prey gained the cover of the trees, still running, and vanished. Michael lowered the rifle and hoped he'd inspired the trespasser to foul his breeches and stay away for good.

Out of habit, he returned to the bushes beneath the parlor window and scanned the area, not expecting to find much in the dark. Peripheral vision detected a wisp fluttering in the breeze, caught atop a bush. He snagged it: a goose feather. Imagination crafted a man-sized goose dressed in a greatcoat, attempting to force Mrs. White's parlor window open. "Holy Christ." He tossed the feather back onto the bushes.

His only weapon the unloaded rifle, he patrolled around the exterior of the house once to confirm that the burglar had brought no accomplices. Next, he checked the stable and kitchen. Ignoring the gouge of cold through his shirt, he circled the expanse of a winter vegetable garden, then visited the vault. Back on the front porch of the house, he stomped dirt and dead grass off the soles of his shoes. The dogs had quit barking.

When he opened the door to the foyer, Lizzie and Sammy welcomed him back with slapping tails and cold, wet noses. Illuminated by two lit candles above the parlor fireplace, Kate whisked the ramrod from the barrel of a musket, no more a stranger to her hands than a tray of tankards from the tavern. A clean click of metal announced that she'd returned the ramrod to its holder. She faced him, a shawl tucked over her shift and petticoat, her stockinged feet stuffed in clogs. "Bear or wolf?"

He closed the door, set down his rifle, and slid the bar into place. "Human."

Above the thrust of her eyebrow, her forehead furrowed. "Human?"

Shivering, he entered the parlor, propped his rifle into place, snatched up his coat, and pulled it on. While he was outside, she'd fanned the coals and cast another log on the fire. He squatted, extended his hands for warmth. "Does your aunt have a neighbor who habitually mistakes her house for his and tries to enter through the front window in the middle of the night?"

"Of course not."

"Then I suspect we've just been visited by a burglar."

The whites of her eyes glittered. She jammed her dangling jaw shut and knelt near him, the musket across her lap. "You caught him trying to break in?"

"Pushing on the front window, in fact."

"Good heavens. Did you wound him with the rifle?"

"Alas, no, and he's off in those woods out there, so we've a murderer *and* a burglar running about Hillsborough." The dogs flopped on the floor nearby and sighed, content. Michael rubbed his hands, still trying to restore sensation. "Frontier lawmaking. Quite like Wilmington before the Eighty-Second arrived. I don't wonder that your brother spoke of moving your aunt out of here."

"He mentioned that to you, did he? Well. Thank goodness she slept through all of this."

"She did?" Michael eyed Kate with astonishment. Her aunt had slept through a rifle shot. "How much laudanum did you give her?"

"Enough to get her through the night." She set the musket on the floor beside her and fanned away a whorl of smoke that escaped the chimney. "Well, perhaps I didn't make myself clear earlier. Aunt Rachel hasn't slept well for ten years. She blamed the elopement on Mr. Griggs's refusal to give Aaron permission to marry Violet. The way she sees it, if Mr. Griggs hadn't been so determined for Violet to breathe wealthy air, we'd have both of them with us today."

Michael cocked an eyebrow at her. "Did your aunt tell Mr. Griggs that?"

She nodded at him. "Apparently she did so about a year after the elopement, right after my uncle Clarence died. Aaron is their only child, you see, so Uncle's death after the elopement left Aunt all alone, very much grief-stricken. I can understand her grief at losing Aaron because—" She jerked her gaze away from him, refocused it in the fire. Her expression convulsed for a second, then smoothed. "That is, I don't understand how she could blame Mr. Griggs all these years for a decision Aaron and Violet made. It was their choice."

Michael studied her profile, curious at the sentence she'd stopped herself from completing, almost certain from the context that it had been Kate's acknowledgement that she'd lost a child of her own. In Kate's case, she hadn't lost a youth poised on manhood, but a babe in arms. Perhaps not even that.

He'd never forget his sister's sobs of anguish over her stillborn daughter. But no way in hell would he get clarification from Kate that moment. The loss of a child was a piece of past presided over and protected by the formidable Ice Widow. He said, "Yes, it was their choice."

Made conscious of his scrutiny by his delayed response, perhaps even aware of how much she'd revealed of herself, she rushed her words along and fluttered her hands, avoiding his gaze. "While you were tending Cleopatra in the stable, I told Aunt of Mr. Griggs's murder. Do you know what she said to me? She said that he deserved it, after selfishly standing in the way of Aaron and Violet marrying in a church."

Michael winced, grasped Kate by the shoulders, and rotated her to him. "Your aunt is a very unhappy woman. Laudanum isn't going to help her."

She swallowed. "*I know.*"

A personal confession, he was certain. Perhaps like her aunt, Kate had blamed someone for the loss of her child. And he was willing to wager that Kate had been inside a laudanum bottle. But he'd never seen any sign of narcotic dependency in her. Somehow, she'd pulled herself out of it. "If you really want to help her, don't give her any more laudanum." He released her shoulders. "Take the bottle from her permanently."

Hell, *he* knew how it was with laudanum, so easy for an officer to access from a surgeon in a major regiment, how much smoother it made him sleep after a gruesome battle. But when a man got to thinking about the poppy more than sunshine, food, and his family, even thinking about it more than sex, it was time to drag himself away from the laudanum.

"Kevin and I want Aunt to sell the tavern and live with us in Wilmington. She's the widow of our mother's brother, and thus no direct blood kin, but we're all she has left. And Kevin and I have so few kin left. Aunt has lived here a decade after Aaron and Violet eloped. She has all these memories festering. Kevin and I think the change of moving to Wilmington would do her good."

"You may be right, but if she's been running a tavern by herself for the better part of a decade, she isn't going to sit in the back of the carriage at your tavern in Wilmington."

"Pah. She's welcome to haggle with our suppliers and pay the bills, as long as I can spend time talking with our customers. That's the part I like the most." She turned from him and concealed a yawn.

He pushed up and grimaced at the clock. "Three thirty. Back to bed."

Frowning, she collected her musket and accepted his extended hand up. "Do you think the burglar will return?"

"No."

She watched him load his rifle, then handed over her musket, which he propped next to the rifle. "Thank you for chasing him off."

"You're welcome. Good night again." He busied himself with replacing the powder horn and bag of shot among his gear, then with repositioning the log in the fireplace so it would burn slower, all the while most of him again hoped she'd just go on up to bed—which she did, but with enough hesitation that he wondered if she were waiting on a goodnight kiss.

He extinguished candles, removed clothing down to his shirt, and crawled beneath the blanket. His brain babbled away, outraged, at finding both a burglar and a murderer running about loose in a backcountry town. What were the odds of that happening? What did it imply about the effectiveness of law enforcement in the town of Hillsborough, North Carolina? In a few hours, *Herr* Schmidt would have much to answer to.

Chapter Nine

THE FISHY TICKLE of hound dog muzzles on Michael's cheek awakened him the second time on Monday the twelfth of February. Dawn light the color of dirty sand trickled between the parlor drapes: enough light for him to discern his assailants' tails swishing the air. "Five minutes," he mumbled, rolled onto his side away from them, and tugged the blanket over his head.

A slimy nose tunneled beneath the blanket and poked warm flesh. Michael's grip on the blanket dislodged in shock and violation. The practiced teeth of the second perpetrator seized the blanket and made off with it. Chill air embraced Michael's naked legs. "Damn!" He bolted upright. "All right, you win!"

Minutes later, fully dressed, he shivered his way out to the vault, Lizzie and Sammy gleefully circling in and about his course, noses to the ground, irrigating the property, mindless of crunchy frost on the foliage. Since the house showed no sign of life, Michael proceeded to the stable, where he shoveled horse dung, spread fresh straw, loaded Cleopatra and Charlie's feed boxes with hay, and fetched fresh water from the well in the yard.

He spotted smoke from the kitchen's chimney and washed up with frigid water behind the stable. His appetite awakened with all the subtlety of a bear's yawn. At the kitchen, he met Mrs. White's freckled, plump household helper, Martha, and her tall, sixteen-year-old son Philip, who was unloading firewood from a cart outside the kitchen. Kate had obviously mentioned her "cousin" Mr. Compton to them, as both welcomed him. Martha shooed Michael out of the kitchen with the promise of porridge in fifteen minutes, coffee in five, back at the house.

Sammy and Lizzie, tails wagging, caught up with him on the front porch. A man's black felt hat dangled from Lizzie's mouth. Michael gawped. Then delight spiraled warmth through him like a swig of Major Craig's brandy. "Heigh, Lizzie, what have you there, eh?" When he tried to retrieve the hat from her, she played the coquette and darted away fifteen feet with it. Despite his gnawing, rumbly stomach, he sat on the top step of the front porch, let Lizzie grow jealous at the sight of Sammy leaning against him and receiving all the petting. She trotted back and awarded him the hat.

"Good girl." He caressed her ears and cheek, stood, brushed dirt off the hat, and smoothed the slobbered, broken feather still clinging to one side. "What have we here—in case I cannot guess? Our burglar made a deposit, and—say, look at this." His forefinger found a hole in the upper right of the hat, and he swaggered a smile at Lizzie. "Too big for a puncture from your teeth. How about that? I actually hit the bugger in the dark with rifle shot. I deserve a raise for that." The inside of the hat around the hole exhibited no sign of blood. His shot had grazed the hat off the wearer's head, consistent with his memory of the man's undeterred run for cover.

Memory tugged his gaze across the yard to the trees bordering Mrs. White's property. Her tavern and house were the outmost buildings on the block: like Ezra Griggs's property, on the edge of town. After a criminal struck, he could hide in the forest. How convenient.

Michael descended the porch steps with the dogs loping alongside him and ambled out to where he'd seen the burglar vanish. A mockingbird sang encouragement from the branch of a taller oak. "Lizzie, where'd you find the hat, eh, girl?" She pranced ahead of him, her sleek neck proud, and sniffed the ground in circles where the cleared land ended. Bruised brush and a snapped branch from a young oak attested to the scoundrel's haste.

Scoundrel? He straightened from his examination of the foliage and angled the interior of the hat to catch the sunlight. Something in his assumptions about the trespasser and the hat bothered him.

The dogs circled back to the house. The hat's label sparked Michael's instant recognition: crafted in Charles Town. All over, delicate, even stitches and black, silk facings complemented the lines of the piece, reinforced the construction of a product that someone had labored over several days, taken pride in. The ostrich feather had been dyed a soft gray.

What was a gentleman's hat doing on the head of a burglar—stolen from a gentleman? Or had the trespasser been other than a common burglar? Why would a man try to enter Rachel White's house at three in the morning, if not to burgle it? Michael's fingernail dislodged several foot-long dark hairs from the felt. Skin at the base of his skull tingled. Was the trespasser a stranger to Mrs. White, or someone she knew?

He flipped the hat right side up and rotated it three hundred and sixty degrees slowly, along the plane of the brim. Familiarity whispered at him. Had he seen the hat before?

Again, his peripheral vision alerted him to minute movement. He looked over the hat to brush broken by the trespasser, and another trapped goose feather waving in the breeze—or was it the same feather from the brush beneath the window? "Attack of the Goose Girl," he muttered. This time, he shoved the feather in his coat pocket.

Lizzie and Sammy's barking rifted his attention. On the front porch, the dogs circled a well-dressed, dark-haired man. Michael squinted. The man removed his hat in response to the invitation of the opened door and stepped inside. Schmidt's minion, O'Toole.

Barbs sank into Michael's disposition. He glanced at his watch. Not yet eight. Surely Schmidt didn't expect him to work that moment. An empty stomach in the morning guaranteed his tetchiness the rest of the day—the worst mind for sifting through a murder scene effectively. He replaced the watch and strode for the house, the trespasser's hat tucked beneath his right arm.

When he reached the front door, he embraced the role of family member and let himself in. O'Toole and Kate had squared off in the foyer, he with an expression that bespoke the blockheaded Gaelic propensity to pine for the unattainable, she with the grimace of a hog farmer's wife who has misplaced her favorite knife on Castration Day. Michael didn't have to feign his cheer. "Good morning!"

A purr slid into Kate's tone. "Michael, my dear, dear cousin, where have you been?"

"Out for a walk."

Kate looped her arm in his, glided up against his left side, and pressed a kiss to his unshaven cheek, her lips every bit as warm, moist, and pliant as he'd fantasized. A galloping horse may as well have bowled him over. Shock and rapture shut his brain down for several seconds.

Then he registered the feral glower spilling into the Irishman's dark eyes, and something headier than lust revitalized his brain. "Mr. O'Toole. It's a lovely day, isn't it? How are you feeling this morning, lad?"

O'Toole grunted like a constipated gorilla. "I've come to fetch you. *Sasanach.*"

Michael presumed Kate didn't speak the Irishman's native tongue and thus wouldn't know that O'Toole had labeled him an "Englishman" with the distinct implication of "you-stupid-nockhole-of-an-Englishman." Time for Kate to move along. He handed her the hat and pried her off his side. She stared at the hat without recognition. So did O'Toole—unfortunate, as Michael would have loved to nab the Irish skunk as the burglar. "And how is Auntie this morning?"

"Her usual feisty self."

"Good. You know I enjoy coffee and porridge with feisty ladies. By the bye, our guest last night left his hat. Carry it to the dining room for me, will you?"

Soon as she left the foyer with the hat, Michael, relaxed and alert, turned back to O'Toole. "So." He slowed the cadence of his sentence. "You've come to fetch me."

"Mr. Schmidt says you're to present yourself over at Mr. Griggs's house at eight o'clock." A smirk ate O'Toole's face. He crossed his arms and spread his legs in imitation of Schmidt. "That's in less than ten minutes."

The furnace in Michael's empty stomach expanded into his limbs. "And you're my chaperone."

"Stop arguing, boy. Let's go." O'Toole jammed his hat on his head and yanked open the front door.

Boy. Michael's higher reasoning reminded him that beneath his skin was no place for Irish maggots. O'Toole was a waste of his energy. But primal fire in his veins clung to the scent of Kate in the foyer with them: Kate hanging on his arm, Kate's lips caressing his cheek.

He lowered his voice to avoid alarming the ladies. "I'm not on Mr. Schmidt's payroll, and I'm not under arrest. I shall have my breakfast first. Run along and tell your master that he can expect me by nine."

"My *master*?" O'Toole's shoulders tensed and hunched. "I'm not Mr. Schmidt's servant."

"His catamite, then. Won't be the first time Prussia has bedded Ireland."

"You son of a—*Póg mo thóin!*"

Michael relaxed further, in anticipation. "Kiss your own arse, boy."

He batted aside O'Toole's punch, swept in for a quick twist of the arm behind the back, and propelled the Irishman face-forward against the opened door, knocking his hat off. "Bloody Irish," Michael muttered in his ear. "Always needing a lesson in manners." His tug on O'Toole's pinned arm squeezed out a groan. "Remember, there are ladies under this roof."

He peeled O'Toole off the door and evicted him onto the front porch. The Irishman tripped, righted himself, and whipped around, hands wrestle-ready, face ruddy. "Come out here, bastard. We'll finish this!"

"Don't bother me before breakfast." Michael skipped O'Toole's hat out and shoved the door shut on the sight of the whitest set of natural teeth he'd ever seen in an Irish mouth. Then he leaned against the door and listened. Porch boards squawked. A furious stomp retreated.

Relief whispered from Michael's lips in a stream. Thank heaven O'Toole had possessed the sense to not force his way into the house and fistfight him.

From the dining room, women murmured and dishes clacked. The aroma of coffee fingered him. Food, yes. He straightened shirt, waistcoat, and coat, and walked to the dining room.

Conversation between Kate and her aunt trailed off when he entered and bowed. Her expression frosting over, Mrs. White set down her porridge spoon and rested her palms on the linen tablecloth, as if prepared to vault over the table at him. He heard Martha singing somewhere outside in the yard.

He proceeded to the chair at the unused setting opposite Mrs. White. "Good morning, madam."

Grooves dug into the skin around her mouth. "You're still here."

Kate hissed like a snake disturbed at sunning. "Aunt Rachel!"

Michael picked up the trespasser's hat from where it lay on the table near his empty coffee cup and returned his focus on the matriarch. "This hat was dropped in haste early this morning by a man who tried to break in your house through the parlor window."

Her head jerked, an angular flick. "Kate told me all about it. I've never seen that hat before in my life. A common burglar in the middle of the night. And Ezra Griggs murdered. Both crimes happened on the heels of your arrival in Hillsborough. What am I to make of that?"

Kate's fist smacked the table. China clinked. "How dare you say that to him?"

"Hold your tongue, Kate."

"I will not. Enough of this, Aunt! Have you lost your wits?"

"You dare speak to me that way when you sit at my table?"

Kate pushed to her feet and flung her napkin onto the table near a bowl containing the flecked remnants of porridge. "I don't have to sit at your table. Neither does my brother."

"Both of you, stop fighting!" Michael's bellow rattled dishes and reverberated off walls, surprising even him. Before either harpy could suck in another lungful of fuel, he held up the hat. "I'm a criminal investigator. I say this piece of evidence does *not* point to a common burglar. The man who tried to break in has money. His hat tells me he has money."

He slid the hat across the table. It skidded to a halt between Kate and Mrs. White. Both sets of gazes latched onto it. "See for yourself that he doesn't need to steal your silver."

Mrs. White sniffed, snatched up the hat, and flipped it to read the label. Michael transferred his attention to Kate in time to catch the dart of her gaze from him to the hat, and the color springing to her cheeks as it had when she'd commented on how different he looked in civilian clothing. For the first time, he wondered what she saw, or imagined she saw, in him without the red coat and epaulet. The thought sent a flutter about his stomach, like a moth trapped in the folds of a cloak. Nine years he'd been a redcoat. What else was there to him?

"You've made your point about the hat, Mr. Stoddard." Rachel White's tone had cooled to neutrality. "But why would a stranger try to break into my house, if not for money?"

"You tell me, madam. And was he indeed a stranger?"

Illumination flickered in her eyes, a sense of suspicion. Michael bent an inch toward her, expectant. Then she blinked and looked away. "I've no idea why someone would break into my house, but anyone who does so would be a stranger."

A muscle in Michael's cheek twitched. Rachel White wasn't a woman to listen to her instincts. Then his mind turned the concept on end, and he held his breath a moment at the implication.

Perhaps she had something to hide, a reason to protect the trespasser's identity. A burglar and a murderer in Hillsborough on the same day—what were the odds, indeed? A horrific possibility shaped itself in his imagination: revenge transacted after ten years, atonement for those who'd caused suffering. Queasiness slid between his ribs and sedimented in his stomach.

Mrs. White would never hear him. Maybe Kate would.

The matriarch slid the hat across the table to Michael. "What of that hole in the upper right of the hat?"

He locked gazes with her, felt her will probe him. "My rifle shot put the hole there as the escaping man ran out to that line of trees west."

"You've quite a bit of skill with the rifle." Chin lifted, the dragoness uncoiled in her chair. Recrimination dissipated from her dark eyes, their new track his height and the breadth of his shoulders, before a final sweep encompassed Kate. "Tell me, sir, did you volunteer to help Georg Schmidt find Ezra Griggs's killer?"

"Not exactly, madam."

"Then explain why you're helping him."

"Because he gave me the choice of helping him or being jailed and interrogated."

She studied him a moment, nodded once, then wiped her mouth with her napkin. "I've business at the tavern this morning, Mr. Stoddard, but do sit at my table in my absence and eat breakfast. I shall send for Martha to bring you coffee, toast, and porridge."

His larynx bobbed, loose at last. He grasped the back of the chair before him and scooted it out. "Thank you, madam."

Chapter Ten

WHILE HE BREAKFASTED alone, Martha lugged his gear upstairs. He finished the meal, went a-hunting, and found he'd been upgraded from the parlor pallet to a sunny room little more spacious than a closet, but with a bed, washstand, and chamber pot. Best of all, he could close the door to prevent Sammy and Lizzie from playing "steal the blanket" again.

At eight-thirty, freshly shaven, his teeth cleaned, he headed downstairs with the intruder's hat for what he hoped would be his only day under Schmidt's scrutiny. The Whites' servant didn't strike him as the nosy type, but even if Martha got bored in his absence, nothing left behind in his room hinted of his true identity.

Aunt Rachel he knew to be at the tavern. Martha was hanging wet laundry, including his traveling clothes, on a line between two posts in the sunlight. He inquired after Kate. The servant pointed to the kitchen.

At a counter inside, Kate rolled out a doughy circle for a tart or biscuits, an apron pinned to her jacket bodice and tied about her waist. Flour streaked her cheekbone like the paint of an Indian. She flattened dough without sparing him a glance. "I'm making a pork pie for supper tonight. Close that door, will you? Keeps the heat in."

Wood smoke, warm dough, and cinnamon apples scented the air, for a moment buoying Michael back to childhood, in the kitchen where Miriam practiced kneading, their mother sliced apples, and he loitered in hopes of sneaking food. He wagered with himself that Kate wouldn't let him sneak dough easily. But like every able-bodied, red-blooded male, he ambled over to the counter to try anyway.

"Martha and I must shop at Market today," she said. "You headed for Mr. Griggs's house?"

"Yes. I've a few questions of you before I leave." He positioned both his hat and the trespasser's an innocuous distance away from the flattened dough.

She slapped the wooden pastry roller on the counter, severing space between hat and dough like a hatchet. The whack of wood-on-wood sent Michael an unmistakable message about the ease of stealing dough in that kitchen. "Interviewing *me*, Inspector?" She faced him and flashed teeth. "I've committed no crimes lately." Her smile faded. "God rest Mr. Griggs's soul. What a horrid way to die. Please find the culprit, Michael."

He made no commitments. The turf wasn't his.

"And you must learn who tried to break into the house. The thought of it being done by someone of means with special intent is frightening. More frightening than a common burglar."

Exactly the first opening for which he waited. "How long has your aunt owned Sammy and Lizzie?"

"Hmm." She sucked in her cheeks. "Kevin and I gave them to her about four years ago. They were both almost a year old. What have the dogs to do with burglary?"

"They've never met your cousin Aaron. If he came to the house, they'd treat him like a stranger. Bark and growl at him."

"Aaron, yes, I suppose so, but—" Her lips separated, made an "o." She pressed her palms to her cheeks. "You think the trespasser was *Aaron*? But why?" Her hands clasped each other at heart level, thumbs kneading floury palms. "Why would he sneak into his own home in the middle of the night, after being gone for ten years? Why not return openly and be welcomed by his mother? Dear heavens, if you but knew how Aunt would rejoice to see him again—"

"I can well imagine, so I see no reason why he'd have been the man who wore this hat." Michael allowed a few seconds to elapse. "However I see a clear reason why he'd murder Mr. Griggs, father of the woman he loves, the man who stood in his way of a church wedding, though I admit not having an idea why he'd wait ten years to do so."

Her hands worried at her apron. Her face paled. "It couldn't have been Aaron last night."

The loved ones of criminals usually commented to that effect. Imploring in her eyes filled his stomach with thorns. "What color hair does he have?"

"Dark, like Aunt's used to be."

"I found dark hair inside the hat."

"No—he has a clubfoot. You said the trespasser ran. Aaron could never run very well."

"This fellow was limping."

A whoosh of air left her. She staggered, the counter supporting her back, and gaped at the kitchen wall as if her long-lost cousin had suddenly peeked through it and winked at her. Behind her, she left the pastry unguarded.

Michael no longer had a craving for it. He closed the distance between them and leaned an elbow on the counter's edge. "Kate, after ten years of absence, why do you think Aaron would return and kill a man? Why would he not reveal himself to his own mother, knowing how she's missed him all these years? And what could he possibly need from his own house that he didn't want his mother to know he took?"

She turned to him, a pulse battering her throat. "Aunt may be the only one who can answer those questions. But if I were you, I wouldn't ask her straight away."

"Not straight away, no. I don't care to sleep in the stable tonight. But I've a hunch she knows a piece of helpful information and is discounting it."

"Aaron, after ten years." Her voice thickened. "I wonder how tall he's grown, if Violet is with him, if there's still any romance between them."

Exactly the second opening for which he waited. He pitched a bland tone. "Why did you kiss me in the foyer?"

She blinked rapidly. "I'm tired of that Irishman leering at me." She spun about, grabbed the wooden roller, and pounded the pastry almost paper thin. "I thought to dissuade him with the appearance of a close relationship with my cousin. Yes, I know it was wicked of me to use you. I apologize."

Surprise drove a sting into his laugh. "Use me all you like. Kiss my other cheek, give me a matched set. And skip the apology next time."

Tiny lines around her mouth deepened. "You're going to be late for your appointment with—ah, blast!" The pastry tore.

Bugger Schmidt. Bugger pastry. Michael wrestled the roller from her, slapped it to the far edge, and backed her against the counter, his hands braced to either side of her.

Fever flooded her face. The streak of flour on her cheek glowed. "What are you doing?"

Her lips were still parted. A faint, floury streak dusted the corner of her upper lip, pale specks pinioned in a film of sweat. Kate had been sampling dough. He knew exactly how the inside of her mouth tasted that moment. Buttery smooth, a hint of salt, moist, hot. Saliva flooded his tongue. Blood steamed from his brain. He swallowed, lowered his voice. "You're capable of gelding a goat like O'Toole without my help. Why do you play this game?"

Her hands slipped between their chests and exerted token resistance against him. "Get on with you. I—I've heard that Mr. Schmidt doesn't like to be kept waiting."

If he'd been O'Toole, she'd have disabled him by then with her knee. She smelled of the baffling women's game of Advance and Retreat. One lesson about women he'd learned early: unlike those who were enthusiastic over a man, a confused woman provided a fellow with little but nuisance. Disappointing, but he admitted that Kate hadn't disguised a single conflicting signal.

Contents of a covered kettle suspended over the hearth reached a simmer, rattling the lid. Kate darted a look at it, then returned her gaze to him. He murmured, "Thanks to your friend Alice Farrell, you and I have been partnered at a social engagement in Wilmington."

"Yes. I know."

"Major Craig has attached a great deal of weight to the event. High visibility. Buttons and buckles shining. Champagne. Seven-course meal. Dancing until the cows come home. My orders are to have a rollicking fun time."

She twitched her hands off his chest and folded them on her breast, above her heart. Chin tucked, lashes lowered, she swiveled her gaze to the kettle. "Oh." Her left eyebrow arched. "Oh." Her lips sealed.

Oh. Unless he was mistaken, Kate had transitioned from confusion to disinterest. At least he knew how to manage disinterest. He pushed away from her and snatched both hats off the counter with more vehemence than he'd expected, as if the conversation had scoured his spleen with sandpaper. He could revel with the best of them, but he was damned if he'd spend an entire party in the company of a woman who yearned to be elsewhere.

The rebuke his shoes made of the wood floor echoed like musket fire. At the door, his back to Kate, he jammed his hat on his head. Her brother's words about Presbyterians singed his memory. "Do make your preference known to Mrs. Farrell. Someone will gladly take your place." He yanked open the door. "Good day."

***

Well before he reached Churton Street, traffic on Tryon Street forced him to calm the storm of his pace. He reminded himself that his objective was to solve Griggs's murder so he'd be free to locate Cornwallis's army, not compete with Kate Duncan for pigheadedness. Aggravation would detract from the concentration Schmidt demanded of him.

The frosty morning cooled his lungs. He took in Hillsborough by full daylight: still houses, the sharp odor of a tannery, fresh bread from a bakery, a farmer guiding his wagon of grain for the grist mill on the Eno River. Goodwives with empty baskets strolled to Market, sunlight yellow on their straw hats. A barking dog chased a cat across the street, the pair racing almost underfoot of a merchant on horseback.

Hedgerows along the northwest corner of Churton and Tryon yielded to a low stone wall that enclosed a graveyard and a handsome little church. Around the corner, Michael found paths and cart lanes crisscrossing the street like threads on a sloppily rolled skein. He dodged another wagon and a rider on horseback to follow a cart lane north on Churton. It veered off northeast and cut diagonally through hedgerows and lots to Queen Street. He stayed with it, and it deposited him just west of Griggs's house.

On the front walkway of the house, Schmidt awaited him in his characteristic stance. He spotted Michael's approach. His feet stayed planted and his arms remained crossed, but his bottom lip jammed into his top lip and dragged the corners of his mouth down, giving him the jowly belligerence of a bulldog. O'Toole, slouching on the top step of the porch, sprang to his feet, circled Schmidt once, and came to rest several feet behind the sheriff's left elbow, a spaniel with sparkling eyes. The remainder of the Schmidt pack, the fellow named Henry and two other men, remained on the porch, their expressions varying degrees of irascibility and boredom.

Five to one. The odds didn't favor Michael Stoddard. He let himself inside Griggs's gate.

Schmidt consulted his watch. Michael knew the shortcut through the hedgerows had allowed him to arrive before nine. He drew up within five feet of the big man and, without investing any warmth, smiled at him. "Good morning, Mr. Schmidt."

Schmidt replaced his watch. "Good morning. Mr. *Compton*."

His address rammed the sensation of ice shavings through Michael's spine, even though there was no way Schmidt or the pack could know his true name. Aunt Rachel and Kate weren't going to divulge his identity. Martha and Philip didn't know. So Michael shoved aside the sensation and twirled the trespasser's hat around his forefinger. "Mr. O'Toole seemed so eager to examine the scene of the crime an hour ago that I expected you fellows would already be hard at work inside."

"We awaited our guest investigator and his porridge." The sheriff's wintry, blue-eyed gaze followed the spinning hat, then shifted to Michael's own hat upon his head. "You are a man who wears two hats."

"I presume you don't intend your statement as metaphor, sir. Actually, this hat is for you." He tossed the trespasser's hat to Schmidt, noting that Griggs's next-door neighbor, an old man with a cane, had emerged on his porch and was again observing them. "It fell off the head of a man who tried to break into my aunt's house around three this morning."

Schmidt's bushy red-gold eyebrows climbed his forehead. "A burglar?"

O'Toole threw up his hands. "We don't have burglars in Hillsborough."

"What can you tell me about this man?" Schmidt's paws turned the hat over and over, in examination.

"As it was nighttime, I noted few of his features, but he was of medium height, had dark hair, and ran with a limp. Judging from the quality of the hat, I'd say he has money. Wouldn't you?"

He watched the tip of Schmidt's forefinger poke the hole. Then the sheriff flipped the hat over, as he'd done, and checked the perimeter of the hole for blood. Michael made the decision to withhold his musings about Aaron White from Schmidt. "I might have made a direct hit had I more light. But a hundred and fifty feet in the dark is a bit of a challenge."

"Sure, and it was but a lucky shot, Compton." O'Toole's consonants buzzed with brogue.

The blue eyes pegged Michael again. "Where did you learn to shoot a rifle so well?"

Michael maintained eye contact and accompanied what he hoped was casual posture with a lopsided shrug. "As Mr. O'Toole says, it was a lucky shot."

Lips closed, Schmidt assessed him, worked his jaw a few times like a bull chewing cud. "Where did this burglar go after you knocked the hat from his head with your rifle shot?"

"Into the woods west of my aunt's house."

Schmidt's forefinger brushed the length of the ostrich plume. "This is no common burglar. What does your aunt believe he was trying to steal?"

Relief cut the road of tension in Michael's gut like cart tracks across Hillsborough's streets. From Schmidt's reasoning, at least intellectually he could relate to the man. "She has no idea what he wanted. We're all a bit nervous this morning, if you can imagine. Who else in town has this scoundrel burgled?"

"No one else. I will keep the hat for further study." Schmidt thrust the hat at O'Toole, then gestured for Michael to precede him to the front door. "For now, let us not pursue this puzzling development, but render our services to Mr. Griggs."

Chapter Eleven

FOLLOWED BY SCHMIDT, Michael headed up the walkway. He noted that O'Toole and the other three men stepped aside, privy to an unspoken signal from their leader. Henry pushed the front door open and drew back.

Electric readiness charged Michael's muscles. He sprang into the house and pivoted to avoid Schmidt's paw swipe. Schmidt kicked the door shut, leaving his lackeys outside. Michael's forearm deflected the second swipe, followed it with a slash from his dagger that snagged Schmidt's sleeve. Then his heel caught on an upturned rug. Schmidt advanced into his stumble, batted the dagger from his hand. It clattered to the foyer floor out of reach.

Schmidt gripped the front of Michael's coat and pinned him to a wall. The frame of a painting ground into Michael's left shoulder. He flailed for a counter hold. His hands bounced off arm muscles like granite. The weight of Schmidt's forearm bore down on his windpipe. He sought breath, found none. Black specks rotated across the face of the belligerent bulldog.

Again, Michael tried to suck in a lungful. Again he heard the rasp of air denied. His deflated lungs felt blistered. His knees rattled. A wave of sweat surged up his legs.

Schmidt's whisper scorched his ear. "I do not like to be kept waiting!"

Dark specks clumped over Michael's vision. His ears buzzed. His legs kicked, involuntary flight in place. Grinding his teeth, he craned his neck for a final gasp. "Bugger yourself!"

Pressure on his windpipe released. Schmidt seized his shoulders and slung him farther into the foyer. Michael slammed a wall, staggered to a crouch, and dragged in air, his throat and lungs aching. The sheriff picked his way over debris, a marauder's measured approach on him, his face the blank mask a warrior wears when his soul has been worn down witnessing the deaths of his fellows. "How easily I could kill you. But I need you."

Bloody hell. Michael coughed, lurched backward in retreat, cast about for a weapon, found none. In his head, he cursed the Army's mediocre hand-to-hand combat instruction and the fistfights he'd endured, a dribble of self-defense training that constituted pitiful preparation against the strength of a giant like Schmidt. Or against a demon that celebrated torture and death, as Fairfax did. His voice emerged scratchy. "Horse piss, you need me. I won't grab my ankles for you like your Irish catamite does."

Brief humor rocked Schmidt like a sneeze. "*Nein, Engländer.* I need your help. You do not live in Hillsborough." He halted his approach, bent over, and picked up Michael's dagger. "You are not bound by its history."

Michael drew another lungful of air and massaged his throat, eyes wary on the dagger. "What history? That of the Regulators?"

Schmidt passed him his dagger, hilt first, waited for Michael to sheath it. "Many expect me to find that Mr. Griggs's killer was a former Regulator, vengeance-minded."

Michael coughed again. "What nonsense. Governor Tryon ran all those men out of North Carolina ten years ago. Even if a Regulator remained here, he wouldn't have retained enough money or power to—" He caught himself. The fetid stench of congealed blood in the house covered him like collapsed tent canvas, chilling sweat on his back and legs. "I see. You must maintain a reputation as the flawless lead investigator in town. I'm to take the floggings for you if the killer's identity displeases Council members. That's how this case works."

Schmidt flashed stained teeth at him and assumed his stance.

"You're a jackass, Schmidt."

"You have your work set before you. Mr. *Compton.*"

"What's the matter? Don't you like my name?"

"It is not your name."

"My parents would take issue with that. I suppose next you'll be claiming that Kate and Aunt Rachel aren't my kin."

"I doubt that, too."

Michael spread his arms and laughed to stuff the wobbly sensation of panic below his stomach, keep it from flitting about his vocal cords. "Who do you think I am, then?"

"A criminal investigator by profession." Schmidt analyzed Michael's carriage, the way he held his shoulders. "Put a sword in your hand, and you become a soldier, an officer."

Michael recalled the sheriff's hollow expression from a minute earlier. He'd seen the same vacancy in the eyes of British soldiers after battle, seen it in his own face in a mirror. Schmidt knew the military world because he'd lived in it.

Dread breached Michael's stomach and clutched his chest. After His Majesty had emptied the royal purse for more than six years on North American chaos, and the Army had hemorrhaged a generation of young men from different lands, did the Hessian or Jäger corps from which Schmidt had deserted matter anymore?

More realization burrowed through Michael's lungs. O'Toole was also a deserter. He and Schmidt had found each other years ago, spun their lies into believable background stories for the people of Orange County.

After six years of war, few in the British Army had the energy or resources to track down the hundreds of men who'd run away from their regiments. Michael, whose critical mission was delivering a message to Cornwallis, certainly wasn't one of those few.

But neither Schmidt nor O'Toole knew that. Thus the sheriff tethered Michael while applying his keen investigative mind toward uncovering his identity. And if he became certain that his guest investigator was a British officer, Michael would never return to Wilmington.

He relaxed his shoulders to help dissipate the dread. "So now you'd pin braid on me and flatter me. I told you yesterday that I have a business to tend in Cross Creek. I don't have time for flattery. And you must be crazy if you expect a man like me to play investigator. Not just crazy, but craven. Find Mr. Griggs's killer yourself." He stomped for the door.

Halfway there, Schmidt's paw hooked his upper arm and yanked him beneath his nose as if Michael were a girl's doll assembled from fabric scraps and cornhusks. Michael smashed his lips together to halt the tremble. His heart slammed his throat.

"*Engländer.*" Schmidt's nostrils bristled with reddish-blond hairs. "You leave town without my permission, and I promise I will hunt you down and kill you."

He shoved him away, toward the front door, as if egging him on to leave. Michael's heart fell back into his ribcage. He hid his alarm by stretching a sneer across his mouth. "Selfish bastard. You've ruined my visit with my kinfolk. No wonder you have problems with the townsfolk's trust. I wager you're as pleasurable at parties as used bum fodder on bread."

The sheriff ignored the insult and swung one arm to encompass the house. "The house is yours. Except to move debris aside so the undertaker could fetch Mr. Griggs's body yesterday, my men and I have not examined the rooms."

The house was his? Michael's shoulders sagged. Schmidt wasn't going to lift a hand to help him. Michael pressed three fingers to the throb of frustration and fear in his forehead, lost to a route out of launching the investigation. "If you truly expect me to investigate Mr. Griggs's death and arrive at logical conclusions, I suppose I shall begin by examining his body—"

"Not possible." A smile slashed the sheriff's face. "The undertaker has already cleaned and prepared the body for the funeral."

No body to examine? What the hell did Schmidt expect from him, miracles? Incredulity swelled in his tone. "How can anyone solve a murder without examining the victim's body?"

"Why should you need to see his body?"

"You said his throat was slit. Had he any wounds on his hands or arms, as if he'd tried to defend himself? Or did the killer sneak up on him?"

Schmidt's smirk broadened. "You are a merchant in Cross Creek? What is your business?"

Michael had anticipated the question, so he gave a vague response. "Naval stores."

"For a merchant who deals in naval stores, you ask questions like a military investigator."

God damn it all to hell. Schmidt had baited him. He'd almost lost his cover. He withstood Schmidt's stare without blinking. "All it takes is one experience of an accountant embezzling from your business, and you never again accept matters at a superficial level."

In silence a few seconds, the sheriff weighed the believability of Michael's words. "You have been upstairs in this house?"

Testiness blasted through Michael's tone. "Upstairs? No, I haven't been upstairs. Why would I have gone upstairs? My purpose here was to convey greetings from my neighbor in Cross Creek to Mr. Griggs, not tour his house. And if you deny me a look at the body—"

"You will find the second floor in as much disarray as the rooms downstairs. And I can tell that you do not need access to Mr. Griggs's corpse to form logical conclusions. In my day, I have dealt with official investigators who have far less sense than you."

A backhanded compliment, if ever Michael had heard one. "You expect me to perform a specific type of research. Isn't a look at the corpse sequitur to the research?"

"Perhaps. But as I said, the corpse is not available for further examination. However, I will see to it that you receive the clothing Mr. Griggs wore when he was murdered. He has a daughter named Violet. You have met her?"

"No." Michael heaved a sigh of sheer frustration. No corpse. Damn. "From what I heard, Miss Griggs eloped with my cousin Aaron ten years ago, when the six Regulators were hanged."

A curt nod indicated Schmidt's validation of the story. "She has a room upstairs. I have inquired of townsfolk, but no one knows how to reach Violet Griggs to inform her of her father's death. So he will be buried this afternoon with no kin to attend him."

"But you'll attend the funeral?"

"Of course."

"Then I shall attend also, and not just as a courtesy to my neighbor in Cross Creek. If I were a murderer, I might not be able to resist the social occasion of my victim's funeral. Naturally, you will provide me with the names of those in attendance who were staunchly on one side or the other of that Regulator business. They must be interviewed."

Schmidt opened his mouth as if to retort, then relaxed his jaw. "Two o'clock. The graveyard at the corner of Churton and Tryon."

"I shall be present. And speaking of interviews, whom have you questioned?"

"The old man next door. He sent someone to notify me when he heard the initial disturbance yesterday."

"Good. I require your notes from the interview." He watched Schmidt's lips roll back and whiten. "Do you plan to withhold more information from me, then?

"I will have O'Toole bring you the notes as well as Mr. Griggs's clothing."

Disapproval reflex twitched Michael's lips. O'Toole. Wonderful.

"You do not like my assistant because he is *Irish*, and you are *English*. I wonder, with such brotherhood, how does King George hold his army together?"

An excellent question debated in coffeehouses and taverns all over Britain. But Michael wasn't about to gulp that bait and verify his identity to Schmidt.

"My *cousin* doesn't like your assistant or his attentions. Mr. O'Toole ignores her rejections. He wants a lesson in manners."

Teeth sprawled across Schmidt's grin, and his eyes glittered, as if he were the owner of a champion fighting cock and had been issued a challenge. Disgusted, Michael reminded himself that O'Toole was a waste of water, food, and air. "Since your lackey's bringing me Mr. Griggs's clothing and your interview notes, you may also send along the names and directions of people still living locally who aligned themselves with Regulators or the land agents. And contact information for any of Violet Griggs's friends still in town."

Dark thunder rolled over Schmidt's face. His eyes narrowed. "Such information requires time to assemble."

Like sabers of two opponents meeting in a bone jarring crash above a battlefield, their gazes clashed and sparked. Ire frothed in Michael's belly. Schmidt had all but imprisoned him in Hillsborough to manage his dirty business, yet he resisted giving him the tools he needed to solve the case. His voice lashed the air. "Then you'd best hop to it. I might get bored and leave town. Despite your bluster, you cannot be certain you'll track me down." He jutted his chin toward Schmidt an inch. "Or what you'll encounter if you do track me." He stalked past the sheriff to the doorway of the parlor, in passage scooping his hat off the floor.

Behind him, Schmidt growled. "*Schwein.* I expect a report from you at six o'clock this evening in my office at the jail."

At the parlor entrance, the stench of blood-soaked rug belted Michael, gurgled porridge in his gut. He shivered, his skin finally registering the temperature in the house. Cold, a tomb buried in snow. All sources of heat had been extinguished for more than twelve hours.

His gaze tracked over a splintered ladder-backed chair, toppled tables, broken vases. This time he noticed a violin smashed to kindling sitting atop the harpsichord, and deep gouges in the wood on the harpsichord. He wondered how he'd missed those details the evening before. They signified a personal attack, hatred directed against someone who had made music in that parlor.

His attention bounced to the slashed portrait of the young lady above the fireplace. On another wall, the likeness of an older woman was undamaged. "Did Mr. Griggs play musical instruments?"

"I never heard him do so."

Griggs's daughter, then, or a long-dead wife. Rage, fear, and powerlessness, the wreck in the parlor also said. *I cannot find it!* Michael spoke his thoughts. "For what was the murderer searching when he tore this house apart yesterday?"

Schmidt's growl converted to a chuckle of condescension. "If I knew that, I would know a good deal more about him, *ja*? More questions, *Engländer*?"

"I presume Mr. Griggs's horse out back has been tended?" Schmidt snorted once, affirmation and annoyance. "What did your men find when they searched the woods?"

"Horse turds several hundred feet in, on a narrow cart track. The killer secured his beast out of sight and entered Mr. Griggs's yard afoot to avoid drawing attention to himself." Schmidt allowed for a pause wide enough to drive a cart of cabbages through. "My men also found feathers."

Michael rotated his head in question, Schmidt's bulk in his peripheral vision. Feathers? Like the feathers he'd found on Rachel White's property? No, surely that was too great a coincidence. He loaded his tone with tartness. "Your men went for a walk in the woods and consider the finding of feathers significant? Do you expect me to believe you have no birds in Hillsborough?"

"Obviously you have not been upstairs. If you had, you would understand."

Curiosity tickled Michael. Although he turned back to the parlor, his senses climbed the stairs. He decided to make examining the second floor his first priority. Besides, Schmidt's men and the undertaker had traipsed in and out of the parlor and disturbed debris to access the corpse, thus diminishing the quality of evidence he'd find in the parlor. "Which town taverns are the best for eavesdropping?"

"King Street, west. The tavern of Blumburg will serve you well."

In a whoosh of stale air, Thor clomped past him. "I will leave my man, Henry, here this morning. If you have need of a messenger, use him. *Und ja*, Mr. Griggs's hands and forearms were cut in self-defense. Now get to work, *du Schlaafsäwwel*."

Door hinges groaned, followed by the front door banging shut. The silence of a sarcophagus embraced Michael.

Chapter Twelve

MICHAEL BACKED FROM the parlor doorway, hung his hat on a peg beside the door, and, from the entrance to the dining room, surveyed the wreck inside. The contents of his stomach shifted, uneasy with the stink from the parlor. Death's reek didn't agree with his gut. It never had. Not on the battlefield, nor the previous June, in Alton, Georgia, where sultry heat had soaked a copse of oaks and dogwoods and amplified the odor spreading from a sheet, fly-speckled and smudged with dried blood, at his feet.

A murdered man had lain beneath that sheet: an enemy Spaniard skinned alive. And as Michael would learn, a fellow officer wearing His Majesty's scarlet, Lieutenant Dunstan Fairfax, had kept the Spaniard's company the night before and slowly entertained him to death.

★★★

The potbellied sergeant assigned to assist Michael in examining the body looked over the lumpy sheet and shook his head. "Poor bastard. Even an enemy didn't deserve to die that way."

Michael said nothing. An impartial violence fueled battlefield death and injury. In contrast, personalized evil hovered over the Spaniard, tangible enough to smear his own skin like filthy oil and almost smother the alarm sent up by hairs on the back of his neck.

The two soldiers knelt, uncovered the body, and severed ligatures on the arms and legs. Fighting flies and gnats, they struggled with the contorted limbs to remove clothing not ripped by the murderer. The victim's stark naked torso, upper arms, and upper legs had been reduced to the appearance of shredded meat.

The sergeant staggered up, lips trembling. "Sorry, sir. It's the stink.

Reminds me of pork."
The suggestion stimulated a gurgling protest in Michael's stomach, ech-
oed in the other man's gut. A greenish cast to his countenance, the sergeant
stumbled away and mopped his face with his kerchief. Michael's forehead
sprouted sweat beads. He pushed to his feet, revulsion and horror hammer-
ing his throat. Waves of hot and cold pulsed him.
Don't puke, man, or I shall lose it, too.

★★★

As if trying to outrun the effect memory had on his stomach, Michael bolted to the foot of the stairs and glared up. Schmidt had made a cryptic comment about the upstairs. More than happy to leave the downstairs for awhile,
Michael climbed to the second floor of Ezra Griggs's house, where he realized
the significance of feathers.

Goose feathers layered Griggs's bedroom, spilled out onto the landing,
their source the gutted feather tick dragged halfway off the bed. Snowdrifts of
feathers coated an open clothes trunk and clothing partially stuffed back in,
linens and a quilt ripped off the bed and pitched to the floor amid a cluster of
rugs, and a table that had held the washbasin, now knocked on its side. The
chamberpot was overturned in a corner, as if flung there. Michael stepped with
cat feet over the floor, hoping to stir as few air currents as possible, but feathers still swirled in his passage. He found the floor beneath the chamberpot dry
and wagered that it had been empty when the murderer grabbed it.

Feathers clung to his shoes and stockings, a fawning retinue of white and
gray faeries. He tunneled beneath the fluffy cloud for anything else hidden
on the floor, but a meticulous search uncovered no object that screamed of
being a clue. Undeterred, he examined the casing for what had once been an
expensive feather tick, perhaps plunder of McCullough's land agents. From the
gash in the casing, and a small amount of dried blood along the edges of the
gash, Michael envisioned the killer going straight from slitting Griggs's throat
to carving his bedding, and not bothering to clean his knife. When Michael
stepped back and processed the ruin, he realized that Griggs's assailant hadn't
spilled feathers just to commit wanton destruction. He'd been searching for
something among the feathers.

The smallest dimension of the tick, its depth, measured about six inches.
That meant the object the killer expected to find possessed one dimension of
less than six inches. Plenty could be hidden there, if embedded and aligned the
correct way. A pistol, a spoon, a book, a portrait, a purse, a small statue, a shoe,
a tinderbox. He recalled the broken vases downstairs. Yes, even a small vase
could be concealed. But he didn't rush to endorse the coincidence.

The coincidence that squealed at him for validation was that of the two
goose feathers he'd found on Rachel White's property. Goose feathers were
common enough filling for fine pillows and ticks, and surely there were geese
to be found in Orange County. But Michael couldn't climb around a dark image
swelling in his head—Ezra Griggs's murderer shedding goose feathers, first
in the woods at sunset during his escape, then on Rachel White's property at
three in the morning. The connection between the Griggses and the Whites an-

chored and fed the image, as did the fact that neither Violet Griggs nor Aaron White could be accounted for.

He pulled the feather from his pocket and gazed out over the ocean of its brethren spread across the bedroom. A fuzzy centipede of fear for Kate and Aunt Rachel crawled up his spine. All hundred of the centipede's icy feet felt like nettles on his nerves.

Sleeping in a comfortable bed upstairs in Aunt Rachel's house wasn't wise. With the door closed, he couldn't hear what transpired downstairs. But knowing what he knew of Kate, if he planned to act as guardian, he'd have to convince her he was tucked into bed before sneaking downstairs. He thought of the couch in the parlor and wondered how many knots in his back he'd awaken with after sleeping on it all night. Integrity was painful business.

He blew the feather from his fingers, watched it laze to the floor and nestle among the others, and picked feathers off his shoes and stockings. Then he left Ezra Griggs's bedroom for that of his daughter.

He needn't have cleaned off the feathers. The bed in Violet's room had also been gutted. Feathers covered a less-widespread but similar chaos to that he'd seen in her father's room—the exception being papers scattered beneath the feathers on the floor, spilled from a leather portfolio. At Michael's feet was a crude charcoal sketch of a horse or donkey, signed at the bottom by "Miss Violet Griggs" and dated "4 June 1766." Violet would have been eleven or twelve when she drew it.

Several dozen sketches had been slung over the floor. Down on hands and knees, Michael brushed away feathers, collected sketches, shook off the portfolio, and slid papers in.

A tree, an apple, the marketplace, and the Griggs's house rendered in charcoal convinced Michael that Violet loved sketching but possessed no great artistic aptitude, like many young ladies whom he'd met. Doting fathers with prospects for placing their girls in comfortable marriages often had them taught to sketch, paint, sing, and play musical instruments like those in the parlor. Lack of talent was no obstacle.

Impatient, he ceased examining sketches and stuffed them straight into the portfolio. Later, at Aunt Rachel's house, he'd have time to examine all of them.

The morning wore on, several hours of feather fighting, before he paused his search to stretch cramped limbs and a tight back. The break provided him with perspective. He'd uncovered no solid evidence. At that rate, he'd be in Hillsborough for weeks. In frustration, he kicked a pile of feathers.

The motion uncovered a paper scrap, a sketch that had been ripped across the diagonal, the upper portion of man's facial portrait. Curiosity over the missing piece buzzed in his blood. He pushed feathers aside on hands and knees until he located the bottom portion of the portrait. Then he rocked back on his heels and fit the pieces together.

He gazed upon a young man seventeen or eighteen years old, plain-faced, unassuming, and kindly. The illustrator had been Violet Griggs, the date 15 May 1771. Curiosity transcended Michael's puzzlement. Who was the fellow— Aaron White? Had Ezra Griggs's killer been the one to deface the portrait? If Aaron had murdered Griggs, why had he mutilated his own portrait?

By then, Michael had collected every sketch he could find. His stomach rumbled. Time to find some dinner, or at least bread, cheese, and ale. He set the portfolio beside the door and rolled the portrait pieces into a cylinder.

With a squeak, the front door opened, and he heard the tread of shoes in the entranceway. He pictured O'Toole in the foyer with the notes and lists he'd requested of Schmidt, and his mood soured until Kate called up, "Michael, are you here? Mr. Henry said I could bring this to you."

"I shall be down straightaway." The rolled sketch jammed beneath one arm, he slapped the latest collection of feathers off his stockings and swept from Violet's bedroom.

In the foyer, Kate juggled a covered hand basket while adjusting hat ribbons beneath her chin. She wrinkled her nose and fanned air before her face. "Ugh! It stinks like a slaughterhouse in here."

He closed the front door on Henry's leer and lowered his voice. "Ezra Griggs's blood. I haven't finished poking around in the parlor yet, so it hasn't been cleaned."

Her squint stung with dubiousness. After shoving the hand basket at him, she transferred her consideration to the parlor. If she'd harbored any attraction for him before, this was surely where revulsion would decapitate the bud of it. His pulse settled to dull rhythm. He straightened, rolled back his shoulders, wrapped his fingers around the basket's handle, and extracted the portrait from beneath his arm. He imagined himself in Yorkshire meeting the parents of a romantic interest. *No, Mother and Father, Michael isn't an undertaker, or even a surgeon, but he does spend a great deal of time with corpses and at the scenes of murders.* Amusing in a dark way. He ought to be laughing.

Kate turned back to him, a grimace from the odor still hovering at the edges of her nostrils and lips, but a practical tilt to her chin. She unfastened ribbons, and off came her broad-brimmed straw hat. "So this is what you've been doing."

A miracle that he saw no rejection in her eyes. He nodded for the stairs. "I spent this morning up there, searching the bedrooms."

"Phew. For what do you search?" She handed him her hat.

He hung it on a peg near his hat, then found a peg for her cloak when she passed it to him. "I search for anything that's out of place. Something that shouldn't be there but is. Or something that should be there but isn't, or has been moved."

One of her eyebrows arched. She plucked a feather from his hair. "Looks like your job entailed a tumble in feathers."

"When a criminal cuts open expensive bedding, feathers are my companions."

She shot a look up the stairs. The other eyebrow rose. "Why would he ruin a feather tick?"

"Possibly for the same reason he made a wreck of the house. He was conducting his own search. Except that I don't think he found what he was looking for." Michael glanced at the basket. "I'm remiss. Thank you for the, er—"

"It's fresh bread I baked this morning. And cheese, and some of Aunt's pickled pears. And some small beer." She rubbed her upper arms. "Although it's so chilly in here that I wish I'd packed some hot coffee."

"It's perfect, all of it. No one has ever brought me food like this—you know, when I've been working." He brushed by her and set the basket on the bottom step of the stairs.

She frowned. "Aren't you going to eat?"

"In a little while."

"Don't tell me you're too busy? I can see why Enid Jones wants to tie you down to a dining room chair."

Enid said that? Uneasy over what else Enid might have said, he watched Kate cross the foyer. The heels of her shoes tapped the wood floor.

She peered into the dining room. "Looks like a band of demons had a party in here." She crossed her arms over her chest. "What on earth was the criminal seeking?"

He craned his neck toward the back door to make sure Schmidt's minions hadn't sneaked in to spy on them. "If I knew that, this investigation would be as good as finished."

She swiveled to him, understanding sparking in her eyes. "Because that would tell you the criminal's motive and rule out other suspects."

Elation spiraled a warm flush over him, like a zephyr across a heathery meadow in May. What a nimble mind she had. "Exactly. Alas, I don't have any suspects yet except nameless, faceless former Regulators."

Her voice lowered. "And Aaron."

After another look toward the back door, he unrolled the two segments of torn sketch. "In Miss Griggs's room upstairs, I found an assortment of sketches that she'd created. This was one of them." He aligned the pieces against the door, so she could better view the whole. In case Henry had his ear to the door, Michael whispered, "Does this fellow look familiar?"

Three steps brought her closer. She cocked her head at the sketch and said, low, "Violet isn't an accomplished artist, but this is definitely Aaron. See the mole on his cheek? Maybe you can see this, too, but he got his pointy chin from Aunt."

He reevaluated the sketch. Now that Kate mentioned it, Aunt Rachel did have a pointy chin, like the subject of the portrait. He pulled the sketch off the door and began rolling the pieces up.

She laid fingers on his wrist, stilling the process. "A moment. Why is his sketch ripped?"

"I don't know. All the others I found were intact."

Her hand fell away. "Maybe the killer was searching the house for Aaron's picture with the intention of defacing it."

He stuck the portrait in the hand basket. "The sketches were slung all over Miss Griggs's room. I think it more likely that the killer happened upon Aaron's picture while he searched the room for something else. The likeness is adequate for those who know your cousin. It triggered more violence, for reasons unknown. In effect, the killer mutilated Aaron in effigy. If the killer were Aaron, I wonder why he'd do that to his own picture."

With the scent of cinnamon, she moved past him to the parlor doorway, her gaze on the wall above the fireplace. "Or why he'd mutilate Violet's portrait."

So that was Violet Griggs. Michael shifted position to stand beside Kate and study the diagonal tear through the canvas, across the face of a young blonde. If he removed the frame, the canvas might relax enough for him to fit the pieces together, as he'd done with Aaron's sketch.

Kate pointed to the portrait of the other woman and murmured, "Violet's mother, long dead."

He'd presumed as much. "Who played the musical instruments in this house?"

"Violet." She sucked in a raspy breath. "I see he damaged her instruments, too."

Michael grasped her shoulders and rotated her to him, commanding her attention. "Was Aaron a Regulator?"

Her gaze made a furtive dart to the right. Blood heated in his ears. Now she was less than forthcoming. He resisted the urge to grip her more tightly but shook her shoulders, once. "Stop that. You want me to help you? Tell me what you know."

"But Aunt—"

"Don't shield her. Don't protect Aaron. Answer my question!"

Her upper front teeth clamped on her lower lip, reddening it. She winced. "I—Aaron—we all knew he sympathized with the Regulators. That was one reason why Mr. Griggs objected to his association with Violet." Her voice dropped to a murmur. "But Aaron didn't fight at the Battle of Alamance. He was here in Hillsborough."

Was he? How did she know? Hadn't she said she was in Wilmington during that time? "What did Rachel and Clarence White think of the Regulators?"

Kate shook her head. "Not sympathetic in the slightest."

He exhaled to purge his lungs of vexation and released her. With a pivot away, he propped one hand on the opposing doorjamb. Not only had Kate's information dug her cousin in deeper as a suspect for Griggs's killer, but it gave Aaron the motive of political differences to break into his mother's home, and it brought in other Regulators as suspects or accomplices. "Who among Aaron's contacts in the Regulators are still in Hillsborough today?"

"I don't know."

He whipped about and saw her recoil, eyes wide. "You don't know? That's what your eyes said a moment ago, and it wasn't accurate."

"I wasn't here in May and June of 1771. I was in Wilmington."

"Yes, you mentioned that last night." His jaw clenched, and he relaxed it. He knew Kate wouldn't respond in a helpful manner to bullying. He softened his tone. "So if you weren't here, how can you be certain that Aaron wasn't at the Battle of Alamance, fighting with the Regulators?"

"Because Aunt Rachel told me that he—" Her sentence trailed into the silence of someone who found herself sprawled on her bum in mud, unable to remember how she got there. Kate averted her gaze to the door. "You think Aunt Rachel has been covering for Aaron all these years." The tempo of her words picked up, and she wrung her hands. "I—I don't care what you suspect, Michael. Aaron didn't kill Mr. Griggs. He couldn't have. He's always been gentle."

Her complexion pasty pale, she dashed past him for the door and snatched her hat and cloak, a woman trying to outrun a specter. Michael, his shoulders bowed, let her leave. The slamming of the door behind her resounded through the house, an echo from the bottom of a waterless well.

Chapter Thirteen

MICHAEL SAT HARD upon the third stair in Ezra Griggs's house. Elbows on his knees, he fixated on Kate's basket of food near his feet and lambasted himself silently. He'd failed to foresee that pursuing Aaron as a suspect would alienate both Kate and her aunt from him.

But what options did he have, aside from pursuing the likeliest suspects? He supported his forehead in the heels of his hands and cursed.

The front door whammed open. Startled, he jerked his head up, straightened. O'Toole sashayed in, his perfect white teeth agleam. "Hoo, Compton, I know what a lady means when she slams a door like that. It means you're not worth a rat's arse, in her opinion. Thank you for stepping on your own stiletto, small as it may be."

Michael stomped to his feet on the first step, shoulders thrown back. O'Toole's smirk faltered over the height differential, then firmed. Michael nailed his gaze to that of the Irishman. "Unless you're making a delivery for Schmidt, you're wasting your master's time and mine."

O'Toole laughed, shrugged the straps of two canvas sacks off his shoulders, and tossed the sacks to the floor between himself and the stairs. "There you are, *Sasanach*. Interview notes, two lists, and one stinking mess of bloody clothing. You're a spy. I shall have proof soon enough. Then you shall be a dead spy."

"You've completed your task. There's the door. Leave."

O'Toole backed a few steps, swept off his hat with a flourish, and tossed it on the floor just inside the dining room. Then he patted his cheek in invitation. "Let's do it now, boy." He closed his fists and raised them, chest high.

Michael's pulse leapt with lust to crack him in the nose. With little difficulty, he imagined the aromas of cinnamon and pastry lingering in the room, Kate's in-the-kitchen scent. He tramped off the step to the floor. O'Toole licked his lips and remained fist-ready. "Go pop a goat," Michael said to him, his tone flat, affecting boredom. "I have my work to do, boy."

The pupils of O'Toole's eyes shriveled. Blood congealed in his face. "*Your* work? This should have been *my* assignment!"

Muscles humming with vigor, Michael straddled the sacks. "You're welcome to it. Beg the job off Schmidt the next time you're in bed."

He bent to retrieve the first sack, his posture creating enough illusion of inattention to catalyze a pounce from his opponent. O'Toole, aiming for the pit of his stomach, landed a punch to the right side of his ribcage instead when Michael twisted in anticipation of him. The lance of pain honed Michael's awareness. He blocked two more swings before clipping the Irishman in the chin. "Who taught you to fight, O'Toole? Your bloody grandmother?"

The other man growled and charged him again. He hooked a foot around Michael's ankle and tripped him. The impact of landing on his side whooshed air from Michael's lungs. He barely managed to roll to his stomach before O'Toole pounced on him and yanked his head back by the hair. His fist glanced off Michael's nose.

Michael's facial muscles clenched and his eyes watered. He pushed up with both arms, dislodged O'Toole onto the floor, and rolled from him. Not quite far enough. The Irishman scored a kick near his kidney. Michael roared with pain. He partially righted himself in the open doorway in time to deflect another swing.

O'Toole pivoted and leered with victory, launched at him again. Michael doubled over. O'Toole's fist met air and threw him off balance. Michael shouldered him into the door, the crash of it echoing down the walkway, and rammed his elbow into the Irishman's stomach. He followed it with a heel jab to the instep.

A half-bray, half severed cough burst from O'Toole's lips. Michael staggered away, dull satisfaction displacing most of his pain at the sight of the hunched, white-faced Irishman propped against the door. By then, he'd had enough. For the second time that day, he tossed O'Toole from a house. This time, the Irishman tripped on the step and sprawled in the front walkway.

Laughter and applause followed. Michael squinted out and realized that Henry and one of Schmidt's other men had been observing the fight's finale from near the fence. Swiping his nose with the back of his hand—no blood, thankfully—he staggered to the dining room, snatched up O'Toole's hat, and pitched it out, earning additional approval from the men at the fence.

Aching and exasperated, Michael brushed himself off and reached for the door. "You horse's arse, I have work to do! Stop bothering me!"

He slammed the door shut lest O'Toole consider the open doorway an invitation to return and resume their sparring. Then he sagged beside the window in the foyer and swabbed dirt, dust, and snot off his face with his handkerchief.

After a few seconds, he spared a glance out the window. His opponent lurched to his feet, fumbled for his hat, and limped out to his fellows. His posture told Michael that he was beaten but not defeated. Michael realized that the Irishman was the sort of lout who reveled in rivalry and clung to grudges. Not by far was O'Toole finished with him.

The prospect of lingering in Hillsborough and wasting more time with a numskull provided him with additional incentive to solve Griggs's murder so he could find Cornwallis. He replaced his handkerchief and checked his watch—well over an hour until the funeral—before gathering up the smaller of the canvas sacks O'Toole had dropped. Then he sat again on the third step and pulled Kate's basket into his lap.

While he munched bread and cheese, he scanned information from Schmidt. Disappointment solidified in his stomach the way day-old corn mush clumped into a block. The sheriff had listed names of just five people living locally who had aligned themselves with land agents ten years earlier. He'd written the names of only one person each for a Regulator sympathizer and friend of Violet Griggs. True, people moved about, especially after traumatic incidents like the rebellion, battle, and executions, but Michael knew how to ask questions that would generate far more names for each category from a hamlet the size of Hillsborough. Schmidt had exerted little effort on his behalf.

None of the names sparked Michael's recognition, but he memorized them, noting in particular Matthew Tierney, former Regulator. His gaze encircled the name Janet Sewell, Violet Griggs's friend, then looped Francis Sewell's name among those who'd supported land agents, connecting the two names with an invisible thread. The directions for the Sewells were the same. Was Janet Sewell the wife or unmarried daughter of Francis Sewell?

Michael replaced the lists in the sack and withdrew Schmidt's notes from interviewing Griggs's neighbor. Within thirty seconds, his perusal deposited the sensation in his belly incurred after gulping down a fatty beefsteak doused in too much pepper. Pages were missing from the interview. Whether that was Schmidt's or O'Toole's doing mattered not. They were withholding information, trying to keep him in town longer.

They didn't expect him to solve the murder.

A chill gouged his back. Maybe they didn't want him to solve the murder. Maybe Ezra Griggs's life had been taken by Orange County's sheriff and his deputies. Michael swore, jammed the interview notes in the canvas sack with the lists, and pushed to his feet.

He dropped the sack beside Kate's basket and the sack of clothing. Twenty-four hours he'd give the investigation. One day to keep his ears open for rumors of Cornwallis's army. If he hadn't solved the case by then or located His Lordship, he'd leave Hillsborough before dawn Wednesday morning and return to Wilmington, report Schmidt as a deserter when he arrived. Schmidt would probably make good on his promise and give chase. But it was better to be hunted down and executed than sit around on his bum in Hillsborough and wait for the knife to find him.

A bitter taste clung to his tongue at the thought of aborting his mission as courier. Not that he'd be the first dispatch carrier unable to deliver a message due to dangerous conditions. Major Craig would rather he didn't die a fool, trying to accomplish an unfeasible task.

Still his sense of duty nagged him. Craig trusted him. Lord Cornwallis and Crown forces in North Carolina depended on him. If he didn't warn Cornwallis about Cross Creek, and His Lordship's strategy suffered because of it, Michael would always remember the stink of failure.

Not unlike the parlor's odor. He grimaced at it, and in the doorway stood still, his gaze cataloguing the general pattern of destruction in the parlor, all funneled to the blood-drenched rug where Griggs's body had lain. Details sprang at him: the slashed portrait of Violet, shattered vases, splintered pieces of a chair, the violin snapped almost in half. Rage. Terror. Greed. Michael distanced his soul from the vast spell of violence left behind by the murderer and forced his attention to the soiled rug.

"Ezra Griggs, tell me how it happened, and why." In a house devoid of life except his own, his voice sounded ineffective, an acknowledgement of futility.

He dredged from memory his single glimpse of Griggs's body, beneath ruined cushions and a broken chair, prone, his feet stretched toward the parlor's entrance, head closer to the fireplace and twisted to his left. Griggs's left arm was cocked beneath his chest, a broken bird-wing, and his right arm—right arm positioned where, how?

Michael's gaze searched the bloody rug, noted the way Schmidt's men and the undertaker had piled debris aside to access the corpse. They'd moved it to Griggs's left because the heavy couch blocked their way to the right. To complete his picture of the body's position, Michael guessed that Griggs's right arm had been thrust in partial concealment beneath the couch.

For the first time, he entered the parlor, two steps in. He bent over and examined the floor between the entrance and the rug. Two steps more, and he found the first sprinkle of dried blood. Closer to the rug, more blood spattered the floor. Blood had sprayed the left end of the couch, too. He straightened and composed a possible picture of the victim's final seconds.

Griggs was in the parlor when he heard his assailant enter the house from the back door. Griggs started for the parlor doorway. His assailant rushed upon him. A brief struggle ensued. Griggs tried to block the knife with his arms. His throat was slit between the doorway and the couch. While losing consciousness, Griggs wheeled for the couch, his blood spewing floor and furniture, and collapsed to the rug, where his heart stopped beating soon after.

Michael propped a fist on his hip. Even allowing for the element of surprise, he wondered why he wasn't envisioning an exchange of angry words before the knife came out. He retraced his impressions from the previous day. The murderer had entered through the back door. Perhaps he'd known Griggs would refuse him admission. Perhaps when the two men met yesterday, they were done talking because Griggs had already denied the killer the object he desired in a charged confrontation that occurred at another time.

Questions for Griggs's neighbors and fellow residents of Hillsborough crowded Michael's brain. He shook his head once, shut out the clamor and concentrated, returned to the picture he'd constructed of Griggs's last moments. Any animal, including a human, that was dealt a mortal blow fought for those final seconds for life. Consequently, murderers and their victims left some remnants of their violent encounter behind. Always.

Even when the murderer covered his trail as cleverly as Lieutenant Fairfax had done in Alton last June.

***

Whistling "Yankee Doodle," the sergeant pulled again with the rake and released the musk of leaf decay in the copse of trees where the murdered

Spaniard had lain the day before. Michael's peripheral vision caught the wink of metal, and he knelt to confiscate a pewter button, clearly the button off a soldier's coat. It must have popped off the uniform of a man who'd helped the undertaker move the body the day before.

Then white flashed at the damp base of the leaf pile. Michael snatched what appeared to be trim torn from a British soldier's uniform. Surprise rocked him, and his thoughts skittered about, seeking reason. A soldier might lose a loose button in the act of shifting a load around. But trim from his uniform would have to be torn off. In a struggle.

He crammed the trim segment and pewter button into his haversack before the sergeant could identify what he'd retrieved from the ground. Cold clambered over him. If a murderer crouched among the men of the garrison, he must keep theories and half-formed conclusions from this phase of the investigation to himself, avoid flushing his prey too soon and alarming the rest of the men. "Keep raking, Sergeant."

Another pull with the rake revealed the button that he'd noticed missing from the Spaniard's waistcoat when he examined his clothing the previous day. Michael straightened with it. "Enough."

Denial in his head shredded beneath the harsh light of logic. In the final moments before he'd been subdued and bound by his murderer, the Spaniard had struggled furiously with a redcoat from the garrison. In the fight, he'd torn off a swatch of the soldier's trim and one of his buttons. And the murderer, in turn, had ripped a button from his victim's waistcoat.

***

Tiny things, buttons and trim fragments, easily overlooked and not screaming for discovery. Michael turned a slow circle, his gaze downward for all three hundred and sixty degrees. He saw the blood fanned on the fabric of the couch again. He also noticed a smear of blood angled away from the rug, around the back of the couch, walked over and bent to study it. From a smaller smear a few feet beyond that, closer to the fireplace, he deduced that he'd found partial footprints left by the murderer, who'd tracked his victim's blood. The stride length marked him as a man of medium height, like the man he'd spotted entering the woods the previous evening. And it appeared that the assailant had walked around the couch waiting for Griggs to expire.

From behind the couch, Michael peered over to where Griggs had lain and imagined how the body would have looked at that angle. Then he picked his way through debris, his shoes crunching broken porcelain, his gaze brushing over the floor, until he stood before the fireplace.

He lifted Violet's portrait from the wall and studied it. The damage prevented his being able to distinguish much of her appearance, but he made out a bound book perhaps half an inch thick that rested in her lap, her plump fingers spread atop it as if guarding it. Most books were bound with black or dark brown leather, so Michael found the choice of cream-colored leather for the binding unusual, perhaps signifying a volume of special meaning for Violet. He wondered whether the book was upstairs, among the feathers, or downstairs in the wreck of her father's study, amid the dozens of books emptied from shelves.

He propped the portrait against the cold hearth. With a pivot, he faced the parlor entrance, the slow sweep of his scrutiny scooping up more debris, fireplace tools, the destroyed violin, pieces of splintered chair. His attention returned to the saturated rug. Again he pictured the body, adjusting for the change in angle. In his mind, he made Griggs's lower right arm and hand vanish beneath the couch. When Griggs had lifted his arms to ward off his assailant, had he clutched at him?

Michael knelt at the edge of the rug, avoided stepping on it because he knew it was still damp. The death-smell embraced him, a dark goddess wet-kissing and hungry. His stomach rebelled. He sealed his lips so he wouldn't taste the stench, forced his attention to the rug. The body had lain prone, head to the left, left arm cocked beneath body. He scanned where the left arm and hand would have pressed to the rug. Nothing.

Lower right arm and hand jammed beneath couch. Michael allowed his gaze to follow the line the limb might have taken. Then he bent a little lower. A pale scrap of something hid beneath the couch like a frightened puppy. He plucked it out. His lips parted in surprise, and he shot to his feet, a warm surge pumping his veins. He'd found three inches of luxuriant lace, like that adorning the front of a dandy's shirt, and smeared with blood.

Michael's attention shot across the parlor to the canvas bag holding Griggs's clothing, just visible at the foot of the stairs. He retraced his path and exited the parlor. At the stairs, he grabbed the sack. He unpacked each article of clothing, unfolded it, and examined it before draping it on the banister. The stinky stiffness of dried blood infused everything.

Well before he located the dead man's shirt, he knew he'd found a piece of the murderer's shirt beneath the couch. Ezra Griggs had worn quality wool, the craftsmanship outstanding, but his fashion tastes were conservative. The blood-soaked, plain, linen shirt he found at the bottom of the bag confirmed his conclusions.

Futility fled Michael's voice. "Thank you for putting up a fight, Mr. Griggs."

He refolded and repacked the clothing. Again he checked the time: almost one thirty. The funeral was in half an hour. He'd return afterwards, continue his search of the parlor.

What was the name of that old man who lived next door, the curious fellow who couldn't resist snooping from his front porch that morning? Michael's fingers closed about the second sack, and he pried it open. He skimmed over the interview notes and located the name: Blake Carroll. He'd just enough time to introduce himself to Mr. Carroll before the world bid adieu to Ezra Griggs.

Chapter Fourteen

BOTH PUPILS OF Mr. Carroll's brown eyes held the first hints of cataracts, more so his left eye than his right. Nevertheless, he jutted a spindly stump of a chin at Michael and banged the end of his cane once on the wood floor of a front porch stippled in shadow by the westering winter sun and leafless branches of an oak. "Hah. Wondered whether I'd meet you, laddie. *You* showed up at Griggs's house yesterday right after the commotion."

"That I did, sir. Compton, at your service." Michael extended his hand, and Carroll reciprocated the handshake with a solid grip. "And you're Mr. Carroll."

He grinned with gums full of long, yellow teeth. "Yah, been Carroll for seventy-six years now. I'm old enough to be your grandfather. 'Cept that accent of yours tells me you was born on the other side of the Atlantic, and I ain't never left North Carolina." Carroll's fingers flexed on the handle of his cane, a hawk's talons upon a limb. "Best land on the face of the earth, North Carolina. So how'd you find out my name when I ain't never seen you in Hillsborough before yesterday? Oh, wait." Carroll snapped the fingers of his other hand. "I heard Schmidt deputized you to investigate the death of Mr. Griggs."

"That's correct."

"God bless Griggs, poor fellow, losing his life. And God bless Schmidt for losing his wits and deputizing a stranger."

"Well, I'm not exactly a stranger. I'm Rachel White's nephew. And you, sir, are a witness to the 'commotion' late yesterday. If you've time, I'd like to ask you a few questions."

"Hrumph. That Irish fop interviewed me yesterday. My supper grew cold before I could get rid of him, so thanks for asking if I have the time, which I happen to have this moment." Carroll sucked his teeth. "Didn't he tell you nothing of what I told him?"

"Very little."

Carroll hrumphed again. His gaze mapped Michael's face. He backed from the open doorway into his house and gestured for Michael to enter. "You got an honest face. More than I can say for Mr. O'Toole. Come on in."

An honest face. Perhaps Carroll's vision hadn't deteriorated yet. Michael removed his hat and entered. Carroll shut the door behind him. Stuffy warmth scented with mustard poultice and wood smoke swallowed them both.

"Set yourself in the parlor. Noah just made a pot of coffee. You want a cup?"

Noah. Who was Noah? "Yes, sir, if you'll join me. Thank you." Michael followed his host and tried not to appear nosy as he glanced about for "Noah." Was he the old man's servant? If so, he'd probably been the one Carroll sent to fetch the authorities when the murderer started making noise next door. That meant he'd have heard the clamor, too. Why hadn't O'Toole interviewed Noah yesterday?

In the too-warm parlor, Carroll said, "Sit, sit." When Michael aimed for a padded chair with armrests and a carved wood backing, Carroll tapped his knee with the cane. "No, that's my chair." He stabbed the cane toward the only couch in the parlor, its original upholstery concealed beneath a fitted cover with a faded, floral pattern. Michael headed for the couch. Skepticism bristled one of Carroll's grizzled eyebrows. "Rachel White's nephew, eh? You don't look a bit like her. Trust me, that ain't an insult. You stay put. I'll fetch that grandson of mine."

Ah, Noah was Carroll's grandson. But why not just holler for him? Michael dropped his hat on a couch cushion and sat near the fireplace long enough for his host's cane-thump to diminish toward the rear of the house. Then he sprang up and peered between curtains draping the front window, assessed how much old Mr. Carroll could have seen of the activity next door, had he been standing in the parlor, and had those cataracts truly not impaired him. The parlor window permitted an unobstructed view of Griggs's front yard. However, the killer's entrance and exit had been through the back door.

The thumping returned. Michael sat. Carroll entered and heaved himself into his chair, a feudal lord presiding over court in his great hall. Soft footfalls preceded the arrival of a man Michael's height and age who, from his jawline, wiry build, and dark eyes, was Blake Carroll minus fifty years, but twenty pounds of muscle heavier. The silver tray he carried bore a coffeepot, cups, napkins, spoons, sugar, and milk. Without allowing the coffeepot to skate around or the milk to slosh, he slid the tray upon the low table before Michael. Then he straightened.

Michael stood. "So you're Mr. Carroll's grandson. I'm pleased to meet you." He stuck out his hand and smiled. "Compton, Rachel White's nephew."

The man hesitated a moment before gripping Michael's hand. Gratitude gathered in his reciprocal smile, and intelligence radiated in his eyes. When the handshake terminated, he looked to his grandfather.

Half a second before Noah made a silent query that involved touching two fingertips to his lips, Michael realized he was deaf and deriving visual cues from Carroll. Apparently, Noah wasn't accustomed to being regarded by visitors as more intelligent than the furniture, which explained his hesitation during the greeting. It also explained why O'Toole hadn't interviewed him. A huge error of omission on the Irishman's part. Noah was clearly not half-witted.

The old man responded with hand signals and another toothy grin. Noah arranged cups and poured coffee. Michael said to Carroll, "Does he understand what we say from watching lips?"

"Fairly well. His speech ain't too good, though. Hard even for me to understand sometimes. Maybe if my son and his wife had lived longer, been able to work with him more—" Old pain and frustration strangled Carroll's sigh. "Near as we can figure, he was born hearing just fine. When he was two, he got him a three-day fever, the one what makes rosy spots on the skin. Most children heal up from it just fine. But that's when Noah stopped hearing."

Noah handed Michael a spoon and napkin, followed by his cup. Then he positioned the cone of sugar nearer to Michael, followed by the creamer. "Choo-gah. Mik."

Sugar. Milk. Michael caught his eye. "Thank you." He reached for the sugar.

Gratitude beamed in the deaf man's eyes again. He served his grandfather black coffee before pulling up a chair. His shoulders straightened, and his gaze darted between the lips of his grandfather and Michael, signifying his intent to participate.

"Noah reads and writes," said Carroll, "but he's best at drawing pictures. We keep slates and chalk handy around the house." He reached behind his chair and withdrew a portfolio like Violet's. "Look here what he drew recently. Miss Griggs taught him long ago."

Michael accepted several charcoal sketches handed to him by Mr. Carroll. While Violet Griggs's own talent had been middling, her pupil's skill surpassed hers many times. A rose, a butterfly, and a cardinal had been drawn to such perfection that they seemed three-dimensional. A portrait of Blake Carroll even captured the cantankerous humor around the grandfather's eyes.

"Excellent work," Michael told Noah and returned the sketches to the old man. He and his grandson were fortunate that they could communicate, which led Michael to speculate what would happen to Noah after his grandfather died. Michael's gaze flicked to the coffee service. Surely Noah yearned to be of more use than a servant to an aging grandfather. What did he want to do with his life?

For that matter, what did Michael want to do with his own life?

He sipped his sweetened, creamed coffee, then cleared his throat over a swell of uneasiness and shoved back the loan of anxiety from the future so he could focus on the dilemma of the present. "Mr. Carroll, at what time yesterday afternoon were you aware of the commotion next door?"

"About four-thirty."

"What did you hear?"

"Dishes breaking, objects hitting the walls, that sort of thing."

"Hear any voices, screaming, yelling during that time?"

"No, none."

Michael swallowed another mouthful of coffee and set the cup on the table. "How did you respond to the commotion?"

"I could tell something was wrong, so I wrote a note about it, gave it to Noah, sent him to Mr. Schmidt. That was maybe four thirty-five." Carroll's chin got that stubborn appearance. "And no, I didn't go next door for a look. Old fellow like me don't need to tangle with human varmints. Although I did load my rifle and keep it handy, in case the varmint got to wandering."

Carroll hadn't reached the age of seventy-six by acting the brash fool. Michael gave him a curt nod of approval. "Did you notice anyone beside Mr. Griggs on his property or entering or exiting his house between, oh, four o'clock and quarter to five?"

"No." Carroll drank some of his coffee and smacked his lips.

"When was the last time you conversed with Mr. Griggs?"

"Saw him out by his stable about four o'clock. Then a few minutes later, he walked back into his house."

"How well can you see at a distance, sir?"

Carroll chuckled without humor. "Yah, seeing at a distance challenges me. But I was in my back yard same time Griggs was in his. We waved to each other. I asked him if he'd rested up yet from that long trip he'd taken, and he said no, not quite. Man rides a horse all that way, he's bound to be tired for days when he gets home."

Michael's scalp felt as if someone traced a wavy line across it with a quill. "Long trip?" He heard the surprise in his own voice and became aware that Noah studied his expression. Reading the quick pulse of curiosity there, no doubt. "Where did he go? How long was he gone?"

"Gone for about ten days. Saturday afternoon's when he got back to town. As for where he went—" Carroll shrugged. "He didn't tell me where he went. Just said he'd be gone about ten days. He traveled a good bit."

Ten days. Horseback. Michael unfurled a rough map of the area in his mind. During that time, Ezra Griggs might have ridden to Bethabara, Cross Creek, Salem, and Salisbury, possibly as far as Charlotte Town, Wilmington, or New Berne. Outside North Carolina, he might have gone into South Carolina. Or Virginia.

His pulse leapt a beat. Major Craig had mentioned Southern Virginia as a possible location for Cornwallis's army. What if Griggs had taken his ten-day trip to seek out His Lordship, and a spy had murdered him?

Bah, speculation. Without more information, Michael had no reason to connect Griggs's trip with his demise. Yet the coincidence was irresistible. "Mr. Carroll, did you find Mr. Griggs's behavior unusual, his leaving for so long and not telling you where he went?"

"Sometimes he'd tell me where he was going. Not always. My neighbor liked being mysterious, heading out, gone a week or so, back again. Pfffft."

In other words, Griggs had acted like a spy with information to transfer.

Carroll unloaded his coffee cup on a nearby stool and pressed forward on his cane, his eyes eager. "You want my opinion? He was involved in something unlawful. Folks talk a good deal about Regulators in this town. There's a reason for that. Regulators, a few are still living here, mostly quiet, not making trouble. But they remember that Griggs worked for McCullough."

Regulators again. The buoyancy Michael had felt moments earlier collapsed. He realized he hadn't wanted Schmidt to be correct in the assumption about the Regulators. He made his tone level. "Thank you, Mr. Carroll."

The old man sat back. "Hah! I understand why Mr. Schmidt deputized you now. He wanted an outsider's neutrality. You don't think my neighbor was killed by a Regulator, do you?"

"I don't know what to think, sir, but would be most grateful if you made a list of Regulators who still live in the area so I might speak with them about Mr. Griggs."

The cane rapped the floor once. "You'll have that list later this afternoon."

Michael considered the information he'd been fed. "Is the name Matthew Tierney familiar?"

As if to ward off the name, Carroll flung up the hand not gripping the cane. "Riff-raff."

"A Regulator?"

"Bah. Regulators wouldn't have him. Not worth their trouble."

A flash of annoyance pressed Michael's lips together. Had Schmidt and O'Toole hoped to send him down a false trail by labeling Tierney a Regulator? "Describe him."

"About your height, dark hair, too. But a rake, a useless dandy in his mid-thirties. Spoiled brat drinking dry a fortune his papa left him." A fusion of cackle and snort emerged from Carroll's throat. "Couple years ago, he got his-self pickled and fell off a balcony of his house. Busted something in his ankle, so he walks with a limp now."

Astonishment seared Michael's blood and bugged his eyes. A man of medium height with dark hair, money, and a limp had tried to break into Aunt Rachel's house last night. How many men fitting that description lived in Hillsborough?

And a *dandy*, Carroll had labeled him. Was it possible that—? Michael fumbled in his coat pocket, extracted the three-inch scrap of bloody torn lace, and tried to settle the excitement squeezing his stomach. "Does this look like it might have come from Mr. Tierney's clothing?"

As soon as he opened his hand to display the scrap, Noah slid forward to the edge of his chair and gaped. "Maan! Yeahh. Maan!" A burst of hand signals and incomprehensible articulations followed. Old Mr. Carroll spread his hands, lost, while frustration screwed up the deaf man's face when he realized he wasn't communicating.

His grandfather grimaced and tried to snag his attention. "Noah! Slow down, slow—ah, it's no use, Mr. Compton. He gets like this sometimes, real excited, and he has to settle down before he can make sense. I think he's saying he's seen this lace on Matthew Tierney before."

Noah, who had been watching his lips, shook his head. "Naaa! Naaa!" He gestured to something over Mr. Carroll's head. "Baa-yaaad, baa-yaaad." He pointed again.

Michael's gaze followed the direction of Noah's finger: outside the parlor, toward the rear of the property. A chill crawled up his arms and wrapped his throat. *Baa-yaaad.* Back yard? He rose from the couch and stood before Noah, commanded his attention by seizing one of his shoulders. "You saw this lace on a man in Mr. Griggs's back yard?"

Light blazed from Noah's eyes. He bobbed his head. "Yezz!"

"Yesterday afternoon?"

"Yezz!"

"I'll be darned," muttered Carroll. "You know, I think he tried to tell me that last night, but I couldn't understand what he was getting at."

Victory dizzied Michael. He sucked in a breath to steady himself. "Noah, was it Mr. Tierney?"

Noah massaged his hairline. His brows lowered, and a crease formed between them. His gaze rolled from Michael's to the coffeepot and back.

Disappointment emptied from Michael in an exhalation. He released Noah and replaced the piece of bloody lace in his pocket. Just this once, he wished the universe had provided him with a clear answer. "Why would Mr. Tierney want Mr. Griggs dead?"

Noah shook his head. Carroll's words were listless. "Them two argued ownership over a piece of land about six years ago, but I heard they'd settled their differences."

Carroll didn't sound convinced of Tierney as his neighbor's murderer. Still, it was something to keep in mind. Michael thought of the expensive man's hat with the broken ostrich feather and rifle shot hole. "Does enmity exist between Mr. Tierney and my aunt, Mrs. White?"

The old man stared at him as if he'd pulled the question from the air. "Never heard of such."

Michael abandoned the tack of Tierney for the moment and returned his focus to Noah. From the way the deaf man sharpened his attention on him, Michael had the company of a fully cooperative witness. Someone who wanted to be useful. "Mr. Carroll—"

"No-ahh." The deaf man patted his chest with his palm. "No-ahh."

"Noah." With the communications barrier, Michael knew he must keep matters as simple as possible, construct more interview questions that lead only to a "yes" or "no" answer. He spoke slowly, enunciating. "Were you in your back yard yesterday afternoon with your grandfather?"

Noah nodded. "Yezz."

"Did you see Mr. Griggs in his back yard, too?" Again, a nod. "Four o'clock?" A third nod. Relief and elation twined in Michael's chest. Noah had confirmed his grandfather's testimony. Now he knew that Ezra Griggs was last seen alive around four in the afternoon, and he could place his time of death at somewhere just prior to four thirty. Michael had arrived at Griggs's house shortly before five. So the murderer had taken about twenty minutes to ransack the house.

"Noah, did you see Mr. Griggs enter his house?" A nod. "The man who wore this lace, did you see him enter Mr. Griggs's house after Mr. Griggs?" Another nod. "How many minutes between them?"

For several seconds, Noah's gaze drifted off Michael. Then he opened both fists twice.

"Twenty? Twenty minutes?"

"Tunnee, yezz!"

"Did the man see you?"

"Naaa."

Michael rolled his shoulders back. He and Noah exchanged a grin, then he turned to the grandfather. "Mr. Carroll, between you and Noah, I have learned that Mr. Griggs was last seen alive a few minutes after four. The suspect was in the house with him twenty minutes later, and your neighbor was dead by four thirty. The suspect spent about twenty minutes in noisy plunder and left a few minutes before five."

"What you reckon the killer was looking for?"

"I wish I knew." A deed to a disputed piece of property, perhaps? That would fit among the goose feathers, as would a ciphered message for the British Army. Michael's mind snagged on the possibility, played with it a moment from another angle. Could Griggs have been expecting Major Craig's dispatch? What if Griggs had found Cornwallis during his ten-day absence from Hillsborough and brought a message back from Cornwallis to Craig? A shudder clawed at Michael's gut. Was a rebel spy proficient at throat slitting stalking *him* that moment?

Generosity bubbled in Carroll's voice. "How's about I fetch paper and charcoal for Noah, see what he can sketch of the killer."

Michael forced back his dread. "An excellent idea, sir." Michael glanced at the clock on the mantle, then swiveled his head so Noah received more than a profile view of his lips. "Mr. Griggs's funeral is at two. I must attend. Will either of you come with me?"

Noah's eyes glittered, and he shifted, faced away from Michael to his grandfather. Furrows carved around the old man's mouth softened, and the bony hitch in his shoulders mellowed, dissolving ten years off him. He chuckled. "Yah, I wager she'll be there, too. Go on, son. If Mr. Tierney attends, show him to Mr. Compton." Carroll's gaze roped in Michael. "Sir, you'll pardon an old man with an arthritic knee for not attending his neighbor's funeral. I'll send Noah to pay respects for the Carroll household. When you get back, we'll start him on sketching the killer."

Chapter Fifteen

BEFORE TWO O'CLOCK, Michael and Noah arrived at the burying ground adjacent to the church. Birds chirped from surrounding trees. Three-dozen townsfolk, their conversations subdued to a drone, had formed a loose circle around a wooden coffin, a six-foot-long hole in the ground beside it, and a mound of reddish clay-dirt on the other side of the hole. Nearby, a couple of stalwart sextons leaned on the handles of muddy shovels, and a minister fussed over a sleeve of his black robe.

Michael tucked items that he'd borrowed from Griggs's house—Violet's portrait and her collection of sketches—and Kate's basket, now empty of food, out of the way against an ivy-blanketed, low stone wall that rimmed the cemetery. After the funeral, he'd drop them off at Aunt Rachel's house before returning to Griggs's house.

Rachel White was among those present: her spine straight as a ramrod, scrutiny cool, and lips compressed. She recognized Michael at the same time he spotted Schmidt lumbering for him, so he hastened to her side, trailed by Noah. He brushed her elbow, relieved that she didn't yank her arm away. Schmidt would have noticed. She and Noah acknowledged each other with polite nods, and Michael said, "I'm surprised to see you here, Auntie."

The compression in her lips glided to one side. "Why? Do you think me a heartless witch?"

"Of course not." He strapped the most beguiling smile he could muster over his lie as Schmidt arrived.

"Just because Ezra Griggs and I didn't agree on one blessed thing is no reason for me to not pay him final respects." Aunt Rachel flung her gaze past Michael to spear Schmidt. Her tone amputated warmth from the air. "I don't approve of your latest choice of associates, Nephew."

Schmidt displayed teeth and evoked his sneeze of amusement. "Come now,

I did not seek to slander your tavern and deprive you of customers. I am clear of those events last summer."

"Clear as a rattlesnake on a rock."

Noah shrank from Schmidt and Aunt Rachel, in no need of sound to identify an old quarrel's grumbly cumulus. Michael eased into retreat alongside him, curious about Schmidt's reference to slander and events the previous summer. How had Kate described her aunt's relationship with Schmidt? The two had "never seen eye-to-eye." That explained the bicker he'd left behind.

Where was Kate? More importantly, was Ezra Griggs's killer among those gathered for the funeral? Michael's gaze performed a search of the crowd.

One hand on Michael's shoulder, Noah paused and pointed across the congregants. Several paces back from the circle, a dark-haired, fleshy fellow in his thirties kept the company of three beribboned, bosomy blondes. An ostrich feather in his hat berated the breeze. Lace spewed from velvet at his cuffs and throat, and leather on his boots gleamed. But three days' beard stubble and the rheumy eyes of a sot skewed his interpretation of macaroni planter to macaroni pirate.

No one else in the churchyard had dressed like him. Michael peeked at the torn lace in his pocket, then glanced across the circle to the billowing ostrich feather. Same fanatical fashion tastes. From Carroll's description, he must be Matthew Tierney. A blonde murmured in the fellow's ear. When he guffawed in response, nearby congregants frowned at the show of irreverence and shuffled away, somber sensibilities bruised.

Noah had slunk off. Michael caught up with him, faced him. "Is that Tierney?" Noah nodded. "Was he the man in the back yard?"

The deaf man craned his head for a look at the dandy. Then he regarded Michael and jerked out a shrug. Michael opened his mouth to ask whether the man in the yard had resembled Aaron White. Then Noah made a gesture of tugging the brim of his hat down to shield much of his face.

Michael exhaled, hard. "Ah. You couldn't see much of his face for his hat."

The minister's voice rose above the hubbub. "Brothers and sisters in Christ, let us begin."

Conversion hushed. The circle tightened about the grave. Noah slipped away, and Michael marked his direct course for a well-gowned but plain, brown-haired woman in her mid-twenties. When she spotted Noah's approach, her mouth sprouted a smile full of crooked teeth, transforming her from plain to ugly. Welcomed within her intimate space, Noah launched into a barrage of silent hand signals that she reciprocated and seemed to comprehend as well as old Mr. Carroll. The resultant sparkle in her eyes and the absence of a retinue of children and husband suggested a longstanding love between the two never consummated in physical marriage.

Before Michael could speculate on which parents had impeded the union, Schmidt's paw whumped upon his shoulder. Testiness flicked Michael's blood. With one quick step aside, he shrugged him off. Schmidt hovered near his ear, his voice low enough to not detract from the minister's words. "Mr. Sewell is bedridden with gout and could not attend the final services of his friend, Mr. Griggs. Otherwise, Mr. Carroll and Miss Sewell would not be standing together over there."

So that was Janet Sewell, Violet's friend, the cryptic "she" to whom Carroll referred when encouraging Noah to attend the funeral. Carroll seemed to have no problems with the choice his grandson's heart made, but the lady's father must object to his daughter marrying a deaf man. Maybe Sewell, like his friend Griggs, had withheld his daughter's hand, anticipating a marriage of wealth.

Michael walked in the opposite direction of the lovers, halted a quarter way around the circle, and scanned all the unfamiliar faces. Schmidt bore down on him and bathed him with a seductive whisper. "The libertine with the blondes is Mr. Tierney. He matches your description of the suspect you saw leaving Mr. Griggs's property yesterday. Does he also match your description of the man on your aunt's property at three o'clock this morning?"

His suggestions burrowed into Michael's imagination, producing images of Tierney's ostrich plume adorning the black hat recovered on the Whites' property as well as the black hat of the man who'd vanished into the woods behind Griggs's house. Michael also envisioned a bull being dragged down a narrow, twisty path by his nose ring. The bull's name was Michael Stoddard.

Schmidt certainly seemed to want Tierney in jail, with Michael the instrument of his arrest. Michael wondered why.

Michael detected looks of impudence that Tierney fired in their direction, as if daring Schmidt to arrest him. No telling what the dandy had done to incur Schmidt's low esteem of him. Intentionally, Michael didn't look at Schmidt. He spoke low. "Who here is a former Regulator?"

"*Former* Regulator? Did you not read my notes? Mr. Tierney *is* a Regulator. He sued Mr. Griggs several years ago. He claimed Mr. Griggs had sold the same piece of property to him and another man as sole owners. Would that not make you want to murder the seller?"

Michael blinked at the similarity to the case he'd turned over to Nick Spry. Then common sense asserted itself. If a type of swindle proved lucrative among land agents and their cohorts, news would spread quickly in the profession, and the mechanics would be copied with alacrity.

Would that not make you want to murder the seller? According to Carroll, Tierney's dispute with Griggs had been settled years ago. Either the two men had recently breathed life into a corpse of an argument, or—he glanced at Schmidt. Again, he had the sensation of being led by a nose ring.

He ambled another ninety degrees around the circle, observing the groupings people had formed. Schmidt trundled after him with the intensity of a butcher hoping to unload a wagonload of rancid meat on an unsuspecting customer. Michael stopped walking again. Schmidt hissed in his ear. "*Engländer*, have you heard nothing that I have said?"

Across the circle in Tierney's group, derision had been discarded, and the "useless dandy" performed a shrewd assessment of Schmidt as if he were his daily opponent in a life-sized game of piquet. He fit his scrutiny around Michael, too, trying to shuffle him into the deck, but from his squint, Michael was a card of arbitrary and unknown value. Perverse pleasure pulsed through Michael at the thought.

He rubbed his forehead. Carroll claimed that Matthew Tierney wasn't a Regulator. Schmidt claimed he was. They couldn't both be correct. Michael needed to interview Tierney as soon as possible, not only to get to the bottom of the Regulator business, but to learn Tierney's whereabouts while Griggs was being murdered. He lowered his hand to his side. "Who here openly opposed the Regulators or aligned themselves with their adversaries?"

Schmidt pointed out four men, all named on the list he'd sent with O'Toole, then scowled at Michael. "You have completed your inspection of the house?"

"No."

Schmidt crushed savagery into a whisper. "Your time here is wasted. You should be back at the house, looking and finding!"

"I've been looking." Michael decided to keep the scrap of lace to himself for the time. He smoothed his tone. "I've found two bedrooms full of goose feathers, as you said I would. Do save us the nuisance, and stop beating around the bush. What else do you expect me to find?"

"*Du bis zu bled, um in den Abe zu kacke!* Evidence! Do not forget our meeting at six this evening. By then, you *will* have made progress on the investigation." He stomped off.

Evidence. A shuddery stream of breath vented through Michael's nostrils. Schmidt clearly expected him to report on more than goose feathers at six o'clock.

Michael settled his pulse and sauntered over beside Aunt Rachel, who clenched his upper arm and pulled him in close to her whisper. "I warn you. Schmidt is a wicked man. And O'Toole lacks a mere teaspoon more brains to compete fully with Schmidt for wickedness."

He coaxed her talons loose, rested them in the bend of his elbow, and tucked her hand against his chest, for all appearances a dutiful nephew patting his aunt's hand in consolation. Across the circle, the sheriff glowered at them. Beneath the stoic exterior that Michael hoped he presented for the public, he wrestled back the shriek of his instincts to abandon Hillsborough.

The vicar launched into a eulogy of Ezra Griggs. Michael scanned the congregants again. Not a teary eye among them. As Kate had opined the night before, the community wasn't sentimental over Griggs. From the enthusiastic reminiscences that the vicar spouted about the deceased, Griggs had likely supported the church in a regular, substantial manner. He may also have spoken with the vicar about marriage plans for his daughter and her romance with Aaron White. Michael added the vicar to his mental list of potential people to interview.

At the conclusion of the service, the crowd around the grave loosened to give the sextons room to complete the burial. Some folks left the site. Others clustered to speak among themselves. Michael released Aunt Rachel. "Where's Cousin Kate?"

She sniffed. "At Market with Martha."

Her reaction confirmed his impression that Rachel White had appeared at the funeral out of duty. His gaze landed on Noah, rapt in conversation with the plain woman. Time to meet the woman who had been Violet's good friend. "Madam, please do me the honor of introducing me to the lady in Mr. Carroll's company."

Chapter Sixteen

AUNT RACHEL AND Michael strolled toward Noah and Janet Sewell. She said to him, "Her father will surely give her an earful when she returns home. Not that it will do much good."

"Looks as though she and Mr. Carroll are in love."

"For more than ten years. You'd think her father would have learned his lesson from what happened with Aaron and Violet. Numskull, like that murdered friend of his."

Michael flinched. Did Rachel White have a compassionate bone in her body?

Noah and his companion ceased conversing at their approach. The women curtsied and greeted each other. Aunt Rachel said, "Miss Sewell, this is my nephew, Mr. Compton, from Cross Creek."

Crooked teeth marred Janet Sewell's smile. She bobbed a curtsy. "Mr. Compton."

"Miss Sewell." He bowed.

"Your nephew has such a candid face, Mrs. White."

Aunt Rachel's responsive smile stopped short of her eyes. Michael, aware that he'd imposed enough on the matron's good will, knew it was time to manipulate conversation toward the investigation. He'd noticed Noah's gaze flitting from lips to lips, so he spoke clearly to Miss Sewell. "Would that the circumstances of our introduction were more pleasant."

"Yes. My father was Mr. Griggs's friend for many years and greatly saddened by the news. He'd have been here this afternoon, but for gout in his knees and general malaise."

"I'm sorry to hear that he suffers. It sounds as though his condition doesn't permit him to leave the house very often." Michael considered Griggs's long trip and wondered how he might learn of any confidence shared between the two men without arousing Miss Sewell's suspicions. "I hope he and Mr. Griggs had spent time together recently."

"Actually, Father invited him for supper about two weeks ago. They played chess afterwards." Her gaze caressed Noah for a second. "I went up to bed."

Michael slid commiseration into his voice. "I heard that Mr. Griggs had returned from a long trip the day before yesterday, so that was probably their last shared meal."

"I suppose so." Miss Sewell appeared bored but polite.

In Michael's peripheral vision, Aunt Rachel crossed her arms over her chest. She was bored, too, and less inclined for politeness. Like a current of sludge, disappointment moved through him. He'd hoped his remark might prompt Miss Sewell to comment on overheard conversation—Griggs telling her father where he was going. Maybe Griggs hadn't discussed his destination in her presence. But that didn't mean Griggs hadn't told his friend. Francis Sewell: another potential witness to interview.

Michael decided to shift the topic. "You were friends with Violet Griggs, weren't you?"

Her eyes lit. "The best of friends." She fidgeted at Aunt Rachel. "How unfortunate that Mr. Griggs was so determined to see Violet marry that land agent."

"He was from a wealthy Northern family." Aunt Rachel tapped her foot. "And such a popinjay. I've been trying to recollect his name but cannot do so. Do you recall it?"

Miss Sewell hung her head. "Not offhand, Mrs. White. I remember that he left town with Governor Tryon the day after the executions." She shivered. "Good riddance. I never liked his way of looking at Violet." Her head bobbed up, and she blurted, "But I so hope that Violet and Aaron are happy together, wherever they are."

Aunt Rachel's lips tightened. Miss Sewell's gaze snagged on something beyond the shoulders of Michael and Aunt Rachel. She cleared her throat and composed her expression.

Michael twisted to glimpse what had encouraged the restraint in Miss Sewell. A grinning Matthew Tierney, trailing blondes, closed on them. His unhurried pace tricked the eye away from a limp and the support a fine cane loaned to his right ankle. "Afternoon, ladies and gentlemen." Leaving his retinue about five paces back, Tierney inserted himself between Michael and Miss Sewell and addressed her. "Er, it isn't a good afternoon for your father. Please convey my heartfelt condolences to Mr. Sewell on the loss of his friend."

Her gaze sought the ground. "Thank you. I shall tell him."

Tierney transferred his cane to his left hand and touched the brim of his hat, the plume waving a greeting. "Mrs. White. Mr. Carroll. Good afternoon." He rotated his torso toward Michael, his expression that of a man who has been transported back in time and halfway across the world to meet Marco Polo. "We haven't yet met, sir!"

Dry humor flavored Aunt Rachel's introduction. "My nephew, Mr. Compton, from Cross Creek. And this is Mr. Tierney."

Tierney intercepted the approach of Michael's hand and wrung the handshake out with energy. "Jolly good to meet you, Mr. Compton!"

"Pleased to meet you, Mr. Tierney."

"Been awhile since I ventured to Cross Creek. What's your business there?"

"Naval stores." Michael's gaze followed the bobbing ostrich feather and explored the lines of the dandy's hat, which bore a chilling resemblance to the hat he'd sent rifle shot through about twelve hours earlier. "Er, your hat—Charles Town?"

What looked like honest surprise and appreciation captivated Tierney's face, and he turned to Aunt Rachel. "By all the gods, madam, your nephew has a keen eye for fashion."

Aunt Rachel's jaw locked. A muscle jumped beneath her eye. Insight and alarm flushed Michael's blood. She'd noted the label on the intruder's hat during breakfast. Matthew Tierney, she now believed, had been the burglar at three o'clock in the morning.

Michael gripped her upper arm briefly and commanded her gaze to meet his. "Aunt, allow me to have a few words with Mr. Tierney before walking you home."

Her response came through clenched teeth. "A few *well-chosen* words, I presume."

Miss Sewell and Noah looked back and forth between Aunt Rachel and Michael, from their expressions baffled at the sudden negative charge in the air. Tierney's giddy smile faded. He seemed just as puzzled by the glower from Aunt Rachel and spread his hands. "What now? Have hats from Charles Town fallen from favor among the fashionable?"

Aunt Rachel bared her teeth.

"Excuse us ladies, sir. This way, Mr. Tierney, and step lively." Michael pivoted and, without a backward look, strode away from the group and the three blondes. After a few paces, with Tierney following him, he realized that his erect posture and the whip of his voice had conveyed an Army officer's order, not the request of a civilian merchant. He relaxed his carriage, allowed the grip of muscles in his hands to subside, and hoped no one had noticed the gaffe.

When he judged the others out of earshot, he awaited Tierney, his stance casual, and studied the dandy's easy gait and the way he used his cane. He tried to picture the intruder's limped escape. Did Tierney have enough power in his right ankle to run without his cane? Difficult to determine when he placed such a theatrical flourish on every movement.

And Tierney was assessing him as he approached. Shrewdness narrowed his eyes when he reached him. "You, sir," said the dandy, his voice low, "were impressed by Schmidty yesterday to investigate Griggsy's murder. Quite a vile welcome to Hillsborough, if you ask me."

Vile, indeed. Michael curbed sourness from pinching up the corners of his lips. Tierney wasn't the directionless fop he passed himself off to be. Behind his irreverence lurked a keen observer with single-minded intelligence. "Mr. Tierney, where were you yesterday between four and five in the afternoon?"

"Ah, that's when Griggsy met his demise, wasn't it? I was at home."

"Any witnesses to that?"

"Certainly." Tierney threw a look over his shoulder, caught the blondes' attention, and blew them a kiss. "Fanny and Lucretia over there." He returned his cheeky smile to Michael.

Michael glanced over the blondes. Irritation peppered his gut. How reliable were Fanny and Lucretia as Tierney's alibi? "Where were you at three this morning?"

"Abed." Tierney wiggled his eyebrows. "I have witnesses for that, too. Fanny and Maria. And while I have your attention, I wish to announce that someone burgled my house early this morning, about four." He grinned at the widening of Michael's eyes. "Coincidence, Mr. Compton? I hear a burglar attempted to enter your aunt's house about the same time."

What the hell—was Tierney trying to throw him off his tail with a lie? "You say your house was burgled. Did you report it to Mr. Schmidt?"

"Of course. As usual, he ignored me."

Michael squinted at the other man and processed what the dandy had fed him. Uncertainty flipped about in his chest. Justice on the American frontier was seldom meted out in fair proportion. A loyalist or neutral civilian in a town controlled by rebels might expect to be slighted. The reverse was also true, as some rebels who'd remained in Wilmington were learning.

But the political stance of men often became subordinate to personal grudges. If Tierney had been burgled, Michael could see the Schmidt-Tierney grudge delving to the depth where the sheriff denied the dandy justice. Schmidt was a monster, not unlike Lieutenant Fairfax. "What did this burglar take from you?"

"I'm not certain."

Exasperation emptied Michael's nose. "How do you know you were burgled?"

"Maria heard someone moving about downstairs. I grabbed a loaded pistol. I arrived in my study in time to see a man crawl over the window sash and make his escape into the yard. I ordered him to halt, but of course, he didn't listen. I fired the pistol out the window after him. Missed, damn his eyes."

"Did you recognize the intruder?"

"No. I didn't see him well enough."

"What evidence do you have of his visit?"

"My window sash is scratched where he made his exit."

"Surely you've gone through your house by now to verify that your property is all there?"

A smirk lifted Tierney's upper lip. "It's a large house. I'm still looking. But if I figure out what he came for—" He tapped Michael on the chest once with his forefinger. "—I promise you shall be the first to know. Don't tell Schmidty I said this, but deputizing you was his first intelligent move in a long while."

"Why is that?"

"You're an outsider, capable of far more objectivity than he is." Tierney leaned back, his gaze raking over Michael the way a chemist catalogued phials.

Michael ignored the stare. "Tell me about your enmity with Mr. Griggs."

Tierney shook his head. "Griggsy and I weren't enemies."

"But you fought in court over a piece of land."

Silk wrapped Tierney's tone. "It was a number of years in the past. The matter was settled to both parties' satisfaction."

"How much support did you give the Regulators during their clash with Governor Tryon ten years ago?"

Tierney's eyebrow lifted, and his head moved in pursuit. "Ten years ago? Why, none."

Michael's gaze tracked the shift of his head. What truth was the dandy dancing around? Removing conditions from the question might generate results. "How much support did you give the Regulators?"

Tierney glanced into the distance. His lips rolled inward and pressed together for a second. "None. Has anyone ever told you that you've a certain style of questioning about you suggestive of the inquiry of a provost marshal?"

"My apologies, sir. A few years back, a former accountant embezzled several hundred pounds from my business, and I've never quite recovered all my charm."

Tierney tittered. "Bloody rotten luck."

Michael studied fidgety facial and body movements that proclaimed Tierney's discomfort. The dandy carried Regulators around in the haversack of his past, but the big question was whether they were also at the bottom of Griggs's murder. Schmidt seemed to think so. "Why does Georg Schmidt hate you enough to aim me in your direction for questioning?"

Astonishment widened Tierney's eyes. "Your aunt hasn't told you?" Michael waited, his shoulders lowered and hands relaxed at his sides, and pondered whether Aunt Rachel figured personally in this latest section of the puzzle, or it was just a conduit for feud gossip. Tierney rested a hand on his hip. "I say, Compton, do you enjoy parties?"

"Of course I enjoy parties." Michael's skin crawled. A little over a week ago, he'd had a similar conversation in Wilmington. "What have parties to do with the murder of Ezra Griggs?"

"I'm having a party tonight at my home on the west end of Tryon. Do come anytime after nine. If Mrs. White hasn't satisfied your curiosity about Schmidty and me, I shall plug the gaps in your knowledge. What do you say, Compton?"

Michael felt his tongue drop in his mouth, like a catfish banged against the ground. If Tierney had killed Griggs, and Michael attended the party, he might be walking into peril.

The west end of Tryon. Tierney and Rachel White were neighbors. Michael recalled an irreverent remark he'd made to Kate about a drunken neighbor mistaking her aunt's house for his own. Tierney may well have been that drunken neighbor.

Interesting possibilities abounded. He flicked a glance at the blondes. A party provided excellent distraction for an investigator who sought to compare testimony from three potential witnesses.

Mobility returned to his tongue. "Thank you, Mr. Tierney. I shall consult my schedule and consider your offer."

Chapter Seventeen

AUNT RACHEL GLANCED at Noah, bustling along several steps behind them on Tryon Street and carrying Violet's portrait. Then she transferred her curiosity to Michael. "Nephew, how did the portrait come to be damaged?"

"I presume by the murderer's knife." In stride beside her, Michael juggled Violet's portfolio open and searched for Aaron's ripped sketch.

She tossed her head and snorted. "Ezra Griggs hired a famous artist to paint his daughter and reimbursed the man's expenses all the way out here. His total bill would have fed several poor families in the area for months. Like a nobleman in London, he hosted a reception for the wealthy in town, unveiled the portrait with pomp. Gossip over his vanity raged for most of a year. Just look at his investment now. Not even fit for kindling. What did you expect to achieve by bringing it back to the house?"

Beneath her haughtiness, Michael felt Rachel White's agony over events that had never supplied her soul with finality. For a decade, she'd bottled up grief in the perfunctory way of women who sealed jars of pickled vegetables. "I plan to remove the frame, relax the canvas, perhaps get a better look at Miss Griggs." In case Noah could understand some of their speech, he added, "I've never met her, you know."

He handed her the halves of Aaron's portrait. "This is for you. I found it upstairs in her room. All of Violet's sketches had been strewn across the floor, but this picture of Aaron was the only one that had been mutilated. Like Violet's painting."

At the sight of the face she hadn't seen in a decade, Aunt Rachel's lips trembled, then compressed inward. For seconds, Michael expected her to weep. But she never missed a step, rolled the sketch into a brisk cylinder, and looked straight ahead. "I had no idea that she'd sketched my son. Yes, I shall keep this. I doubt it's of use to anyone else."

Michael wondered whether Kate had managed the loss of her child with such fortitude. Then he reminded himself to keep an objective distance from both women while Aaron stood in the center of the stage of suspects.

They marched up the front walkway to her house. "Sammy! Lizzie!" Aunt Rachel scowled and, reaching the steps to the house, twitched her petticoat aside with one hand so she could stomp onto the porch. "Where could those dogs be? Sammy, Lizzie!"

Mounting the steps after her, Michael frowned. "Did you hear them bark just now? Listen."

"Bah, they're probably out chasing rabbits." Aunt Rachel scraped the soles of her shoes on the doormat and fished around in her pocket for the key to the padlock on the door.

Noah steered the portrait up the steps. Michael walked to the edge of the porch and cupped hands around his mouth. "Sammy! Lizzie!" He whistled. The hounds barked in the distance, a sort of helpless, muffled sound.

Aunt Rachel hrumphed. "How do you like that? Kate and Martha didn't close the padlock."

Her hearing wasn't as sharp as Michael's. Hair sprang to attention all over his neck. He heard a faint thump from upstairs and pivoted around. "No!" he hissed. In two steps, he yanked the woman by the arm away from the doorway to the edge of the porch, motioned Noah over beside her. Then he returned to the door, studied the partially open padlock and said, low, "Maybe they did lock it, and it was picked while all of us were gone."

Aunt Rachel's expression shriveled. Noah, his gaze darting between them, comprehended. He set down the portrait, squared his shoulders, and lifted his chin.

Another thump from the second floor informed Michael that an intruder was still at it. In broad daylight. This person was desperate. Michael's hand signal ordered Aunt Rachel and Noah to remain on the porch. He eased off the padlock, pushed the door open. Hinges emitted a deep groan. Upstairs grew quiet.

Furniture in the parlor had been flung aside or turned upside down, the mayhem resembling that in Griggs's house. Leaving the door open, he tiptoed to the foot of the stairs. A thud sounded from above: the clamor of a window sash being shoved open. With a curse, Michael whipped around the banister and took the stairs three at a time.

He arrived in his room too late to apprehend the intruder, who'd just exited through the open single window. The straw tick hadn't been slit, but it was doubled over on the floor like a fellow who'd been punched in the stomach, and the bed was wedged between him and the window. No way was he getting a quick view out.

Downstairs, Aunt Rachel hollered in alarm and warning. Noah shouted, "Maan!"

Michael galloped back to the bottom floor and out onto the front porch, where Aunt Rachel leaned over the railing around the side of the house and pumped her fist. "Get him, Noah! Yee-aww, look at that lad run!"

"Find those dogs, madam!" Michael vaulted over the railing, took his bearings on Noah, who pursued a dark-haired man fleeing toward King Street, east of direct south, and sprinted after both of them.

Her cackle followed him. "Huzzah! Nab that rogue, Michael!"

Noah, fleet-footed, had closed the distance between himself and the scoundrel to within ten feet when the escapee squeezed between two horses trotting eastbound on King Street. The second beast startled and reared. Noah skidded to a halt and sprang back several feet, his agility sparing him a blow from the horse's hooves while its rider gained control of his mount.

Michael marked the track of the fugitive, in among the alleys and close quarters of merchants' stalls cluttering the opposite side of the street. When he drew up abreast of the deaf man, they exchanged a look of united purpose, sucked in a breath each to replenish what the chase had thus far driven out. Then Michael gestured southeast, and they bounded across the street in pursuit, avoiding a wagon.

A blur of cheeses, fabric bolts, root vegetables, and leatherwork streamed past in Michael's peripheral vision, accompanied by snatches of bicker and barter, and whiffs of tobacco smoke and sour milk. "What's your hurry?" a man called out. "Why are they running?" hollered a woman. Noah at his heels, Michael dodged carts, cats, and baskets, awarded occasional glimpses of their quarry until the miniature bazaar opened up onto Margaret Street.

Both men hauled up short, chests heaving. The rogue who'd climbed out of Aunt Rachel's window was nowhere in sight. Michael instructed Noah to comb a section of stalls and meet him back on King Street.

The fallacy of his plan, he soon learned, was that from the rear, many men appeared as their quarry did: dark-haired, medium stature, dark coat over tan breeches, black hat. And every one of them had decided to spend his coin between King Street and Margaret Street at three o'clock that afternoon. After Michael had poked his nose around stalls and lifted cloths to peer beneath tables for five minutes, he couldn't remember whether the rogue had been limping or even guess his approximate age. But he sensed their fugitive watching him from a place of hiding.

On King Street, the sight of Noah's scowl confirmed that they'd lost their quarry. Dejection dragged the spring of Michael's stride into a trudge. He patted the other man's shoulder. "Come on, lad. I'll buy you a beer."

They'd happened to meet in front of Blumberg's Tavern, recommended by Schmidt that morning as a good place for eavesdropping. But the hitching post was empty, and Noah pulled away from the place, as if he didn't care for it, so Michael aimed them farther west, toward Aunt Rachel's property.

During the walk back, he wondered whether the intruder had found what he was looking for in the house and made off with it. If he wasn't the scoundrel Michael had seen leaving Griggs's house yesterday and also the burglar at Aunt Rachel's house that morning, a troupe of evil-intentioned, middle stature men with dark hair must have descended upon Hillsborough. What was the thread that connected all the incidents? Regulators? Aaron and Violet? Spies?

The seemingly random clues tugged Michael's reasoning about. Not for the first time, he longed for the company of Nick Spry, and the ability to bounce his ideas off his impartial assistant. Noah, bless him, was intelligent and alert enough to be an assistant, but his deafness drove a wedge through language, obscured many nuances that communicated the subtle patterns in clues. Alas, the only point of which he was certain was that Matthew Tierney wasn't the fugitive he and Noah had chased. No, this scoundrel had been about his breaking and entering during Griggs's funeral—which implied that he'd known when the occupants of the house would be out and why.

And what had happened to the dogs?

He and Noah passed Aunt Rachel's tavern. The post out front was also empty. Granted the afternoon was young, but somehow he'd expected to see business there already.

Sammy and Lizzie bounded toward them from the direction of the stable, ears flapping with jubilation. Aunt Rachel emerged from behind the stable dusting off her hands, spotted the two men, and, from the drop in her shoulders, realized that they hadn't caught the intruder. She walked out to meet them, her mouth a slice of grimness.

"Lost him in Market," said Michael. His jaw relaxed when he reached down to pet Sammy. Lizzie butted Noah's hand with her nose, and he stroked her head. Neither hound looked the worse for the adventure.

The woman ejected a sharp sigh of frustration. "At least you two are unhurt. And I'm grateful that you came home with me. I shudder to imagine what might have happened had I encountered the burglar by myself."

Michael shoved away the mental image of Aunt Rachel beating the burglar bloody and senseless with her bare fists while screaming for help at the top of her lungs. "Where did you find the dogs?"

"Locked in the stable with the horses. You should see the size of the two fresh beef haunches that rogue gave them to lure them in." Aunt Rachel measured the air with her hands to show him. "Hrumph. Some watchdogs those two are. Seduced by food."

"Don't be so quick to judge them, Aunt. In the middle of the afternoon, with so many people about, occupying dogs with food provides a burglar with a quiet means of retaining the seat of his breeches while he thieves."

Noah had been watching their lips. His eyes lit with comprehension. "Boocha. Boo-cha."

"Butcher, yes indeed." Michael shared the smile with Noah. "And since the haunches were fresh, a butcher in town likely sold them to the criminal this very morning. In a town this size, how many people would purchase *two* haunches of beef in one morning?" Beef wasn't cheap. The burglar had money and plotted in advance to neutralize the dogs. Michael thought of the expensive hat he'd shot off the head of the trespasser not twelve hours earlier. The two crimes reeked of the same perpetrator.

"The butcher is near King and Churton." Aunt Rachel waved a hand east.

"On my way back to Mr. Griggs's house, I shall stop in for a chat with the butcher, see how well he remembers this morning's customers. For now, I promised this good fellow here a beer to moisten his throat after the chase."

"Come along to the tavern with me. You can both have a beer. I owe you that much for chasing off the rogue."

Michael grasped Aunt Rachel's upper arm to halt her advance toward the tavern. Much as he'd appreciate a beer that moment, he was running out of winter daylight and time to hook more clues together. "I shall have a look in the house instead, before people move furniture back into place, make certain the intruder hasn't left a piece of his identity behind."

"Very well. I shut the front door but didn't lock it. Couldn't bear to look at the chaos."

He firmed his voice, held onto her arm, and commanded her to meet his gaze. "What was he looking for?" She hesitated. He waited, then shook her arm a little. "Come on, tell me. I can see it in your eyes. You have a hunch."

"You shall think me daft."

He brought his face closer to hers by several inches. She tried to pull away. "Aunt Rachel, if he didn't find what he was looking for, he may come back. Out with it."

Frustration screwed up her expression. "Violet's journal." She twisted away from him and snapped, "Absurd, eh? I told you so."

"Whoa!" He held both hands up, palms outward. "Violet Griggs's journal? Why would anyone look for the journal of a woman who has been gone ten years from Hillsborough? Why would they look in *your* house for it?" He stepped toward her, arms lowered, hands consciously relaxed from fists. Again she retreated. He watched her gulp. "*Who* would look for the journal in your house? Aaron? Is that what this is about? Aaron? Did he kill Mr. Griggs? You may as well tell me now. If he did it, there's no way he'll get out of it."

She slapped her hand over her mouth and shook her head. The shimmer of tears sprang to her eyes. Michael shoved down a surge of compassion, glad that Kate wasn't present to shield her aunt, prevent him from probing Rachel's pain like a surgeon digging grapeshot from a screaming soldier's leg. "You've seen Aaron in the past twenty-four hours, haven't you? Surely you know you cannot shelter him—"

"Leave me be! I haven't seen my son in ten years! Oh, damn the Regulators! Damn Henry McCullough!" Her voice hoarsened. "Damn Ezra Griggs! Damn Georg Schmidt! And—" She bit back her final sentence, although Michael heard it in thought and clenched his teeth against the spiritual slap. "You! You leave me be about Aaron! My son didn't kill anyone!"

With the seal on her grief rent, she floundered off toward her tavern. It was her refuge, Michael realized, her bolster against reality. The dogs trailed after her a short distance. Rebuffed, they circled back to Michael and Noah.

Michael studied Aunt Rachel's retreat a moment, then headed for the house. Violet Griggs's journal? He realized he hadn't asked the distraught woman the most important question: why she'd suggested a journal to begin with. That must be clarified later.

Noah paced him. Old loss mobilized the deaf man's features. Violet had been his neighbor, a friend who taught him to sketch. Perhaps Aaron had been Noah's friend, also. Noah could use that beer. Before they left the side yard and emerged onto the front walkway, Michael faced Noah and pulled out his purse. "Aunt isn't of a mood to pour you a draught right now, so here you go, a beer on me. Or have a shot of rum, if it's more to your taste."

Noah waved away the coin.

"Well, then, I'm good for it anytime." Michael fit the purse back into his pocket. "Thanks for your help in the chase."

"I help. Maan." Expression determined, he jerked his thumb over his shoulder in the direction their fugitive had taken. "Maan. Ehra Grizz. Baa-yaaad.

Baa-yaaad."

Surprise hitched Michael's breath. He made himself speak slowly, so Noah could follow. "He was the same man you saw in Ezra Griggs's back yard yesterday?" Noah nodded in confidence. Victory hopped a jig in Michael's pulse. He grinned. "That's twice you've seen him. Do you recognize him?" Confidence wobbled in Noah's expression. He wasn't certain. Michael considered other routes to pinning down more evidence on the intruder. "Can you sketch what you saw of him?"

"Yezz!" Self-assurance radiated in Noah's eyes.

"Go home, then. Sketch him. Bring me the sketch. I shall be here, or the butcher shop on King and Churton, or Mr. Griggs's house."

Noah nodded, hesitated, glanced toward the tavern. "Mizz Why no yu ahnt." He pierced Michael with an expression of deep perception. "No yu ahnt."

Not your aunt. Caught off-guard, Michael blinked and recoiled, searched for his voice. He must have blundered his phony identity far worse than he'd imagined.

"She like yu. Ah see more." He glanced around once to insure their relative seclusion from the street before pressing a forefinger to Michael's chest once. "Yu." He mimicked a private saluting an officer. "Only ah see." Smiling, he twisted about and took off at a trot for his home on Queen Street.

A flare of panic urged Michael to give chase, spin balderdash to convince Noah his perception was skewed. Then he steadied his nerves and forced himself to mount the steps calmly onto the porch. *I see more. Only I see.* Perhaps it wasn't that his portrayal of a naval stores merchant was poor, but that the eyes of a man not distracted by sound perceived far more than the eyes of his fellows blessed with hearing. At least Michael hoped that was the case.

Besides, he suspected Noah was a man who kept his perceptions to himself, having years ago learned that he couldn't convince others of the value of seeing beyond their own limitations.

He lugged Violet's portrait and sketches inside, set them at the base of the stairs, and toured the disarray on the first floor. Almost nothing had been broken. If the intruder was indeed the same man who killed Griggs and laid waste to the interior of his house, as Noah had suggested, the criminal had learned the value of quieting his search. This time, he'd kept rage, desperation, and fear controlled.

Michael checked his watch. Barely two hours until dark. In addition to interviewing the butcher and poking about Griggs's parlor, he needed to walk the track into the woods that the murderer took to escape the scene—while daylight remained. He couldn't trust the reports of Schmidt's men. At no time had he felt the absence of Spry's assistance more than he did that moment, when he raced the waning daylight alone.

Disorder reigned in the two larger bedrooms on the top floor. Ladies' clothing had been emptied from chests and valises. Furniture was overturned. Difficult to tell whether any personal effects were missing, but nothing appeared broken or ripped.

On the window sash of his room, he discovered scuffmarks from the intruder's shoes and a two-inch piece of dark blue wool fabric snagged on a rough and warped section of wood—torn, he guessed, from the man's coat when he hastened his exit. He enclosed the scrap in his waistcoat pocket with the ripped and bloody lace. Then he reassembled the bed, righted the washbasin in his room, moved the portrait and portfolio inside, and closed window and door.

What a relief that he'd left nothing behind that morning to identify him as Lieutenant Stoddard on detached service from the Eighty-Second Regiment in Wilmington.

Chapter Eighteen

"HOW MAY I help you, sir?" The butcher's smile was missing a couple of teeth but amiable enough. He waddled out from behind the counter, exposing more of the gore-stained apron tied above his girth, his shoes dragging clumps of bloody sawdust over the packed dirt floor.

The shop appeared empty of assistants. Michael said, "My name is Compton, from Cross Creek. I'm visiting my aunt, Rachel White, for a few days."

"Ah, yes, I know Mrs. White well. Welcome to Hillsborough, Mr. Compton."

"Thank you. Hmm." Michael pretended perusal of a couple of gutted, plucked, and beheaded chickens and a leg of lamb on the counter. "I thought I might surprise Aunt Rachel with a haunch of beef tonight." He spread cupped hands. "About yea big, if you have it."

The butcher grimaced. "Eh. A fellow bought both my beef haunches this morning. I shall have more on the morrow, first thing, if you can wait. Or how about this pork loin tonight? Makes lovely chops. I shall give it to you for half price, since it's the end of my day."

Irresistible, even with Michael's short supply of coin, and he did wish to repay Aunt Rachel for her hospitality. "That pork looks good. Four chops, please."

"Very good, sir." The butcher retreated behind the counter, hefted the pork loin to a sturdy table, and turned his back to sharpen his big knife.

Michael spotted Noah peering into the shop through a window and waved him in. The bell over the door jingled, a sound as cheery as the ebullience of success on Noah's face. While the butcher was occupied hacking off thick pork chops, Noah removed a cylinder of paper from a tote bag slung over his shoulder and unrolled the cylinder for Michael.

There wasn't much to see of the fellow's face, as Noah had captured him in charcoal from an angle of three-quarters turned away, but his clothing, physique, and middling stature were apparent. Michael studied the line of the man's jaw, grateful and amazed at the level of detail Noah had captured, eerie familiarity pricking him. He could easily be the man he'd seen entering the woods near Griggs's house and the man who'd lost his hat to Michael's rifle shot, except that the man on Griggs's property hadn't been limping.

The butcher gave Noah a nod of familiarity and plunked a package of pork chops before Michael. Michael rolled up the picture, handed payment to the butcher, and shoved the package beneath his arm. "The fellow who bought those beef haunches this morning—he was about my height and weight, and had dark hair?"

"Yes, sir."

"Dark blue coat?" The butcher nodded. "Who is he? Do you know his name?"

"No. Never saw him in town before this morning."

Michael batted away the grasp of disappointment around his heart. "How long have you lived in Hillsborough?"

"Almost eight years."

Maybe the butcher didn't recognize him because he'd moved to Hillsborough after the suspect left town. Michael unrolled the sketch and showed it to the man behind the counter.

A grubby forefinger tapped the paper. "Yah, that's him." Brow lowered, the butcher braced one hand on his hip and jutted his chin. "What's this about?"

Again Michael rolled up the sketch. "About an hour ago, while all of us were about town, that fellow used the beef haunches to lure my aunt's dogs into the stable and lock them in so he could have free access to the house. We arrived in time to catch him in the act, but he jumped out an upstairs window. When we gave chase, we lost him in market."

The butcher's jaw slackened, and he whumped a stout fist on the counter. "The devil! And the scoundrel used *my* beef haunches for such a dastardly act! I thought there was something weird about him. And he was nervous."

"What made you think he was nervous?"

"Couldn't stand still. Nearly wore a trench across my floor there with all his pacing, back and forth. Bugger drummed his fingers on everything. His cheek, his thighs, my countertop."

"Nervous" fit the disposition of a man whose fear fueled the destruction of furniture, a man who had murdered. Michael pressed on. "Since he apparently isn't from around here, I thought we might get a better description of him before we report him to investigators."

"Surely, I'll help you any way I can. Fellow was in his mid- to late thirties, I'd say. Well-dressed, one of them dandies. Lace at his throat and wrists. I presumed he had plenty of money. Why he'd burgle a house is beyond me."

"We wondered as much. Mr. Carroll and I didn't get a good look at his face."

"He had sort of a sallow complexion." The butcher licked his lips, considering. "Like maybe he powdered his face a good bit and didn't see much of the sun."

Aware that Noah's gaze tracked the words from the butcher's lips, Michael considered the detail of sallow complexion. The butcher possessed good observation skills: a boon to any criminal investigator. He hoped he was up to cataloguing so much detail. "Thin face? Plump?"

"Neither thin nor plump. In between."

Noah coughed to shift attention to himself. "Ah draw maan face." He opened his tote bag and withdrew paper and a piece of charcoal. "Draw!"

The butcher frowned in surprise, darted a look between Michael and Noah. "I thought Mr. Carroll here was deaf. His grandfather sends him in with notes for his orders. Can he hear us?"

"To some extent. He picks up a great deal by watching our lips while we converse."

"Yu tell maan face." The blank paper in Noah's hand wiggled at the butcher. "Ah draw!" He sounded insistent.

Skepticism jumbled Michael's thoughts. From the sample he'd produced, the deaf man possessed advanced skill at sketching. But identifying a suspect based on a sketch was an unreliable strategy. Too much depended on memory and talent, both subject to human interpretation. And sketching anything required time, of which Michael had little that moment.

Noah smiled. His gaze, alert, shifted between the other two men. Instinct prodded Michael. Most residents of Hillsborough had relegated Noah, a man with acute perceptions, to life's margin. But Noah wanted them to engage him in this experiment. He was asking for the opportunity to prove his unique value in the community.

If the experiment were a success, he wouldn't be the only winner. Michael would have something solid to show Schmidt at their meeting in about two hours. A visual record not just of the rascal's features, but also of his disposition, wealth, and complexion.

"I say we try it." Michael directed his words to the butcher. "Have you a back room affording the three of us some privacy, and an assistant to mind the shop for a quarter hour?"

"A quarter hour, you say? Surely." Game for the venture, the big man relaxed his shoulders and called back into the shop for his apprentice.

***

Twenty-five minutes later, Michael, his back to Noah and the butcher, gazed out the window at the long shadows and flattened disappointment in his voice. "What of his eyes? Have we sketched them too close together?" He twisted about to the men.

"I—I don't know." The butcher, seated beside Noah at a table in a cramped office that smelled of blood and resin, pushed up and flicked his hand at the portrait Noah had constructed, the bust of a man face-on. "To be sure, it's close, but somehow not quite right. And I apologize, but I must return to my business. We've already given this sketch more than a quarter hour."

Noah followed the discourse. He set down his piece of charcoal and briefly bowed his head.

"I appreciate your time." Michael signaled Noah, who rolled up the portrait and collected his materials. They shook the butcher's hand and were shown from the shop.

The wrapped pork chops beneath his arm, Michael walked north on

Churton, Noah glum at his side. They picked up the cart track that provided a shortcut to Queen Street and in minutes found themselves before the Carrolls' house. The house next door exuded a sinister feel. Michael loathed his return to a dead man's parlor that stank like a butcher's shop.

He said to Noah, "Thank you for sketching the burglar. The butcher doesn't think the portrait is exact, but it may be good enough for someone's recognition and help us nab the rogue." From comprehension in the deaf man's eyes, he seemed to understand. "I shall need to show it to Mr. Schmidt." Noah hesitated, bowed his head again, and handed over the sketch.

Michael realized that he was proud of the picture, even though it wasn't "quite right." He didn't grudge him that pride. Noah had worked hard. Too bad the match hadn't been clearer.

The finished product was smeared from Noah's attempts to modify details for the butcher. Desperation, volatility, and arrogance shot from the subject's features and clouted Michael, along with a nudge that he'd seen the face, or pieces of the face, somewhere else. His brain struggled, searched for a name. Violet's ripped portrait of her sweetheart popped into his mind, along with a thrill of horror. Might desperation contort the features of Aaron into *this* mask?

He rotated the sketch to Noah. "Aaron White?" Noah's shoulders slumped in fatigue, and he shook his head. "No, or you don't know?" Noah spread his hands.

Still uncertain, was how Michael read him. Aaron would now be about twenty-eight years old. The butcher had said that his customer that morning had looked ten years older than that. But years of hardship could weather a man's face, age it faster.

Noah pointed to the face of the suspect. "Ya-nett. Sho Ya-nett."

Ya-nett? The communications barrier thrust hard between them, punched a sigh from Michael. "What is Ya-nett?" Then his ear picked up on the spoken pattern. "Janet—Miss Sewell? You wish me to show the sketch to her?"

"Yezz." Noah's cheeks colored. Fatigue melted from his expression.

The request made sense. Daughter of a wealthy man, Janet Sewell had shared her father's culture, socialized with land agents a decade before. If Regulators had murdered Griggs, showing Miss Sewell the sketch might open a break for him. He agreed to seek her out the following day and tucked the rolled sketch in an inside coat pocket, beside Noah's full-length portrait. Then he shook Noah's hand and bade him good day.

The interior of Griggs's house had grown colder, drearier since he'd left. Michael set the pork chops on the dining room table, found four undamaged candles and a tinderbox, and placed them beside the chops so he could find them when he returned. While light remained, he must search the track where the suspect had vanished about twenty-four hours earlier.

From Griggs's back yard, he picked up the entrance to the track. He looked for nothing in particular as he walked, but stayed relaxed and alert. His gaze swept over ground, winter-bare brush, and trees. The general south-southeast wind of the track grew rugged. Fading light encouraged him to miss his step several times, once landing his foot in a rut an inch from a horse turd, another time almost twisting his ankle. He wondered what distance Schmidt's men had followed the track and wagered with himself that they hadn't walked as far back as he.

Within ten minutes, the track intersected with a well-traveled road, likely the Indian trading path coming out of Virginia. When he turned about to retrace his steps, he realized how overgrown the track was in comparison. Indeed, travelers on the Indian path might not spot it when passing through. For someone familiar with Hillsborough, though, the poor maintenance of the track made it an excellent route for secrecy.

In dusk's chill he shivered and wished he'd brought his greatcoat from his room. After blowing on his hands, he proceeded back to Griggs's house on the overgrown track.

Half a minute in, a fox startled him by darting across, a mouse dangling from his teeth. "*Bon appetit*, brother," Michael muttered, his gaze following the beast, then he squinted at dead branches piled off the path. Was that someone's attempt at concealment? He picked his way over to the mass. The noise of snapping twigs beneath his shoes was loud enough to scare off local varmints. He dragged branches away.

A new gig lay on its side—from what he could tell untouched by weather. The leather seat and woodwork bespoke expensive tastes of the owner. Stumped as to why anyone would leave such quality transportation out there where the elements could destroy it, Michael ran hands along wood trim and swiveled about for a better look at the vehicle. Then he noticed the axle had cracked, making the gig useless. Still, an axle could be repaired.

The manner of concealment suggested that the owner considered the gig disposable. Michael straightened and brushed off his hands, disgusted. Some people possessed entirely too much money. Those were the foolish men arrogant enough to drive a fine, new gig down a beaten-up track, where ruts could catch a wheel, crack an axle.

At the thought of such foolishness, cold not of winter's making drove down beneath his coat. In disbelief, he dragged all the branches off the gig and backed away toward the track for a bigger look. Not so much foolish as *desperate*. That gig had been driven by Griggs's murderer, he felt certain. Two more steps back to where he thought the track was, and one of his heels dropped into a rut. Down he went, rolling with it to avoid straining his ankle.

And that, he realized, stunned, sitting upon the ground, was exactly what had happened to the murderer. Fleeing the crime scene, he'd cracked the gig's axle, dragged the vehicle into the brush to conceal it, and unhitched his horse. And when he'd backed up to admire his clever work, he stepped in a hole with less grace than Michael and twisted his ankle.

Michael picked himself up and checked his limbs for damage. He then resumed his return to Griggs's house, albeit with care to avoid duplicating the injury of his quarry—a man who he now realized was stuck in Hillsborough with no transportation out, unless he rode his horse.

But the murderer wasn't ready to leave yet. He was still searching. He'd visited Rachel White's house at three in the morning, deposited at least two goose feathers from Griggs's bed on her property, limped an escape from Michael, gotten his hat blown off by rifle shot, and returned to the house during Griggs's funeral for his search. Perhaps he'd bandaged his ankle for support, for he was no longer limping quite so much during the afternoon chase.

Michael emerged in Griggs's back yard about seven minutes later, an array of potential conclusions spinning his head. Aunt Rachel had suggested that the murderer was searching for Violet's journal. Damned if he knew why. He couldn't see how musings a seventeen-year-old girl had written in her journal a decade past might threaten a wealthy man in the present. Still, he must follow up and question Aunt Rachel.

He more easily imagined Griggs riding into Virginia to meet Lord Cornwallis, an exchange of information. On his return trip, Griggs had picked up a tail: a rebel spy, who'd murdered him so he could search for military intelligence. Such a spy would already be aware of Michael's prying. Michael reminded himself to remain vigilant.

Had Schmidt's men penetrated the track a little farther, they might have spotted the gig. Then Michael's reason snagged on another theory. He'd assumed incompetence on the part of Schmidt's men, when the sheriff might already have known about the gig. If Griggs had returned from his long trip with evidence that Schmidt was a deserter, not a Moravian, Schmidt had a solid motive to slay him.

In the house, Michael lit candles and checked his watch. What additional evidence could he find before his appointment with Schmidt at six o'clock, in less than half an hour? He retraced his steps in the stinky parlor around the couch, illuminated the room with all four candles, and surveyed his surroundings from before the fireplace.

The broken violin lay atop the gouged harpsichord, to his right. If the murder occurred the way Michael had assumed, the perpetrator would have damaged the musical instruments during his rampage after Griggs lay moribund on the floor. Michael remembered noticing the condition of the instruments that morning while Schmidt breathed down his neck. He resurrected his memory of the parlor from yesterday evening, when he'd first come upon Griggs's body, and before Schmidt, his men, and the undertaker's apprentice had traipsed through, shoving things about to access the body.

Try as he might, he couldn't remember seeing the violin the evening before. Maybe it had lain on the floor among the clutter surrounding Griggs, and the undertaker's journeyman had set it atop the harpsichord to move it out of the way.

He walked to the harpsichord, the third such instrument he'd seen in his life. Never had he expected to find one in a frontier hamlet. Griggs must have paid through his teeth to have it shipped across the Atlantic, then carted overland to him. Further evidence of his vanity.

But how wretched, that the perpetrator had defaced so exquisite an instrument. The gouge in the wood of the side showed up with a pale cast against the black paint, a deep ugly gash, like a man's cheekbone laid open by a claw of ragged glass. Try as he might, he also couldn't remember seeing the gouge the evening before. Perhaps he'd had far too much horror to absorb during those seconds before Schmidt banged upon Griggs's front door.

The lid on the harpsichord was lowered all the way. He stretched around, slid one hand beneath the lid, depressed a key toward the middle of the bank, and was rewarded with the pleasant but muffled vibration of plectrum on string from within. Memory abducted him back a decade to a warm summer night when he'd crouched in secret outside Lord Crump's parlor window, the scents of Lydia's lust and perfume on his skin, and listened to her seduce melody from the harpsichord inside, to the delight of her all-male audience. He shoved away the memory and walked his fingers up an octave on Griggs's harpsichord, enjoying the resonance with each key.

At the top of the octave, a pressed key brought forth a dull plunk, as if the associated strings were stifled in releasing their vibration. He fingered other keys in the vicinity with the same result. He imagined Griggs's murderer unsatisfied to merely brutalize the harpsichord's exterior, but taking perverse pleasure in damaging the inner workings, too. What a waste.

Dejected, he transferred the violin to a nearby chair, then shuffled about to open the harpsichord's lid for a look at the strings. Before he could raise the lid, though, the toe of his shoe knocked something across the floor beneath the harpsichord, into the wall. He bent over to identify what he'd kicked: what appeared to be two sticks. He knelt and retrieved them. Shock rolled through him. He'd found the snapped halves of a gentleman's fine cane of oak, the splintery raw edges ground down, flecks of black paint peppering the edges.

After setting the broken cane atop the harpsichord, he gripped a candlestick and passed illumination the length of the instrument's great wound. Splinters from the oak cane were stuck in the gouge. Michael straightened, traded candlestick for cane atop the harpsichord, and rotated ruined oak pieces in his hands. Easily he envisioned the depth of rage that fueled the murder extending to the cane: the perpetrator snapping it in half and digging raw edges along the side of the harpsichord, symbolic effacement of Ezra Griggs. The lunatic who embodied such rage must be captured, incarcerated before he killed others.

His thumb brushed over metal embedded in the head of the cane. He held the piece closer to the light and distinguished the letter "T," scripted with great flourish.

T. Tierney.

Michael rechecked his watch. Five minutes to six. He'd have to sprint to his meeting with the county sheriff. But he'd make room in his schedule later to attend the town rake's party.

Chapter Nineteen

AT SIX O'CLOCK, Michael discovered that he had only to present himself in the vicinity of jail before Henry and another of Schmidt's lackeys materialized out of the night to escort him the remainder of the way. He made his voice chipper. "I wondered where you lads had gotten off to this afternoon. Went back to the house after the funeral. All of you were gone."

Mute, they showed him to Schmidt's snug den jammed into a corner of the jailhouse. Henry's hand on Michael's shoulder encouraged him to sit on a stool facing a stained wooden table that resembled a stunted, inbred cousin of Major Craig's table in Wilmington.

Someone had boarded up the only window in the area. Two lanterns suspended from the ceiling by hooks illuminated little. When Michael realized how much the room reeked of puke and piss, he wished he'd checked the seat of his stool for moisture before he sat. From another part of jail, he heard a man's protracted wail of agony and despair.

With a creak of wood, Schmidt heaved his chair forward onto all four legs from where he'd perched it in partial shadow on two legs, against the back wall. His sneeze of amusement accompanied the chair's settling on the other side of the table from Michael. He looked three sizes too large for the chair. "*Engländer!* I have anticipated this moment all day!"

Henry and the other man stood so close behind Michael that he could hear their breathing. He hoped his smile reciprocated the frigidity in Schmidt's face. "Yes, I'm sure you have."

"You worked hard today. You bring me evidence?" The big man gestured to the two canvas sacks Michael had dropped at his feet when he sat.

Michael lifted the sack of Griggs's bloody clothing and tossed it atop documents littering a corner of the table surface. "I return Mr. Griggs's clothing to you." He reached in his pocket and retrieved the bloody lace. "The clothing was crucial in confirming that this piece of torn lace I found beneath the couch in the parlor didn't come from Mr. Griggs's garments. I speculate that it came from his killer's shirt, and that in a brief struggle for his life, Mr. Griggs ripped it off. As he collapsed, his hand wedged beneath the couch. He dropped the lace when he died." He flung the scrap at Schmidt.

The sheriff caught it mid-air between clapped hands, then spread open his palms. Sly wonder smeared his expression and leaked approval into his voice. "A dandy would wear this sort of lace on his shirt." Henry stepped forward for a look, and his exhale squeaked with excitement, as if a booger had blocked one nostril.

Like a member of the Sidhe grown overly fond of darkness and thus outcast, O'Toole dislodged himself from shadows behind Schmidt and sniffed at the lace before slinking back into gloom. Michael thought he spotted a bruise swelling the Irishman's handsome mouth, and he repressed a smile over the memory of their scuffle just after noon.

Sanction oozed from Schmidt, and he caressed the lace between his fingers. "Well done, Mr. Compton. What else have you for me?"

"The suspect was also wearing a dark blue coat and tan breeches. Aunt Rachel and I arrived at her house after Mr. Griggs's funeral in time to interrupt the rascal as he made a search of the house. Here's the piece of his coat that he left on a window sash upstairs when he made his escape." Michael tossed the fabric piece at Schmidt.

This time, Schmidt made no effort to catch it, just watched, perplexed, when it landed on his table beside a half-eaten hard roll. He dropped the lace beside it. "You then gave chase?"

"Of course, but I lost him in the marketplace south of King Street." Michael paused several heartbeats to savor the effect of the two grenades he prepared to lob on Schmidt, then extracted them from his coat pocket. "Here's a picture of the scoundrel as he was running away from my aunt's house this afternoon."

Noah's first sketch, unfurled on the table, drew the men behind Michael plus O'Toole forward to cluster about the table. Michael darted a glance at the Irishman. By God, what a stunning bruise that was decorating O'Toole's upper lip. He wouldn't be kissing any women for awhile with that thing in his way. Warm pleasure swirled through Michael. "And *this*, gentlemen, is our suspect up close. Anyone here recognize him?" Michael succumbed to a smirk while he unrolled Noah's second picture atop the first sketch.

The pitch of Henry's nasal whistle increased. "Bloody hell, how'd you come by this?"

"It's sheer bog, Compton." O'Toole's swollen lip muddied his pronunciation.

Schmidt squinted at Michael, and his voice blended disbelief and disappointment. "Did you sketch it yourself?"

"I don't possess such talent. Noah Carroll sketched it."

O'Toole laughed like a deranged leprechaun and slapped his knee. "That deaf-mute idiot? I don't believe it."

Injustice simmered in Michael's gut. He visualized the Irishman's bottom lip swollen to match the top lip. "You'd believe it if you'd had the brains to interview him yesterday in addition to his grandfather. He's neither an idiot nor a mute. Aunt and I are fortunate that Mr. Carroll was with us when we returned to her house this afternoon. He helped in the chase."

Schmidt poked a forefinger at the facial sketch as if the suspect were prepared to jump out atop him. "Mr. Carroll saw the suspect up close, then?" His eyes glittered.

Michael realized he might place Noah in danger by identifying him as a close witness. "No. Mr. Carroll wouldn't recognize him. He sketched that portrait from a description the butcher at King and Churton provided for him. The suspect purchased two beef haunches from the butcher this morning for the purpose of placating Aunt's dogs while we were out, so he could gain access to the house—"

"Mr. Carroll is an unreliable witness because he cannot hear and cannot communicate with anyone except his grandfather!" O'Toole pounded a fist on the table. "Those pictures are worthless!"

Michael studied O'Toole's reddened face, and a small, mean part of his spirit hoped the Irishman would take a swing at him, give him the excuse to become the divine instrument by which those uneven lips became matched. "Mr. O'Toole is a shoddy investigator because he judges based on preconceived notions and misses the testimony of valuable witnesses."

"Sure, and I'll beat you within an inch of your life soon, boy."

"Soon?" Michael smiled and pressed forward, hands on knees. "What's wrong with this moment, *boy*? I'm glad to throw your arse out the door for a third time today."

Without removing his scrutiny from Michael, Schmidt shot his left arm out horizontally, a cord of iron across the Irishman's midsection to halt O'Toole's lunge. "Enough of this, both of you." He retracted his arm. O'Toole backed a few steps gripping his stomach, gasping.

Michael focused on Schmidt. "No one answered my question earlier. Who is this man? Do you recognize him?"

Henry's whistling nostril had quieted. "Never seen him before."

"Nor I," said the other henchman.

Schmidt shook his head. O'Toole muttered something in Gaelic that probably didn't answer the question and would have earned him a trouncing upon translation.

"Were any of you gentlemen residents of Hillsborough during the Rebellion?" Again, more mumblings of negation. "Ah, as I thought." Michael snatched both sketches from beneath the sheriff's paw and defused Schmidt's lowering scowl by saying, "Since none of you know him, I shall show these sketches around town to people who resided here while that Regulator business was happening." He rolled up the papers and thrust them back in his coat pocket.

The disbelief and disappointment creasing Schmidt's face appeared to have deepened. Michael cocked his head. "Chin up, my good fellow. With luck, one of the residents will recognize him, and you shall have an arrest within twenty-four hours. In the mean time, I suggest that you circulate a description of the man." Michael snapped his fingers. "I almost forgot. Alert anyone in the area who sells gigs or repairs axles. Our suspect may approach them about purchasing a new gig or repairing his broken one—"

"A broken gig?" Deep grooves appeared around Schmidt's mouth. "You are saying that this suspect drives a gig? Where is it now?"

Schmidt's bafflement looked genuine, so it was Michael's turn to taste disappointment. He'd been sure that he knew about the gig. "It's pitched over to the side of the most rutted portion of the track connecting Mr. Griggs's back yard to the Indian trading path. My theory is that in the suspect's haste to flee the scene of murder yesterday, and in the darkness, he adopted an injudicious speed and cracked the axle on his gig—"

"You're lying. Dibble and me searched the track this morning in full daylight." Henry sounded like a thunderstorm five miles away and closing quickly. "We didn't see a gig."

"Perhaps you didn't walk far enough. It's within a minute of the Indian path."

"Horse piss!"

"You will investigate his claim, Henry, first light on the morrow." Schmidt's glare pulsated. "You, Dibble, and Franklin. If you find a gig, you will impound it to prevent the murderer from retrieving his vehicle."

While Henry grumbled assent, Michael's relief streamed out through his pursed lips. Schmidt's order to Henry was the first sensible thing he'd said that evening. Michael seized the other canvas bag by its handles. "It sounds as though our business for now is concluded. I'd love to stay and chat more, but Aunt's cook, Martha, probably has supper ready for me."

"Sit, Mr. Compton." Schmidt bunched one fist within the other palm at the apex of an upright triangle created by bracing both elbows on the table. "Tell me what else you found in the victim's house."

Michael planned to question Matthew Tierney about the broken cane before revealing that evidence to Schmidt. "Nothing else. Aren't feathers and a piece of torn lace enough for one day?" But from the tensing of Schmidt's lips, he could tell that they weren't enough, that Schmidt was somehow expecting more. "See here. I'm exhausted. I want a hot meal and a good night's sleep. I'm sure I shall find more evidence on the morrow. And as I said at the funeral, if you believe there's something in particular I should be looking for in the house, do tell me."

Skin beneath Schmidt's eyes puckered. "What is in that bag?"

"Pork chops." And the broken cane below the pork chops, wrapped in canvas the same color as the bag.

Schmidt jerked his head, and Henry snatched the bag from Michael. Michael subsided back onto the stool, fear nipping at his composure. How would he explain his lie to Schmidt's satisfaction? Maybe he should have admitted the find—but no, instinct had guided him to tiptoe around it for now.

Henry lifted the package of chops from the bag and sniffed it. "Yah, smells like pork to me." He shoved it back into the bag, somehow managing to not clack the wood pieces around, and dropped the sack in Michael's lap.

Michael channeled relief into a sulk and hoped that in the poor lighting, which had undoubtedly kept Henry from spotting the wrapped canvas at the very bottom of the bag, the sweat on his forehead wasn't noticed either. "I paid half-price for those chops. End of the day special."

Schmidt hadn't moved. "You have an answer for everything, do you not?"

When Michael remained silent, he added, "Who are you?"

At least that question Michael could answer. "Michael Compton, naval stores merchant from Cross Creek. I'm also Rachel White's nephew and Kate Duncan's cousin."

"This neighbor of yours in Cross Creek who knew Mr. Griggs ten years ago. What is his name?"

"Kirkleigh."

"He is the same fellow who courts Mrs. White with love letters?"

Tension hardened Michael's throat. He sensed a trap in the weaving. "Yes."

"On the morrow at nine o'clock, you will bring me Mr. Kirkleigh's love letter that you gave your aunt yesterday."

One of Michael's hands cut the air, and he scowled. "You're no gentleman if you're asking for that. Besides, I doubt she shall let me have it." Especially since it had been reduced to ashes in the parlor fireplace the previous night. "You know how ladies are with love letters. Or maybe you don't know."

"You refuse to bring me the letter?"

"Why would you even want it? If stories filled with carnal perversion are what you seek, I suggest that you purchase one of those cheap magazines printed by—"

"Mr. Compton, you do not need to know why I want your aunt's letter. But if you fail to supply me with it by nine on the morrow, I will lock you in jail and search Mrs. White's house myself for the letter. And you will remain in jail until I have that letter."

Damnation. The very thought of sampling Schmidt's hospitality in jail cramped Michael's bowels. He sensed that the sheriff lusted for an excuse to intimidate Aunt Rachel by searching her house. And he received the distinct impression that Schmidt was the last person in Hillsborough whom Aunt Rachel wanted rifling through her house. His shoulders slumped with resignation. "Well, then, I shall persuade Aunt to loan me the letter."

"Good." The beneficence of a minister blessing a congregation wreathed Schmidt's face. "You may leave now. Enjoy the pork chops. May no burglars darken your dreams tonight."

Chapter Twenty

A SHORT AMBLE on Churton brought Michael to King Street, where he paused to suck in lungfuls of frosty air untainted by torment, terror, and the nefarious ambitions of deserters. His stomach and bowels settled, but not all the way. Where in the name of heaven would he find a love letter to Aunt Rachel from a fictitious old flame named Kirkleigh by nine the next morning?

He'd have to write it himself, of course. His gut tensed again. Never in his life had he written a love letter. He'd never been in love. And now that anxiety and necessity speared him to the wall about it, he wasn't sure he could fake declarations of love with any greater conviction than Craig had achieved in his letter.

Gods, what a stodgy old fart he was turning into. Where was Spry's blithe humor when he needed it?

Men's laughter to the east drew his attention. He didn't have to walk far to discover the source of merriment: a group of fellows walking home after fortifying themselves in one of three taverns hunched together near the end of King Street. Numerous horses waited at the posts for each tavern, and the sounds of jollification proclaimed that business was healthy if you owned Faddis's Tavern, Courtney's Tavern, or Reed's Ordinary.

Michael still needed to work in a bit of eavesdropping that night in hopes of hearing buzz on the location of Cornwallis's army. He considered the tavern Schmidt had recommended but couldn't imagine commerce better there than at the trio of taverns before him. Besides, the fact that Schmidt had recommended a tavern was good reason to avoid it. So after supper, after accomplishing the daunting task of writing a heartfelt love letter to a harridan old enough to be his mother, he'd hop about the establishments on the east side of town, soothe his nerves with claret, and listen to gossip.

On the opposite end of King Street, only a couple of horses stood hitched before the tavern Schmidt had lauded. The same slow night blighted the tavern of Aunt Rachel. From the business he'd seen at the taverns down the street, Michael knew the demand for drink in Hillsborough was robust. He couldn't imagine any town having too many taverns. Too many churches, yes, but not taverns. Odd.

His arrival at the house coincided with his conscription into manual labor: righting the couch, then the dining room table while Kate and Martha watched, both women dusty and weary from straightening out the house for several hours. In the dining room, Martha blotted her forehead on her apron. "I apologize that I haven't anything prepared for supper, Mr. Compton. I'd planned to bake Mrs. Duncan's pork pie, but that wants time and careful watching, and your cousin and I have been cleaning up all afternoon after that scoundrel. If only I'd something quick to cook you."

Michael dug into his sack and handed over the package from the butcher. "Fried pork chops."

"Ooh." Martha produced what he suspected was her first smile in several hours. "Such a thoughtful fellow. Thank you." She sashayed for the front door.

"The pork chops are much appreciated." No humor flavored Kate's sigh. A dark streak of grime wandered off her chin and vanished beneath her tucker. "Aunt told me what happened this afternoon. Michael, you *must* apprehend the lout who did this."

Again, he made no promises. Instead, he set the sack near the dining room door, fished out Noah's sketches, and passed them to her. "Tell me if you recognize him."

From her lifted eyebrows, recognition glimmered, but as quickly as it sparked, it submerged into the sag of her shoulders. "How peculiar. I feel as though I've met this fellow somewhere, but I'm not sure when or where."

"You told me earlier that you weren't in Hillsborough when the Regulators were stirring up trouble."

"I wasn't." She handed the pictures back to him. "What have the Regulators to do with this rascal?"

"Of all the people to whom I've shown these portraits today, the only one who vaguely recognizes this man was a resident here during the Regulator Rebellion. I've now a strong feeling that this rogue was in some way connected with it. Are you certain you weren't here then?" She drew back from him, frowning, and he held up the facial sketch. "Is this Aaron?"

"No, it isn't Aaron." Her chin lifted, and her lower lip quivered. "Take another look. There's no pointy chin. Aaron has Aunt's pointy chin, I told you."

He reexamined both pictures and saw no sign of a pointy chin. The flicker of hope he'd held out sputtered and extinguished. Michael walked away from Kate and stared out the window at night. Whoever the man was, his identity wasn't forthcoming that evening. Mute, he again returned the sketches to his pocket.

"Who sketched those pictures?"

"Noah Carroll."

"Goodness. I didn't know he'd such talent in him." Kate's tone softened. "You've had a long day, too. May I fetch you some brandy?"

The dreaded task of crafting the love letter now stretched before him. Maybe brandy would loosen the noose on his anxiety. "Yes, thank you. And Kate, will you kindly supply me with stationery, quill, and ink?"

"Certainly. The study is still somewhat jumbled. You'd do better writing in here. I shall bring a few more candles in for you." The tap of her heels faded.

He paced. From the pieces of family history he'd heard, he patched together a background in his head. Aunt Rachel had married Clarence White when she was about twenty and birthed Aaron at twenty-two. Aaron and Violet had eloped when she was about forty. She'd been widowed a year or so later.

The fictitious Kirkleigh fellow supposedly grew smitten with Rachel before she'd married, possibly before she'd met Clarence White. Kirkleigh, recently widowed, had resumed wooing the love of his youth. Was it an easy correspondence? Would a woman like Rachel White have harbored a sentimental spot for him after three decades?

Michael continued pacing, cleared his throat, and tested salutations aloud. "My precious Rachel. My beloved Rachel." He felt his nose wrinkle, stopped pacing, and faced the window again. "Rachel, radiance of the sun in my life." Damn, that line tasted vile. Why had it succeeded for a junior officer he'd known in New Jersey? "Sweetest Rachel, vision of all glory and, ah, damn this isn't working."

It sounded inauthentic because guesting beneath Rachel White's roof for a scant twenty-four hours hadn't let him know her. He didn't have the slightest idea what tickled the woman and made her smile. *If* she still smiled, which he doubted. Tragedy in her life had atrophied the muscles around her mouth. She was a long way from woo-able.

Breath whooshed from him. He squared his shoulders. "Darling Rachel, my life's partner—" His hands implored the dark window. "—my beloved nymph and goddess—" He froze, stunned by the appearance of faery-like lights in the window. Then he spotted Kate's reflection from where she stood in the doorway, a tray in her hands, lit candles upon the tray the source of faery light in the window. A lava flow of humiliation spilled through him. He was too mortified to move. Whatever she'd heard, he was sure it had been too much.

After a second's hesitation, she entered the dining room, and the illumination in the room swelled. He heard her set candlesticks on the table, rustle paper. "Here's your brandy and writing materials." Her tone sounded both perplexed and mechanical.

"Thank you." His voice cracked like that of a youth. He gritted his teeth. Sweat slicked his palms and beaded on his brow. He grimaced, willing her to go away.

She stood fast, her face turned to him. "Michael, is there anything you need to talk about?"

Of a sudden, it occurred to him that Kate might be able to fill in some of Aunt Rachel's character for him, give him more to work with. He doused humiliation and faced her at last. "I need your help."

A shaky laugh gusted from her. "It sounds that way."

"It isn't how you think."

"Really? How is it, then?"

Her smile bore a razor edge, not quite the wariness of a niece protecting her aunt from predation, but a sentiment of sibling nature. He saw no way to soften the explanation, although he lowered his voice in case Martha was nearby. "I told Schmidt that the cipher from Major Craig to Lord Cornwallis was a love letter to your aunt from an old sweetheart in Cross Creek."

"Mr. Kirkleigh, I remember you said his name."

"Yes. Schmidt is suspicious of me as a spy. He expects to see the letter by nine on the morrow or he throws me in jail, and he ransacks your aunt's house."

Kate gripped the back of the nearest chair with both hands. "Ye gods."

"I must falsify a letter from this Kirkleigh fellow. But I don't know your aunt, so perhaps you can help me determine what a man might say to appeal to her."

"All right." She released the chair and emitted a ragged sigh. "I—I admit, I thought—"

"—you thought I was debauching your aunt, taking advantage of her. No, not at all."

They stared across the table at each other two seconds, then rocked the walls with nervous laughter. She gestured to his place. "Do sit. Let's see what I can think of to assist you."

He pulled out a chair and seated her first before realizing how his hands shook. When he assumed his own seat, he downed all his brandy and welcomed its firestorm down his throat. What a foul snare lies wove.

Stationery that Kate had placed before him appeared similar enough to that used by Major Craig. He doubted his deception would trip on it. But the paper was blank, and no amount of staring at it would produce words upon it.

Pinning his gaze to the top sheet, he said, "What qualities do you think your aunt possessed in youth that might have attracted this Mr. Kirkleigh?"

"She had very lush, dark hair, like a Spanish *doña*. And although she's still tall for a woman, before she birthed Aaron, I'm told her waist was quite slender."

Michael ventured a glance at Kate, found her gazing at her hands upon the table. "But did she have a special quality in her personality that would appeal to a man, make him continue to think of her after they'd been separated three decades, make him intent on wooing her?"

"Aunt is a very honorable woman." Kate's erect posture dared him to say otherwise. "I imagine that in her youth, she may have impressed many suitors with her virtue, by not succumbing to their shallow charms and tumbling in the hay with every swain. Surely this Mr. Kirkleigh would remember such a characteristic and speak highly of it in his letters to her."

Michael tried very hard to stop his jaw from dangling in dismay but managed only to keep his lips shut. His stomach clenched again. Was Rachel White's character where Kate got her Ice Widow inspiration? He swept his gaze about in search for more brandy, but he'd drunk everything in his glass. "Let me see if I understand you, Kate. You believe Mr. Kirkleigh should remember your aunt for more than thirty years because she never let him kiss her?"

Her jaw cocked. "I've the impression that you and I aren't in agreement. If my interpretation isn't correct, why does it always happen that way in novels?"

Novels? Novels were fiction. Besides, Kate was clearly reading the wrong novels.

The page before him was still empty. The night was going to be long. "Have you more brandy?"

She sat rigid in her chair. "You're mocking me."

"Not at all." His gaze locked with hers. "But I believe that one way for certain that Mr. Kirkleigh would remember Rachel White for three decades is if she'd made love to him—"

"That's outrageous!"

"—even if it were only once. He'd remember her through a successful marriage, through children and grandchildren. A man doesn't remember with *fondness* what a woman kept from him three decades earlier. He remembers with fondness what she gave him with her heart." He opened the inkbottle, snatched the quill in his right hand, and dipped the tip in ink.

"I see. You're telling me that a man doesn't remember a woman unless she's lain with him."

His breath snagged over the sting in her voice. Had he said that? He didn't think so, and his first inclination was to fling sarcasm at her. Then he regained rhythm in his breathing and reassessed his words. He maintained a low tone. "No. That isn't what I said. And I can tell you that a courier running a dispatch through hostile territory would long remember the courage and sacrifice of a woman who gave him shelter. Even if she'd never lain with him."

Her lips parted, and she broke eye contact. Her hands slid into her lap. Her gaze followed. Michael felt his lips twist around satisfaction, then he relaxed them. At last, she'd taken notice that the yardstick by which she measured men was warped, stunted.

"Promise me you won't write something carnal about my aunt."

Schmidt wouldn't believe the letter unless it contained something carnal. Michael averted his gaze to the paper and silkened a lie upon his tongue with as much finesse as the amoral villains in the novels Kate read. "Very well, I won't." In the top right corner, he scripted the date five days earlier, then studied it. If he were Schmidt, he'd compare penmanship. Fortunately, his left-handed script passed for that of an older man with a rickety grip on the quill. He readied the underlying sheet of paper and switched hands with the quill.

"Why are you writing with your left hand?"

"So Schmidt won't recognize my script." This time, the date bore little resemblance to his usual writing. His quill hovered above the space for a salutation. He'd leave Rachel White's name out of it. That way, Schmidt would have a rough time using anything in it against her.

He slithered a glance at Kate and found her inspection of him wary. By candlelight, her hair was almost the color of a ripe, golden peach. He imagined licking peach nectar off her naked throat and wrote: *My darling Peaches.*

"You acquiesced on this issue too easily, Michael. I suspect you're really writing depravity."

"What's a walk like along the Eno River in summer?"

"What? Why?"

"Because in this letter, Mr. Kirkleigh reminisces about a stroll that he and your aunt shared on the bank of the Eno River when they were both seventeen. They brought along a basket of food and a blanket." And ripe, golden peaches in the basket. He fantasized about Kate eating juicy peach slices from his fingers.

"Oh!" Wonder chased suspicion from her expression. "Lovely! In novels, the hero usually treats the lady to such an excursion—with the chaperone a discreet distance away, of course."

"Of course." Michael made a silent note to frolic that pesky chaperone with the driver at least a half mile away, if necessary. Kate's prattle about the Eno River became a drone. His pen visited another world.

You lay on the blanket, the dapple of sunlight and leaf shade across your bodice, your smile soft and moist from kisses. I unbuckled first one shoe, then the other. You laughed when I tossed them aside, kissed your wrist. And oh, the lovely arch of your throat when I slid my fingers up your leg to your garter, and the glitter beneath your half-closed eyelids when the stocking whispered off your toes, your moan when my thumb stroked the arch of your foot. Your skin, so delicate, like the silk of your hair.

The brandy hit about then. Inspired, Michael removed the other stocking and graduated the foot massage to an ankle and calf massage that incorporated lips and tongue. He left off with lust-maddened, partially disrobed Peaches tackling the lucky Mr. Kirkleigh to the blanket and covering his face with kisses, and his own heart hammering as if he'd run the length of King Street. Anyone with half a brain could figure out how the fictional couple's next few hours were spent, and why Mr. Kirkleigh still remembered his Peaches with enough fondness to woo her thirty years later.

Nowhere in the letter did he describe Aunt Rachel to distinction or mention her name. He'd preserved her honor. He deserved a raise for *that*.

Kate's tone bubbled with cheer. "And don't forget that afternoons along the Eno River can be steamy and stormy."

"You're absolutely right." He grinned with perhaps too many teeth and blew on the ink.

"Finished already?" She frowned. "Are you feeling well? Your face is flushed."

"It's the brandy."

"When do I get to read what you wrote?"

He laughed and fanned the page faster, trying to dry it so he could fold it up.

Her expression sealed closed. She rose and pointed a finger at him. "You let me read that letter, sir."

"Madam, I respectfully decline." He folded the letter, leapt from his chair ahead of her lunge, and held the letter above his head, arm outstretched, just out of her reach.

"I knew it. I can see it in your face. You've written filth that besmirches my aunt's reputation. I cannot allow you to present that *thing* to Mr. Schmidt. Give it to me."

By all the gods, she looked magnificent standing beneath him, fear and anger vermilion on her cheeks and trembling in her chest. What he would give to preserve that sight. With no difficulty, he imagined his free arm encircling her waist and reeling her up against him so he could shock her with a kiss, just like the rascals in those novels she read. Maybe Kate's problem was that she had no rascals in her life, just a bunch of insipid heroes who felt blessed with the arms' length distance she imposed upon them.

"Michael, give it to me, or you are no gentleman."

Disappointment scoured his glee, pickled his expression. How could she so quickly dismantle what she knew of his moral fiber and fall back on whatever hellish lesson she'd learned from Daniel Duncan about the honor in men?

He lowered his arm and placed the letter in her hand. "No gentleman at all." Then he brushed past her and left the dining room.

Chapter Twenty-One

MICHAEL MADE A foray to his room for his great coat, then stomped down-stairs for the front door and snatched his hat off the peg beside the door. Poised to yank open the door, he remembered the broken halves of cane at the entrance to the dining room. When he grabbed the sack, Kate ignored him, her gaze rigid on the content of the letter between her hands.

A muscle in Michael's cheek twitched. He swept outside before spite steamed up his belly and scalded his lips. All that work he'd put into the letter, all the anxiety he'd suffered over it that had left the inside of his gut feeling skinned—to no avail. His first ode to Eros would become blackened ash within five minutes. Even worse, he'd have to browbeat himself into writing *another* such letter, and tonight. Well, spirits at that trio of taverns would ease the burden.

Nine minutes later, he found himself in Faddis's dim, smoky tavern wedged onto a bench between two loggers who smelled of pine resin and garlicky sweat. A slab of black bread sat on the trestle table before him alongside a steaming bowl of bean and turnip soup. Halfway down the table, a brunette serving wench tucked the top of her shift under to expose more skin at her bodice and positioned her prodigious cleavage at the lower edge of a smooth, wooden ramp set upon the table. She held still, pink tongue caught between wet lips, while a logger readied a coin on its rim at the top of the ramp.

The table of men hushed. The coin released, tinkled smoothly, skirted a knot, wobbled, then popped neatly into the gap of the woman's stays. Men at the table howled approval and clapped the champion coin-roller on his back. With a good-natured grin, the wench spanked hands off her rump and climbed out from behind the men to return to work.

A redhead rubbed Michael's back with her breasts while she lowered his claret onto the table before him. He paid for the wine and glimpsed a pucker around her mouth when he applied himself to his meal instead of encouraging her advances. Yes, indeed, a year of abstinence had cured him of hankering for the shallow romps supplied by barmaids and laundresses. Maybe Kate Duncan had cured him of all women for awhile.

The logger to his right prodded his shoulder and showed brown teeth. "Too bad you missed the whole show, lad. Competition started half an hour ago."

"Couldn't get out of the house fast enough." Michael shoveled bread in his mouth.

"So don't tell the wife next time. Now, Fred over yonder, he was our reigning champion before tonight."

"So this was an unexpected win."

"Yah. We all thought Toad lacked the proper twist in the wrist, you know." The logger studied him. "You ain't from around here."

Michael wiped his right hand on his breeches and shook the fellow's callused hand. "Compton, from Cross Creek. Visiting my widowed aunt for a few days."

"Gurney. All us fellows move about chopping pine for naval stores."

"Thirsty work, no matter the weather."

Gurney swigged from his ale, then wagged a forefinger at him. "You sound like a redcoat."

"You'd sound like one, too, if you'd lived in Bristol four years."

The logger swabbed his nose on his sleeve. " 'Course, it don't matter to me. We'll have moved on farther west by then. But I think redcoats are coming to town soon."

Hair rose along the edges of Michael's scalp. He dredged a chunk of bread through soup and crammed it in his mouth so he'd have to talk around it, garble his accent. "That's what they all say. Redcoats would be crazy to come here." He chewed, swallowed. "Not enough recruits."

Gurney reached around him, tugged on the sawdust-speckled shirt of the logger to Michael's left. "Froggy, tell Compton here what you lads seen out the Road from the Haw Field Saturday."

Froggy turned bloodshot eyes on Michael and breathed rum fumes in his face. "Redcoats."

Michael didn't need to fake astonishment. "Infantry?"

"Nah. Dragoons. About a dozen of them rode through our camp." Froggy contorted his facial expression to convey haughtiness and moved his head about on his neck to exaggerate the posture of a dragoon in the saddle, walking his horse. Gurney chortled at the unflattering imitation. Froggy added, "They looked like boards got shoved up their bum-holes, like all us men ought to be shitting our breeches at the sight of 'em."

"Maybe one of you should have shit his breeches, give 'em a warm welcome." Gurney barked a laugh. "Make 'em feel special. What unit were they from?"

"The ones with skulls on the front of their helmets, and red horsehair sticking out the top."

Gurney volunteered, "That's the Seventeenth Light. Wicked buggers, they are."

Michael's heart skipped a beat, hammered three beats. Seventeenth Light.

Reconnaissance and advance guard for Lord Cornwallis.

He gulped wine on a throat suddenly dry and felt for his dagger.

Seventeenth Light. Lieutenant Fairfax's unit.

Froggy shrugged. "I don't care, long as they keep passing through, don't get in the way of me cutting pine, and ain't being followed by Continental dragoons."

"Here, here." Michael lifted his goblet. The loggers tapped it with their tankards, and all three drank.

"Eh." Froggy sniffed. "Mark my words. Lord Charlie will be camping in someone's yard soon enough. That's the reason he sent them dragoons through. Checking the climate."

A logger across the table, who'd helped himself to more beer than he ought, along with an earful of their conversation, deepened what looked like a perpetual scowl trudging down the corners of his mouth. "Naa. It's a spy they're looking for, a civilian rumored to be leaking Cornwallis's movements to Nate Greene." He stared hard at Michael.

Gurney leaned forward on a bent elbow. "How you know that, Dismal?"

"Dragoon described him to me Saturday. Medium height, lean build, mid-twenties, dark hair."

Michael tacked the information to memory and spooned in another mouthful of soup. The dragoon hadn't been looking for Ezra Griggs. The murdered man had been a generation older. And sometimes, intelligence about such spies was incorrect.

Derision soured the laughter of Froggy and Gurney. Gurney wiped his eyes. "Much help that is! It fits the description of half the men in this tavern."

Dismal's expression continued to live up to his name. "He said the spy had an accent from across the Atlantic." He rammed a glare at Michael. "Like *you*. He offered a reward for his capture." The word "reward" was pronounced "ree-ward."

Michael straightened on the bench and held the drunken logger's glare. "My family might pay you for taking me off their hands, but my hide won't fetch you a penny from the redcoats."

Gurney and Froggy roared with joviality, thumped Michael on the shoulder, and told Dismal to bark up another tree for his beer money. Not amused at their suggestion, the dour logger pushed up from the table and lumbered off into the crowd.

***

In half an hour, Michael changed his venue to the next tavern over, owned by one William Courtney. His seat near some men enabled him to overhear their discussion of the huge crowd of people attending a riveting sermon preached the previous year, there at Courtney's, by a visiting Methodist minister named Francis Asbury. To Michael, it seemed that backwoods congregations might achieve better attendance at sermons if they took a hint from Asbury and met in taverns.

The men moved on. Two codgers occupied the space beside him on the bench. Ale had already loosened their tongues. Michael bought them an additional round each.

Conversation glided from Methodists to Baptists. One man pressed a fore-finger to the side of his nose and leaned toward Michael to confide that one of the six Regulators hanged a few hundred yards east of them, beside the Halifax Road, had been a Baptist.

The old fellow grinned, pleased to have an opportunity to hang out Hillsborough's muddy laundry for a visitor. "I won't forget his last words, a Psalm of David, before they shoved the barrel from beneath him. I might fault him for being a Baptist, but while he was kicking in that noose, I was thinking, 'Don't you worry, lad. You are going to meet Our Lord.'"

Disgust stung Michael's stomach. Some comfort that thought was to a man whose life was being strangled out of him. With effort, he replenished the po-liteness of his smile.

The other fellow moped a little. "One of the six Governor Tryon pardoned that morning was another Baptist. Don't know why Tryon pardoned him. If it had been me, I would have hanged both those Baptists while I was at it. Good riddance."

The first man's head wagged in eagerness to protract the tale. "The only man alive who knows where the Regulators are buried is Abijah Pratt, the un-dertaker."

"And he isn't doing too well. Within a week, I wager he'll take that secret to the grave."

No doubt about it, the two men were part of Hillsborough's formative years. Excitement built within Michael at what history they could possibly recall for him. "Both of you have lived in the area a long while?"

The question sent them reminiscing with vigor about buying land in the '50s from William Churton's original grant and raising their families in town. Yes, they remembered Henry McCullogh and his lads, like Ned Fanning. The parties, the pomp, the ladies and their jewels. Ah, those were the good years. But now this damned uprising, six straight years of war, taxes around every corner, and decent trade disrupted. To be sure, they'd heard—*everyone* had heard by then—that General Cornwallis was camped northwest of town, ready to swoop in and raze Hillsborough at any moment. A shame two men who'd worked so hard their whole lives couldn't have some peace in their twilight years.

Michael agreed as he slipped Noah's portrait of the scoundrel from his coat. When the men's jabber eased off, he unrolled the picture on the tabletop. "Either of you ever seen this fellow?"

Both sets of eyes widened. The dam burst again on the natter.

"Say, I know him!"

"Sure, he was one of McCullough's boys. Cannot recollect his name, though."

"Yah, seems to have vanished right after the executions. With Tryon."

"One of them Northerners." The old man poked his friend. "Wasn't he sup-posed to marry Violet Griggs?"

"Maybe." The other man frowned in concentration, wiggled a finger in his own ear, as if trying to loosen wax. "She ran off with White's boy, Aaron."

"Ah, Ezra Griggs, God rest his soul." The first man regarded Michael straight on. "I can say that because Griggs wasn't a Baptist. And no one can fault him for trying to settle his girl in a wealthy marriage. Hmm. Could be I'm confusing this fellow in the portrait with Matt Tierney."

Puzzled, Michael injected, "How so? Does he look like Mr. Tierney?"

"A bit. But I recollect that ten years ago, gossip was that Griggs talked marriage a short time between Miss Violet and Tierney."

Startled by the revelation, Michael scooted toward the men. "Violet Griggs and Matthew Tierney were to be married?"

The second codger rubbed a bristly chin. "Well, I cannot say how formalized the arrangement ever became. See, Tierney once showed great promise as a naturalist. He traveled all over the Carolinas collecting trees, flowers, birds, bugs, and other critters. But even then, he was too fond of drink."

A naturalist? Michael couldn't envision the drunken dandy he'd met after the funeral turning loose one of his blondes long enough to study and sketch the intricate construction of a butterfly's wings. "I hear that Miss Griggs enjoyed sketching. Perhaps that allowed them to find a common interest."

"Maybe. But Griggs put an end to it when he found out Tierney was helping the Regulators. Griggs hated those Regulators, you know."

Tierney had dodged questions about Regulators. If Griggs had once considered Tierney a credible contender for the hand of his daughter, then shut him off from marriage due to political differences, Tierney might have been angered, indeed. But would the dandy have waited ten years to kill Griggs over it? Michael found it hard to believe, even if his gut wasn't already telling him that Tierney hadn't killed Griggs.

Bolstered by rumors he'd heard in Faddis's Tavern about the British Army in the area, Michael revisited his earlier theory about Griggs being followed home from a ten-day mission to meet Cornwallis, then losing his life to the rebel spy who'd tailed him. Some pieces felt as though they fit well with that particular theory. Other pieces dangled, at odds with the shape of the puzzle. Without a doubt, though, he had serious questions for Matthew Tierney that night.

Both gentlemen had fallen quiet, immersed in their study of the portrait. Michael pitched his tone easy, gentle. "How about it, now. What's the fellow's name?"

One man shook his head. The other said, "Haven't seen him in these parts for ten years. If he'd been a troublemaker, he'd have stood out, and I'd have easier remembered him. But he wasn't so." He handed the paper back to Michael. "What more interests me is the sketch itself. Best I've seen in these parts for a long while. I'd like to hire the artist for some family portraits."

Warmth trickled into the coolness in Michael's soul. The solution to Griggs's murder may be eluding him, but at least he could set a deserving man on a path that utilized his talents. He rolled up the sketch. "The artist, gentlemen, is Mr. Noah Carroll."

For several seconds, the two old men regarded each other, stunned. One said, "I didn't know he could sketch portraits."

Michael patted the outside of his coat, above where he'd lodged the portrait. "Then he's possibly Hillsborough's best-kept secret. As for family portraits, my suggestion is that you seek him out on the morrow. Soon as word hops around, his schedule will become quite full."

***

Around nine-thirty, Michael departed William Reed's Ordinary, third of the drinking establishments, and made his way back to Churton. Of an agreeable disposition thanks to several glasses of wine, more than ready to tackle the quill again for an erotic letter, he wasn't so eager as to forget that he'd been invited to attend a party. Nor was he so mellow that he was unaware of acquiring a shadow after departing Reed's Ordinary.

Simple to guess that Dismal was barking up the bounty tree for beer money, but a bit more complex to figure out who in town had loosed that dog of a logger on him. Since he didn't want Dismal and his handler following him to Tierney's jollification, he ducked into a narrow alley between little shops on the northwest corner of King and Churton and played a game of hide-and-seek among shops. Dismal, whose sobriety hadn't improved over the course of the evening, quickly lost his quarry, evinced in his voluble string of curses.

Michael reversed roles and tailed Dismal, following him to a shuttered shop on the southeast corner of Churton and Tryon. The door never opened to Dismal's rap, so Michael sidled closer, where he distinguished O'Toole's muffled, angry berating of the logger through the door.

O'Toole. Of course.

Dismal stumped away, pockets empty of beer money. Michael waited at least five minutes before slipping from between the shops and resuming his original course for the dandy's house on Tryon Street. This time, he wasn't followed.

At Faddis's, Dismal had been the one to volunteer the tale of a spy sought by dragoons of the Seventeenth Light. He and O'Toole might have fabricated the entire spy story, intent on overpowering and assaulting Michael, or dragging a stunned Michael back to O'Toole so the Irishman himself could revel in the battery.

But if the story about the spy was accurate, Michael could think of no one who better fit the part than O'Toole. The Irishman could divert suspicion off himself by presenting Michael to the dragoons as the spy for whom they'd been searching. And the Seventeenth Light, efficient as always, would dispense justice as soon as rope was strung upon a branch of suitable height.

The farther west he walked on Tryon Street, the more boisterous became the swell of noise signifying a party at full-gallop. If the number of gigs and horses on the street weren't enough of a clue to point to the source, anyone would have figured out by the din where to find Matthew Tierney. Michael strode up the front walkway of a sprawling two-story manor diagonally opposite Rachel White's house on Tryon and banged on the front door. Laughter like a chorus of lunatics responded from deep within the house. No one answered his second pound on the door, so he tried the handle, found the door unlocked, and entered the foyer.

The house smelled like an over-warm wine keg seasoned with roasted turkey and beef. After another blast of riotous laughter from somewhere on the first floor, Michael stripped off his greatcoat, found a peg for it and his hat among twenty-odd greatcoats, cloaks, and hats clinging to the wall, and stepped forward with the canvas sack of cane halves. "Hullo! Mr. Tierney? Hullo!" His voice echoed.

The foyer opened to a lovely staircase that curved up to the second floor. Wall sconces lit the open area and the stairway. Michael fanned his face, then dabbed sweat off his forehead with the back of his hand. Tierney liked his parties warm.

Double parlor doors banged open. A jowly man in his thirties, his nose the shape of a tulip bulb, caught sight of Michael, and started. Then delight suffused his ruddy face.

Michael gaped, unable to believe the fellow's clothing: some sort of linen tunic, storm-gray in color, which barely reached his fat knees and exposed naked lower legs. At both shoulders, the pinned tunic allowed his chubby, naked arms freedom, and although a belt of soft silvery material crossed his ample belly, the tunic barely closed on the sides, revealing pasty skin all the way down to his bare toes.

The man whooped with glee and whipped about to a parlor full of people, flashing bare buttocks at Michael. "By all the gods, friends, we are saved! Ares has arrived!"

Chapter Twenty-Two

CLOSE TO TWO-DOZEN jovial, inebriated men and women stampeded from the parlor and encircled Michael as if he were a rare songbird arrived to perform just for them. Each person was garbed in a linen tunic of a different hue, belted at the waist. The women's tunics were ankle-length, slit on the sides. Michael ogled a naked thigh on blonde Fanny, a naked hip on blonde Lucretia, and a naked calf on blonde Maria. The room pulsated and grew warmer.

"Compton, so good of you to drop by!" A tunic-clad Tierney approached from the parlor, goblet in hand, cane thumping the floor every other step. "Welcome to Mount Olympus!"

Michael forced his gape off the women and focused on Tierney. He opened his mouth. No words emerged. He cleared his throat. "I—I thought this was a party. Looks like I interrupted the rehearsal for a play."

"It *is* a party, lad." Tierney's guests split the circle and allowed him to close on Michael. "Forgive me for not explaining this afternoon. I host parties with themes. Last month, we explored Egypt and the Ptolemies. For this party, we've recreated the Greek pantheon. And what we need to do this moment is find you a tunic. Fanny, love, please do the honors."

She bustled from their company back into the parlor, the sway of her hips beneath the thin linen commanding Michael's eye for several seconds. He blinked, returned his attention to his host. "A tunic?" A mental image of his own legs, leanness enhanced by nakedness and flimsy linen, fired through Michael's imagination and floated a flush up his neck. "Why?"

"Because no one else wants to portray Ares, the god of war."

"I don't care to wear a tunic, thank you."

The fellow with the jowls tittered. "Look there, he's blushing. Isn't that divine?"

Michael backed for the door. "See here, you're obviously occupied tonight,

Mr. Tierney, and I've a few questions of a business nature to ask you, so I shall return on the morrow." A fellow about eight inches taller than he, with a deep chest, black hair, black eyes, and a black tunic blocked Michael's access to the door. Michael eyed him up and down. "Who might you be?"

The corners of the man's eyes crinkled. Teeth showed in his smile. "Hades, god of the underworld."

"Here we are, Matthew honey." Fanny wiggled over to Michael with a patch of scarlet linen barely large enough to cover a greyhound. "Just the right size. God of war, take your clothes off."

Michael's eyes bugged, then he glowered at Tierney. "No. Good night."

The dandy sighed with forbearance, swapped with Fanny the red linen for his cane, and hobbled forward to drape the arm with the goblet over Michael's shoulder. "Compton, I can tell you've a deficit of true fun in your life. And you must be thinking all of us are a little strange."

Eyes narrowed, Michael drew back a few inches. Tierney had embraced the hedonic lifestyle of London's nobility. Now Michael had an idea why Griggs warded his daughter off marrying the dandy. And Tierney's limp did look substantial enough to prevent his running.

"Tell you what, then." Tierney poked his shoulder. "I shall bend the rules, just for you. You can wear the tunic over your clothing." A couple of women oohed in disappointment. "But do stay with us awhile, enjoy the camaraderie, sample the wine, the roast. If you wish, I shall answer your questions later, after we've worked through at least one of our skits."

"Skits? You said this was a party, not a play."

Tierney dragged the red tunic over Michael's shoulder and hobbled back a few steps to retrieve his cane. "We enact some of the more popular myths and have such fun with it."

Fanny clasped the tunic at Michael's shoulders, smoothed it over his coat, and tied a belt of soft leather at his waist. He tugged the canvas sack out from beneath the tunic, then grunted in surprise when her hand squeezed his right buttock. "Where's my script to rehearse?"

"We don't use scripts. We don't rehearse. We just roll with the fun of the moment. That's what this is about, spontaneity." Tierney shook him a little by the shoulders, somehow managing to not slosh purple wine from his goblet. "Loosen up, lad. In no time at all, I guarantee you that your nasty fun deficit will vanish." Tierney swept his arm about to encompass his guests. "Let me introduce you to your fellow Olympians."

Michael heard the acerbic edge to his own voice. "Let me guess, Tierney. You're Zeus."

"Wrong," said Tulip Nose, protracting his consonants. "*I'm* Zeus."

"I'd have taken you for Dionysus."

"*I'm* Dionysus," said Tierney and swigged wine from his goblet for emphasis. Michael should have presumed as much from Tierney's tunic, purple as autumn grapes.

Fanny winked at Michael. "And I'm Aphrodite." Beneath her rose-colored bodice, her breasts undulated like melons loose in a cart and draped by canvas.

One by one, the gods and goddesses introduced themselves, while Michael sweltered in the heat of the house. Tierney announced to his friends, "Since we've Ares with us, I recommend that we skip ahead to the sixth myth so we can all participate."

Agreement swelled from the people clustered around the base of the stairs, while Michael's heat-befuddled head worked hard to recall Greek myths. In which ones did the entire pantheon participate? Alarm spiked him with a thought. "Tierney—er, Dionysus—surely you don't plan to recreate the Trojan War?"

Guests laughed. The god of good times grinned at him. "Ares, my fine fellow, do these folks look ready to lose their lives in battle?"

No, most of them looked ready to lose consciousness: droopy eyes, wobbly stances, reddened faces. "Then why do you need a god of war?" They laughed again. Michael recognized that he was the only one present who hadn't received movement orders. His ears buzzed with annoyance.

"Because you're living proof that no one is always a warrior, Ares. Now, please be kind enough to follow Aphrodite upstairs and assist her with the final preparation of props."

Michael's tone snapped like a pennant in the breeze. "What preparation?" If Tierney wanted to trap him, he might lure him upstairs with a request as absurd as "preparation of props."

"Aphrodite will show you everything."

Zeus giggled through his nose. "Quit dawdling, you lucky devil. We've seven other skits for the night, and the ladies might contract the vapors if they have to wait much longer."

Aphrodite/Fanny tickled Michael beneath the chin and mounted the stairs flaunting a shapely ankle and calf. If Michael had planned to single out Tierney's blondes for questions in connection to Griggs's murder, following Fanny would provide him the privacy to do so. One palm on the banister, the other hand gripping the sack, he climbed after her, earning applause from the Olympians.

On the second floor, Fanny seized a candle from the sconce and vanished into a room, leaving the door opened behind her. Michael reached the top step. His heart hammered, and his surroundings pulsated more. Must be the heat. At the foot of the stairs, all the Olympians watched him, waiting, good humor wreathing their faces. A homely, scrawny fellow in a dun-brown tunic who stood next to Tierney waved special encouragement. Michael couldn't remember which god *he* portrayed. Yet not a one of them, even Tierney, exhibited any expression that might feed Michael's suspicions of walking into a trap.

Maybe he wasn't walking into a trap.

After a glance around to verify the absence of gorgons, furies, and three-headed hellhounds, he entered the room to find Fanny lighting candles. Active coals in the fireplace pumped in even more heat. A big, four-poster featherbed dominated one corner of the room. Overhead in the room's center, the ceiling was swathed in some sort of canopy that receded into shadow.

"Ares, darling, close that door, will you?"

He complied and became aware of a seashore smell. Hadn't Zeus birthed Aphrodite from the foam of the ocean or some such nonsense? Over at the mantle, Fanny finished with the candles. Her tunic slid off one smooth shoulder. The pendulous curve of her breast beckoned before she tugged the tunic back into place with a little hitch of frustration to suggest that her usual attire didn't include clothing. Michael's groin tightened. Abstinence and Aphrodite: no contest there. He'd told himself last night that abstinence was a foolish idea, anyway.

Like an internal chaperone, a voice in his head nagged a reminder that Fanny wasn't really a goddess. Chaperone. Damn. Kate's chaperone must have followed him. Kate. Oh, hell. He shoved the inner voice away.

Memory served a sluggish reminder that he had business to conduct. He yanked blood back into his brain and cleared his throat again. "Er, Fanny, I've a few questions of you."

"Aphrodite, darling." She smiled sheer radiance, blew out the candle she'd used on the others, and set it on the mantle. Through a thread of smoke, he saw her tongue trace a round of her lips. His heart kicked a few beats. She pointed across the room. "This skit requires that the divan over there be repositioned to the center of the room right here. I'm sure you're strong enough to manage it by yourself."

After strutting to the indicated divan and dropping the canvas sack atop the velvet upholstery, he dragged and pushed the furniture, which surely out-weighed a workhorse, to the center of the room where the blonde waited. He hoped he hadn't gifted himself with a hernia. Panting, he straightened. "So tell me, Aphrodite, where were you yesterday between four and five in the after-noon?"

Her golden eyebrows dipped. "Yesterday? I was here. But why worry about yesterday?"

"Here in this room?" He sniffed. Weird. The smell of the ocean seemed stronger.

"No, honey, in the room next door." She made a kissing motion with her moist lips and glided to his side of the divan. "The bed in that room holds more people than this bed does."

Did Tierney have enough beds to sleep a Greek pantheon? More impor-tantly, Fanny's skin gleamed with sweat down the front of her tunic. Michael wasn't the only one in the house who was hot. His groin throbbed. "Who—ah—was with you in that larger bed?"

"Matthew and Lucretia—I mean, Dionysus and Persephone." She tugged a ribbon in her hair, loosened a tumble of golden curls around her damp shoul-ders.

Like a gnat, the chaperone buzzed in with the thought that Fanny was Tierney's playmate, and not so different from barmaids and laundresses when it came to the depth of the play. Michael ought to smell how fishy it all was, especially with the fishy odor to remind him, but he couldn't stop looking at that lovely blonde hair. Peaches, like Kate's hair. Damn, why should he think of *her*? Breath emptied his lungs in a hard rush. "Where were you at four this morning?"

"Such funny questions. In the same bed, with Dionysus and Iris, of course." She flicked fingers over the clasp on her left shoulder. The fabric flopped down at a diagonal, exposing her entire left breast. "Do you find me pretty?"

Saliva squirted inside his mouth. What emerged from between his lips sounded more akin to *ye-oh-aw* than the King's English. His head bobbed like that of a village idiot.

Her breast heaved. "Oh, I'm so glad!"

His arms filled with succulent wanton, pliant in the right places, possessing the too-good-to-be-true urgency of wenches who inhabited publications that circulated in an army camp's shadows. Her tongue performed a twisty, twirly duet with his. He lost himself in the caverns of the kiss, shocked that after more than a year of abstinence, he'd almost forgotten how a woman tasted. Fanny guided his hands on an efficient tour above and below her tunic, tugged to liberate the leather belt constricting his waist, and raked her nails down the buttons on his breeches.

She released his mouth and sank like a sylph to the divan, where she shoved the canvas sack onto the floor and reclined to expose the full lengths of both legs. "Hurry, honey," she whispered, lips wet.

Panting, pulse whamming his ears, he stripped off the red tunic and flung it aside. "Why hurry? What if I want to take my time with you?"

"Later, I promise." She dropped the other side of her bodice and wiggled both nipples at him. "Let's get you out of those clothes first. They'll be here any moment."

Her words penetrated the haze dampening his reason, stalled his fingers at the top button of his breeches. He heard his own ragged breathing catch, and he straightened his shoulders. "What do you mean?"

"Oh, I'll help you." In exasperation, she sat and reached for his breeches.

He backed just out of reach, ears attuned to a scraping noise outside the door, and spun about. The door crashed open. The scrawny fellow in brown burst in swinging what looked like a claymore in the dim light, a feral scream tearing from his throat. He kicked the door shut, homed on Michael, and charged.

Michael yelped, jumped away from Fanny, and dodged the swing. He didn't know how the little fellow lifted a claymore—leave it to the Scots to befriend a weapon too heavy for many men to wield with accuracy—but he didn't plan to volunteer as the man's target. He scrambled for the door.

Somehow, the homely fellow intercepted him, elevated the blade between Michael and escape. "Ah ha! I caught you abed my wife! You shall pay for this!"

Desperation pitched Michael's voice an octave higher than usual. "You crazy son of a cur, why didn't you tell me downstairs that she was your wife?"

"Come on, Ares, do *something*." Fanny sounded bored, not at all terrified. "I really needed another five minutes."

Michael glanced at her, found her at ease upon one elbow like a painter's voluptuous model, breasts dangling, the tunic a strategic tangle atop her crotch. When his attention returned to the other man, he found the blade had dropped a foot. He gaped at his opponent, baffled.

The man's face screwed up. "Compton, isn't it? Well, Fanny isn't my wife. But since I'm Hephaestus, and she's Aphrodite, that means we're married in the myths, and you know Ares and Aphrodite couldn't keep their hands off each other. So here we are." The blade popped up. "Enough talk. Get over there with her."

Michael's pulse stammered. He staggered toward Fanny. "You cannot mean to murder us!"

Fanny and the man in brown laughed, and she said, "Oh, that's rich!"

As he reached the divan, Michael's gaze focused more sharply on the blade. Then anger and humiliation exploded through him at what he recognized: wood painted gray. He lunged out, yanked it from his opponent, and snapped the play-Claymore in half across his thigh. "God damn you to hell!"

The pieces, hurled away, clattered against a wall. Fanny sat up and applauded. "Bravo, honey! I knew you could do it!"

Hephaestus sulked. "I can see I won't be using that forge again."

"You call this fun, do you?" Michael balled his fists. "How much fun will you have while I'm beating the snot out of you?"

The little man sneered. "Typical of you, Ares. Fortunately, the god of fire and metalworking has always been much more intelligent than the god of war." He reached up, pulled a cord Michael hadn't noticed dangling from the canopy, and sprang for the door.

A net flopped down atop Michael and Fanny, knocking him to the divan beside her. The reek of rotten fish and stale seawater expanded from the net, and Michael, coated with the stink, realized where the smell of ocean had come from earlier. Hephaestus whooped with glee.

Rage pounded Michael's throat. He moved to disentangle himself. The net encumbered his struggles.

"Ugh!" Fanny wiggled beside Michael, her naked thigh against the fabric of his breeches. "This stinks! I shall have to bathe afterwards."

The little man swept to the door and tugged it open. "Olympians, let it never be said that Hephaestus cannot capture two sneaks! Come see what fish the loan of my uncle Poseidon's enchanted net has caught!"

In disbelief, Michael listened to the paddle of naked footsteps upstairs. He worked his dagger loose and sawed at the net, but the lighting slowed his progress. The room's population swelled with drunken deities. Women squealed and men howled with hilarity. All congratulated Tierney for his clever design of the skit's props and the little man in brown for playing the plot so smoothly. Michael, his ears aflame, kept sawing.

He'd half-pawed his way out of the net when Tierney and his cane thumped to his side. His breath bathed Michael in wine fumes. "My dear Mr. Compton, allow me to help you out of the tangle. That was spectacular! How about another skit, eh? Was that one not fun?"

No man in his right mind would relish being thrust into the role of the booby. Once upon a time, Tierney might have had a future as a naturalist. But inebriation had pickled his brain, transformed him into an even bigger booby than Ares.

Michael batted the dandy's hands away, climbed from the mess unassisted, scooped up his sack, and straightened. Bubbly laughter of Olympians faltered to silence in his glacial glare, which he slid from them onto Tierney. "You can meet me in your study in two minutes for questioning. Or I can leave this house now, and you can expect Georg Schmidt to arrest you on the morrow for the murder of Ezra Griggs." Without waiting for Tierney's response, he stomped for the open doorway and the stairs.

Chapter Twenty-Three

MICHAEL THRASHED ASIDE cloaks and greatcoats in the foyer until he retrieved his own property. That a somber-faced Tierney plodded down the stairs after him, his cane making a hollow smack on each stair, supplied him with no satisfaction.

How arrogant he'd been at Faddis's Tavern, imagining himself impervious to manipulation. Outwitting O'Toole's inebriated henchman had boosted his conceit. By thinking with his groin, he'd left himself open to entrapment and attack. If Tierney or his friends had wanted to kill him, he'd be dead by now. Some fine, seasoned investigator he was.

Tierney arrived at the entrance to the foyer, his face taut. "This way, Mr. Compton." His hand, minus a goblet, gestured left. Michael followed him, ready, alert.

The dandy entered his study with a lit candle, leaving the door open. The study felt cooler than the rest of the house. It also smelled musty, unused. Supporting that observation were books from shelves, boxes, and documents all strewn upon chairs, a couch, the desk surface, and the floor. The study functioned as an unkempt storage area only.

Tierney lit more candles. Michael shut the door to prevent Olympians from eavesdropping, and he walked to the only window, from which Tierney claimed a burglar had escaped. After he piled his greatcoat, hat, and sack atop a nearby chair, he bent over to examine the sash.

"Do you see the scratches where that devil climbed out my window at four this morning?"

Michael ran his fingertips over scrapes on the wood, consistent, he supposed, with damage from shoes. Even by direct candlelight, though, he'd be unlikely to spot the subtle catch of clothing fibers in the wood of the window frame. That sort of detection required daylight. He straightened, displaced several books off the seat of a ladder-backed chair, and planted the chair on a portion of floor barren of rugs. "Sit, Mr. Tierney."

The other man complied. Michael walked past him, idly curious about the titles still lodged with crooked abandon in bookshelves and gathering dust. In passing, he sneaked a study of his host. Tierney's purple tunic brought out pastiness in his skin, the bloat of face and limbs. Often enough, Michael had seen such men drinking themselves toward their final breaths. The demons that rode them arose from loss, frustration, anger, and horror. And sometimes from guilt.

Tierney's swollen fingers drummed his thighs. "I figured out what the burglar stole from me early this morning."

"And what was that?"

He tittered. "A cane. Isn't that absurd?"

"*A* cane? How many other canes have you besides the one you're currently using?"

"Ten or so. I match them with my attire and the social occasion."

Michael strolled over, picked up Tierney's current accessory, examined it, then returned it to him. He saw no reason why the particular cane Tierney had chosen should match a wine-purple faux-Grecian tunic better than any other cane. "What was special about the stolen cane to make it worthy of theft?"

"I don't know."

"Where do you store your canes?"

"Various places about the manor. Rooms I most often frequent."

The more Michael questioned him, the more random the man's responses made the theft seem. An excellent strategy, if a guilty party wanted a reported burglary to seem, at the same time, more real yet more difficult to solve. "What about one of your canes would distinguish it from those of another fellow in town?"

"A metallic letter 'T' is embedded in the head of each of my canes. For Tierney, you know."

Michael approached the nearest bookshelf. "Why would anyone break into your manor and steal a cane?"

Again, jumpy laughter from Tierney. "I don't know. There's plenty else here that's more valuable."

Tierney kept fidgeting. Was he culpable over a crime or nervous at being questioned? Michael pulled a book off a shelf and opened it. Excruciating detail, handwritten, proclaimed the description, habitat, and diet of skinks. He flipped pages, blew off dust, skimmed over similar details for more lizards than he'd expect to find at a meeting of politicians.

A pen-and-ink drawing of a reptile accompanied each entry. Michael studied a few drawings more closely. The artist's skill, while passable, wasn't outstanding. The style seemed familiar, basic, almost childlike. On the front page, Tierney's name appeared as author, the year 1769. No artist was credited. Michael slid the book back to the shelf and returned observation to Tierney. "Tell me about your years as a naturalist."

The dandy completed a brisk rubbing of his bare upper arms with his hands. "There isn't much to tell. And it's rather nippy in here. Might we move into the parlor?"

"No. And unless you start answering my questions instead of dancing around them, I promise the temperature in here will grow even nippier."

Tierney pushed to his feet, wobbled, then concentrated a snarl at Michael. "This is *my* house, Compton, and you're one of the most hopelessly stodgy men I've ever met. Get out!"

A hiss emerged from Michael. "Sit and answer my questions, or Schmidt throws you in jail on the morrow. You don't seem to comprehend that I'm all that stands between you and him." Tierney's chest jerked, as if Michael had physically pushed him, but he remained standing, scowling. "Look at you. You're nothing at all like the man who wrote those journals twelve years ago. What happened to you?"

"Why do you care? No one cared back then. Nothing I do now makes a difference." Tierney flopped down on the chair hemorrhaging self-pity.

"How did you injure your ankle?"

"While I was traveling the North Carolina backcountry studying evergreens, I fell off my horse. No, I wasn't drunk, not *then*. A snake startled my mount. I managed to climb back into the saddle and ride twenty miles to the nearest farmstead."

"Impressive." Michael thought of Blake Carroll's story of Tierney's injury: a drunken fall from a balcony upstairs. "But that isn't the truth. You were drunk and fell out a window."

Tierney's pupils contracted, imparting upon him the visage of one of the skinks sketched in his portfolio. "*That* incident happened a year later. I re-injured my ankle in the fall. It never healed. I've not been able to ride a horse since then." He pouted.

Michael flung up his hands. "Just like that—*pfftt!*—you gave up and dove into a wine bottle because you couldn't access the backcountry personally? I find it hard to believe that a man who wrote those journals, a man who invested such passion in studying nature, would give up his life's calling, merely because of an injury. You still had your wits about you. More importantly, you had money. You could have trained assistants. But you *chose* not to do so."

The skink eyes seared. "Who are you, Compton? I doubt you're my neighbor's nephew. The way you collect information, the way you process it, you're no naval stores merchant. You're analytical, like a naturalist." Victory gleamed in his eyes. "But more like a military strategist. An officer of the Crown, even. Is Compton really your name?"

Michael's pulse hopped about over his own poor acting. While he waited for it to settle, he reflected Tierney's glare back to him. Neither man spoke for a long moment. "One reason a man might choose to abandon his calling is crushing loss." Hands clasped behind him, Michael paced, slow, before Tierney, aware that the dandy tracked his movements with a predator's eye.

He halted, resumed the stare with Tierney. "I shall reconstruct that pivotal year of 1771 for you, what drove you to cast aside your potential and become the sot you are today, disrespected by so many in town."

Tierney laughed, a harsh sound that invited more winter into the study. "Fool. You cannot reconstruct a man's road into hell."

"Can I not?" Michael grabbed at a hunch derived from his conversation with old Mr. Carroll. "First of all, your father died."

Tierney's eye twitched. "Hardly a 'crushing loss,' as you'd so label it. His death meant I finally had control of all his money and property."

"True, but money can neither substitute for nor purchase character. Your father's reputation in Hillsborough was excellent." Michael's gaze took in the study, once opulent, and he protracted his hunch. "He supported your career, gave you credibility. When he died, you lost your greatest advocate."

"Wrong. When he died, I lost my greatest source of harassment."

Michael ignored Tierney's denial. A muscle in the dandy's cheek had jumped. "I'm curious. After your injury, why didn't you train assistants, fund their excursions into the backcountry to fetch samples of evergreens and skinks?" His eyes narrowed on the dandy. "Did you injure your wrist in the fall, making you unable to sketch?"

"I didn't ske—" Tierney accompanied his abrupt truncation of the sentence with a cautious regard of Michael.

Michael leapt into the silence. "You weren't the sketch artist. Who was your artist?" In the next second, the answer became clear to him, prompted by the familiar style. "It was Miss Violet Griggs. When your father died, you lost your intercessor for her hand in marriage."

"Bah! She was nothing to me."

Michael laughed. "Do you think me an idiot, Tierney? How many young ladies have the fortitude to sit and patiently sketch lizards? Miss Griggs was your *partner* for a time. And even if you insist that you never cared for her, I know you must have accorded her some amount of deference because of her money."

A corner of Tierney's mouth creased with sarcasm. "Certainly. What man would turn away money?"

"Thus it was another crushing blow for you when Ezra Griggs broke off his daughter's association to a man who was a *Regulator*. You were deeply involved in the movement. Mr. Griggs's society opposed it."

Tierney's lips pinched shut. Michael dove in on him. "In 1771, your father died. A second accident reduced the utility of your ankle, preventing you from pursuing your occupation. Ezra Griggs cut you off from the only woman who might ever have been your partner in life because you supported an opposing political view. Then the *coup de grâce*. The entire movement that you'd believed in collapsed. That's why every day, you drink yourself toward an early grave—"

"I know where this is going!" Tierney stood, winced when he placed too much weight on his ankle, and corrected his stance. "Yes, I admit that 1771 was not a good year for me. But I didn't kill Griggsy yesterday!"

"Isn't it the truth that you hated him? And you hated Violet for running off with Aaron White when she should have run off with you?"

"No, I didn't hate any of them!" Tierney's shoulders hunched. "And I didn't kill Griggsy!"

"Mr. Tierney, hatred is a powerful motive for crime. This morning before dawn, you broke into Mr. Griggs's house with an extra cane." This part Michael admitted to himself was far-fetched, but the pieces meshed with a decent fit. "Enraged, you snapped the extra in half and gouged the side of Violet's harpsichord with it. In a mad fit, you flung the broken cane to the floor, then broke her violin. All of it in effort to efface her because she torments you still.

"Another man eloped with your woman, and there isn't a damned thing you can do about it. Thus you concocted the story about a burglar stealing your cane at four in the morning. No wonder Schmidt doesn't believe you. I don't believe you, either."

The defensive line of Tierney's jaw melted. The glare faded from his eyes. "What are you babbling about, the harpsichord and violin?" His eyes widened, and his neck extended. "Wait a moment. Are you telling me that you found my missing cane in Griggsy's house?"

The scaffold upon which Michael had hung pieces of the puzzle wobbled. Tierney's open, erect stance proclaimed that he was awaiting news, not hiding crimes. But the dandy might be looking to weasel out of *something*. Michael mustn't communicate his doubt.

He bustled to the chair near the window, snatched the canvas sack, and thrust it at Tierney. The dandy plunged a hand into the sack and withdrew the halves of cane. His mouth and jaw rippled and tensed. When he spoke, the pitch of his voice was higher. "Do you know how much this cane cost me? Damn his eyes! He broke it!" When Michael retrieved the cane and sack, Tierney started after him, his pupils still contracted. "Say, give me back my cane!"

"Later. Right now, it's evidence, Mr. Tierney."

"Evidence? Evidence against me! That's what you're saying, isn't it? Give it back!"

Michael deposited the sack atop his greatcoat and swept back to the distraught dandy. "When I first saw Mr. Griggs's parlor late yesterday afternoon, minutes after his death, the harpsichord was undamaged by the murderer's rampage. But this morning, when I began my investigation, the harpsichord and violin were damaged as I've described. Here's what I think happened. Denied revenge for ten years, you saw an opportunity to sneak in and exact a final bit of retribution on a man who'd hurt you, and cleverly pin your vandalism on the murderer." He stepped toward Tierney, forcing him to retreat one step. "The truth now."

The culpability postures Michael expected didn't manifest in Tierney. Instead, Tierney eyed him with keen interest, his back straight. "I don't know what this is about, the harpsichord and violin damaged." Words cascaded from him, a tribute. "Violet loves music and her instruments. Especially that harpsichord. It's sacred to her, like an extension of her. Griggsy knew that, and she knew what a fortune her father had paid for it. I would not have damaged such fine instruments, irreplaceable here in Hillsborough."

Cold in the room crept beneath Michael's shirt. Would Violet have abandoned her beloved harpsichord for a man's love?

Tierney drew a shuddering breath. His tone soured. "Someone broke into my house, stole one of my canes early this morning. You say you found that cane over there in Griggsy's parlor. Suppose I'm telling the truth about the burglary. What does that suggest to you?"

What it suggested, since Michael was now certain that Tierney hadn't murdered Griggs, was that the dandy had somehow angered the true perpetrator enough to get himself framed for murder. The criminal had broken into Tierney's house, stolen the cane, and planted it where an investigator could find it and arrive at the pat conclusion.

Michael proceeded to the window and stared down at the bag containing the wrecked cane. Stripes of ice hurtled up his back, embedded into the base of his skull, and sent his hair on end. Foul blood, he knew, existed between Schmidt and Tierney. Twice, Schmidt had questioned him about what he'd found in the house, expecting him to declare some object in particular. The county sheriff now looked complicit in the murder of Ezra Griggs.

That wasn't the news Schmidt expected to hear at nine on the morrow. But giving Schmidt that news would most certainly earn Michael imprisonment. Then he would mysteriously die within a day or two.

And what of the man whose face Noah Carroll had sketched, a man who a few recognized as belonging to a dark, decade-old past of land agents who defrauded their clients? Was he a rebel spy who had followed Griggs back from a meeting with Cornwallis? Or had Schmidt hired him to murder Griggs and frame Tierney, specifically because he hadn't been seen in town since the Regulators were executed ten years earlier? And why the expression of rage in the destruction of Griggs's property? For what was the murderer looking?

"Mr. Tierney, I haven't had the opportunity to speak with my aunt about why she and Mr. Schmidt dislike each other so much. I gather that it relates to the enmity between you and Mr. Schmidt." Tierney chuckled behind him, the sound of dead leaves scraping brick. Michael pivoted. "Enlighten me as to your histories, the three of you."

Tierney leaned on the cane. "Last summer, Schmidty became a secret partner in the purchase of the tavern across the street from your aunt's tavern. He desired no competition, so he started a rumor that all the beer and ale served in your aunt's tavern contained horse piss. Your aunt lost eighty percent of her business overnight. I uncovered the source of the rumor and made it public knowledge, earning Schmidty's wrath. Business at his tavern also collapsed. Alas, business for your aunt never recovered. No one wished to bother with the lingering hostility. Men took their thirst elsewhere, profiting the town's other taverns."

Michael's heart felt pinched and achy a moment. At last, he understood Aunt Rachel's mysterious lack of business. There was nothing left for her in Hillsborough. She must be hoping for a miracle involving Aaron and Violet.

Schmidt possessed a strong motive for framing Tierney and ridding the town of the drunken chatterbox who'd exposed his dirty business dealings. Yet dread, rather than elation, lumbered up Michael's back. He might be able to stall for time in the morning, but if he concluded that the perpetrator was someone other than Tierney, Schmidt would kill him. Then Schmidt would fabricate proof of the dandy's decade-old grudge against Griggs and kill Tierney.

If Michael fled back to Wilmington, Schmidt would still murder Tierney. More ice shoveled up his spine. He imagined Schmidt so immersed in murder that he used the heat and smoke over Tierney to rid himself of his hated competitor, Rachel White. And her niece. Both women had lied to protect Michael's identity. Michael's gut knotted fire. Schmidt just might allow O'Toole to amuse himself with Kate first. Damnation.

Upon his honor, he couldn't leave Hillsborough with the lives of three other people hanging upon his next moves. But he hadn't the slightest idea how to extricate all of them and himself. Aware that Tierney scrutinized him, Michael dredged discipline from his bone marrow to deflect a display of trepidation from his face.

Noah's portrait of the murderer rustled in his coat pocket. Glad for the reminder, he brought out the picture and unfolded it for Tierney. "Who is this fellow?"

The dandy's brow lowered—not a scowl, but a measure of his search of memory. "If he's who I suspect he is, he might have been one of McCullough's minions here ten years ago."

"What's his name?"

Tierney's frown didn't waver, and he shook his head. "Memory fails me there." Premature wrinkles deepened on either side of his mouth. "He and Griggsy talked briefly of him marrying Violet, but she wouldn't have him."

"Why not?"

Tierney stared at the portrait as if squaring off with a fiend. "Something not right with that one." He pointed in accusation at the sketch. "Too quick to anger, always. I never cared for the way he watched Violet, as if she were not a woman, but an object to possess."

How weird. Janet Sewell, Violet's friend, had said something similar after the funeral. On the morrow, he must interview Miss Sewell, pin down what she meant.

A heartbeat later, he realized that Tierney had revealed his true feelings for Violet. Faint humor found its way to his lips. "I thought you said that Miss Griggs didn't matter to you."

Tierney's shoulders rolled back. "I was ever aware that Griggsy had cultivated her to be some man's perfect wife and companion. *That* fellow, though, didn't care." A frown forced his eyebrows closer. "Perhaps this may sound peculiar. I don't think he wanted her as a wife, but I got the impression that he didn't want anyone else to have her, either."

Peculiar, bah. Characteristic of a very selfish individual. Michael secured the portrait in his pocket.

"Who is he, Compton?"

"Someone with whom I'd like to speak."

Tierney squinted at him, curiosity prying at Michael from his gaze. "Someone connected with Griggsy's murder?" When Michael ignored his question and fetched his belongings, Tierney joined him at the window. "Hah! I can tell that you don't think I killed Griggsy. Or that I vandalized Violet's musical instruments."

Michael swung his greatcoat over his forearm and stood still, again locked in a gaze with the dandy. "No, I do not."

Tierney's jaw bobbed up and down a few times. "By all means, make your conclusions known to Schmidty on the morrow."

Much good it would do either of them when Schmidt had already made up his mind and colored evidence to bolster his decision. The dependency Tierney placed on his cane caught Michael's attention anew. He studied the disability a few seconds. *I've not been able to ride a horse since then.* "You didn't recently purchase a gig, did you?"

"Actually I did. A month ago. My old gig wore out, with all that I've driven it."

Now Michael's heart felt like it had been knotted in an anchor's cable and tossed overboard with the anchor. What a bloody wretched coincidence. Were he the lead investigator in the case, the purchase wouldn't have been recent enough to incriminate Tierney. But Schmidt was building a case of circumstantial and false evidence. Tierney's gig was fodder.

The dandy's cheeks emptied of color at Michael's expression. "What has my gig to do with Griggsy's murder?"

It was another nail in the coffin Schmidt was building for all of them. "Unless I've misjudged Mr. Schmidt, he will attempt to use your recent purchase of an operational gig against you. My suggestion, Mr. Tierney, is that you send all your guests home and treat yourself to sobriety, wherein you might more competently watch your own back for the next day."

Chapter Twenty-Four

ON TIERNEY'S FRONT porch, Michael sucked in a lungful of winter night—crisp, quiet, scented with wood smoke—then coughed in revulsion. Trapped in a sea trawl: that described his new fragrance. Would sneaking a cold-water dunk in the dark behind Aunt Rachel's stable be enough to rid him of the maritime essence? He decided no. His clothing reeked. Best to seek soap, a towel, and warm water inside the house.

The last time he'd seen his spare clothing, it was hanging out to dry early that morning. No telling what Martha had done with it since. Maybe the garments had appeared in his room during his absence.

Before leaving the porch, he attuned his senses to the night and surrounding shadows. He'd been followed during the evening's tavern hop. If someone tailed him from Tierney's home or awaited him at Aunt Rachel's, he'd correct the situation before he reached the front door. But his only encounter, two cats coupling on the street before Rachel White's house, served as a reminder that he had a love letter to compose for the second time that night. Huzzah.

On Aunt Rachel's front porch, he heard Lizzie and Sammy sniffing at him through door cracks. Light filtered through the parlor's drapes. As soon as he opened the door, the hounds, tails awag, dragged their noses all over him, delighted to partake of the delectable scent in which he'd doused himself. He hung his greatcoat and hat on pegs while fending off the dogs' frisk.

Kate's tone bubbled from the parlor. "My, they certainly seem pleased to see you!"

Still in the foyer, he faced her: happy, hospitable Kate sitting near the fireplace, her needle and thread posed over a man's coat in her lap. His gaze enlarged. That was *his* spare coat, and the main seam was split like a dead deer's belly. A cough rasped from him. "M-my coat."

She held up the eviscerated garment. Satisfaction relaxed her face. "I noticed it seemed a bit snug across your chest yesterday, so I'm letting out the seam a bit. Your waistcoat, too."

Flames highlighted the gold of her hair. Her smile was sweet. Peaches.

He closed his dangling jaw. He had no change of clothing and reeked of fish. What power women held.

"Now, now, don't fret, Michael. I shall have it ready for you soon." She stood, placed the mending on her chair, and approached him, full lips curved like Cupid's bow and moist. "I wronged you earlier. I'm so sorry." The love letter he'd written emerged from her pocket intact, no sign that it had ever faced the fire of her disapproval. "You never once mentioned Aunt's name in this letter, you never described her."

She extended it to him. Stunned, he snatched it from her lest she change her mind.

"There isn't anything here that might be traced to Aunt and shame her," Kate said. "You truly are a gentleman. On the other hand, I behaved like a shrew, and I so want to make it up to you. The least I can do for you is—"

She broke off, sniffed. Her eyes narrowed. Her smile faded. She sniffed again.

Michael slunk back a step from the bounty of indebtedness she'd aimed at him. The nose of a hound prodded his thigh with bliss. He bumped the dog away. "Kate, might I trouble you for a bucket of warm water upstairs in my room?"

Her nose wrinkled. The Cupid's bow of her mouth upended. "My God, is that *you*?"

His hopes for a more personal expression of her gratitude shriveled before they shaped. "And—and a towel. And soap."

"What happened to you? How did you find—ugh!—the Atlantic Ocean this far inland?"

Not if hell froze would he admit the truth. Besides, she wouldn't believe him if he confessed. One quarter of a lung participated in his laugh. "Oh, this quirky sort of thing happens all the time during criminal investigations."

"Criminal investigations?" She coughed. "No wonder the dogs gave you such a hearty welcome. You're stinking up the house. Don't you dare go upstairs smelling like that." She grabbed the nearest lit candle in holder and thrust it at him like a sergeant distributing a musket to a private. "Pile everything except your shoes at the foot of the stairs and report directly to your room. Fortunately, I've water warming on the hearth. I shall bring some along to you shortly and use the rest of it to soak those clothes overnight." Her eyelids spasmed shut. "Ugh."

He resisted hanging his head like a naughty boy. "Where's your aunt?" Too well he could imagine the reaction of Rachel White if she rounded the corner at the foot of the stairs to behold a redcoat not only out of his uniform but also out of his clothing.

"Still at the tavern, although I don't know why. She has so little business." Kate fanned the air before her nose. "I expect her home within the hour, so do hurry. If she arrives and catches a whiff of you before we get rid of this odor, you'll be sleeping in the stable tonight."

"Yes, madam." He headed out of Kate's sight for the foot of the stairs, stripped down, then scurried up with the candle and love letter, his shoes and garters, and the canvas sack containing his watch, Noah's sketches, and Tierney's cane. The majority of the stench did seem to have lodged in his clothing, for which he was thankful.

In the little room, he closed the door and drew the curtains. His spare shirt, neck stock, breeches, and stockings lay folded on the bed—little more than his underwear, but at least he wasn't totally without clothing. A minute or so later, Kate left him soap, a towel, and a bucket of warm water outside his door. Finally, he rid himself of the residue acquired during his romp among the gods. Dressed as well as he was able, he emptied the wastewater out the window and poured the remaining water from the bucket into his washbasin for the morning.

Before he could tie back his combed out hair, Kate's voice quested through his door. "I've sewn up the seams on your coat and waistcoat. Let me see whether these fit better than before."

That was quick. He opened the door to receive his garments. Her gaze lingered on his hair, shoulders, and hips before she turned aside, appearing to comply with cultural dictates for modesty.

Surprise shot through his veins. Satisfaction simmered in atop it. Kate wanted an eyeful of him.

He took his time shrugging into and buttoning the waistcoat, a casual, inverse strip. Her gaze, flecked with sparks of hunger, snaked over the lines of movement created when he rolled back his shoulders. He smiled. "A much better fit. You have my gratitude."

"Now the coat. We must be certain of that, too."

He complied because by then, even though they both knew the coat would fit him, they were enjoying the tease of a game that mandated his dressing fully. And when the coat did indeed fit, he thanked her again.

"After your other set of clothing is clean and dry, I shall alter it, too."

He bowed his head, polite. Waiting. Kate wasn't the sort of woman to plug a silence with natter. She was working her way around to asking him something.

"I suspect you plan to be courageous tonight, sneak downstairs to the parlor with your rifle to guard the house after Aunt and I have gone to sleep. Martha and I devised an alarm system." She pressed fingers to her mouth, stifling humor. "Pots and pans beneath the windows, rope tying them together. If the criminal breaks in, he'll create a dreadful racket, tangle his feet."

Michael chuckled at her scheme. But the man wasn't going to return that night, instinct told him. They weren't dealing with a fool.

"At which point, Sammy and Lizzie will detain him until we apprehend him."

We. Kate was too funny. "Thank you for sparing me guard duty all night." He brought the empty bucket out of his room and set it on the landing, at the top of the stairs, then leaned against one side of the doorjamb.

She moistened her lips with her tongue and leaned against the side of the doorjamb opposite him. She took a deep breath. Her tone silkened. "I have a question."

He relaxed, his stance casual, receptive. "Ask."

She took another full breath. "Do you expect Mr. Schmidt to believe that what Mr. Kirkleigh wrote to his Peaches might have actually happened?"

"I do. Why wouldn't he believe it?"

"Because it's a fantasy." Gentle laughter rippled through her. "You know, for a man to seduce a woman merely by massaging her feet. It wouldn't really happen that way."

He blinked several times, not certain he'd heard her correctly. Then he realized from her expression that she wasn't joking with him. Not only had a foot massage never led to seduction for her, but her personal experience with seduction was so limited that she didn't conceptualize the possibility of seduction by foot massage.

Maybe she'd never been seduced. Maybe the Ice Widow awaited the touch of an adept fellow before thawing. Michael's groin stirred.

Whatever Daniel Duncan had done to her, he'd surely—bah, forget the dead husband. He was gone, in the past. Pieces of Michael's conversation with Kate in the dining room earlier returned. The realization clouted him, and his gaze pinned her with incredulity.

Even though Kate might allow every would-be suitor to believe that Duncan the dead husband was his competition, neither Duncan's memory nor any man of flesh and bone guarded her heart. Michael's competition was the heroes in those damned novels she worshipped.

"Kate, has it ever occurred to you that those novels you read, the ones with the chaperones, might actually by authored by women who are writing under men's names?"

"Well, yes, actually."

"And that those women might never have understood how a man thinks and feels? Perhaps most of them have never even lain with a man?" Even in the semi-darkness, he saw color surge to her cheeks. Not embarrassment, but acknowledgement that yes, that thought, too, had crossed her mind. "Well, then, I'd rid myself of those novels, if I were you. They don't represent reality."

Her pupils enlarged. "So what you wrote in that letter isn't fantasy. It's, um—" She caressed her upper thighs with her palms, one slow arc down, then up. Hands loose, chin angled up, she peeled her back off the doorjamb and swayed half a step toward him. "It's *feasible.*"

His gaze dallied over the path her palms had promised and lodged in the confluence of her upper thighs. A flush fired the length of his neck into his cheeks and ignited a bonfire in his groin. In his imagination, he tasted summery peaches dripping with syrup, sliding around on his tongue, and the naked arch of Kate's foot, then her calf, so smooth beneath his fingers, and pressed to his lips. His chest expanded. How splendid that her mind wasn't set about this matter. The two of them might travel the road of feasibility together. All she had to do was specify when. An uninterrupted two hours of when. He opened his mouth to offer encouragement.

Downstairs, dog toenails skitter-crashed across the foyer to the front door in an explosion of sound. Startled, Michael jerked his interest to the stairs. From the first floor he heard a happy-panting welcome precede the creak of the door, and Aunt Rachel's weary voice. "Imps. Missed me, did you?"

Obviously, this wasn't the *when* for which Michael had hoped.

Kate scooped up the empty bucket and slipped past him, nymph-like in her descent of the stairs. "Aunt Rachel." Dry duty in her voice displaced the softness of her tone seconds earlier. "How was business tonight?"

***

Michael expelled disappointment, retreated to his room, and shut the door. *An uninterrupted two hours of when.* Who was he fooling? On the morrow, he must do battle with a ruthless band of deserters. Unless he found a way to placate them while saving four lives, any dreams of uninterrupted time with Kate Duncan were as flat as paper.

Paper. His gaze jumped from Violet's slashed portrait to her portfolio of sketches, resting beside her portrait. Tierney and those fellows in Courtney's Tavern said they thought Ezra Griggs might have talked marriage between his daughter and the mystery man sketched by Noah. Michael hadn't examined all of Violet's sketches yet. Had Violet sketched the man, even though neither Tierney nor Janet Sewell had thought her fond of him?

He opened Noah's sketches on his bed, then fetched the portfolio and pulled out the pile of sketches. Aaron, he decided, was beyond the inner circle of suspects for Griggs's murder.

He tied back his hair and paged through the sketches, one by one. If he could better identify the suspect, even give him a name, he could present irrefutable evidence to Schmidt that Tierney wasn't Griggs's murderer. Faced with a mountain of evidence and testimony of numerous witnesses in town, Schmidt would have to back off Tierney and hunt the real killer. To do otherwise would expose him as intent on personal revenge, not justice.

As Michael examined sketches, he confirmed that Violet's proficiency had improved a bit as she grew older. Her middling skill enabled her to sketch a variety of lizards, snakes, centipedes, and spiders, each the sort of critter that ran shivers and squeals through most girls, each with the same simplicity that she'd used for Tierney's naturalist's books. She and Tierney truly had been suited for each other.

A seed of suspicion that had nagged Michael for several hours sprouted. Griggs had liked neither Tierney nor Aaron. Violet had at least shared a bond with Tierney. He saw no evidence of a similar bond shared with Aaron. If Violet was certain to anger her father with her choice of a man anyway, why had she eloped with Kate's cousin instead of with a man whose work she'd shared?

A crowded sketch full of confusing images, unlike the others, sent him to the candle for better light. There he saw that, instead of a natural creature, some sort of monster, part-man with claws and fangs like a cougar and horns upon its head, dominated the sketch in profile, its mouth gaping above a tiny, supine girl-like figure. She lay draped over an altar, boneless, like rolled pastry over a tart pan before it is trimmed.

Michael recoiled. Moisture vanished from his lips and throat. His gaze flitted over the sketch. No signature. Yet the style was the same as that in Violet's most recent pictures, dated 1771.

The child in the picture wasn't just boneless. She was broken, non-existent.

His gaze darted from the monster-man to Noah's sketches. The one of the man fleeing Aunt Rachel's house was close to profile. What now—was that a resemblance between the two sketches, in the nose and chin?

He evaluated what he'd observed in the development of Violet's skill. He compared pictures again. Try as he might, he couldn't escape the growing belief that Noah and Violet had sketched the same man.

He sucked in a breath of revulsion and held the monster sketch out, away from him, as if the death stench in Griggs's parlor had channeled through it and smeared over him. What kind of animal was he dealing with?

Janet Sewell whispered in his memory. *I never liked his way of looking at Violet.* He heard Matthew Tierney's words. *I never cared for the way he watched Violet, as if she were not a woman, but an object to possess.*

Violet. Michael's mind twisted her name. Violate. A child. Gods, no, how wrong, a child!

Wrong? murmured Lydia from memory, sliding her arms around his neck. *Why do you say wrong? How can this be wrong, my pet?*

He dropped the monster sketch atop Noah's portraits and stepped back from it. He'd been fifteen when Lydia, a grown woman, had seduced him the first time. Fifteen was more than child, on the verge of becoming a man, as most would point out. But by her relentless pursuit, Lydia had carved her name in his being.

Two years later, his father, his uncle, and Lord Crump had opened the escape for him, into the Army. But like a miller's mule grinding corn, he'd gone nowhere, year after year, plodding the same circle over women and sex and love. Tavern wenches and laundresses found him easy prey. And Fanny. Fanny resembled Lydia. He hadn't realized it until that moment. The full breasts, the curly hair.

But Kate was different.

He drew closer to the bed. The girl figure in Violet's sketch was many years younger than fifteen. A great sigh emptied Michael's mouth. Whoever that whoreson had been, he'd robbed Violet, her father, Matthew Tierney, and Aaron White.

If the monster had returned to Hillsborough after reportedly being gone ten years, and he'd murdered Ezra Griggs, what was his trigger, his motive? What had caused all the rage? Could he really have been looking for Violet's journal in Griggs's house? In Aunt Rachel's house, too, as she'd suggested?

Agitation caught him up, propelled his feet into pacing the tiny room. What if Violet had documented in her journal the man's unnatural attentions upon her for years, and he sought the journal to destroy evidence, to spare his character? What might have caused him to suddenly seek the journal after so much time? Perhaps he hadn't expected Griggs to be home when he broke in, and he'd been forced to kill him.

In the next heartbeat, Michael shook his head to dismiss the theory. What bothered him about it was the decade that had passed since Violet and Aaron left Hillsborough. Even if Violet's testimony about such depraved attentions came to light through her journal, would a judge consider any of it relevant when the incidents had occurred so long ago? Did such a testimony even possess the weight to ruin a man's reputation? And why, ten years after the fact, would a man ascribe so much power to the words of a young woman that he'd murder her father to get his hands on her journal?

He heard footsteps on the stairs, and the murmurs of Aunt Rachel and Kate. That afternoon, Rachel White had advanced the notion that the burglar was searching her house for Violet's journal. It was time for Michael to find out why.

Chapter Twenty-Five

THE WOMEN ARRIVED on the landing as he opened his bedroom door. Aunt Rachel drew back at his appearance and tucked her chin. Flickering light from the Betty lamp Kate carried flung shadow over her. A few steps below them, the hounds paused their ascent.

"My apologies for startling both of you." Michael directed his words at the older woman. "May I have a moment of your time before you repair for bed?"

Aunt Rachel stroked down her throat twice. "I'm exhausted. On the morrow, at breakfast."

"This won't take but a moment." Sensing the buildup of a protest from Kate, Michael moved in on her aunt. "This afternoon, you told me you thought the burglar was looking for Violet Griggs's journal in this house. Why was that?"

"It was an absurd thing for me to say." Her hand waved the air, as if to fan away smoke.

What in hell was she hiding? The shortened fuse on Michael's temper sparked. He backed her closer to one of the other bedroom doors. "Madam, you know something about this investigation that you aren't divulging. By withholding that information, you could be endangering the lives of several people in Hillsborough, including your life and that of your niece. Out with it, once and for all!"

Her mouth twitched, a failed attempt at pulling her lips into a line. Her chin dropped another inch, and she shifted her gaze past his shoulder. "Violet's journal was here."

Surprise shoveled Michael's eyebrows up, hiked the pitch of his voice. "Today? Where? Did the burglar steal it?"

"No, not today." Aunt Rachel's head jerked back and forth, like a swimmer shaking water from his ears. "Two weeks ago. Ezra Griggs came to my door and gave me a wrapped package. Rot him! He told me he was leaving town for a few days, and if he wasn't back by Sunday the eleventh, yesterday, I was to take the package, unopened, to Schmidt and tell that beast that the package was evidence that Griggs had been murdered."

"What?" Kate's near-shriek made two syllables of the word. "Aunt, you never spoke of this to me at all!"

Michael jutted up his hand, palm outward, to silence Kate, and bored his gaze on Aunt Rachel. In his hour of need, Ezra Griggs had trusted a woman who disliked him and a man who Michael himself wouldn't have trusted as far as he could throw him.

At that instant, he understood the source of the older woman's reluctance to volunteer information. He soothed the bark in his tone. "Naturally you were curious about what was in the package after he'd made such a claim. Anyone would be curious. And Mr. Griggs put you in an awkward place, asking that of you when the two of you were barely on speaking terms, and when so much bad blood existed between you and Mr. Schmidt."

"Bad blood?" Kate sounded huffy. "Aunt Rachel, what's happened between you and Mr. Schmidt? I know you two don't care for each other's company, but this sounds like more than that."

Michael stayed focused on Aunt Rachel. "What a tarnish it would put upon your reputation of integrity if word leaked into the community that you'd had a peek at someone else's property. Of course, Kate and I won't tell anyone."

Aunt Rachel stomped her foot. "Rot Ezra Griggs!" This time, the invective rang against the rafters of the house.

"So you carefully opened the package and found that it was nothing more than a journal."

"Violet's journal. Can you imagine the conceit of Griggs, presuming that the blathering of his daughter was important enough to get him killed? He was crazy, I tell you!"

"How much of it did you actually read, madam?"

"The first three pages." She tossed her head. "A girl's journal is a secret thing, a private place to openly speak her mind and heart, where no one will censor her. I didn't need to read more than three pages to know what else was there. The nerve of that coot, toying with me in such a way."

"What did Violet write about?"

Her scowl buckled to create a clench of embitterment. " 'Today, I sketched Jimmy.' "

Michael's attention perked. "Jimmy?" His gaze darted back and forth, between the two women. "Who was—is—Jimmy?"

"The Griggs's horse," said Kate, her tone bland.

While Michael ejected a hard sigh of disappointment, Aunt Rachel pursed her lips into a girlish simper. " 'I adore my harpsichord. Papa wishes me to perform for his friends. I am the best harpsichord player in Hillsborough.' " The simper dissolved into disdain. "What a silly twit! She was the *only* harpsichord player in Hillsborough! You see what I mean? There was naught in that journal except Ezra Griggs's arrogance and Violet's vapidity." She rubbed her brow. "Whatever did my son see in that girl?"

Aunt Rachel hadn't read but the first three pages of the journal. Details for which a man might kill could well have lurked elsewhere among the reminiscences of a pampered girl. "So you wrapped up the package exactly as Mr. Griggs had given it to you, with him none the wiser when he came to fetch it after returning from his journey. Was that Saturday or yesterday?"

"Saturday."

"The killer conducted a messy search of the likeliest places in Mr. Griggs's house where the journal might have been hidden. Having failed to find it there, he came here for a similar search. Why? Was it because he knew there was once a connection between your two families?"

A thought snagged him, followed by horror rolling over him with the suspicion of what may actually have happened. Hoping the killer would spare his life Sunday, Griggs blurted out that the journal was hidden in Rachel White's house. But the killer had been unmoved.

Michael watched bluster on Aunt Rachel's face transition to puzzlement. He dared not frighten her with his suspicions about Griggs's final, desperate ploy. "Madam, I believe the murderer was, indeed, looking for Violet's journal, and that he believed it to contain information of a damaging nature to him. Do either of you have an idea where Mr. Griggs might have hidden it? A favorite spot in the yard, perhaps? Or in the stable with Jimmy?"

Both women shook their heads. Kate said in a practical, quiet tone, "Michael, that journal could be anywhere."

"But I feel certain that Ezra Griggs put it in a place nearby where he knew it would be safe, undisturbed. He expected to use it. That reminds me." He ducked into his room and retrieved the ruined portrait of Violet. "Is this her journal?" He held up the painting by the frame and pointed to the white book resting in Violet's lap.

Aunt Rachel fluttered her hand at the painting. "Yes, that's it."

A needle in a haystack, that's what Michael was looking for. He studied the canvas a few more seconds before returning the portrait to his room. Out on the landing again, he brought his attention back to Aunt Rachel. One of the dogs panted in the lull of conversation. The older woman fidgeted. One more piece of business to manage that night. "Madam, do you intend to tell your niece and nephew the full state of affairs between you and Georg Schmidt?"

Rachel White crossed arms over her chest. "I will not be driven out of Hillsborough."

"What?" Kate looked between them. "Aunt, what's going on? And how is it that Michael knows so much of it, and I, your own family member, know so little?"

Michael measured Aunt Rachel's attempt at bluster. "You know that this goes beyond what happened between you and Mr. Schmidt last summer."

"Indeed it does!" The older woman shook her finger at him. "Clarence and I have operated that tavern for almost thirty years."

He felt the agony beneath her bristle. "No one's questioning that, madam. But this isn't about your business competence. This is about something more important. Natural change that you've resisted." He glanced at Kate and found her expression one of bewilderment. "Change in the direction of fullness in your life, into the lives of two people who love you."

"See here, young man. Every business owner knows about the peaks and valleys of commerce. I've seen the cycle repeat for longer than you've been alive. Business is slow right now, but it'll pick back up again."

"Not this time. You know it as well as I."

"How dare you stomp into my life and tell me how to run my business, my family?"

"Pride is no substitute for family. As I understand it, Kate and Kevin are all the family you have left." He jutted his chin at Kate. "Look at your niece. Do you see how much she loves you? Hiding from her the truth of what happened last summer with Mr. Schmidt and Mr. Tierney doesn't change the business decision you must make. But it does deprive you of the counsel of another competent business owner, also a woman. You tell her the story, or I shall do so myself." He backed into the doorway of his room, a message bearer bowing out after completing his task.

To her credit, Rachel White straightened her arms and turned to her niece, responsibility composing her expression. "Very well. We will speak of this now, Kate."

Her expression mingling curiosity and apprehension, Kate followed her aunt into one of the other bedrooms without further acknowledging Michael. Meanwhile Lizzie and Sammy completed their hike to the landing and tried to dash past him into his room. "Ah, no you don't." He pointed for the women. "Go with them." And wet-nose someone else at five in the morning.

They complied. He withdrew and shut himself into the room. Weary from the day's many chases, he'd earned a night in bed, upstairs. Kate's alarm system, crude as it was, was adequate to penetrate his sleep.

Nevertheless, sleep eluded him like Ezra Griggs's killer. The sole dream he remembered was no stranger to him, but fragments from a nightmare he'd experienced several times. On his knees, immersed in the stench of the decomposing Spaniard's corpse on the ground before him, he anticipated the clout to the back of his head that shoved his face forward, almost into the flayed flesh of the Spaniard's torso. He also expected the harangue of Lieutenant Fairfax down his neck. "Here you are again, Stoddard, like a common idiot! And just as before, it stinks."

Michael gagged but didn't take a swing at Fairfax. Stomach muscles contracted just short of a heave, kept him sweating, panting like one of Aunt Rachel's hounds. Slathered in the miasma of decay, he grimaced. "Let me guess. The solution is right beneath my nose."

Fairfax shoved him between the shoulder blades. "If you know that much, why did you come back here? Why do you need my help solving this murder? Why am *I* your teacher?"

Michael awakened on the floor, where he'd sprawled, one leg tangled in the blanket on the bed. Jolted, achy, and stiff, he extricated himself from the snare and crawled back into bed. For the remainder of the night, clues, images, and evidence paraded across the insides of his eyelids every time he shut them.

Before dawn on Tuesday February thirteenth, he rose, lit the candle, and shocked his face with a splash of icy water from the washbasin. After dressing and pushing the curtains open, he completed his perusal of the sketches he'd collected from Violet's bedroom floor. At one point, he heard the dogs sniffing beneath his closed door, but he ignored their invitation to visit. No more pictures of fanged, horned monsters presented themselves from Violet's portfolio, but that didn't mean she hadn't drawn them. The quantity of feathers on the floor of her room had impaired the thoroughness of his search the day before.

The longer he studied the disturbing sketch, the more convinced he became that being incriminated as the molester of a young girl almost two decades in the past wasn't the scoundrel's primary motivation for wanting Violet's journal. A man who could afford quality products like a gig and two beef haunches, then discard them, had the resources to hire attorneys with the power to bury the words of a child who'd been the object of his carnal attentions. Unless Violet had detailed immutable proof in her journal that the man was some sort of spy or an assassin, Michael couldn't imagine what was in that journal to harm him.

Something else Tierney had said about the man in Noah's sketch returned to Michael. *I don't think he wanted her as a wife, but I got the impression that he didn't want anyone else to have her, either.* Beyond invincible selfishness, what did that imply about the murder suspect? Utter ruthlessness? Murderous rage? But why the ten-year gap in action?

Where had Ezra Griggs hidden his daughter's journal?

A light tap on his door drew him to the realization of a sky brightened with dawn outside the window. He left the sketches on the bed and opened the door to Kate's sleep-deprived and grim visage. "Martha arrived and started coffee. I think she's making flapjacks."

He nodded. "Where's your aunt?"

"In her study, looking over her finances." Kate's lower lip trembled, then stiffened. "She's agreed to put her property up for sale and move to Wilmington with Kevin and me."

Distress puckered Kate's mouth, creased her brow. Michael's congratulatory smile faltered. "Isn't that what you and your brother wanted?"

"Yes, but—" The tremble resurfaced in her lip. Her voice faded to a whispered stream of outrage. "Ye gods what Schmidt did to her. I never knew. Why didn't she tell us? I cannot imagine. I'd like to slap him across the face. If Kevin were here he'd demand that her honor—"

Michael seized her hand and yanked her into the room with him, surprising her, cutting off the cascade from her lips. "Listen to me," he said, low, still gripping her hand. "Keep your head down around Schmidt. And O'Toole, and all of Schmidt's minions. His story about being a Moravian is a lie. He's a deserter from a Hessian or Jäger regiment."

Her eyes widened. "How do you know this?"

"You think one soldier cannot recognize another?"

Her eyes widened even more. "But then that means he recognizes you."

"Yes. We've been playing quite a chess game with each other since I arrived on Sunday. O'Toole is likely a deserter, too—bloody Irish troublemaker—as are the rest of Schmidt's band. Most came from militia companies, I wager. Schmidt has the bearing of a regular, an officer. I also suspect that O'Toole may be in contact with Crown forces, posing as their loyalist spy while passing along information to the Continentals. And that means you and Aunt Rachel could be in great danger. Schmidt carries a grudge against your aunt, and you've both lied to protect my identity."

Her eyes narrowed, and the clasp of her hand with his firmed. "Schmidt won't learn that information from Aunt Rachel or me."

Her constancy chased the chill from the room, and in her eyes, he imagined the flecks of hunger that he'd seen the night before. His hand repositioned on hers with greater dedication. "He possesses contacts of which I'm unaware. Please, Kate. Don't underestimate him."

Much as he would have enjoyed taking advantage of intimacy invoked by proximity, stealing a hug from her or more under the guise of consolation, he allowed their fingers to slide apart. "I've something I want to ask you. It depends on how well you know Violet."

"Not extremely well. I think I told you that already."

He swiveled from her to pull the sketch of the monster-man off the bed and face it toward her. "I found this among her sketches. What does it suggest to you?"

She squinted at the sketch, her brows jammed inward. Michael watched her gaze rove across and process the details. Then her nostrils flared. Her shoulders drew upward. She covered her mouth with both hands and retreated a step. "Ugh! Oh, poor Violet!"

"My reaction, too. Let me show you something else." He laid the sketch on the bed beside Noah's near-profile sketch of the suspect in flight and pointed out the similarities in nose and chin shape. "Do you think Aaron or Mr. Griggs had an idea that something bad like this had happened to Violet?"

She shook her head. "I cannot say. I simply wasn't here enough. Janet Sewell would be a better resource for you. She was Violet's confidante."

"I plan to visit her this morning after breakfast. But Kate, I've only just met her. I doubt she'd open up to me about something like this." He drew a breath. "And I'm a man."

"Then I shall go with you. Perhaps my presence as a woman will help."

He smiled at her. "Thank you."

Her scrutiny returned to the sketches on the bed, and she dragged the bust shot atop the others. "You know, I had a dream about him last night." She shuddered. "You shall think me daft, but I dreamt he was chasing me through the streets of Wilmington."

Wilmington.

Michael whirled, hard, on Noah's sketch, his jaw dangling in shock. Beneath his nose, indeed. "It's the hair." He flipped sketches over, shoved them atop Noah's sketch to cover the suspect's black hair. "There. You see? Concentrate on his face, not his hair. We don't know him with dark hair—"

"—no, we know him with a powdered wig."

They gaped at each other and blurted in unison, "Horatio Bowater!"

Chapter Twenty-Six

OVER FLAPJACKS AND coffee in the dining room, Michael showed Noah's sketch of Bowater to Aunt Rachel. She recognized him and produced his name, the name she'd been trying to remember after the funeral the previous day. And she reiterated that he'd had an "unwholesome" way of looking at Violet Griggs.

His voice low to prevent Martha from overhearing, Michael informed Kate and her aunt of the investigation he'd turned over to Nick Spry in Wilmington: how Bowater swindled at least two clients on the same piece of land and set traps to deter access to his records books in his absence. Michael theorized that Ezra Griggs's long trip had been to Wilmington and back. Alice Farrell witnessed him challenging Bowater early on the morning of Monday the fifth of February. Bowater gave chase in his gig, expecting to overtake Griggs within a day and murder him. But Griggs made it home the following Saturday and retrieved Violet's journal from safekeeping with Aunt Rachel.

Kate drummed her fingers on the tabletop a few seconds. "If all that is what happened, explain why Mr. Griggs didn't kill Mr. Bowater at his office in Wilmington."

"Too many witnesses, such as Mrs. Farrell." Michael considered Griggs's parting words to Bowater: *You'll hang, just like all of them, and be buried in ground just as unhallowed.* "And since both men had originally opposed the Regulators, I suspect that Mr. Griggs wanted the satisfaction of seeing Mr. Bowater hanged, like a Regulator, a criminal."

She frowned. "But surely Mr. Griggs wouldn't have ridden ten days, just to confront Mr. Bowater about carnal designs on Violet years ago."

"I agree." Aunt Rachel emitted a brittle sigh, sat back, and crossed her arms over her chest. "Men can visit their vile acts upon children and elude punish-ment, but I tell you, if women could be jurors, verdicts would be vastly different for such scoundrels." She shot a glance at Michael. "You said that Mrs. Farrell in Wilmington mentioned a hanging, and burial in unhallowed ground. I'm afraid no judge will execute a man and bury him in a criminal's grave for fondling a young girl." She sniffed. "Men such as Horatio Bowater have enough money to hire attorneys that squeeze them out of those sorts of charges anyway. Likely the charges would have been dropped, and the creature would never have appeared in court."

Michael nodded. "So it must have been a crime in addition to this suspected inappropriate contact with Miss Griggs. As for the ten-year gap, perhaps Miss Griggs identified the crime worthy of execution in her journal, but her father only recently found her journal and read it."

Kate sipped coffee, set her cup on the table. " 'Crime worthy of execution.' Sounds like treason or murder to me. And we know from his actions—attempted maiming, burglary, murder—that the man is desperate to conceal his secret from ten years ago."

"That journal." Michael smacked the table once with his palm, clattering dishes. "I *must* find it. Mr. Griggs intended to use information in it to expose Mr. Bowater. He knew the value of the information, and he put it someplace safe. Mr. Bowater didn't find it when he turned the house inside out. It's still safe. I ask again, do either of you have any idea—" He trailed off, a bitter taste flooding his mouth, at the sight of both women shaking their heads in negation.

"Seems to me that even without the journal, you've enough evidence between Mr. Carroll's sketch and all the witnesses to have Mr. Bowater arrested under the suspicion of killing Mr. Griggs and burgling my house." Aunt Rachel cackled. "Take your evidence to that beast of a Prussian. He'll lay paws on him all right." She rubbed her palms together. "A few of his practices definitely didn't come from the Moravians. Rest assured that Mr. Bowater will confess within a day of his capture."

Michael's mouth dried. She had no idea of the brutality she was calling down upon Bowater. Outside, Sammy and Lizzie barked, indicating the arrival of a visitor. "Madam, Mr. Schmidt was never Moravian. He's a deserter from the Hessians or Jägers, trained to kill. His deputies are all deserters." He swallowed. "Stay clear of Georg Schmidt for at least another day while I tie up the ends of this inquiry." And he hoped he could tie up the ends.

Aunt Rachel's face paled. She whispered, "How do you know all this about Mr. Schmidt?"

Renewed barks from the hounds preceded a firm knock on the front door. The two women stiffened. A chilly scrawl of premonition scrolled over Michael's scalp. He let out a held breath and pushed to his feet, depositing his napkin beside his plate. "Martha is likely out in the kitchen. I shall answer the door." Without waiting for their response, he left the dining room.

The window closest to the door allowed him to see the dogs sniffing with curiosity at the shoes of a fellow in his early twenties dressed entirely in black and standing with otherworldly calm before the front door, his hat still between his hands. Michael recognized him from two days earlier, the town undertaker's journeyman. His eyes darted to the street, where a wagon had parked before Aunt Rachel's walkway. More chills stalked his scalp. He opened the door.

"Good morning, sir," said the soft voice that communed with the dead. "Is Mrs. Rachel White at home?"

"My aunt is at breakfast. May I deliver a message to her?"

"Yes, sir. My master, Abijah Pratt, has sent me to fetch her with all haste. He's on his deathbed, has information he must convey to her about her son, and begs her to tend him."

Michael's stomach squeezed and twisted the flapjacks he'd eaten. Secrets carried to the brink of death weren't usually good secrets. A glance past the journeyman took him beyond the wagon. He realized that the street was empty, uncluttered from various conveyances of Matthew Tierney's Olympians. Maybe the dandy had listened to him the previous night. Michael opened the door wider for the journeyman. "Come in. I shall fetch her."

From the rack beside the door, he grabbed the cloaks for Kate and her aunt, as well as their hats. Then he bustled into the dining room and proclaimed the news. While helping an ashen-faced Aunt Rachel into her cloak, he assured her that he'd tell Martha about her abrupt departure. He bundled Kate out after her. "Stay with her," he murmured. "When you learn what Mr. Pratt knows, come find me."

Her cheeks had paled. "Where will you be?"

"Where does Janet Sewell live?" Not that he expected Violet's friend to confide in him, but at least he must try to learn what she knew. Kate gave him directions for the east end of Tryon Street. "I may be there, or at Ezra Griggs's house. Possibly Mr. Schmidt's office at the jail, a bit later. I must still deliver the love note to him before nine."

He saw both women seated in the wagon and watched them drive off with the journeyman at the reins. Foreboding dried his lungs with every breath he took of winter morning. He whipped about and strode for the kitchen, where he updated Martha.

With the love letter, sketches, and canvas bag of cane halves, he strode east on Tryon Street until he found the brick manor, so like Tierney's, home of gout-ridden Francis Sewell and his daughter. Michael had no idea whether Miss Sewell was even awake. He manipulated a brass knocker on the front door to bang out his presence on the step at quarter to eight in the morning. A butler in dark gray wool much finer than the fabric of the suit Michael wore answered the door. The servant's gaze grazed the length of Michael like the jagged edge of a glacier. Michael said, "Mrs. Rachel White's nephew, Mr. Compton, to see Miss Sewell, briefly."

The butler's nostrils expanded. "Have you an appointment?"

"Tell her I've news of her friend, Violet Griggs."

Michael barely sprang back before the butler pushed the door closed. Blood seethed in his veins over pompous gatekeepers who possessed no concept of stakes larger than their own ingratiation with their employers. He counted to thirty before his breathing resumed a rhythm less ragged with rage. "Bum fodder," he muttered.

Less than a minute later, the door was whisked open by the lady herself, fully dressed and quite awake. "Mr. Compton?" Anticipation and perhaps dread widened her eyes. "Stiles says you wish to speak with me about Violet?" The butler scowled in the shadows over her shoulder.

Michael inclined his head. "Madam. Are more private circumstances available than your front step for our conference?"

"Come with me." She opened the door wider and admitted him. Michael followed her, the plod of the butler behind them.

After he'd been directed into a spacious, book- and map-lined study, Miss Sewell blocked Stiles's access at the double doorway. "Mistress," the butler said from without, "I remind you, your father ordered that you not be alone with—"

"Then awaken him and inform him of my defiance," she barked. "Not until three this morning did he find sleep, so great was his pain." She shoved the doors shut on the butler.

For a quarter minute, she stood with her back to Michael, the wild expansion of her ribcage calming. Then she faced him, a composed hostess. "Would you care for coffee?"

"No, thank you."

"Please, be seated." She indicated a chair with gold-embroidered upholstery and took a seat beside him in a matching chair.

Stiles might be so crass as to disturb the pain-tormented slumber of an ailing gentleman. Michael bypassed the chitchat and withdrew Noah's sketch of Bowater's face. "Let me show you a portrait of the man who most certainly murdered your father's friend, Ezra Griggs, on Sunday." He unfolded the paper toward her.

A rattle trailed from her throat. In a blur, she evacuated her chair and stood between him and the doors, as if prepared to flee the room. "No!"

Puzzled, Michael rose and glanced from the sketch to the woman. "What is it? What's wrong?"

She aimed a trembling forefinger at the sketch. "It's—it's him!"

"Do you recognize him? What's his name?"

"B-B-Bowater. He's the one." Her palms folded over her throat.

"He's the one?"

Miss Sewell pressed fingertips to her lips and shook her head, her eyes imploring.

He put away Noah's portrait, then withdrew the monster-man picture. "Violet sketched this picture. What do you make of it?" He flipped the paper about to face her.

A lamentation, half-moan and half-shriek, tore from her, and she pivoted from him. Michael saw her fumble in a pocket for a handkerchief and stagger a step away. From the intensity of her reaction, he was willing to wager that she'd witnessed Bowater afflicting Violet with his affections when the two girls were quite young. Breakfast turned to vinegar in his stomach.

A shudder convulsed Miss Sewell. Alarmed that she might be woozying into a faint, Michael dropped the sketch on the seat of his chair and rushed to her side. "Miss Sewell, I apologize—"

"Dear God, you say he killed Ezra Griggs?"

"Yes, madam, he did. And he burgled the home of my aunt, Rachel White. I'm so sorry to distress you. May I assist you back to your chair?"

"No." She shrugged his hand off her elbow. "Mr. Griggs wanted that rascal to marry Violet."

"Yes, I've heard."

"So very wicked." Her voice lowered. "He should have been executed long ago for his crimes." In profile, her eye glimmered with tears. She hung her head.

Her gaze wandered the rug the way a mariner adrift for weeks in fog searched the sky for stars. Her fingers twisted the handkerchief.

The language of her anguish hooked Michael, snaked back in time and anchored in the anguish of a seventeen-year-old, withdrawn and haunted, even after his tormenter had returned to her London town home. "You're too clever to spend your life cleaning the mews," his family and Lord Crump cheerily told him, "so here's your chance to make something of your life." He accepted a uniform, an ensign's commission, and a voyage to the other side of the Atlantic: traded the ravage of sex for the ravage of war. Nine years later, was the seventeen-year-old still searching for clear sky?

Harshness infiltrated Janet Sewell's whisper, recalling Michael to Hillsborough. "I would kill him myself if I could. We were only eight years old."

We. The room tilted. *Eight years old.* Nausea gripped Michael's gut, then retreated on a storm of virulent fury. Violet hadn't been Bowater's only victim in Hillsborough. His mind clutched a fact from memory. Bowater had originally come from the North. Was it possible that he'd been molesting young girls in his home colony, and some relative had shipped him to North Carolina to diminish scandal, foist the problem onto others?

Color forsook her face. Her lips moved, a testament barely audible. "He favored Violet."

Michael stared, empty of words, the lameness of any dialogue at that point aching and apparent. Janet Sewell knew she was ugly, knew her own unattractiveness had repulsed a man's unnatural affections onto her dear friend. She'd hung back, a child with no voice in the justice system, unable to do anything while Violet's childhood was ruined.

Sometimes the witness to a crime suffered even greater torment than the victim.

Miss Sewell lifted her head but didn't look at him. "Violet so deserves love. Aaron was sweet on her, but I didn't think she cared that much for him. I hope she's grown to love him."

Desperation surged in Michael's chest. He had to walk back to his chair to hide suspicions that tensed his jaw. For the moment, he let Miss Sewell believe that Aaron and Violet had eloped, a happy ending like those in Kate's novels. That morning, though, he'd begun to wonder whether the couple had, indeed, run away together.

With the sketch of the monster folded and put away, and his back to Violet's friend, he said in as soothing a voice as he could manage, "Miss Sewell, I believe that Mr. Griggs found his daughter's journal several weeks ago and read it. Something she wrote in it revealed dangerous information about Mr. Bowater. Information that he was involved in a crime that could get him executed. Mr. Griggs then challenged Mr. Bowater with the truth and was murdered several days later." Over his shoulder, Michael regarded her. She hadn't moved. "Mr. Bowater came to Hillsborough and ransacked Mr. Griggs's house in search of the journal, but it appears that he's been unable to find it. Have you any idea where Mr. Griggs might have hidden it?"

"No." She swiveled back to him then, her face blotched with unshed tears, and he turned to face her full on. "I heard about his house being destroyed during the search." Her lower lip trembled, and her crooked upper teeth caught it, stilled it. "Her harpsichord, vandalized." She sighed, gripped her hands as if in prayer. "Do you know who told me that?"

He shook his head, watching the tremors in her hands and the quiver of handkerchief between them.

"Mr. Tierney told me. He came by at seven-fifteen this morning to tell me."

Mild surprise wound through Michael. Had Matthew Tierney been romantically involved with Janet Sewell, too?

"He was sober." Irony tinged her short laugh. "The first time I've seen him sober in many years. You might not know this, but he was sweet on Violet once, too. He told me this morning that Violet's harpsichord had been intentionally damaged in the attack. You cannot imagine how wicked and cruel it was of the criminal to do such a thing.

"You see, Violet loved that harpsichord. And her father was delighted that she adored his gift to her. So for someone to destroy such a priceless treasure—" She broke off, dabbed her eyes with her handkerchief.

Violet loved that harpsichord. The message, spoken now by a third person, at last carried the weight to slow the forward motion of babble in Michael's brain, force him to halt and examine in memory the harpsichord as he'd experienced it the evening before. Sturdy. Unassuming. Lid lowered all the way.

Memory repeated the octave-long stroll his fingers had taken upon the keys until denied pleasant melody by a dull, plunking sound. Damage to the inner workings of several keys, he'd assumed, vandalism committed out of rage. But what if the explanation for the malfunctioning keys were simpler than that?

He shouldn't have let himself be distracted by the proximity of his meeting with Schmidt the previous evening. He should have followed through, opened the harpsichord's lid.

Excitement swelling in his chest, he collected his belongings. "Miss Sewell, I appreciate your audience. Your information has been quite helpful."

"It has?" A blend of sadness and hope transformed her face from ugly to plain. "Will you be able to bring Mr. Bowater to justice for killing my father's friend?"

With pertinent information from the journal pegging Bowater, Schmidt would be forced to act out of justice, search for and arrest the land agent. "It looks that way."

He obtained Miss Sewell's assurance that she'd be in town that day, should he have further questions of her. Then he accepted her escort to the front door. Outside, he noticed a cart track curving northwest from the east end of Tryon Street. With luck, it would deposit him on Queen Street, near the Carroll and Griggs houses. He set off at a trot, less than an hour remaining before Schmidt expected him to produce Mr. Kirkleigh's love letter to Peaches. But hope buoyed him for the first time in nearly two days.

Chapter Twenty-Seven

THE FRONT DOOR of Ezra Griggs's house was padlocked shut. The back door was locked from the inside. Excitement that had pumped Michael's veins moments before dwindled.

Of course Schmidt had locked the house. It was the scene of a murder under investigation. But Michael didn't want those deserters present when he found Violet's journal. He wanted the opportunity to examine the evidence himself, discover what information the young woman had written that so threatened and incensed Horatio Bowater.

On the west side of the house, he pushed at windows. The study window shifted about a quarter inch and stuck, as if humidity had pasted it. Unable to wiggle his fingers beneath the sash and gain leverage, Michael shoved at it more, but it refused to budge. Perhaps he'd have better luck with a dining room window on the east side.

He swiveled about and spotted Noah's approach from his back yard, a foot-long crowbar in one hand. Blake Carroll waved to Michael from the back step. "Morning, laddie. Thought you might could use this here tool for your work."

Relief and gratitude trickled through Michael. "Thank you, Mr. Carroll."

"Never thought I'd be an accessory to breaking into my neighbor's house." The old man flashed a crooked smile and reentered his house.

Noah reached the west side of Griggs's house and handed the crowbar to Michael, who nodded his thanks, then worked the window open and gained leverage for his hands. He returned the crowbar to Noah and shoved some more. The wood emitted a bad-tempered groan, but the window rose, creating enough space to crawl in.

Noah signed his desire to join him in the house. Michael hesitated, his initial thought to work alone. But he considered that if he were wrong about the harpsichord, Noah's sharp eyes might help him detect evidence he'd overlooked. "Come along, then." Noah clambered inside at his gestured invitation, and they shut the window.

Michael trod with care around the wreck of books and furniture Bowater had made in the study, relieved that Noah mirrored his caution. In the foyer, Noah grimaced at the stench of death, which had intensified overnight. Michael directed him to the foot of the stairs, handed him the canvas sack, and asked him to wait there.

In the parlor, he retraced the route he'd taken around the couch until he reached the harpsichord, aware that Noah observed his actions. After setting the violin on the floor, Michael lifted the lid on the harpsichord with one hand.

The cream-colored book that had rested in Violet's lap for her portrait lay atop the strings for several keys, impeding the resonance produced from jack and plectrum. Michael whooped with victory, then hollered, "Thank you, Ezra Griggs!"

He claimed the journal, lowered the harpsichord's lid, almost tripped over the violin in giddy delight, then replaced it atop the harpsichord. Noah awaited his return to the foyer with a grin, responsive to the visual language of triumph. Michael held up the journal when he reached the other man. "The killer was searching for this."

"Vy-let write." Noah tapped the surface of the journal.

"Yes, and now I must read."

Noah nodded, sat on the third step and waited, patient, pleased to be part of action that extended beyond his property, action that involved justice. Michael entered the dining room and selected for himself a chair with a seat that had escaped Bowater's blasts of broken china. When he made himself comfortable, he flipped pages to the end, for Aunt Rachel had already apprised him of the journal's beginning. The final entry was dated June eighteenth, 1771, the day before the Regulators were hanged. Stark and short, it read: *Dear God, Mr. White's plan failed abysmally. Mr. Bowater must actually have mistreated girls in New York, too! We called his bluff. Now he's threatened and angered. He follows me everywhere. I fear for my life. I see no choice but to leave.*

Michael shuddered, certain that if winter rain had dribbled beneath his collar, it could not have coated his skin with a more thorough and frigid film than Violet's fear. The unambiguous nature of her fear shocked him, even with Aunt Rachel's words in memory: *A girl's journal is a secret thing, a private place to openly speak her mind and heart.* He felt guilty reading words that Violet had never intended for the eyes of another person.

Nevertheless, he reread the entry. *I see no choice but to leave.* Strange that she hadn't added "with Aaron." And that was when he realized that she'd called him "Mr. White," not "Aaron," which would have signified intimacy.

Maybe she hadn't left with Aaron. Although Aunt Rachel believed that Aaron and Violet had eloped, and town folklore perpetrated the legend, neither Violet's best friend nor her former suitor seemed convinced of a love bond between Violet and Aaron. The curious lack of intimacy in her reference to Rachel White's son substantiated that. But if Violet had run off by herself, where was Aaron all these years?

Michael thumbed back about ten pages, several weeks before the executions, and read: *Mr. Bowater laughed at my refusal and told me he wouldn't have me for a wife. But if I marry another, he said he would kill me.*

As Michael read farther back in time, Violet's story crept over him, sinking more hooks of horror and disgust into his soul. The pattern emerged: Violet trying to tell her father about how Bowater frightened her. Ezra Griggs always occupied with a business meeting or a social event. Either Bowater hid his abuse of Violet, and Griggs never saw it, or Griggs denied it to preserve business contacts. Not only had he never become his daughter's advocate, but he'd narrowed her world: *We are not to be married after all. Papa doesn't want a son-in-law who has sympathy for Regulators. Part of me is relieved to bid adieu to the fuss, yet after all our work together, I fancy I might not have been too unhappy as Mrs. Tierney.*

She had earlier mentioned "Mr. Tierney," not Matthew. No one, not even the dandy, had gained access to Violet's heart. Horatio Bowater had seen to that.

The faint queasiness filtering through Michael's belly affirmed his understanding on the most primitive level. He'd felt safe romping with tavern wenches and laundresses. None of them had sought his heart—but then he hadn't been capable of giving it.

Nine years of war's carnage wasn't the culprit. His gaze shot across the foyer to the harpsichord. Memory called up Handel, rendered by Lydia's fingers on the keys of Lord Crump's harpsichord less than an hour after her fingers had played across Michael's naked thighs.

In the foyer, Noah stood to stretch his legs. He ambled to the front window, where he leaned against a wall, out of sight of anyone looking at the house, and gazed out at the morning. Michael regained his concentration and returned to Violet's journal.

After the spring of 1771, he picked out Violet's references to "Mr. White," descriptors such as "kind," "cheerful," and "courteous." Apparently, because she reflected those qualities back to Aaron, the idealistic young man with a clubfoot grew smitten with her. By early June, he'd wrangled pieces of the Bowater history from her. From that point onward, Michael realized that Aaron became Violet's champion—and Horatio Bowater's competition.

Bowater had delighted in harassing Violet. Aaron the knight stepped forward with a plan to save his princess. The two of them would challenge the dragon, claim that they had evidence of his past misconduct in his home colony of New York. They would order Bowater to leave Violet alone, or they'd ruin his career by telling Governor Tryon of his peccadillo.

Aaron and Violet couldn't have acted in a more foolish manner. The dragon hadn't backed down. Michael's stomach churned with grief, anger.

If Ezra Griggs had read the entire testimonial two weeks ago and paid attention, he'd have recognized that he failed his daughter on an epic scale, worthy of the quill of Will Shakespeare, maybe even that of Homer or Euripides. It would have seemed as obvious to Griggs as it seemed to Michael that Violet and Aaron hadn't eloped ten years ago—that in the chaos of the Regulator trials and executions, and all the comings and goings of so many strangers in Hillsborough, Bowater had found a way to quietly kill the young couple and dispose of their bodies, then leave town in Tryon's entourage the day following the executions, and get away with two murders.

"Damn you, Griggs!" Michael slammed the tabletop with his fist. Broken china jumped and clattered with the vibration. Noah pushed one step from the window toward the dining room and stood straight, shoulders back, his wide, questioning eyes on Rachel White's nephew.

Michael ignored him and brushed off his fist. Chill hollowed his bones. If he'd been Griggs, sitting alone in his house and grown older alone, a discovery of probable murder that had deprived him of children and grandchildren, even ten years after the fact, would have supplied him with plenty of motivation to hunt down the dragon, ride more than a week on horseback for the satisfaction of challenging him. No, Griggs wouldn't have killed him. Griggs had waited ten years for justice. He could wait a bit longer to taste the revenge he wanted most: seeing Bowater thrash in a noose, destined for the same unhallowed ground as their adversaries a decade earlier.

The information in Violet's journal reinforced Michael's impression of Griggs and curtailed any empathy he might have felt for him. The man had used Rachel White. He'd placed her in the position of presenting evidence to Schmidt, whom she despised, and he'd likely routed Bowater to her house in search of the journal. For many years, Violet had been clear about her torment. From the words she left behind, Michael saw no indication that she was ever happy, except when she played her harpsichord. What a pathetic life. He bowed his head. The emptiness of the house resounded in his heart.

Noah gave his shoulder a brisk shake. Then he pointed to the front door. Michael had heard no knock. Someone must be approaching the house. He stood, slid the chair beneath the table, snatched up the canvas bag, and strode to the closest window, the journal still in his hand.

Kate jogged up the walkway, one hand lifting her petticoat enough to allow easier strides, the other gripping a shawl about her shoulders. Her cheeks and nose were flushed, and she bit her lower lip. She hauled up short at the sight of the padlocked door. Her expression crumpled.

Michael thrust the journal and canvas bag at Noah and fumbled open the window. "Kate, go round to the back door! I shall let you in."

She nodded and flew for the side yard. He slammed the window shut and motioned for Noah to follow him. When he slid the bar aside and opened the rear door, Kate awaited him on the back step. She rushed inside, her breath ragged. After he slid the bar across on the closed door, there was enough light for him to discern her eyelashes, dampened and darkened.

"Abijah Pratt the undertaker has died." Her voice sounded thick. "But not before he t-told Aunt." She smashed her palm to her mouth a few seconds, as if by holding in her words, she could hold back the truth an instant longer.

"At dusk on the day the six Regulators were executed, a m-man drove up in a wagon before the shop and spoke with Pratt, alone. Said he w-was one of Governor Tryon's officials. While the governor's men were rounding up rebels that afternoon, one man had resisted arrest and been killed. A militia surgeon had dressed him for burial, loaded the b-body in the wagon."

Kate sucked in a hurried breath, as if afraid someone would interrupt her. "P-Pratt's visitor said that Tryon's orders were that the criminal be cast in the c-common grave with the six criminals hanged that morning. No further words were to be spoken of it, or the undertaker would experience penalties directly from the office of the royal governor."

Dread compressed Michael's breath, stiffened his face. Beyond Kate's shoulder, Noah's eyes had widened with apprehension.

Kate gulped, steadied her next breath, loosened her shawl. "Pratt and an apprentice unloaded the b-body from the wagon. The man drove off. They carried the body out b-back, loaded it on their wagon with the wrapped bodies of the six hanged men. The apprentice stepped away for a moment. Then Pratt noticed that the shroud wrapping the s-seventh man had loosened about the f-feet. When he rewrapped it, he recognized the c-clubfoot." Kate flailed her hands about, trying to find more words.

Michael leapt into the tight silence. "Did Pratt name the man who brought the body?"

She stared at the floor and shook her head, a jerky motion. "He d-didn't know him by name, but he'd seen him in town, a fellow of medium height and d-dark hair, always in the company of Tryon's land agents. He'd no r-reason to believe the story was a lie. Rumors circulated that Violet and Aaron had eloped. He didn't have the h-heart to tell Aunt Rachel and Uncle Clarence that their Regulator son had been k-killed that afternoon while resisting arrest."

Dull finality bowed Michael's shoulders, certainty without satisfaction. "I'm—Kate, I'm sorry, so sorry. This is—it's terrible." Ever awkward around grieving women, Michael winced at how lame his words sounded. He hadn't the slightest idea what to do for her, beyond keeping his mouth shut of any platitudes. For sure, it wasn't the precise moment to tell her that Horatio Bowater had likely murdered both Aaron and Violet. And Aunt Rachel was probably wild with grief back at the house. "Why—why did you come all the way over here? Why didn't you send Martha to tell me?"

He glanced at Noah. The deaf man gaped at him, hard, as if Michael were a celebrated actor who had irreparably botched his lines on opening night at Drury Lane, with a full house, and nobility in every box. Perplexity blasted Michael. He straightened and stared back, anxiety a hot lump in his throat. What? *What* had he done wrong just now?

Kate lifted her head, eyes brimming with unshed grief. "Because I—I came here b-because you—" Her hands raised, palms up, beseeching. "You—"

In Michael's peripheral vision, Noah hugged himself, blatant cue from the irate stage director. Less the investigator, more the friend, Michael realized. He could have kicked himself for being such an insensitive oaf. He clasped Kate's hands and guided her into his arms. She released a wail and sobbed into his shoulder. Noah dispensed a curt nod of approval, tucked the journal inside his waistcoat, and wandered off toward the front of the house.

Michael's sister Miriam's firstborn had been a stillbirth. The role of comforter fit him no better in 1781 than nine years earlier, when he'd held Miriam in his arms, his throat devoid of words to ease the sorrow. To his bemusement, after Miriam had drenched his shoulder with her tears, she'd kissed his cheek and thanked him for the wordless solace. A lesson learned: those who grieved the loss of a loved one didn't need that void filled with words.

Kate spent her tears quickly but didn't rush to unfold herself from the curved warmth of their bodies. Not in the slightest did he mind the minutes he spent listening to her breathing return to normal, his hands on the small of her back. At last, she said, muffled, "I wasn't here much in 1771, but I find it so difficult to believe that Aaron has been dead all this time, that he'd become deeply enough involved with the Regulators to die for their cause."

He decided not to keep his findings from her any longer. His murmur brushed her lace mobcap. "I think your instincts are accurate, Kate. I found Violet's journal and read it. Horatio Bowater pressured her constantly, made her fear for her life. Aaron thought to rescue her and concocted a plan, a bluff of blackmail. But he drew Bowater's wrath upon both of them instead."

She trembled. "Oh, dear God! You believe the man who delivered Aaron's body to Pratt was Mr. Bowater." Her head shifted, and she nestled her cheek against his shoulder so she could speak easier, but she still made no move to dislodge herself from his arms. "If Aaron didn't elope with Violet—"

"All these years, Violet must be dead also."

Her sigh sounded pitiful. "Yes. Ezra Griggs found out Mr. Bowater's secret by reading the journal. And now he's dead, too." He didn't imagine reluctance in the lift of her head off his shoulder, or in her step back from him.

He dropped his hands to his sides. Her expression needed no translation. He knew his moral duty. "I will apprehend Mr. Bowater and bring him to justice. I hope Mr. Schmidt will work with me." But he had a bad feeling Schmidt wasn't going to cooperate.

Noah rushed back to them in a blur that was, to Michael's amazement, almost silent. Apprehension tensed the deaf man's face. He pointed to the front door and performed a perfect pantomime of Schmidt's carriage and expression. Michael heard Schmidt's voice approaching, in conversation on the walkway. The sheriff must have brought henchmen with him.

Michael squashed down the swell of panic in his stomach. Cold sweat broke out across his forehead and on his palms. Was he late for his nine o'clock appointment at jail? Had someone reported his break-in through the study window? Maybe Schmidt had decided to plant more false evidence in the house. Since he had to meet with Schmidt anyway, he knew he had to act as a front guard and protect the two people with him. He grabbed the canvas bag from Noah, tiptoed for the stairs, and gestured for both the deaf man and Kate to hide upstairs.

Noah motioned for Kate to precede him, gripped the crowbar with determination, and followed her up. In the foyer alone, Michael blotted sweat off his face with his coat sleeve, fumbled for his watch—eight minutes to nine—then composed emotion on his face to belie his vulnerability and the hammer of his pulse.

The padlock clattered off the front door. He backed from the door a few steps to give the men room. The door swung open, flooding the foyer with sunlight, and Schmidt stomped in. His entire, huge body wrenched in shock at the sight of Michael.

Michael grinned. "Good morning! Lovely day, isn't it?"

The foyer filled with Schmidt's deserters. They surrounded him, ten men total. Schmidt barreled up to within a foot of him, nose hairs bristling. "*Schwein!* What are you doing here?"

Spittle flecked Michael's face. He forced himself to not flinch or reach for his handkerchief. But he dropped the smile. "I'm not due to present my aunt's love letter to you until nine, and you seemed disappointed last night by my progress on the investigation. So I thought to drop by Mr. Griggs's house before our meeting, see whether daylight would help me find additional—"

Breath whooshed from him as Schmidt shoved him backward with a push to the chest. He landed almost atop O'Toole, who sneered and balled his fists. Michael swallowed, regained his poise and some distance from the Irishman. This was not going as well as he'd hoped.

Schmidt's eyes had narrowed on him. "How did you get in this house?"

Without taking his gaze off him, Michael pointed over his shoulder. "Study window. It was unlocked."

Schmidt scoured his men with a glare. His fists punched air once. "*Lappeduddelen!* Which one of you forgot to lock the window?" The pitch of his voice ascended as he delivered the question.

Men shuffled their feet. No one confessed. Much as Michael would have enjoyed watching Schmidt pound away on his minions until he obtained a culprit, there were two people upstairs who needed his protection, so he must move the festivities in the foyer along. He dropped a dollop of practicality into his tone. "No harm done, I assure you, because in addition to having my aunt's letter for you this morning, I have learned the identity of Mr. Griggs's murderer."

Men stopped shuffling and grew still. Schmidt's blue-eyed gaze wheeled about and nailed Michael with a hard frost. "What is the name of this murderer?"

"Horatio Bowater." Michael pulled Noah's facial portrait of Bowater from his pocket. "Remember this sketch? I showed it around several taverns last night. A number of fellows who'd lived here from the days of the Regulators identified him for me."

His face empty of expression, Schmidt pawed the portrait from Michael's grasp, folded it without so much as a glance at it, and shoved it in his pocket. "Bowater does not reside in Hillsborough."

"Not any more. He left Hillsborough in June of 1771 with Governor Tryon, right after the executions. Witnesses believe he has been living in Wilmington all this time."

"*Du Dummbeudel.* What motive would he have for coming back here and killing Mr. Griggs ten years later?"

Michael thought of the journal upstairs, in Noah's waistcoat, and instinct screamed at him to not deliver it into the hands of Schmidt. "Good question. I wondered that myself." He licked his lips, aware that his pulse hammered in his temple, aware that Schmidt was wholly unimpressed with his presentation but smelled his nervousness the way a bear sensed fear in prey. "As it turns out, witnesses also informed me that Mr. Griggs had affianced his daughter, Violet, for a short while to Mr. Bowater. Mr. Bowater grew enraged with jealousy when Miss Griggs refused him in favor of my cousin, Aaron White."

Dizzy over the precipice of fear, Michael balanced himself on a blade-edge of truth. "My family and I believed all this time that Aaron had eloped with Violet right after the Regulators' execution." He gulped again. "But the undertaker told Aunt Rachel from his deathbed this morning that Mr. Bowater had brought him Aaron's body, wrapped for burial, the night of the executions and claimed that Aaron was a Regulator who must be buried with the six hanged men."

Schmidt's eyes had begun to glaze. Michael was losing him. He hurried the rest. "I assure you, Aaron wasn't a Regulator. Mr. Bowater murdered him and covered the crime with the Rebellion and executions. Since Violet vanished at the same time, I presume that she, too, was murdered. Somehow, perhaps Mr. Griggs recently came across evidence that pointed to Mr. Bowater as his daughter's murderer. He might have thought to extort money from Mr. Bowater. We all know how being extorted angers a man. So Mr. Bowater drove his gig all the way here from Wilmington, arrived late on Sunday, parked his horse and gig down that trail behind the house, and murdered Mr. Griggs. He tore the house apart looking for whatever piece of evidence had alerted Mr. Griggs of the murder but was unable to—"

"Enough of this, *Engländer!* O'Toole, search him!"

Chapter Twenty-Eight

THE IRISHMAN BOUNDED forward like a blooded terrier scenting another dog in the pit, yanked the canvas bag from Michael, and tossed it to Schmidt. Then he used a body search to repay Michael for the knee to the groin. Michael anticipated it, deflected the worst, and doubled over to look the part and please O'Toole.

The Irishman relieved him of dagger and purse, then confiscated Noah's other sketch, Violet's monster sketch, and the love letter to Peaches. The first two he passed to Schmidt, who pocketed them after a cursory examination. But O'Toole waved about the love letter. "Hoo, listen to this, lads!" Apparently somewhat nearsighted, he brought the letter beneath his nose. " 'You lay on the blanket, the dapple of sunlight and leaf shade across your bodice, your smile soft and moist from kisses.' " O'Toole chortled. Several other men sniggered.

Michael's spine stiffened. What if he hadn't made the references in the letter obscure enough, and Schmidt found a way to shame Aunt Rachel after all? "By God, I didn't think I'd ever meet an Irishman who could *read*."

"You *Sasanach* pile of shit!"

Schmidt's paw shot out and collared O'Toole in mid-lunge. He pinched the love letter from the Irishman and shoved it in his pocket, then flung him away. The halves of Tierney's cane gripped in one hand, he stalked Michael. "Explain this cane."

Michael didn't have to fake a stammer. "I-I found it beneath the h-harpsichord." He forced his chin to rise. "From the gouges on the side of the harpsichord, I deduced that someone broke the cane in half, vandalized the instrument with it."

Schmidt's thumb stroked the metal initial set in the head of the cane. "The letter embossed in the head of this cane is a 'T.' The name Bowater starts with a 'B.' "

"Even more peculiar is that neither violin nor harpsichord was damaged Sunday, when I arrived in the house just after Mr. Griggs's murder. Someone entered the parlor later with this cane and damaged the harpsichord. I don't believe Mr. Griggs's murderer was responsible for it."

Schmidt extended his face toward Michael, as if prepared to kiss him. "The murderer," he said softly, "was looking for Miss Griggs's journal." Teeth showed in Schmidt's smile. "Mr. *Stoddard.*"

Michael felt his face grow rigid before he relaxed his jaw. "My name is Compton." He held Schmidt's horrible glare. Beneath his shirt, a thousand ants of terror scouted his skin.

How had Schmidt learned his name? How had he figured out that Bowater was looking for Violet's journal?

Teeth took over the sheriff's face, filled Michael's field of view. "Lieutenant Michael Stoddard of the Eighty-Second Regiment, currently occupying Wilmington, commanded by Major James Henry Craig." Schmidt chuckled. "I left two men at jail to arrest you when you arrived. I planned to search this house for the journal. Then I planned to search the house of that lying shrew, Rachel White, and deal with her. But finding you here and listening to how well you spin *Scheiße* has been even more entertaining.

"You will come with me to jail now, Mr. Stoddard. All night long, a friend has been waiting there to be reunited with you. I will search houses after I finish with you."

Michael departed Griggs's property encircled by deserters. His wrists ached, bound behind him. His knees wobbled a sailor's gait, and a pulse of peril hammered inside his ears. Desperate as his own situation looked, though, his consolation was that Kate and Noah might escape Griggs's house undetected, for every man from Schmidt's posse strutted around him to celebrate the successful hunt. And before a brutal deserter finished amusing himself with a British officer in jail, maybe Kate would have time to withdraw to a safe location with Aunt Rachel.

All night long, a friend has been waiting there to be reunited with you. Obviously Schmidt had captured Bowater, who had recognized Michael during their chase in the maze of market stalls the previous day. Schmidt interrogated Michael's identity and the information about the journal from the land agent. The sheriff would heave Michael into a cell with Bowater, let the two of them explore the permutations of justice delivered with fists, and watch the sport through the grate on the door. Better than dogfights and cockfights. And because Schmidt was motivated to make sure the winner, whoever he was, never left jail alive, the streets of Hillsborough would be purged of murderers and British officers alike.

What Michael didn't understand was why Schmidt hadn't pulverized him first. Plenty of opportunity to do so in Griggs's house, and he knew Schmidt personalized his job with such practices. Not that Michael was complaining, but with the exception of O'Toole, whom Schmidt kept on leash, all the deserters treated him with tender care.

No stool awaited him in Schmidt's dingy den this time, although the reek of piss and puke seemed to have intensified overnight. Michael slouched before the desk, clinging to the identity of Compton, naval stores merchant from

Cross Creek. The chair behind the desk groaned torment when Schmidt lowered himself onto it. O'Toole assumed position behind his master. Multiple footsteps approached, men bringing Bowater. Michael maintained his stare on the man sitting behind the desk, resolved to reveal no recognition when presented with Bowater. Compton of Cross Creek wasn't supposed to know Bowater of Wilmington.

Perhaps the desire to exhibit no recognition was what kept his heart from smashing through his ribcage and his horror submerged when the men arrived, and he turned to behold not Bowater, but Private Nick Spry, garbed as a civilian and, from Michael's furtive assessment, unharmed, although his wrists were also bound behind him. Thank the heavens that his assistant from Wilmington possessed the discipline to control his own expression at the sight of his commander.

Michael faced Schmidt, who'd been studying his reaction. "Where is the man you believe is my friend?" Schmidt smiled and pointed to Spry. Michael jutted his chin toward Spry. "I've never seen him before in my life. And he doesn't look like the man in my sketches, Bowater."

What in hell was Spry doing in Hillsborough, in the same nightmare as Michael?

Schmidt inundated him with his smile. "His name is Spry. He is a private in the Eighty-Second Regiment. He is your assistant at criminal investigation."

Michael let out a sigh and glanced aside. "Is that your name, man? Spry?"

"Er, no. It's Miller. That's what I told this gentleman last night, when they brought me in."

Michael turned back to Schmidt. "Mr. Miller here doesn't look like a drunkard or a troublemaker. Is he a stranger to Hillsborough? Is that what you do with people you don't know? Pick them up and lock them in jail? That's essentially what you did to me."

"Like you, Mr. Stoddard, this fellow was seeking Mr. Griggs, a man brutally murdered. Do you not find the coincidence great?"

Spry's digging about in Bowater's records back in Wilmington must have convinced him his commander was riding into a trap perilous enough to dent the efficacy of Crown forces in North Carolina. Otherwise, Craig would never have sent Spry in pursuit. And Michael hoped that Spry had, indeed, received Craig's permission to leave Wilmington. But to arrive in Hillsborough only one day after Michael, he must have left Wilmington the day after Michael had left—

Ye gods, Spry's leg! Could it possibly be healed enough for him to spend five days in the saddle? Michael didn't see how. He dared not spend more than casual attention on his assistant.

Schmidt was still monitoring him, convinced of his trap. Michael shook his head. "I see your point about the coincidence. But surely you know that Mr. Griggs had many contacts, received many visitors from outside the area, traveled a great deal on business. It isn't justice to arrest two men who come looking for him right after he happens to get himself murdered, then claim they aren't who they say they are. It's piss-poor investigation, that's what it is."

"Where is Miss Griggs's journal, Lieutenant Stoddard?"

"I don't know where her journal is. I didn't know she had a journal until you told me about it fifteen minutes ago. And as I said, my name is Compton. I'm Rachel White's nephew, and Kate Duncan's cousin, and I'm a naval stores merchant from Cross Creek." He again jutted his chin at Spry. "Did he tell you my name was Stepford, or Stanford, or whatever you said?"

Nothing Michael said took a bite out of Schmidt's freezing, evil smile. The sheriff enjoyed his feints. Michael realized then that Spry hadn't told Schmidt their identities or divulged his business in town, other than to seek Griggs. And Spry couldn't have known about the journal. But Horatio Bowater knew who both of them were, and he was looking for the journal.

Michael's stomach filled with acid. Bowater had bought off Schmidt—no, that was grotesque. Surely Schmidt would not have fallen for that. He leaned forward. "See here, do you intend to pin Mr. Griggs's murder on me or Mr. Miller? If you do, may the devil damn you black. I've already told you that Mr. Griggs's murderer is named Horatio Bowater. He's the one in all those sketches you took from me, sketches produced during my interviews with witnesses."

In response, Schmidt extracted all three of the sketches and the love letter from his waistcoat. One by one, he touched them to the flame of the candle on his desk, and allowed them to disintegrate to black ash in a metal tray already loaded with ashes. Evidence against Bowater, gone. It was what Schmidt planned to do with the journal, too, if he located it.

Despair covered Michael like the net in Tierney's ridiculous skit. In the cloud of smoke created from incinerated paper, he coughed, aware that his expression reflected desolation. Schmidt sat back and interlaced fingers over his belly, lapping up every bitter bit of despair he could squeeze out. Still smiling, he said, "As one military officer to another, Mr. Stoddard, I give you my word that I will not charge you or your assistant here with the murder of Mr. Griggs."

No relief hit Michael's bloodstream. An even worse fate than being hanged for murder, at least in Schmidt's estimation, awaited Spry and him. He could hear it hissing in the wick of the candle, see Schmidt's eyes sparkling with the unholy light of it through the billowing brimstone of burned evidence.

"You have heard that General Cornwallis and his army are in the area, *ja*? They are looking for a spy from Britain who is suspected of passing military secrets from Crown forces to the Continentals. He is your stature and has your hair color." Remorse crossed Schmidt's face, a brief flash. "Unfortunate that he made an error in judgment that allowed him to fall under suspicion. But he will not make that error again. Will he?"

An Irish-accented voice groveled from the shadows near Schmidt's chair. "He will not."

"It is his good fortune that you have crossed his path. We will offer you to Cornwallis in his stead. We have already set up the meeting for noon. And we have been instructed that you are worth more delivered undamaged. I do not doubt that his Lordship will be pleased to discover that we have netted a second spy in the process, your assistant.

"*Ja*, Lieutenant, he will expect you to proclaim innocence, concoct a number of reasonable sounding explanations for why you are here, out of uniform, instead of in Wilmington." Schmidt repositioned his fingers higher on his belly. "Major John André must have wiggled the same way last October, before the Continentals hanged him."

Spasms of unreality rocked Michael. His left eye twitched. "Schmidt, I don't know why you've arranged our execution by redcoats. Are you saying that you'll let Bowater go free? For God's sake, that's his gig lying wrecked on the track in the woods near Mr. Griggs's house. He's committed murder! The people of Hillsborough will expect a criminal to hang!"

"A criminal will hang, I assure you. Upon closer examination, it appears that the wrecked gig did not belong to Mr. Bowater after all." Schmidt bent down, pulled the canvas sack off the floor, and sat it in his lap. From it, he extracted the head of the cane. "The letter 'T.' Tierney."

Michael's jaw dangled. "Damn you! Mr. Tierney is innocent of this crime! One of you stole the cane from him, planted it in Mr. Griggs's house to implicate him!"

"You are mistaken, Lieutenant. Mr. Tierney has carried a grudge against Mr. Griggs for ten years, ever since Mr. Griggs terminated plans for his daughter to marry Mr. Tierney. And there was that dispute over land a few years ago. You see how well it all fits. When the dust has settled from these events, and no murderers or British soldiers remain in town, citizens will thank us for restoring safety to the streets of Hillsborough."

A primal snarl contorted Michael's face. "You whoreson, bought by Bowater! You're letting him go!" Despite his bonds, he vaulted at Schmidt.

Two henchmen snagged his shoulders from behind, while a third forced on a gag and tied it above his hair ribbon. Just before a sack stinking of moldy cabbages dropped over Michael's head, he spotted a gagged and struggling Spry being subdued on the filthy floor of the jail.

***

Stumbling blind and unbalanced, Michael was yanked along from jail. Outside, birds chirped overhead, and the sun charmed the air to thaw. His captors hoisted him onto the bed of a wagon. Then a body-sized mass landed on the wagon bed beside him with a grunt: Spry.

Michael coaxed his galloping pulse and ragged breathing off the ledge of terror, then relaxed his legs when someone bound them at the ankles. He determined the advantage of listening to what transpired around him. Schmidt's implication that redcoats would hang him without hearing him conflicted in logic with his report that General Cornwallis preferred to receive a captured, alleged spy who hadn't been beaten to a pulp. Someone on the receiving end of this deal had requested that he be delivered intact, and thus might not be in such a hurry to execute the prisoner. Michael's confidence clawed its way up the side of the pit.

A wide swatch of canvas was flung across Michael from head to toe—probably also over Spry. Hiding two captives from view discouraged the curiosity of Hillsborough residents. Above the stench of cabbages drenching the sack on Michael's head, he could smell nothing, but he heard multiple horses and tackle being readied, and he picked out at least eight different voices, including those of Schmidt and O'Toole. Flanked by men riding horses, the wagon lurched into motion. The party of captors ceased talking.

At his side, Spry made no noise. Michael sensed him concentrating, listening. The bustle of town faded. Their captors made no attempt to negotiate the Eno River Ford, south of Hillsborough. From the angle at which sunlight struck them, and from the area roads he knew to be passable for a wagon, Michael deduced that they were headed north, on the road to Virginia.

One driver rustled about in the bed of the wagon near Michael's head. "Bloody hell, I left my cartridge box behind!"

"You brought a musket? Idiot. All you need is what's on you." The wagon hit a rut. The man cursed the road and added, "Just enough to have some fun with his Lordship. Let the marksmen worry about the firearms."

Michael didn't recognize either man's voice. His breathing as soft as possible, he perked his ears to absorb their conversation.

The first man snorted in glee. "Can't wait to see the surprise in his face."

"Make it a tomahawk in his face instead, lad."

Raspy breath issued from Spry. Michael stiffened over what the men's conversation implied. Schmidt's band of deserters would somehow ambush and assassinate Lord Cornwallis when he met them to pick up his spy. His breathing grew harsh, too.

Logic braked his panic. Would Cornwallis make such a trip himself? No. The general would send a subordinate to collect a spy. The task was too menial for Cornwallis, whose mind, like that of any general, meandered the cirrus of battle tactics, instead of toiling in the trenches of spy apprehension. But Michael had misjudged Schmidt before, and he admitted that he'd done a poor job of anticipating the sheriff's strategy that morning.

The wagon ascended yet another hill, and horse hooves approached from the north. In seconds, Michael heard a horse pacing the wagon, and Schmidt's growl. "Why do you talk? I told you, no talk now. We will have plenty of time for talk later, at the rendezvous."

The men driving the wagon grumbled assent. Schmidt rode away. The drivers fell silent.

About thirty minutes after departing Hillsborough, the wagon executed a left turn, westbound upon a track more rutted than the road to Virginia. Dried grass and bushes clawed at the sides of the wagon in passage, and the harsh caws of crows increased. Up ahead, Michael heard the sigh of water. The wagon neared what sounded like a mid-sized stream and halted. The drivers scrambled down.

Horses and wagon eased forward, and a man's call wafted to them from far ahead. "To the right! No, no, steer the team *right*! Watch that front wheel!"

Sweat burst out on Michael's forehead and down his back. Wobbly wood replaced packed clay beneath horse hooves and wagon wheels. Below them, the stream sang like an Odyssean siren. One second of inattention, and the wagon would plunge off the narrow bridge, death by drowning or crushing for its bound occupants. But Schmidt's men wanted their bounty and thus took care to transport their captives to the opposite side of the stream, where drivers climbed back aboard and resumed the route west.

The trip consumed the morning and merged into teeth-jarring, road-rutted wilderness. Michael thought of Bowater—rot the man's soul—most likely headed back to Wilmington by then, if he'd understood Schmidt's implied agreement with the murderous agent. *Leave Hillsborough, never return, and I will not arrest you for murder.* Then there was Tierney, sober for the first time in years, but too late to save himself from false evidence. And Aunt Rachel, grief at the loss of her only child delayed and hardened by a lie that had lasted a decade. And Kate, frantically trying to move her aunt to safety, seduction by foot massage forgotten.

Forgotten. Vanished. He and Spry, two soldiers disappeared on a mission, gone like winter mist in the mountains. Unless Cornwallis listened to him and spared them.

The track widened. Multiple horses surrounded the wagon with hoof-thump and harness-jingle. The entire party pushed on another minute before stopping. Boot steps crunched pine needles and dried twigs on the ground. Off whipped the canvas that covered the prisoners.

Chill swathed Michael, froze his sweat to his skin. In a silence that stretched out strange and too long, he felt a gaze of arctic ice finger the length of his body, explore his shape with leisure and intimacy and welcome. Hair sprang up the length of his neck.

An image of Violet's crude sketch of the fanged, horned monster sprouted in his imagination, and his pulse pumped with the screaming need for flight. Might Schmidt's talk of turning him over to Cornwallis have been a lie? Maybe Schmidt intended to leave Spry and him to animals in the wilderness. He imagined rubbery slobber dangling from a maw, a red tongue swabbing jaws, and behind that tongue a set of teeth meant to flay a man's flesh off his body.

From the head of the wagon, Schmidt was in a jovial mood, like he'd just become a proud, new papa. "Two is better than one, *ja*? The spy was working with an assistant, so we brought them both." Coins, many of them, clinked in a pouch, bounced together a couple times. Schmidt laughed with surprise. "Why, thank you very much! It is a pleasure to be of service."

Men grabbed Michael off the bed of the wagon, carried him a short distance, up steps. Sunlight dimmed. Shoes and boots scuffed across planks. Like a rolled rug, he was dumped upon a gritty, splintered floor. Footsteps retreated.

Indoors? Why had he been deposited inside some sort of building, instead of on the forest floor? He tested his bonds. They held fast. He squirmed about, tried to free his wrists from another angle. Splinters snagged his sleeves. He stilled his efforts when the shoes and boots returned, bypassed him trailing muffled curses. Spry. Michael listened while the footsteps and curses dwindled, then halted. Again, the shoes and boots passed him. Spry, he realized, had been dumped nearby in the building.

He felt a swish of cold air near his hands and received O'Toole's croon in his ear: "*Sasanach*, it doesn't matter whether she's your cousin. You'll be gone, and I'll be in Hillsborough. With *her*." Michael tensed for a kick to the midsection, but the Irishman's shoes clomped for the exit.

Outside, the wagon clattered off. Amiable men's voices, companions who'd completed an onerous task and were ready to celebrate, faded into the forest. Several of those men—five? six?—sounded as though they'd come from Britain. Horses cantered away. Silence gripped the building, but not a peaceful silence. Even the crows were still.

Terror rippled him. Damn, damn, damn. He writhed in his bonds, haunted by visions of a fiend that was inspired by Violet's sketch. Panic lodged in his breath.

A single set of boots mounted the steps. The thing that had fondled Michael with its gaze entered the building, its tread quivering the floor, coursing toward Michael like the wake of a shark sniffing a meal. Michael burned his wrists on rope, then gasped around the gag when a knee pinned him on his side. Hands yanked off the cabbage sack. His head banged the boards.

For several seconds, he blinked, established that he was facing the wall in a hovel that reeked of wood rot, mold, and animal feces. Then he shimmied into a crooked sitting position and twisted his neck for a look up at his host.

The gag muted his yelp of horror and recognition, yet still his cry was loud enough to resound through the hovel and escape through the patchy roof. Survival instinct jerked him halfway to his feet. He tripped over the bonds around his ankles, smacked the wall, and flopped to the floor.

Light from an open window illuminated the muscular form of Lieutenant Dunstan Fairfax glowering down at him, the scarlet of his coat like a spill of gore over his chest, his eyes frozen chips of green glass ground into his handsome face.

Michael's failed attempt at flight fired phosphorescence in Fairfax's eyes. Ecstasy resonated in his voice. "Don't leave just yet, Stoddard. I've waited almost a year for this."

In a blur, his right fist whipped out and delivered a backhand to Michael's jaw that sent him sprawling on his face in a nebula of swirly stars stinking of animal turds. Before the turds had a chance to stop spinning, Fairfax hauled him up by the hair and hovered his face in close. "Tried your hand at solving a murder in town, did you? You fell short, let a killer go free. Time you learned from the Master. Time for a lesson on interrogation."

Chapter Twenty-Nine

SOMEONE ELSE'S MUFFLED curses pierced Michael's pain fog. Fairfax released Michael's hair and straightened. "Ah, the comrade." Michael sagged back to the rotting floor. Grit crunched beneath Fairfax's boots in a pivot.

Michael's vision steadied on the image of Fairfax sauntering toward Spry's trussed, tousled, and upright form on the other side of the hovel. Fairfax dragged the private past a fusil propped against a wall and a large canvas bag on the floor to a spot six feet to Michael's right, then wrenched the sack off his head and flung it aside.

Horror oiled Michael's joints, squeezed his heart. Gagged gibberish emerged in place of his shout, "It's me you want! Leave him be!"

Neither Fairfax nor Spry paid attention to him. Michael tried to catch Spry's attention, command him using the language of his body not to confront Fairfax. But Spry was too absorbed in sizing up the russet-haired lieutenant from the Seventeenth Light Dragoons. The private sat taller, and his eyes narrowed.

In response to the private's silent challenge, Fairfax flogged him with a glare. Michael had yet to see anyone withstand that archangelic fever. Sure enough, within seconds, Spry's shoulders and gaze lowered.

A darted look around what had once been someone's single-room dwelling confirmed to Michael that he, Fairfax, and Spry were the only occupants. Where were Fairfax's dragoons? Outside on guard? Not likely. Fairfax conducted business with his "clients" alone. No witnesses.

Some men who'd departed the site minutes earlier had sounded like Britons. Fairfax's patrol must have left with Schmidt and his deputies. Michael and his assistant were truly alone, at Fairfax's mercy. Breath shuddered from Michael's lungs through his nostrils. A fetid taste invaded his mouth.

Fairfax paced over to tower above him. The stance obscured the fact that he was the same height as Michael. It emphasized at least twenty-five pounds of muscular advantage that Fairfax held in his shoulders and chest.

Softness padded Fairfax's tone. "When I ask questions, you shall answer. If your answer doesn't provide me with the information I seek, I shall encourage you." The floorboards creaked beneath his tramp back to Spry. "And I shall bestow twice the amount of encouragement upon your associate here."

The rotation of Spry's head toward Michael in puzzlement terminated with Fairfax's double slap to the face. Like pistol shots, the cracks echoed through the hut and revitalized the ache in Michael's own face. Rage burned his wrists with rope. Landing one good, solid punch on Fairfax's face: that was all he wanted that moment.

Reeled back onto one elbow, Spry shook his head, dazed. Any trace of insolence and challenge in his expression had vanished, replaced by tremors of hatred, fear.

Spotless, shiny dragoon boots strutted back to Michael. "Last December, you rode out to the camp of the British Legion. Why?"

To find you and kill you, blot a fiend off the face of the earth.

Fairfax made no attempt to remove the gag, so Michael responded around it the best he could: "Dispatches." He strove to enunciate. "I ran dispatches. Dis—"

A backhand to the other side of his face severed his sentence. He'd seen it coming. His captor wasn't concerned with his response. In that moment, his back and palms clammy with sweat, Michael envisioned the breadth of Fairfax's sport. Over the next few hours, the monster would thrash all manner of truths and lies from them as they sought to produce whatever combination of words that ended the torture.

After Fairfax became caught up in his sport, the result was always the same for his victims. What a fool Michael had been earlier, imagining he'd have the option to negotiate, simply because Schmidt had been ordered to not damage his prisoners in transit.

Spry cringed from Fairfax's approach and tried to shield his face. After receiving his second double-dose of encouragement, he rolled onto his side and groaned. Fairfax smiled down at him.

Michael cursed through the gag, his thoughts spiraling with rage. Rage failed to subordinate the terror tangling his pulse. The previous summer, Fairfax had lured him back to that copse of trees where he'd butchered the Spaniard. He'd subdued him and pressed a dagger to his carotid artery, then taunted him with why he sported with his victims. The only reason he'd released Michael was because he'd staged an ambush for him later—an ambush that failed. But at his worst moment last summer, with Fairfax's blade biting his skin and drawing blood, there hadn't been a second life at stake, someone beside himself to command his concern.

His face expressionless, Fairfax ambled back to Michael. Nausea kneaded Michael's stomach. Did Fairfax care what he had to say? If not, Michael could expect him to never remove their gags over the course of the afternoon. Rancid desolation filled his mouth. It was what each of Fairfax's victims had tasted as they realized there would be no rescue.

His heart skipped two beats, then resumed a hard rhythm when Fairfax reached around the back of his head, untied the gag, and whisked it away.

Twining the cloth between his fingers, he moved back two steps. His face still empty of emotion, he waited.

Michael realized that he waited for curses or pleas from his victim, now that he'd allowed him his voice. In memory, Schmidt said: *He will expect you to proclaim innocence, concoct a number of reasonable sounding explanations for why you are here, out of uniform, instead of in Wilmington.* Of course.

"December 1780, Stoddard. The camp of the British Legion." Fairfax found a soothing tone to commiserate with Michael's dread. "A portable desk with hidden compartments. I know that you used one of those compartments to communicate with at least one confirmed spy in camp."

Michael had used the desk to collude with the double spy, Adam Neville, hoping to pin down Fairfax's schedule, isolate him. Neville, one of the disaffected, wouldn't have minded seeing Fairfax killed. But Neville also enjoyed watching all the factions in the war squabbling with each other and kicking up more chaos.

Both hands braced on his thighs, Fairfax bent nearer. "The desk belonged to a woman named Helen Chiswell. Surely you know of her association with the St. James family of rebels."

Michael felt his brow lower. He hadn't realized that Enid Jones's mistress was acquainted with the St. Jameses. But to his knowledge, only one member of the family officially qualified as a rebel: the patriarch, Will St. James.

Fairfax murmured, "Her *intimate* association." Concupiscence sparked in his eyes.

Dread dribbled over Michael, as rank as the contents of a chamberpot.

"She told me that you spoke with Neville at camp. You spoke with her, too, didn't you? Did you also speak with Jonathan Quill, her lover who traipsed into the backcountry with her?"

Michael knew that Mrs. Chiswell had left the backcountry of South Carolina and was headed home to Wilmington. But good gods, what had Fairfax done to her before she'd gotten out? And who was Jonathan Quill?

"What have you to say about those visits to the Legion, now that I know you colluded with at least one traitor?" Fairfax straightened. "How about this? 'I passed along Lord Cornwallis's movement plans to Neville.'" More silk draped his tone, as if he were a father consoling a son who'd stolen sweets. "'My information confirmed for the Continentals that Lord Cornwallis was too far away to assist Tarleton's Legion. I assisted Morgan's Continentals in destroying the Legion.'" His expression glowing, Fairfax drew back to assess the effect of his words. "Tell me, does that summarize it, Stoddard?" And he nodded, agreeing with himself.

Blood tainted the inside of Michael's mouth, metallic and foul. He could only imagine what Spry tasted. He tried to steady his breathing. His gaze met green eyes devoid of humanity. He said to Fairfax, "Tell Lord Cornwallis that interference from the rebels prevents Major Craig from establishing a supply depot in Cross Creek. If Lord Cornwallis hinges a strategy upon replenishing supplies in Cross Creek, his initiative will fail."

A crease appeared between Fairfax's eyebrows, as if Michael had lapsed into another language. "If this information were true, Major Craig would have sent you with a dispatch for Lord Cornwallis." The gag twining his fingers suddenly became a noose, popped taut between his hands. "I would examine the dispatch."

Despite the cold, sweat streamed down Michael's back. In his peripheral vision, Spry struggled to a sitting position. Blood glistened on his nose. Michael rushed his words out. "I arrived in Hillsborough Sunday evening. My contact in town had just been murdered. I had to burn the dispatch to keep it from falling into the hands of Georg Schmidt." Sarcasm hammered his tone, despite his vulnerability. "You know, that Prussian you wasted your money on earlier."

The gag whipped around his throat, abrupt interruption to his air supply. Fairfax hoisted him off the floor by the gag. "You jackass. Schmidt told me everything."

Black specks swirled through Michael's vision. Instinct's supplication for life kicked and bucked his legs, his torso. "Fool!" said Fairfax. "You call yourself an investigator? You showed up Sunday evening in the house of a man newly murdered. You befouled evidence, insinuated yourself into Schmidt's investigation, and accused the wrong man of murder!"

Fairfax pressed harder, found Michael's carotid. Specks in his eyes clumped together, darkening the face full of divine glory that bent over him. His tongue beat his clenched teeth in effort to damn the dark angel back to hell. But lack of breath denied him his voice.

Buzzing in his ears swelled, faded Fairfax's words out and in. "He thinks you're the spy . . . *I* think you're the spy . . . by this evening, Cornwallis needn't concern himself further with the spy."

Some portion of Michael retained consciousness, for he remembered a rubbery numbness that cushioned his plop to the floor. He gasped lungfuls of air, his breathing no longer constricted, the carotid artery free again.

A thumping noise vibrated the cabin, rocked the floor. He squirmed about. His sight filled in, presented him with the visual duet of Fairfax choking Spry with the gag, and Spry kicking for his life. Thump, thump. Thump, thump.

Exaltation owned Fairfax's face. He twisted the gag tighter, depressed Spry's artery, and inhaled his mortality. Spry was going to be dead within minutes. Fairfax was clearly finished with him, ready to devote the bulk of his attention to his fellow officer.

"Moravian," Michael croaked. He coughed, firmed his voice. "Fairfax! Did Schmidt tell you he was Moravian?" Spry stopped kicking, went limp, unconscious. Michael coughed again, his throat and neck aching. "He lied! He's a deserter!"

Spry slumped to the floor, face pallid. Fairfax dropped the gag beside him, inhaled again, and rolled back his shoulders. One of Spry's hands clenched air, then relaxed. Not dead yet, but dead the next time Fairfax dallied with him.

Fairfax turned on Michael then and stroked the flat of a dagger blade in his right hand the way a man caressed his lady's inner thigh. Sweat on Michael became pebbles of ice. His lips trembled. "All Schmidt's men are deserters. That Irishman, O'Toole, is the spy you're seeking."

His captor took one step toward him. Reflex scuttled Michael along the floor the equivalent of one step away. Panic dragged his gaze to the bag lying beside the fusil. His imagination populated it with various types of blades, cleaned and well-sharpened. Fairfax adored honed steel and all it could accomplish: flay, eviscerate, behead, dismember.

Eyes radiating rapture, the dragoon crooked his left forefinger at Michael. *Come.*

Spry coughed. Blood oozed from his nose. He tried to sit, and collapsed. His actions earned Fairfax's calculating regard. Vomit churned Michael's gut. Fairfax timed his slow approach on him to culminate with the point at which Spry regained full consciousness, so the private wouldn't have to guess at his fate in the next act.

Another step from Fairfax in his direction earned a second retreat from Michael. "They're *deserters*, Fairfax. Didn't you hear me?"

"Oh, that's cheeky, Stoddard. But you just aren't that bright. Halfwit commoners like you have been watering down officers' ranks for decades. Something must be done about it."

Who else in the Army did Fairfax plan to prune? By then, Spry was sitting up, wobbling. Michael scuttled and felt his back graze the wall. Fairfax had closed the distance between the two of them with a third step. It brought him almost before the window that spilled raw light upon the scene.

Fairfax had disregarded his warning about the deserters. He didn't believe Michael. The only thing he cared about was his own glorification, or perhaps his amusement.

At some distance from the house, a branch snapped. Both Michael and his captor glanced to the window. Fairfax returned his concentration to Michael. But Michael again thought of the dragoons with whom Fairfax rode. Pieces of overheard conversation during his wagon ride that morning connected, took on a sudden, chilling implication. "Where are your men this moment?"

Fairfax laughed. "Why do you care? They aren't outside, listening, ready to rush in and help you when you scream for your miserable life—if that's what you're hoping."

"You sent them to rendezvous with Schmidt. Didn't you?"

Fairfax stiffened, his step delayed, the brilliance of his smile diminished.

Loss flooded Michael, exploded in his voice. "Ye gods, you've sent those men to their deaths!"

"Where did you hear of this?" Fairfax stepped toward him, full light from the window igniting anger on his face.

"From Schmidt, riding alongside the wagon that transported us this morning—some sort of trap he'd planned to kill all of you!"

The report of a rifle firing preceded the whiz of shot in the window. It missed Fairfax's nose by no more than an inch and imbedded in the rear wall. Fairfax dove out of sight. Spry flattened himself to the floor with a muffled shout. What sounded like twenty men outside released a huzzah of triumph that surrounded the building.

"You bloody fool!" Michael hollered to Fairfax, who leapt across the floor to his canvas bag. "They're *deserters*! What do you expect?"

Fairfax had worked a sword shorter than a saber from the bag before five civilian men burst in through the warped door. With a demon-scream and a spring like a starved rattlesnake, he flew at them, partially decapitated one with the sword, and ground his dagger into the abdomen of another. The second man fell across Spry, whose bellow of pain was almost drowned out in the injured man's screams. Collapse of the first man's body knocked down a cohort.

In the confusion and hesitation that followed, one of the two men who remained standing readied his tomahawk but circled too close to Michael. Rocked back on his bound hands, with his legs curled to his chest, Michael pumped his legs out, booted the man in the buttocks, and sent him straight into impalement upon Fairfax's waiting sword. The tomahawk clattered away. Another demon-scream later, the fourth and fifth rebel lay upon the floor, writhing and dying.

Rifle shot again blasted through the window. Men outside shouted. The rumble of running feet approached the house. Fairfax vaulted over bodies and yanked Michael upright. "Earn your life, bum fodder!" He hacked his dagger blade downward, severing the ropes that bound Michael's wrists, then thrust the handle of the blade into Michael's grasp.

Chapter Thirty

REBELS IN HUNTING shirts huzzahed into the room. Michael sliced through the bonds on his ankles, then arced the dagger from his feet up into the groin of a man who tried to club him with a tomahawk. He swapped hands with the dagger, gripped the tomahawk, and rode the wild wagon driven by combat at close range.

Ducking every time he neared the window, for the rifleman outside continued to mark as a target any man who presented himself, including two of his own comrades. Maneuvering several men into the terminal embrace of the demon in the red coat. Stabbing kidneys and groins, bludgeoning faces. Fight or be slain. Backcountry brawling knew no stand-and-deliver code of honor like field battles, demanded no emotion except for harnessed terror.

Fairfax must have freed Spry. The private wielded loaded pistols from the canvas bag. Each time he plugged an assailant with shot, the report rang in Michael's ears.

What seemed like years later, burned powder stench mingled with death-stink, two dozen times more metallic than what Michael had smelled in Griggs's house Sunday afternoon. Powder smoke cleared. Slippery death mounded the floor. Dying rebels bleated and thrashed. Only Michael, Spry, and Fairfax remained standing.

Michael, his chest heaving, stared at a seeping gash on his left forearm. Then his right hand, as if operated by someone else, whipped the handkerchief from his waistcoat pocket, shoved back sliced shirt and coat sleeves, and wrapped the gash quickly. *Not too deep,* the surgeon in his head commented. Maybe it would stop bleeding on its own.

Another rifle shot plowed through the window and skimmed Spry's coat. He barked in fright and ducked. Michael realized that while the rifleman lived, he'd pick off any of them leaving the hovel. His head throbbing from two blows collected during the brawl, he seized and loaded the fusil, made his way among bodies to the window. Behind him, the dark angel visited the dying, his dagger dispensing eternal silence, one by one.

Crouched beside the window, Michael felt the stiffening, aching constellations of bruises on his ribs, back, and arms. He shoved hair off his face, grabbed the nearest corpse's handkerchief, and waved it in the open. The rifleman rewarded him with a shot and divulged his location, partial concealment behind an oak tree about fifty feet distant. Michael dropped the handkerchief. "Spry."

"Sir." The private sounded out of breath, confused.

To his knowledge, Spry had only been in one combat situation before: at night, with little bloodshed. Michael had puked after his first three *real* battles. Spry needed a good puke. But before that, Michael needed his help. "Stand on the other side of that window, in cover. Use your handkerchief. Draw out the rifleman."

Spry gulped. "Sir."

Michael readied the fusil from a corner of the window and sighted. In his peripheral vision, the handkerchief fluttered. Half the torso of the man outside presented itself, more than enough target if the fusil's quality were good. He squeezed the trigger.

Powder ejected from the touchhole, spattered the side of his face, and remained plastered there by battle's grime. His ears rang. Smoke cleared.

"Got him, sir." Spry slurred his words like a drunken man. He slunk from the window.

Michael stared across fifty feet of woodland. Within a pile of winter-brown leaves, a heap of clothing twitched. Michael lowered his gaze to the weapon in his hands. Trembling hands, as always. He clenched them around the fusil, saw a smear of another man's blood, now dried, on the back of his right hand. He closed his eyes.

Agony in the hovel behind him had quieted. The soft clicks of a firearm placed on full cock sprang him to his feet. A pistol in his extended hand, Spry had taken aim on Fairfax, who stood in almost-reverential stillness above the final rebel that he'd dispatched, gory dagger still in his grasp. Rebel blood bathed the left side of his face, stained the neck of his white shirt.

Michael felt giddy. He slowed his breathing. "Spry. You loaded the pistol?"

"Sir. Yes, sir. Pistol is loaded." Contusions swelled Spry's face in several places. Blood caked his nose. Sweat streaked through filth on one cheek. But unlike moments before, he was alert and focused, prepared to be the instrument of his commanding officer.

Michael snatched a pistol from a dead rebel's belt and checked it: still loaded. He cocked the pistol and sighted Fairfax. For almost a year, he'd dreamt of being in this position. Glory expanded in his chest. Serenity infused his voice. "Drop the dagger, Fairfax."

Fairfax complied. His lips curved, soft and seductive. "You cannot kill me."

"Argue all you like with two pistol balls. This is the heroic end you've wanted, surrounded by two-dozen rebels that you slew single-handedly. Your story shall make the front page of *The London Chronicle*."

"Execute me, and Schmidt and the Irishman go free." Fairfax waved a hand over the carnage at his feet. "See for yourself. They aren't among the dead here."

Michael's gaze skittered over bodies. He recognized several deputies from

Hillsborough and Dismal the logger. The rest were strangers: fellows recruited from the wilderness, backwoodsmen who'd never bargained on battle with British regulars or a fiend worth five men in combat. But no Schmidt. No O'Toole. And no Bowater.

The revelation sheared away Michael's grandeur. Had Schmidt and O'Toole headed back to Hillsborough? He envisioned both deserters arriving in town, making good on their promises to Matthew Tierney, Rachel White, and Kate Duncan. After they'd ensconced themselves in their stronghold, neither he nor Spry would be able to move in the city openly and render aid. His stomach burned. He spat, "Why should I release you? We don't know where to find those two before they return to town."

"But I do. They shared with me the location of their rendezvous."

Spry's voice sounded hoarse. "He's lying, sir."

Rendezvous. Schmidt had spoken of it earlier, during prisoner transport. In his arrogance, he may very well have blabbed the location to Fairfax. The sheriff hadn't expected the three of them to survive. Michael felt sickened. His decision was no longer pristine.

"I've never felt that deserters are worth the effort of being returned to their units. They merit only one judgment." The green of Fairfax's eyes became malachite. "If you were correct about the rendezvous, Schmidt and his man butchered my patrol. No one kills my men and gets away with it. *I* must track down the deserters and dispense retribution." He touched his tongue to the corner of his lips. "And unless I've misunderstood, Schmidt allowed a killer to go free. *You* must capture the killer and bring him to justice. You cannot do that *and* hunt down deserters."

"Don't listen to him, sir." Spry drew a shaky breath. "Poison talk, like the devil himself."

Michael's voice emerged harsh. "Do you think me a fool, Fairfax? You expect me to just let you go. I know you haven't the means to track down Schmidt and O'Toole. They're on horseback. Even if you tethered a horse nearby, those men will have made off with it."

"I assure you, they did not make off with my horse. I never leave my mount where it can be found by an enemy." Coyness flashed in his smile. "Or even an ally." A cold chuckle emptied his lips. "What's wrong? Afraid I won't keep my word, rid the earth of a deserter and his arse-kissing associate?"

Gods, no, that wasn't what Michael feared. He had no doubt that Fairfax would hunt down the pair if he let him go. All morning, the monster had savored the thought of torturing two men to death. Schmidt and O'Toole would satisfy him as well as Stoddard and Spry.

"No, wait a moment." Fairfax's chest swelled, and his smile dissolved. "That isn't it. You know I shall keep my word." Luminosity exploded in his eyes. "By all the gods, you're afraid you won't get another chance to kill me!" He laughed full out. "Yes! That's what your trip to the Legion camp in December was about. Delivering dispatches, bah! You missed a chance to kill me then. If you let me go now, you've missed a second chance, haven't you?" He took a step toward Michael—over a body. "*Haven't you?*"

As if Michael had received another slap, his head and shoulders recoiled. Although he corrected his posture in the next second, his body had confessed. The devil! Was Fairfax certain that he'd intended to kill him in December, or was he bluffing?

"Ahhh." Fairfax's gaze ploughed the length of him, dragging a sneer with it. "Stoddard, I didn't think you had the stones for such scheming. You risk court-martial and execution to kill *me*. How splendid, how worthy!"

How could Fairfax have learned what Michael plotted? What if he'd tortured some sort of confession out of Adam Neville or Helen Chiswell? Michael realized that he didn't know, and in that moment, he couldn't know. Nothing in Fairfax's stance revealed the cards he held at the table.

Michael felt as if a half-dozen of Bowater's traps had snapped shut on his chest and crushed his ribcage. Broken bones raked his throat, shredded his vocal cords. His enemy had stolen his breath, his voice.

Fairfax turned his empty palms toward the men holding pistols on him and tilted his head slightly to present them with his carotid artery. "Either you two have done with it and shoot me, or I shall recover my gear, walk out that door, and hunt the deserters."

That son of a mongrel, inverting order and justice, taunting him! A vision boiled in Michael's imagination. He saw himself squeezing the trigger, savoring the wet rip of a pistol ball through Fairfax's upper left chest cavity, followed by Spry's pistol ball a second later. And the shock and agony supplanting Fairfax's sneer as he collapsed atop dead rebels.

Spry's voice, drenched in dismay, rent the fantasy. "Sir?"

Teeth still bared, Fairfax absorbed death, grew taller. The temperature in the room plummeted. "Stop wasting time, Stoddard. I want those deserters. You want the murderer. You have my solemn promise that you shall receive another chance to kill me." He clenched both fists. "Should I find you in Hillsborough, when my Lord Cornwallis moves through, that opportunity will come sooner, rather than later. And rest assured that I shall give you more sport than you could ever imagine as you *try* to kill me, you pustule."

Horror whistled through Michael's soul. What sane man called down a pact like that upon himself? His voice trickled back around a clenched jaw. "This isn't about sport."

"Perhaps not. But you couldn't live with yourself if you allowed Schmidt and O'Toole to return to Hillsborough. You know they'd continue to inflict cruelty upon those poor, defenseless civilians." The thunder of Fairfax's mockery reverberated off bodies. "Lieutenant Michael Stoddard, defender of all that is good and just. Yet there you stand, indecisive, like a schoolboy. You know what's to be done. All it will cost you is some self-respect. Well worth the price, I'd say."

Were the roles reversed, were Fairfax holding a pistol on him, Fairfax would kill him and, without compunction, let a murderer go free, and leave the civilians of Orange County to a sheriff who dispensed justice based on personal grudges.

Michael couldn't apprehend the deserters *and* Bowater, yet somehow they must all be apprehended. He saw no other way to accomplish that than by releasing the monster.

Manipulated by the Master. Manipulated with his own *integrity*. Defiled self-respect tasted of bile and blood, disillusionment and damnation. Michael swallowed it, kept Fairfax in the pistol's aim. "You bloody son of a whore."

"And should you make it back to Wilmington, be warned. Mrs. Chiswell is a rebel spy, as is her lover, Jonathan Quill."

A snarl ripped from Michael's mouth. "Go! Out of here, before I change my mind!"

Chapter Thirty-One

MICHAEL AND HIS assistant plodded eastward on the Road from the Haw Field, an empty logger track. Leaves and twigs crunched beneath their shoes. Pines scented the chilly afternoon, smelling a good deal better than either man. Although both had washed off as much as possible in a creek that wandered north of the track, the stink of skirmish clung to them, stained their clothing, their breath.

Before setting out from the hovel, they'd taken dead men's pistols, daggers, money, and food. Michael had gauged that they could reach Hillsborough by nightfall if they kept to a steady pace afoot. That meant Bowater, likely headed south in Tierney's stolen gig, would be as much as a day ahead of them when they took up the chase before dawn on the morrow. However Bowater wasn't Michael's immediate source of concern.

For at least the fourth time since they'd begun walking, he glanced behind, imagining a malachite green stare empty of humanity searing his shoulders, sighting between them down the length of a pistol barrel. Higher reasoning assured Michael that Fairfax had kept his word in this instance. Nevertheless, he craved safety for Spry and himself, a way to breathe easy, without the constant tension of wondering what hostile force might cross their path in the wilderness five or ten minutes hence. They lived only because of the rebels' combat inexperience and Fairfax's change of mind.

Shock over the massacre in the cabin had claimed Spry's tongue. He'd spoken mostly in monosyllables during the walk.

Michael remembered. The sergeant who'd caught the cannonball in his stead at Brandywine had been a fellow Yorkshireman. He'd had a wife and children. After each of Michael's early field battles, shock had knotted his tongue, as if by not commenting on what he'd seen and done, he could erase the dark, unholy shame that came from taking human lives, erase the horror of dangling over the pit of losing his own life and surviving when others had died. Even later, when he exchanged words with other officers about the rawness, he found it eased his horror little and left him with the sensation that he'd been plunged in a filthy trench, where pieces of his own humanity were sliced away and replaced by parts of reptiles.

Each soldier had to climb his own path out of that trench. Or not.

Spry also favored the leg injured twelve days earlier. While a man's own medicine was a mysterious gift from the Divine, any man would be unwise to deplete his gift so soon after such trauma. Spry had ridden five days straight to reach Hillsborough. Hardly the "light duty" prescribed by the surgeon. Michael had to get his assistant back to civilization, and, since their only source of locomotion was their feet, keep his mind off his injury as they walked.

He made the inflection of his tone neutral. "I'm curious what you told Major Craig to convince him to send you here."

Spry stirred from his daze, cleared his throat. "I told him what I found the morning you left town. First, a letter Bowater had kept for ten years, sent to him by Ezra Griggs, your contact."

Michael felt his eyebrows crawl up his forehead in brief surprise. "I thought Bowater would have been more clever than to retain such damning evidence."

"The content of the letter by itself didn't damn him. Griggs merely griped that his daughter had eloped with the local clubfoot, and he railed at Bowater for not marrying her instead."

Understanding filtered through Michael. "Ah. Bowater kept that letter because he wanted to reread it, to gloat over the misery he'd caused two families. But you didn't know that."

Spry shrugged, his gaze on the track, as if he were having trouble concentrating. "I still thought it odd that he'd keep such a letter. Suspicious that it had come from your contact in Hillsborough. So I requested an audience with Mrs. Hooper."

A pulse of surprise traveled Michael's veins. Wives and families of several rebels had taken refuge in Wilmington just prior to the Eighty-Second's occupation, trusting to Major Craig's mercy rather than the mercy of the King's Friends in the countryside. These families kept a low profile in exchange for not being singled out by the redcoats. Anne Hooper was the wife of one of the signers of the Declaration of Independence. Easily, she might have regarded Spry's request as harassment. "Mrs. Hooper? Why Mrs. Hooper?"

Spry's words came more freely. "Sir. I interviewed Mrs. Farrell. She told me that William Hooper was acquainted with Bowater from the days before either of them lived in Wilmington. I wondered whether Mrs. Hooper might have known enough about Bowater to contribute to the investigation. That bunghole bodyguard of hers made me wait forty-five minutes outside her door in the rain. I was soaking wet by the time I got in to see her." The swelling on Spry's face made his smile aimed at Michael lopsided. "She gave me a towel."

A breath of relief hissed from Michael. "And then she told you something she and her husband knew about Bowater that made you realize he must be apprehended, right?"

"No, sir. The Hoopers haven't kept Bowater's company since prior to the Regulator executions. They didn't like him. Mr. Hooper was the King's Deputy

Attorney General in the Salisbury District Court, where Regulators kept brewing trouble. In court, repeatedly, Mr. Hooper heard the side of farmers and planters who were allied with the Regulators. They complained of government officials who cheated men on the sale of land. These brokers would charge double what the land was worth. Or perhaps impose exorbitant interest rates. Or 'lose' records of the sale and claim it never happened after a farmer had already cultivated the land. Over and over, Bowater's name came up in association with those abuses."

Michael snorted. "Judging from the situation we encountered back in Wilmington with Bowater's clients, it doesn't sound as though his ethics have changed much across the years."

"No, sir. He's just become more devious."

Spry had settled into a walking rhythm. His stride had opened, and his limp hadn't deepened. Perhaps the walk wasn't aggravating his injury. Some of the tension dribbled from Michael's chest. Spry had done well to extract such background from Mrs. Hooper. He must have set her at ease. "Did Mrs. Hooper speculate on why Bowater relocated from the interior of North Carolina to the coast?"

Spry chuckled. Maybe the shock was wearing off, and his leg wasn't hurting him badly. "Like everyone else, sir, she'd expected him to accompany Governor Tryon to New York after the Rebellion was squashed. But she recalled that Tryon received a mysterious dispatch from one of his agents already in New York. Although the governor didn't make public the content of the dispatch, he called Bowater in for a private conference and dismissed him from his company. Many people conjectured at the time, but no one ever came up with an explanation that fit."

"Hah!" Michael clapped his hands together once. "You amaze me, Spry. All that information from a woman who considers us her enemies. I commend you." He raced his words to keep up with the stride of his conclusions. "My guess is that the dispatch to Governor Tryon contained information about Bowater's illicit past in New York. Tryon determined that it was unwise politically for him to keep company with Bowater. Bowater saved face by stepping down from the entourage and making a life for himself in the obscure little town of Wilmington."

"And what might his illicit past in New York have been?" Curiosity. Some of Nick Spry was finding its way out of the trench.

Michael returned sobriety to his tone. "I think he had a peccadillo for young girls, and his father hastily packed him off to Hillsborough ahead of a posse of enraged fathers." He informed Spry of what he'd learned about Violet, her journal, and Aaron White. Then he advanced the supposition that Griggs had confronted Bowater in Wilmington early on the morning of Monday February fifth, only to call down death upon himself when he returned home days later.

"So when you arrived in Hillsborough on Sunday, sir, you discovered Griggs's body right after he'd been murdered?"

"Correct." Michael squinted at Spry. "But I doubt Major Craig released you to detached duty, just on the basis of a ten-year-old letter and the statement of the wife of a Signer."

"Oh, no. There's more. A witness I interviewed insisted that he'd seen

Bowater take the northwest road to Cross Creek in his gig on Monday the fifth. The timing was less than an hour after he'd seen a stranger gallop from Wilmington on the same road. This stranger fit the description of the man whom Mrs. Farrell had witnessed arguing with Bowater."

Spry's bruised lips parted in a grin. "Bowater's records book included his contacts among known rebels. Three of them were in custody in the pen." Spry chuckled again. "Some of the men and I, well, we spent a rewarding half-hour learning how much the prisoners knew of Bowater's politics. He spies actively for the Continentals, sir. On February the fifth, he pursued an agent of the Crown out of Wilmington, intent on malice. And *you* were headed into that storm bearing Major Craig's dispatch to Lord Cornwallis. What motivated the major to send me to Hillsborough was his desire to ensure that the actions of a proven rebel spy didn't prevent his dispatch from reaching Lord Cornwallis."

His tone lowered, along with his spirits. "Much good my haste did any of us, sir. Mr. Griggs is dead. You had to destroy the dispatch. You and I were almost killed back there. And Bowater has been set free." Cynicism corroded Spry's tone. "I don't understand it. Schmidt is the county sheriff. From what I heard, you gave him plenty of evidence that Bowater killed Mr. Griggs. How can Schmidt not want to jail a murderer?"

"Because he carries a grudge against a Hillsborough resident named Matthew Tierney and plans to sacrifice him instead." Michael recounted Rachel White's altercation with Schmidt and the role Tierney had played in it.

Anxiety elevated the pitch of Spry's voice. "Schmidt is a brute, and a bloody deserter atop that! He should be exterminated!" He caught himself and grunted. From the tense silence that swallowed his stride, and the jerkiness of his gait, Michael knew his assistant was digesting the suitability of the punishment Michael had imposed upon the sheriff back in the hovel, in his act of releasing Fairfax to hunt him down.

Spry's breathing grew uneven and hoarse. "You relayed Major Craig's message to Fairfax. I don't think he heard you at all. He won't deliver it. He isn't natural. He's a damned monster!" Spry gaped at him. "You let him go! Just like Schmidt let Bowater go! Fairfax manipulated *you*! Sir!"

Outrage and indignation spun Michael's pulse, flamed his face. He'd witnessed men fueled by post-battle horror, forgetting their station, snapping at officers, earning the penalty of at least several hundred lashes for themselves. He'd witnessed the resentment in the eyes of those men, long after their flogged backs had healed to a lumpy, misshapen patchwork of scar tissue. And sometimes, he'd witnessed the junior officers responsible for those men reprimanded, their credibility demoted.

Spry presumed upon the bond between them, a bond necessitated by the investigative work they shared. But the fact was that most soldiers didn't forget their place, no matter the horror they experienced. If Spry didn't learn his boundaries that moment, the next time he was exposed to the horror of battle, he'd earn a flogging for himself. Or worse.

In two long paces, Michael bisected his path, pivoted, and stood to face him, block his way forward. "Take care!"

Routine roused reaction in Spry. Halted, at attention, he stared ahead past Michael's shoulder. Confusion clouded his expression.

Shoulders back, Michael glared at him. Fairfax *was* a monster skilled at manipulation. But defiance in the Army brought a man nothing but punishment. "In His Majesty's Army, private, the penalty for insubordination comes in various forms, none pleasant, all designed to ensure that a man who steps out of line once never does so again. Do you understand?"

The pink on Spry's cheeks deepened. He firmed his chin. "Sir."

"I cannot afford an assistant who is insubordinate, though he may be otherwise correct, courageous, humorous, and quick-witted. There are men in the Eighty-Second Regiment who meet my criteria for an assistant but would never exhibit insubordination. Do you understand, private?"

Color drained from Spry's face. "Sir."

"Major Craig doesn't care who I select as my assistant as long as he's competent and observes proper protocol." Michael doubted that and suspected that Craig had, by now, taken a personal interest in what Spry could accomplish. But if Spry knew that, he'd ignore the critical lesson on defiance presented to him on the Road from the Haw Field. And he might destroy his own credibility before it had the chance to become established. So Michael squeezed a few yards from the doubt. "When we return to Wilmington, you could serve the King just as well by working with the rest of the men. Constructing those fortifications around the town. Running messages. Digging latrines."

Sweat beads popped out above Spry's upper lip. The skin on his face adopted a greenish pallor.

Interesting. From his assistant's reaction, Michael judged that the dull, physical labor that occupied most privates of the Eighty-Second resided in a level of hell even deeper than that of combat. When Spry had joined the Army, perhaps he'd expected to be marching from one end of the colonies to the other, not holed up in a port town building redoubts. Now he knew what he'd signed for and how seldom the Army provided opportunities for a private to use his intelligence. And Michael hoped he was also figuring out when and how to keep his mouth shut.

Time to balance the protocol lesson and ensure that he wasn't creating a poppet. "A minute ago, you asked a question about strategy and decisions. Rephrase that question in a manner that no one would mistake for insubordination."

Still sweating, Spry gulped. "Sir. You released Fairfax with the understanding that he was to track down and eliminate Schmidt and O'Toole—"

"It's *Mister* Fairfax, should you find yourself in the unfortunate position of needing to address him again. He's a Lieutenant in the Seventeenth Light Dragoons."

"Sir." Spry gulped again. "How do you know Mr. Fairfax won't ride to rejoin Lord Cornwallis's army straightaway, without an encounter with Schmidt and O'Toole?"

That same concern had crossed Michael's mind. But Michael knew enough about Fairfax to dismiss the concern. A more chilling question to ask might be, *How will we know when Fairfax has accomplished his task?* But Spry didn't yet know enough about Fairfax to assemble that question. "From personal acquaintance, observation, and history, I doubt Mr. Fairfax will return straightaway to Lord Cornwallis."

The greenish tinge to Spry's complexion became more pronounced. He hadn't liked that answer. One of his eyes twitched, perhaps a deferred reaction to combat, and memory of the monster choking life from him. "Personal acquaintance, observation, and history, sir?"

"Last summer, in a town in Georgia, Mr. Fairfax tortured a Spanish assassin to death. For sport. He set up everything to implicate local Indians. Clever and efficient. I solved the murder, figured out what he'd done. But when I presented evidence to my commander, he—" Bitterness released into Michael's mouth. "Mr. Fairfax had received movement orders out of the area. The Spaniard's missing partner was easily blamed for the murder. The investigation was closed."

Spry's voice lowered in shock. "Your commander released him. And Mr. Fairfax knew you'd figured out what he'd done."

"He tried to kill me, twice. Clever and efficient. Weeks later, while I was on detached duty in Camden, South Carolina, I discovered that he tortured to death several rebel spies. Again, he set up the murders to implicate others. Clever and efficient." Spry, still staring ahead, moved his mouth as if his throat had shrunk to half diameter. "Mr. Fairfax has convinced me that whatever he does, it will be clever and efficient."

"But—but what action do you and I take if he fails? Suppose we arrive in Hillsborough to find that Schmidt and O'Toole have preceded us?"

An excellent question, one that had eroded Michael's confidence the entire time they'd walked the track eastbound. After all, Fairfax hRegad pitted himself against *two* men, and Schmidt was physiologically more powerful than Fairfax. If Michael and Spry returned to a reunion with Schmidt and O'Toole in Hillsborough, they'd be executed immediately.

But Fairfax had the element of surprise in his favor. Michael had seen evidence from his history to indicate that surprise was all he needed to gain the upper hand on an opponent.

Michael and his assistant also had the element of surprise in their favor. Schmidt expected them to be dead.

"Our return to Hillsborough shall be discreet. I've an idea where we might shelter in town for the night." Spry's stomach gurgled. He looked wretched, ready to puke. Standing at attention made it worse. "Are you clear on this issue of insubordination, Spry?"

An almost-inaudible squeal left his lips. "Sir."

"Stand at ease."

Alone, Michael meandered east on the track, then stopped to gaze ahead at the miles they must still traverse that afternoon. His ribs still ached, as if splintered by steel traps. In bushes at the side of the track about twenty feet behind him, Spry heaved up horror—for many men, an essential rung on the ladder out of the trench, after battle had claimed a piece of their humanity.

At least now Spry knew the full scope of the horror.

As for the impending exchange between Schmidt and Fairfax, Michael couldn't summon the enthusiasm to cheer the victory of either man. Unless they managed to exterminate each other, a monster in the guise of a human would prevail. And Michael would eventually have to deal with that triumphant monster.

Chapter Thirty-Two

LIGHT IN AN upstairs window told Michael the old man was home, in the process of retiring for bed. He tapped a second time on the back door, louder than before, still keeping the volume down. Regardless of whether Schmidt had returned, he had no wish to attract attention from neighbors on Queen Street.

The upper-floor window cracked open to divulge crankiness. "Who's that bothering me after my supper?"

Carroll, prudent, hadn't poked his head out the window to make a target of himself. Michael detected a twitch in drapes covering the window of the room adjacent to the old man's. Must be Noah. "It's Compton, sir."

"*Compton?* Good God, laddie, you're alive! Be right down." The window snicked shut.

Relief whooshed from Michael, transformed by the frosty night into a whorl of breath. He clasped the shoulder of Spry, who'd sagged against the outer wall. "Chin up, lad." Although fatigue stripped away his words, Spry's head bobbed in gratitude. Close to ten miles they must have walked, scrambling from sight off the main road to Virginia every time they heard the approach of horses, unsure whether it was enemies.

Light swelled between seams in drapes near the back door. Shoes inside shuffled. The bar slid away. Then the door opened inward to a room near the stairs and back-pounding welcomes for Michael from the Carrolls.

Spry limped in. Noah winced at bruises mottling the private's face and rushed to bar the door behind him. Michael made a quick introduction of "Miller," his companion.

The old man's tone roughened. "Let's get you lads cleaned up. There's left-over stew and bread that'll go to waste if you don't eat it. You can tell us later what happened."

Michael lifted his chin. "Mr. Carroll, I must warn you. Georg Schmidt has tacked a price upon our hides."

"Bah. Nobody's seen him or most of his men since this morning. He left a couple of rats guarding the jail, then most of them rode north, escort for you two all hog-tied and covered up in that wagon. Oh, yes, Noah witnessed everything." Carroll cackled. "When Schmidt returns, he'll surely have to dance a jig for the Committee of Safety to explain his absence.

"Now, get on with you both, into the dining room." Carroll jabbed his cane toward the front of the house. "I ain't hearing a word of your story until you relax."

Noah swept ahead of them, his lamp the beacon of a pilot boat in the darkness. Michael followed. The foyer sprawled before them, a pit of shadows. Floorboards creaked on the second floor at the same time peripheral vision alerted Michael to movement on the stairs. Within one hard heartbeat, he leapt back into the skin of a soldier and snapped about to face the stairs, a hand on his dagger.

Lamplight picked up a peachy luster of blonde hair. The swish of descending fabric resolved itself into petticoats. Kate launched herself into Michael's arms. "Oh, thank heaven you're safe, Michael! After this morning, I thought I'd never see you again."

In the semidarkness, he sank into her embrace with a swiftness that shocked him, immersed him in softness and cinnamon-scent. At one with warmth and welcome, he forgot where he was. Matthew Tierney's words whispered to mind: *You're living proof that no one is always a warrior.*

Noah meandered back from the dining room, lamp in hand, to shed light upon the reunion. Over Kate's shoulder, Michael saw bawdy humor balm the weariness on Spry's face. What was the Widow Duncan doing in Hillsborough, and how had she and his commanding officer arrived at such a cozy, first-name basis?

Michael cleared his throat, untangled Kate's arms from around his neck, and set her back from him. The air about them trembled, resistant to the separation. Then puzzlement dashed away the hunger in her eyes. She stepped away farther, wrinkled her nose. "What's that weird smell on you? Last night, it was dead fish. Tonight it's like—"

"Yes, thank you, Kate." He preferred that she not speculate upon what dead species had supplied his current reek, especially since Rachel White had descended the stairs after her niece.

Neither Kate nor her aunt had been physically harmed. From the way all of Carroll's drapes were drawn, the old man and his grandson must have sheltered the women most of the day. More gratitude swept over Michael.

Kate spotted Spry and rushed to him, abandoning Michael like a bucket dropped in dirt. "You look terrible. What happened to your face?" She tugged Spry toward the dining room and motioned Noah to follow her with the lamp. "Sit before you fall over with fatigue. Here, now, let me take a look at you. You fellows were in a huge fistfight, weren't you?"

Spry groaned on cue, not even attempting stoicism when Kate's fingers explored the knots on his face. Michael's lips pinched shut. Damn it, Fairfax hadn't exactly been easy on *his* face. Maybe he could look forward to having

Kate clean and re-bandage the cut on his forearm. Mid-afternoon, it had had the grace to stop bleeding.

Aunt Rachel opened her embrace to him. "What a blessing that you've returned."

Considering that forty-eight hours earlier, she'd nearly cast him out into the night, her hug seemed more miraculous than Kate's. They separated, and he noticed that grief over the second loss of her son bloated her face. "Madam, I'm so sorry for your loss. Would that I hadn't been the instrument of—"

"Oh, hush." Her voice was hoarse. "After ten years, my wait is finally over." She regarded him with resolve. "I've had the day to think about it. I've no reason to remain here. Time to sell my property, indeed, and move on to Wilmington with Kate and Kevin."

In Michael's peripheral vision, Kate peered into the cavern of Spry's mouth, at teeth the size of those on a workhorse. Spry lounged back in a chair, docile, allowing her to reassure him that no teeth had been knocked out. Michael slammed back envy with an extra-big smile for Aunt Rachel. "Marvelous. That will make them quite happy." Then he craned his neck toward the stairs. Odd. He'd heard a scuffing noise from the second floor, above the back-and-forth of the two Carrolls, who prepared the dining table and spread a late supper for their guests.

Aunt Rachel prodded him in the chest with her forefinger, redirecting his attention back to her. "You, sir, have unfinished business here in town. Tonight."

"I do?" Premonition crept up his spine at her smile, not unlike glee in the face of a Greek goddess just before she dispensed a ghastly punishment upon a mortal. Michael felt his larynx bob in a swallow. "Tonight? Why tonight?"

"Right after Mr. Schmidt apprehended you and escorted you to jail, Kate returned to the house. She warned me of the danger and assured me that Mr. Carroll would hide us. As we prepared to flee, deputies came marching down Tryon Street. However they went to Mr. Tierney's house, not mine, to arrest him first." Aunt Rachel stretched the suspense with her smile. "Mr. Bowater was among them."

Michael caught his breath. "What time was that?"

"About ten." She gripped his upper arm. "You'll never guess what Mr. Bowater expected out of his inclusion in that arrest party."

The pieces came together in Michael's head. "Mr. Tierney's gig."

Her eyes widened in amazement, and she released his arm. "Aren't you the clever one? How did you figure that out?"

"Schmidt awarded the gig to him, under the condition that he leave town and never return. Schmidt planned to pass Bowater's broken vehicle off as Mr. Tierney's, more wrongful evidence against him."

"I see. Well, then, the universe has corrected such a grievous imbalance. Mr. Tierney anticipated the pivotal role required of his conveyance. When Mr. Schmidt's men and Mr. Bowater arrived, they found the gig partially disassembled and rendered incapable of travel."

Sobriety had worked wonders for Tierney. "How in the world did you find all this out?"

Ruthlessness split Aunt Rachel's lips. "Aren't you going to ask me instead when Mr. Bowater left town?"

"When did he leave town?" Michael spread his hands.

"He *didn't* leave town."

He caught his breath. "He's *here*? Alive?"

She nodded, crisp and curt. "He has already paid a wainwright, Mr. Spears, to reassemble the gig and have it ready for his departure first thing on the morrow. Meanwhile, he's parked his wretched carcass in Faddis's Tavern for the night, where he awaits delivery of his transportation."

Gratitude spun Michael's thoughts. What an advantage the universe had dropped in his lap. "That fool imagines he's safe. That Schmidt has neutralized me and won't begrudge him the extra day in Hillsborough while his transportation is repaired."

"So it seems. Noah has kept Violet's journal secure and will give it to you, critical evidence you need for a conviction. So fortify yourself with supper." Aunt Rachel's chin quivered, but she stilled it. She patted his shoulder with the encouragement bestowed upon a prize-winning boxer. "Then head over to Faddis's Tavern. Fetch the scoundrel who murdered my son. Tonight."

Bowater had proven himself wily and violent. Michael rotated his head and studied Spry's sluggishness. From the aches in his own body, he could gauge the restorative effect of a good night's sleep on his assistant and himself: their coordination, judgment, dexterity, strength, and mental alertness. He and Spry needed their faculties replenished before they challenged Bowater.

More importantly, the apprehension scene that Aunt Rachel anticipated would draw plenty of attention in a busy tavern at night—not necessarily a beneficial sort of attention. Bowater might even find a way to elude capture during chaos, while Michael had no authority in Hillsborough to arrest the land agent or command the assistance of civilians in apprehending him. And he didn't want to advertise his presence to any of Schmidt's men.

Far better to make Bowater's capture as discrete as possible, then leave Hillsborough soon afterward, if not immediately. Genesis of a plan filtered into his reasoning. "Is my mare still in your stable?"

"She is. Around five this evening, Martha sent word that my property hadn't been disturbed in our absence. Her son Philip has cared for the horses and dogs."

Tired as he was, Michael knew he had to sneak to Aunt Rachel's that night and retrieve Cleopatra and his belongings. Spry had told him earlier that Schmidt confiscated his gelding, tackle, and pack at the jail. Somehow, they must also retrieve Spry's gear and mount. And he must locate a wagon for prisoner transport. Not even if Bowater were bound and gagged would he allow him in a saddle. He mused over obstacles in the plan. "Where is Mr. Spears the wainwright located?"

"King Street, just west of my tavern."

"Has Martha's son Philip experience handling a gig?"

For a second, Aunt Rachel's eyebrows pinched. Then her dark eyes flashed as she fingered threads of fabric from the tapestry he wove for the morrow. "Yes. And it doesn't sound as though you're planning to apprehend Mr. Bowater tonight."

"No, not until the morrow, when we're fully rested." He watched the press of her lips, caught one of her hands in his, and claimed the posture of an officer.

"Hillsborough deserves peace, not more turmoil or bloodshed. While I manage Bowater's capture and removal, and *quietly* ensure that justice is served back in Wilmington, you must ensure the safety of yourself and your niece." He kissed her hand. "Promise me you shall do so."

The guard in Rachel White's eyes lowered, perhaps for the first time in years. One solemn twinkle garnished her gaze. "Fie on you, Michael," she whispered. "You haven't been paying attention." Her regard flicked to Kate, who, despite all the fuss she'd lavished on Spry, hadn't hugged the private once. "I can see to Kate's physical safety. What she does with her heart is up to her."

The scuffing noise he'd heard upstairs earlier caught his attention again. He started toward the stairs, restrained by Aunt Rachel's hand on his arm just long enough for her to whisper, "Tierney has hidden up there all day. He seems to be ill."

So that was how she'd known about the disrepair of the dandy's gig. Michael summoned energy and bounded up the stairs. Tierney shrank from his approach and wrapped himself in shadow, like a grieving Spanish widow. But Michael snagged his shoulder and pinned him against a closed bedroom door. "What in hell are you doing up here?"

He heard ragged breathing and saw the sheen of sweat on the dandy's brow. "What does it look like I'm doing? I'm hiding behind a blind man, a deaf man, and two women. Hillsborough is full of heroes, don't you know?"

Tierney didn't sound well. Michael backed off him a step. "If I'd been in your shoes, I'd have hidden, too. Where's the glory in awaiting Schmidt's pleasure in jail?"

Tierney drummed fingers against the wood of the door behind him, as if stillness eluded him. "Hang that son of a whore."

Michael kept his voice low. "That sentence isn't mine to carry out."

"I see. Well, then, you'll need a wagon for prisoner transport on the morrow, yes? I'll give you a wagon, and you can give me back my gig in exchange. No need to return the wagon."

"Thank you. That's generous of you." More pieces of plan for the morrow clumped together in Michael's imagination, more things to do before he could rest that night.

Savagery slathered Tierney's shaky whisper. "But do kill Horatio Bowater before you reach Cross Creek. Or wherever the hell it is you're really from, because it isn't Cross Creek, and you don't know a bloody thing about naval stores."

Uneasy, disturbed, Michael stared at the dark blob of dandy splayed against the door. "Mr. Bowater must have a trial. I cannot blatantly kill him, Mr. Tierney."

"But you can. You've killed men in battle." He coughed, ceased drumming his fingers. "You killed men today. I smell death on you. So just pretend that he tried to escape, and you had to shoot him. Then leave him for scavengers."

Michael's disquiet deepened. "Are you well? You don't sound like the same man as last night."

"Last night." Tierney laughed, the eerie titter of a mind unhinged. "I thought she was happy last night." His laughter subsided into soft gasps. With a pang of pity and shock, Michael realized the man was sobbing. "With Aaron White."

Bitterness choked back the sobs, tangled his tongue. "But she was dead! Bowater killed her. I should have done something ten years ago. I sensed it was wrong, the way he looked at her. I should have dueled with him. Killed him."

At his party, Tierney hadn't impressed Michael with being so very smitten with Violet as to collapse into heartbreak and madness. Perhaps multiple stresses of the day had sent him reeling. But still, he couldn't imagine Tierney dueling with anyone. Some portion of the man's emotion seemed shammed. "See here, why don't you join us downstairs while we eat supper, settle your nerves with brandy—"

"No. I'm done with spirits. Almost a day since I touched any."

The explanation for his overly emotional state became obvious. Those dependent on spirits seldom gave them up without tumult. Too much like losing a lover. "A wise choice. But go easy on yourself these next few days."

Tierney babbled as if he hadn't heard him. "Schmidt impounded your man's horse and gear when he arrived last night, yes? You need a way to retrieve it, a distraction, while you slip into jail. I've a plan. I'm a fugitive. Early on the morrow, I shall turn myself in. I can create a great drama for those two curs guarding the jail. At least five minutes of drama. They'll never see you sneak in and make off with the horse and gear."

Michael stared at him, incredulous, wishing he could read inside his skull. The more Tierney talked, the less sense he made. "No one's asking you to make that kind of sacrifice."

"I make it freely."

Such a cavalier attitude toward danger reeked of ulterior motive. Michael listened to giddiness in the other man's breathing. "A more helpful sacrifice on your part," he said cautious, still listening, "one that requires no danger to you, would be giving us an extra horse and some traveling gear."

'No. I shall create drama at the jail."

Tierney's motive sprang out at Michael. "You pathetic louse." A growl roamed his throat. He shoved Tierney's chest, slammed him against the door. "You're working up the nerve to incite those two deputies into shooting and killing you. You're more afraid of *living* than dying."

"Violet's dead!" Venom loaded Tierney's whisper.

"Don't tell me you haven't suspected it all these years. You're too intelligent for that." Michael heard his voice rise in fury and made himself pause a moment to drop the volume. "This isn't about your heartbreak over learning that she's dead. This is about your self-pity. You could be helping people with your skills, but no, your body of work gathers dust in your study while you wallow in self-pity."

"You expect me to resume my work as a naturalist? Not a respectable act for a gentleman."

"And getting two deputies to shoot you is? Come on, Tierney, grow up. The field you're in is well-respected. You're telling yourself lies."

"With Violet gone, I have no artist!"

The solution spread through Michael's soul like a wind shredding clouds, rolling them back to reveal a clean, blue sky. Noah sketched people, a rose, a butterfly, and a cardinal. Noah wouldn't be squeamish about sketching caterpillars and skinks. "Violet's student possesses far greater talent than his teacher."

"Student? What student? What the devil are you talking about? Where?"

"The portrait I showed you last night was sketched by Noah Carroll."

Tierney exhaled into the darkness and muttered, "He's deaf."

"Not completely. And his eyes are better than those of anyone in Hillsborough because of it." Michael softened his voice further. "Hire Noah Carroll as your artist. He needs the work, the respect that comes from being able to use his calling to help others." His forefinger tapped Tierney's chest once. "No man has to die to be a hero. Resume *your* calling as a naturalist."

He pivoted for the stairs, fatigue weighing down his legs as if bags of clay had been strapped to his stockings. He took a deep breath, then said over his shoulder to the dandy, "Noah's grandfather will show you pictures he's drawn. Come on downstairs. Have a look at them."

A quarter way down to the first floor, Michael heard Tierney following him. And he smiled.

Chapter Thirty-Three

AROUND FIVE-THIRTY THE next morning, the fourteenth of February, Michael observed Tierney and Spry's return from their foray to the dandy's property. At the front window, he watched them park darkness-cloaked forms of a wagon and horse in the street and slip around for the rear of the house. Stiff and aching from the previous day's skirmish, he scuffed back to meet them just inside the door, and Noah shut out the cold. The dandy and the private hadn't been followed. Michael congratulated them on their stealth.

Back at his post up front, he rotated his shoulders to loosen muscles and peeked out the drapes. A horse hitched to a gig had joined the conveyance in the street: Bowater's horse and Tierney's gig. Excellent. The first phase of his plan was complete. Martha's son, Philip, had fetched the repaired gig from Mr. Spears on King Street. Michael rubbed his hands together and again headed for the back door, this time to thank Philip.

But as soon as Noah ushered Philip inside and closed the door, the lad released a stream of babble, his arms flailing about. The commotion drew everyone else in the house to them: Spry, Kate, Aunt Rachel, Carroll, and Tierney.

At first, Michael thought the wainwright had harassed Philip, questioned his story about being tipped by Bowater to deliver his transportation to the doorstep of Faddis's Tavern before dawn. Then he sorted out the words "death," "demon," and "devil" from Philip's gibberish. A deeper concern stabbed him. He seized the youth's shoulders and shook him, once.

Philip gaped, his face whiter than fog by the light of Noah's lamp. His blather dribbled away. Queasiness whirred in Michael's stomach. His voice snapped. "Did someone follow you here?"

"N-n-no, sir." Philip shook his head as if trying to dislodge water from his ears.

"What frightened you, then?"

"The d-devil is out there. And dead men." He broke free of Michael and pointed in the direction of town center.

"What twaddle is this, Philip?" Aunt Rachel's voice grated like pumice. "You've more sense than to fear the dark. My nephew asked you a question. Answer him."

"M-men's heads. They b-bounced. I s-saw them."

Tierney thumped the floor with his cane. "Bounced? Where? What are you talking about?"

"On the r-road b-before the jail."

"I'm not drunk anymore. Am I the only one here who's confused?"

"No, Mr. Tierney, you aren't the only one who's confused." Aunt Rachel stepped between Michael and Philip. "Young man, I insist on a proper accounting from you. Start from when you left Mr. Spears's shop on King Street with the horse and gig."

Philip sucked in a breath and nodded. " King Street was quiet when I headed east toward Churton. But near the cross streets, I heard a horse on Churton, south of me. I pulled the gig before Dowell's Ordinary, just before the corner, where we wouldn't be seen by anyone northbound on Churton."

Philip clawed at his cloak where it closed at his throat. "I got out, peeked around. A m-man in a greatcoat. On horseback. Stopped just outside the jail. He emptied a s-sack hooked to his saddle. They rolled out, bounced on the road. T-two men's heads, they rolled and bounced. Their hair—" His finger traced a shaky arc through the air, a visual recounting of the floppy motion of loosened human hair on a severed, bouncing head.

Oil in Noah's lamp sizzled. Philip gulped. No one moved.

Michael's gaze slithered to Spry at the same moment his assistant's gawk sought him. A muscle twitched beneath the private's left eye. Michael swallowed, and it felt like he was forcing down an oversized hunk of week-old bread.

"He rode north on Churton." Phillip's whole body shuddered. "I waited there, out of sight. C-couldn't get my legs to move for five minutes."

Michael brushed past Aunt Rachel and Philip to stand beside Spry. "Miller and I shall assess this development before we commence with the next phase, make certain we don't have to revise our plans."

The bleak eyes of Martha's son tracked Michael. "Today's Valentine's Day, sir." His voice squawked, a boy on the brink of manhood. "It's the day to give a kiss to your sweetheart. Who would give severed heads instead?"

Spry coughed with discretion. "Er, I need a bit of fresh air." He jammed his hat on his head and rushed out the back door. One of his hands clenched the sheathed dagger at his hip.

The blast of winter night created by his departure cleared Michael's head. He glanced at his watch. They had less than an hour of darkness left. He swung his greatcoat over his shoulders and settled a loaned hat on his head. "We shall return in fifteen minutes. Philip, you remember what to do next?"

"Sir. Switch the two horses out front." The lad's voice firmed as he spoke. Occupy a soldier with a crucial task after battle, and he could distance himself from the nightmare.

"Correct. Be quick about it. Have the gig and wagon ready when we return. Everyone else, remain inside while we're gone." He collected his rifle and ammunition from beside the door.

"Be careful, Michael." Spunk forsook Kate's voice. Fear tunneled her eyes.

His gaze lingered on her lips. Valentine's Day. The image of severed heads bounced through his imagination. He let himself out into a frigid night's grip upon Hillsborough.

Beside the back step, Spry's breath formed pale mist. He stamped his feet for warmth and said, low, "We confirm what the devil left us in front of jail for Valentine's Day. Then we bag Bowater and take our leave of this town. Right, sir?"

Michael sighed, hard. "Agreed."

***

Early risers were up and about by wagon, foot, and horse: a dairyman, a baker, a farmer. Keeping to the shadows, the two soldiers trotted for town center. Michael muffled the clank of his rifle.

Their guarded approach allowed them the view of two round, head-sized objects on the ground, dark and still, about five feet out from the jail's entrance. Jail itself appeared quiet, as if the humans associated with it were asleep or had abandoned the building.

Michael, crouched with his assistant behind a hedgerow opposite the entrance, tugged Spry's coat sleeve and murmured, "Whoever enters or exits jail won't miss those things."

"Meant to be tripped over, sir." Spry kept his voice low. "Any moment now, one of the men Schmidt left behind could spot them and raise an alarm."

His exhale, laden with reluctance, informed Michael that Spry loathed the thought of the next step: drawing close enough for positive identification of the objects. Michael glanced inside the low palisade wall beside the jailhouse. One horse minus saddle and tackle hunched near the building, head low. The beast appeared cold, dispirited. "Is that your horse?"

"Looks like it."

"Sneak over. If it's yours, locate a gate and bring him out here with us. Probably too much to hope for, that your gear is stored nearby. But if you recover any of it, be quiet. The goal is to not draw attention to ourselves, not start a row." Michael fixed his gaze on the two objects in the road, preparing himself.

"Sir." With a whisper of sound, Spry stood, scanned the street in both directions, and slunk across to the fence.

Before Michael could lose his nerve, he crept to the jail's entrance. One of the heads on the ground before him angled a handsome, cleft chin to the sky. O'Toole. About nine inches away, Schmidt's right cheek had lodged in a fresh horse turd. *Scheiße*, indeed.

Michael's stomach lurched. Implicit in the delivery of Schmidt and O'Toole's heads was Fairfax's contract. He'd sliced clear the way for Michael to administer the King's justice upon a murderous, greedy land agent. Now Michael was in his enemy's debt.

Silly of him even to have entertained the slightest hope that Schmidt, O'Toole, and Fairfax might exterminate each other during their confrontation. That sort of easy ending occurred only in plays and novels. While his brain sputtered out the rationale that Cornwallis's army could march north on the morrow, and thus there was no immediate worry for him, his instincts insisted that somewhere down the road, regardless of where Cornwallis marched, the devil would expect to collect on their bargain.

Michael groped his way to the palisade, where he gripped a foundation picket and hauled in several lungfuls of frozen air to settle his gut. Within the enclosure, Spry, his back turned, fitted a bridle on his gelding, alternating with motions and murmurs that soothed the horse. Michael opened the gate and let himself in.

The private paused his ministrations to study his commander's approach. Michael muttered, "Orange County needs a new sheriff."

Spry nodded once, mute, then hefted the horse's saddle, bedroll, and saddlebags off a rack built onto the side of the jailhouse. Michael caught the reins in one hand, his rifle held in the other. Without further talk, they guided the horse from the enclosure and eased the gate shut behind them. Michael located a cart track back to Queen Street.

As they walked, his disquiet increased. Spry's horse had been fed and groomed, but why had the gelding and gear been left unguarded? How had they been allowed to recover all of Spry's belongings except his rifle, dagger, and money without being challenged? The deputies inside must be enjoying the repose of the complacent, overconfident in the return of their sheriff.

Before full daylight, hell would unleash in Hillsborough. If neither deputy stepped outside first and found the heads, an artisan or sutler would be sure to recognize the sheriff and his minion when traffic picked up on Churton Street. The Committee of Safety would impose a curfew. The lives of two soldiers disguised as civilians would become even more imperiled. Resourceful as Bowater was, he might escape amidst the fear and confusion.

Michael had paid far too high a price to allow that villainous land agent to escape.

In the street before Carroll's house, he noted that Philip had switched the horses and left both vehicles and horses facing east. The two soldiers led Spry's gelding to Carroll's stable, where Cleopatra and the gelding nosed each other in recognition and welcome. Since the mare had been readied for the day's ride earlier, Michael left Spry to saddle his own horse, then proceeded to Carroll's house.

The six people inside were waiting where he'd left them, near the rear door. Lamplight wavered, plunged six pairs of eyes into shadows. With the impartial tone of a senior officer's spokesman, he said, "Mr. Schmidt and Mr. O'Toole are no longer capable of keeping the peace in Orange County."

He quieted the murmur of consternation and fear with raised hands. "I can speculate what happened. I told you last night that Lord Cornwallis's army appears to be camped within a few days of Hillsborough, and that dragoons from the Seventeenth Light helped my man and me escape execution at the hands of Mr. Schmidt's men. Mr. O'Toole was apparently spying for the Continentals and slipped up, revealed himself to Crown forces. Mr. Schmidt planned to pass me off as the spy. Instead, it appears that the dragoons pierced Mr. Schmidt's deception and executed two enemies of the Crown. I would expect no less of them."

Aunt Rachel pressed knuckles to her lips. Kate stroked her aunt's upper arm once. Tierney flopped into the chair nearest Michael, defeat rasping from him, the sweat of withdrawal beading his forehead. "Brilliant. Schmidty already advanced his theory to the Committee that I'm Griggsy's killer. Now Schmidty's dead, and I had the best motive of anyone in Hillsborough to want him dead."

"Quite so." Michael didn't dull the razor of sarcasm in his tone. "But four other people have lodged with you beneath this roof for the better part of the past twenty-four hours and can testify that you'd neither the opportunity nor the means to kill Mr. Schmidt or Mr. O'Toole. I'm afraid you must go on living awhile longer. And as the deaths of the two men will be discovered at any moment, do have the sense to stay hidden until the worst of it blows over."

He ignored Tierney's groan to face the others. Somberness displaced his sarcasm. "Miller and I must leave now, move forward quickly with the rest of the plan. If we're successful, he and I won't be coming back here. Philip and Noah will return with Mr. Tierney's gig and horse. Philip." He addressed the boy. "Ready to drive the gig to Faddis's?"

Philip thrust back his shoulders. "Yes, sir!"

"Noah." Michael looked the deaf man square on to ensure that he had his attention. "Ready to drive the wagon?"

Noah grinned, his eyes aglow with purpose, and bobbed his head.

Michael nodded, then sought Noah's grandfather. "Mr. Carroll, Miller and I are grateful for your generosity. We can never repay you."

"Sure you can, laddie." Rapacious teeth flashed. "Rid Hillsborough of that scoundrel who killed my neighbors." He offered Michael a firm, warm handshake.

Aunt Rachel cleared her throat with all the subtlety of a wagonload of barrels dumped and clattering loose down the street. She imprisoned Michael in her imperious hug, then set him out from her and passed a critical eye from his head to his toes. "The next time I see you, nephew, I expect you to be properly attired."

In other words, in uniform. Michael's eyebrows loped upward. "Yes, madam."

She guided him left, to the attention of her niece. At the sight of Kate's soft, parted lips and receptive gaze, Michael's arms ached. What a bother, that the two of them stood in the company of so many people who must continue to believe them cousins. He attempted a blithe smile. "Alas, Mrs. Farrell must cancel her social event. The guest of honor won't be in town."

"Cancel? Hardly. I expect Mrs. Farrell to reschedule the event. And Peaches now expects a long walk beside the river with Mr. Kirkleigh."

Heat surged through his neck into his face. Never had such incentive to apprehend and secure a criminal been dangled before him. He passed the tip of his tongue along his upper lip. "Lucky Mr. Kirkleigh."

Even the brevity of his filial hug didn't prevent the current of unity from unfolding between them. Probably for the best that Spry timed his entrance then, leaving the back door ajar. "All ready out there, Mr. Compton."

Her carriage straight, Kate lowered her gaze and sidled close to Aunt Rachel. Michael had seen the adieu in camp, whenever a woman sought the solace of other women after bidding farewell to a man who held her heart: a soldier prepared to storm down the throat of hell with his fellows on a battlefield. No woman had ever favored him thusly before. The ache in his arms leapt into his heart and squeezed.

He spun about, the heels of his boots scratching brusqueness upon the wood floor, and made for the chill of the opened doorway with a wave of his arm. "Very good, Miller. Philip. Noah. Attend us."

Chapter Thirty-Four

SINGLE-FILE, WITH PHILIP in the lead, they traveled a cart track around the east edge of town to the Indian trading path, then picked up King Street to Faddis's Tavern, avoiding the jail. A couple of groggy grooms at the stable recognized Philip and Noah and allowed them to back the gig just inside and park the wagon outside. Michael pressed the remaining coins he'd taken from dead rebels into the grooms' palms: a guarantee that they'd enjoy mulled spirits beside a fire, stay out from underfoot for at least half an hour.

The grooms left, and Philip hurried for the tavern to inform the wainwright's customer that his transportation was repaired, awaiting final approval in the stable. Michael and Spry tethered their horses beside the wagon, loaded at Tierney's manor with a naturalist's camping supplies and provisions. Noah concealed himself nearby.

Daggers and coiled rope at their belts, Michael and Spry hid in the stable, on either side behind the double doors. In shadows created by the golden glow of lanterns hanging on wall pegs, Michael remembered the traps that Bowater had left behind in Wilmington. He rechecked his rope and dagger, then let out a tense breath.

In about ten minutes, with the sky paling and a bit of breeze creaking branch and beam, Michael heard the approach of Philip, his tone chirpy: "My master wanted you to be satisfied, sir. If anything's amiss, I shall drive the gig back, and we shall repair it while you breakfast."

Michael's lips peeled back from his teeth when he recognized Bowater's grouchy assent. Straw on the ground swished with the passage of Philip through the stable's entrance. "*That?*" said Bowater. "That isn't my horse!"

Michael peered around the edge of the door. Bowater, minus his wig, hat, and greatcoat, looked rumpled, as if he'd thrown on clothing as he walked out. The land agent also appeared unarmed of even a dagger and stood just inside, before the head of Tierney's horse. Alas, too close to the doors. At that distance, he might run out before Michael could close him in.

Philip spread his hands, and his tone bled with innocent dismay. "Not your horse, sir?"

"Pimply brat, you've hitched the wrong horse to my gig!" Shoulders hunched, Bowater stomped in for Philip.

"But I thought for certain—" Philip backed from Bowater, eyes widening and jaw trembling, unfeigned. "Which was your horse? The b-b-brown mare?"

Veins bulged on Bowater's neck. The pitch of his voice rose. "You know it was the brown mare! You're trying to swindle me with this older gelding!" He punched air near Philip's nose. "Dolt! I should beat you before I send you back to your master for the correct horse!"

Bowater was, by then, well inside the stable. The ruse had played out long enough. Alarmed for the lad's safety, Michael swung shut the door he'd hidden behind, followed a second later by Spry. The clatter echoed, startling Tierney's gelding and several horses lodged in stalls.

Bowater whipped about in surprise. Philip sprinted from around him. Spry allowed the boy to scamper past. Philip departed the stable, on his way to his final task: clearing Bowater's belongings from his room.

The land agent's sallow complexion reddened upon recognition of the two soldiers. A snarl wavered over his lips. "*You!* You're dead!"

Michael didn't transfer his stare off his fugitive. "Odd. I don't feel dead." He made his voice calm, flat, unlike the rabbit-leap of his pulse. He took a step away from the doors, toward Bowater. "Do you feel dead, Mr. Miller?"

"Not at all, Mr. Compton. In fact, I feel like taking a trip south, riding for a few days." Spry planted his feet beside Michael and popped his knuckles once, loudly.

"Gah!" Bowater jumped into the gig and seized the reins.

While he fumbled for control, the horse skittered around. Michael and Spry dodged hooves and pounced into the gig from both sides. From Michael's first experience with the land agent in Wilmington, he expected that he and Spry would subdue him quickly and be on their way.

But Bowater thrashed between them like a wildcat caught in the metal trap he'd laid below the floorboards of his office. The soldiers slammed and bounced against upholstery and frame. The frightened horse neighed and yanked the gig forward, jerking all three men around.

Bowater punched Michael's stomach and clipped his chin, already tenderized by Fairfax. Over the red-hot buzz of pain, Michael heard Bowater butt Spry's head with his own. He lunged for Bowater. The gig jerked again. His face smashed the seat, wrenching his neck.

The land agent kicked out. Spry plummeted from the gig and thudded to straw-covered dirt near the wheels. Bowater, tangled in reins, was dragged partway out.

Tierney's gelding continued his nervous dance. Michael scrambled for the reins. Bowater heaved himself back into the gig and elbowed him in the shoulder. The two grappled and punched. Michael tasted blood. Locked together, they tumbled out the other side. On his back, Michael absorbed the impact of his fall and Bowater's. Pain blasted his torso.

Bereft of breath, hips and shoulders pinned, he gaped at the downward arc of his own dagger in Bowater's fist. Strength surged through him. His hand shot up, caught Bowater's wrist. The land agent's teeth bared, and he bore down. The point of the dagger hovered above the hollow of Michael's throat, a lantern-lit, lethal faery.

Michael shoved more strength into twisting Bowater's wrist. The dagger remained firm an inch from his throat.

Out of the shadows thundered Spry to straddle them both and whip rope about Bowater's neck. The land agent flailed in the noose and dropped the dagger. Michael regained just enough leverage to dodge the plummet of the point into dirt beside his neck. Bowater bucked, clawed for the rope. Michael rolled from beneath him to his knees, where he sucked in air.

The stable door, left ajar by Philip, creaked open wider on the breeze, followed by a metallic whisper of sound, like a ramrod locked into place. Sensing the chance for flight from the chaos, Tierney's gelding hopped about. The gig collided with Spry, dislodging his hold on Bowater. The land agent kicked him again.

A yowl tore from Spry. "My leg! Son of a—damn you! My leg!" He tottered against the gig clutching the leg injured in Wilmington.

Bowater flung the rope from around his neck and darted for the opened door. Michael sprang for him and seized a fistful of stocking. Wool ripped away. Michael swore.

The land agent bolted for freedom. But in the doorway, he brought himself up short, his legs braced apart, and his ribcage a bellows of exertion. His hands flung up, a gesture of warding off. He staggered three steps backward, into the stable.

Janet Sewell advanced three steps in after him, a pistol steady in her hand and aimed for Bowater's chest, her face a Medusa-mask. When Bowater tensed to leap, her grip firmed on the pistol, and she jabbed the barrel toward him, forcing him to retreat another step. About five feet behind her, Noah hove into view, his expression laden with horror. Young Philip, wide-eyed and riveted, peeked around the edge of the door.

"My father taught me to use this pistol." Her voice sounded rough, the salt-crusted tone of a pirate's mistress on the open sea. "I've killed plenty of scampering rats with it."

Michael's pulse bumped like a runaway cart on a rocky trail, and boulders rolled into his stomach. Without a doubt, if he didn't seize control of the situation, someone would be killed. He staggered to his feet and scooped up his dagger and Spry's rope, hardly taking his gaze off his fugitive and the woman who had placed him on her executioner's block. He steadied Tierney's gelding. Then he foisted the rope off onto his assistant, who still grunted with pain. Slowly he approached the land agent.

Bowater spotted Michael's approach. He lowered his arms. His lips quivered with cunning. "Madam, do you know who I am? I'm a patriot, like yourself."

Spry hobbled up beside his commander. Michael drew a breath of confusion. Did Bowater not recognize Janet Sewell?

The agent jabbed a thumb over his shoulder. "Those two are redcoats.

Lieutenant Stoddard and his lackey, Spry, have tracked me from Wilmington. But patriots govern *this* town."

Desperation surged through Michael.

"And if you allow me to pass, madam, I shall be about the Congress's business in town."

The hand with the pistol remained steady. Half a second only did the woman holding it spare a glance for the soldiers. Then Medusa recaptured Bowater. "Do you know who *I* am?" Her tone became soft but not soothing. "I was your first victim here. Ten years ago, when the Regulators were hanged, you murdered your second victim, my best friend."

Bowater's head wrenched, as if her words had driven needles through his earlobes. From the side, Michael saw the land agent's face sag. One of Bowater's cheeks twitched with the realization that he'd gambled and played his worst possible card.

Miss Sewell licked her lips. "September of '71, a boy fishing downriver on the Eno found remains of a young woman weighed down in the water. The body was unidentifiable from long exposure to the elements. Thus was the crime unsolvable. However, as I lay abed this morning, I realized that the body must have been Violet's. We thought all this time that she'd eloped with Rachel White's boy. But you murdered him back then, too, as old Mr. Pratt testified from his deathbed yesterday."

Bowater shook all over. His knees wobbled. His throat made noises like pecking chickens.

" 'Congress's business in town?' " A sneer teased the woman's lips before folding back into softness. "Bah. This past Sunday, you murdered Violet's father, *my* father's best friend. Just think, Horatio Bowater. Had my sweetheart not come to me last night and told me where to find you this morning, we'd have missed each other.

"Now I don't know whether those two men behind you really are redcoats, sent to apprehend you. But you're such a miserable excuse for a human being that even two redcoats will look the other way while I deliver this pistol ball exactly where it belongs."

She shifted her aim to Bowater's groin and cocked the pistol fully. His eyes bugged, his chicken scratch became blubbering, and his hands covered his crotch.

Michael inched forward. "Miss Sewell, please don't squeeze that trigger." He winced as he heard himself. Although he'd tried to pitch his tone calm, the fire in his pulse tainted his voice, made it more rigid than relaxed.

"Why should I not kill him? You know as well as I what happened. You've made yourself familiar with the history that binds together the Sewells, Whites, and Griggses."

"If you kill Bowater, you become a murderer." Michael recognized the furrow on Noah's brow, the glistening of his eyes. His spirit dropped inside the deaf man's heart, and anguish scored his own heart. "I doubt very much that the man standing behind you wants murder for your future. As of last night, he has a very different, very rewarding future spread before him. He wants you to share in it." Michael fished after conjecture, knit it into possibility. "It's a future which your father would approve."

Curiosity chipped at the shield of vengeance on her face. The pistol trembled. Then she steadied it. "Do you ask me to let this murderer face judgment here in town?"

"I ask you to let him face judgment, yes. But in Wilmington, not here."

She swallowed, kept her stare on the land agent. The pistol trembled again. "The King's justice? Is it true, what Bowater said of you?"

Michael felt as if he were teetering upon a cliff ledge. "Yes. I'm Lieutenant Stoddard. This is my man, Spry. We're from the Eighty-Second Regiment, out of Wilmington."

Philip's lips made a little "o," then spread into a grin for Michael. Oh, the tales the lad would tell his friends.

Miss Sewell's lip jerked. "How do I know that the King's justice will be served? Wealthy men like this pig have bought their way from jail cells and into low-security situations from whence they escape. Bowater has wealthy family in New York."

Time to ease her of her burden. "Miss Sewell, we possess substantive evidence that Mr. Bowater murdered *three* people. That makes him an extremely dangerous criminal—"

"Substantive evidence? I doubt it." Bowater laughed, shrill. "You'll never make any of what you think you have stick to me!"

"Oh, but I will. I have Violet's journal and all her details of how you threatened her life in her final days." Bowater flinched as if a riding crop had whacked his cheek. The fire in Michael's pulse subsided. He smiled. "As I was explaining, Major Craig of the Eighty-Second doesn't hold dangerous criminals in jail to await trial. He transfers them to a prison ship."

Bowater jaw dropped. "No! Not a prison ship! You cannot be serious!" He groaned.

Miss Sewell's face relaxed. "A prison ship, you say? He might not survive to face trial."

Michael nodded once. "Lamentable, but true."

Medusa disappeared, replaced by a mortal woman. "Take him, then, Mr. Stoddard."

Michael motioned Spry to step forward with his rope. Bowater flinched at the rasp on his wrists from behind. Not until the land agent was bound did Miss Sewell lower her pistol. Noah slid his arms around her waist from behind, gently slipped the firearm from her hand, and released the pistol from its cocked position. She sank into his warmth, and her eyes closed with the spasm of a sojourner who has traversed a nightmare.

The soldiers marched Bowater to the wagon, where they ensured his lack of concealed weapons, took his purse, bound his feet, and gagged him. Michael retrieved his own rifle and ammunition, and after Spry accepted Bowater's rifle from Philip, the lad placed the land agent's valise in the wagon. Bowater was hoisted in and covered with canvas, just as Michael and Spry had been transported from Hillsborough almost twenty-four hours earlier. Philip soaked up all the activity with unabashed enthusiasm in his expression.

In the background, Noah and his love had been conversing in their peculiar language of gestures and half-words. Hand-in-hand, the couple approached Michael while Spry was roping Bowater's mare and the wagon behind his gelding. Pale sunrise spread over Janet Sewell's face. Michael watched her shrewd study of the wagon and its contents, and he said, low, "I thank you for your assistance."

Her gaze captured his. "How long will your return to Wilmington take, laden like this?"

They'd head east on the Halifax Road, a longer route back to avoid Hillsborough jailhouse as well as the wheel-miring mud at the Eno River Ford, south of town. "At least ten days."

"Have you all the supplies you need?"

In memory, he catalogued food stored in the wagon and coins he'd counted in Bowater's purse. "I believe so." When she extracted a purse from her own pocket, he held up his hand to refuse. "Our fugitive's purse is adequate to fund our return."

"Noah told me just now about Mr. Tierney's plans to use his artwork." Tears sparkled in her eyes. "You arranged it between them. This money is the least I can do to thank you."

The gratitude of women took many forms. In Janet Sewell's eyes, he read that she'd handed off an eighteen-year-old nightmare to Lieutenant Stoddard of the Eighty-Second Regiment, and he'd opened a future for her and the man she loved. He bowed, accepted her purse, and lodged it in his pocket with Bowater's money. Besides, he'd be a fool to turn down extra money.

From the direction of town center, he detected the rising hum of commotion. Someone had found Fairfax's gift to the community. The others except for Noah tilted faces in that direction. "Ah." Michael clapped his hands together, regained their attention. "It's time for us to move along. Philip, Noah, we thank you for your part in this. We couldn't have done it without you."

The soldiers shook hands with Martha's son and the deaf man before mounting their horses. Spry walked his gelding and the wagon for King Street. Michael rested his rifle across his thighs and saluted the three afoot. "Be quick about returning Mr. Tierney's gig and horse to him. But be slow to judge his whining. His mood will improve in a few days."

"Ah see Tierney. Ah see." Noah patted his chest. "Big. Tierney heart big."

Indeed. The wagon and its travel supplies cost far more than the money Tierney had accepted for them. Michael clicked his tongue for Cleopatra to follow the wagon. Then he waved a farewell from the saddle. "Yes, my friend Noah, you see it *all*."

Chapter Thirty-Five

WHEN BOWATER ATTEMPTED escape the second time on Wednesday, Michael decided to cut the prisoner's food ration in half. That way, if he succeeded in slipping away, debilitation from lack of sustenance would ensure that he didn't travel far before the soldiers tracked him down.

Wednesday night, Spry placed Bowater's meager meal before him and removed his gag. Before he could untie Bowater's hands, the land agent cursed them for starving him. Michael directed his assistant to gag the prisoner and throw him back into the wagon, unfed. Then the two soldiers partook of their own supper plus Bowater's.

Fine with Michael if the prisoner didn't want to cooperate. The open road made soldiers hungrier than ever. Bowater's half-ration wouldn't go to waste on the journey.

The land agent was amazingly compliant by suppertime Thursday night.

The demands of the trip settled the soldiers into a companionable quiet, providing Michael leisure to speculate on Kate's abrupt, amorous interest in him. He'd witnessed similar behavior often enough in the aftermath of battle. Cloaked by night, beneath a wagon or behind a bush, soldiers and camp women who scarcely knew each other defied death with a five-minute entanglement in spontaneity and sweat.

A woman like Kate expected far more than a five-minute futter when she ignited a man's desire. Obviously the shock of having Aaron's death confirmed had rattled her, catapulted her into Michael's arms. Much as he would have enjoyed a lusty adieu from her, the enforced speedy departure from Hillsborough had spared them awkwardness, provided them pause to recover poise and retreat behind the lines of propriety.

You have my solemn promise that you shall receive another chance to kill me.

As if he'd been jabbed between the shoulders with a dagger point, Michael swiveled and scoured the road behind with his stare. Empty. Breath hissed from his tensed lips. He returned his attention forward, eased back in Cleopatra's saddle.

Ensconced in their fortress of propriety, Kate and Aunt Rachel would be safe, beyond reach of Fairfax when he came calling to collect on his debt. Michael's soul ached where a piece of self-respect had been cored from it Tuesday afternoon, in that hovel of dead men. He'd given Fairfax too much already. Let the mutinous mutterings of his own heart be ignored. He refused to hand Fairfax the fuel of a romance.

***

On Saturday afternoon the twenty-fourth of February, southbound on the sandy road that cut through New Hanover County, Michael checked his watch and glanced at the private, who rode abreast of him where the road was wide enough. "Less than an hour out of Wilmington, lad. Which is it you're dreaming about, Enid's cooking, or fair-haired Molly?"

Spry stirred, eyed the canvas-covered, listless mass of Bowater in the wagon, and lowered his voice. "Tell me about the St. James family, sir."

Michael angled back from his assistant. "How did you—?" Then he remembered, and he appraised Spry anew. Even battered by Fairfax and dazed, the private had been paying attention to the conversation. Michael held his voice low, too. "They hail from Alton, Georgia, where I was stationed last summer. The father, a printer, is a rebel. The children are mostly neutral. As Mr. Fairfax sees it, since the father is a rebel, each family member and associate must be treasonous."

"Sir, people change sides in this war quicker than clouds change shape."

"True. And a pistol pressed to the temple leads to quick conversion."

For several seconds, Spry twisted his lips back and forth, all the while squinting at the top of his gelding's head. "We're quartered in the home of Mrs. Chiswell, sir. Enid says she's a loyalist. Mr. Fairfax says she's a rebel. She cannot be both." He cocked an eyebrow at Michael. "Er, can she? What would you call her, then?"

One might call such a person a double spy. Had Mrs. Chiswell split her loyalties in such a way? Fairfax would like a North America filled with double spies. Even better, he'd like a seat in Parliament, conferred upon him after he'd revealed a North America filled with double spies.

Michael's incidental meeting with Mrs. Chiswell at the Legion camp hadn't allowed him enough exposure to her to form an impression of her loyalties. However, he could guess what form of pistol Fairfax might press to any woman's temple. And what of the man whom Fairfax had mentioned, Jonathan Quill? Too many unanswered questions. Prudence dictated that this was a situation best monitored from beneath Mrs. Chiswell's roof.

He patted his belly once and quirked his eyebrows at his assistant. "You know, I rather enjoy Enid's cooking."

"Oh, me, too, sir." A grin never failed to emerge from Spry at the mention of good food.

"And I prefer to keep enjoying it. Mrs. Chiswell is due back from South Carolina any day. You and I mustn't disrupt her routine. It would wreak havoc on trust. She must be allowed to go about her business, whatever her business may be, with two trusting, well-fed, complacent redcoats quartered at her house."

The grin ebbed from around his assistant's eyes but remained on his mouth. He knew his commander's opinion on the merits of slow, steady surveillance. "Yes, sir."

$$* * *$$

Just after four o'clock that afternoon, Spry and two soldiers from the Eighty-Second Regiment escorted the shambling, shackled land agent to one of two crowded cells in Wilmington jail. In the jailer's office, Michael signed admissions and transfer documents, then paid camp boys to deliver news of their arrival to both Major Craig and Enid.

He doubted that capturing a rebel spy but not delivering Craig's message directly to Lord Cornwallis would earn him another glass of his senior officer's excellent brandy. Michael guessed that his account of Bowater's capture would earn him but passing interest from his benefactors: his blacksmith uncle Solomon Stoddard, Lord Crump, and Major Hunt, the commander beneath whose nose Fairfax had sneaked his sport of the Spaniard last summer. But Michael was certain where he could find an excellent supper, clean water for bathing, and at least seven hours' undisturbed slumber in a warm, comfortable bed.

He and Spry retrieved personal gear and surrendered the wagon with supplies and all three horses to the garrison. Just outside the barracks, a private running communications caught up with them long enough to relay the message that Major Craig expected Michael and his written account of the Hillsborough affair in his office the next day at noon, after the regiment's vicar delivered the Sunday sermon. Exhausted, Michael and his assistant trudged for Second Street.

After a minute, his voice soft, Spry said, "You *did* intend to kill him in December, when you ran those dispatches to the Legion."

Michael gazed down the block, where a dog chased three boys running hoops, and gossiping goodwives stepped from the street to allow the passage of a horse team and wagon. The full measure of his foolishness flooded him. Ordinary mortals didn't slay dragons unassisted. That had been his mistake in December. While he'd never expected gods to descend from Olympus and grant him a magic sword or winged sandals, he wondered what he *had* anticipated. Had he expected to fail?

I shall give you more sport than you could ever imagine as you try to kill me, you pustule.

Michael's stomach knotted. His attention darted over shadows between houses, but he resisted looking over his shoulder. When the cup passed to him again, he must be better prepared for the poison. He steadied his breathing, felt the knot in his gut loosen, and offered his assistant the mute, solid gaze of a man who hadn't given up his intention.

Spry massaged his own jaw a couple seconds, as if to remind himself of bruises that had faded. His shoulders straightened, and he walked taller. "You'd have died for me back there off the Road from the Haw Field, sir. No need to go it alone next time. Call on me to watch your back."

Michael drew an unguarded breath for the first time in almost two weeks. Warmth thawed the ice-rimmed hole in his soul. An ally couldn't be bought. An ally was a gift from the gods.

Spry didn't expect a torrent of gratitude from him. Michael responded with a brief nod.

They turned the corner onto Second Street. The private's nostrils quivered into the breeze, and he smacked his lips. "I smell Enid's beef roast, sir."

Michael's sniff sorted through the usual municipal blend of slops, rotting vegetables, Atlantic Ocean, and sandy dirt with a baked pastry or two struggling to compete. "Keep dreaming. She hasn't had time to cook for us since we arrived. Maybe on the morrow."

A shawl-wrapped, grin-laden Enid bustled toward them from the side yard of Mrs. Chiswell's house half a block ahead. "There you two are! Been waiting for you. So good to see you." She reached them and bobbed a curtsy, her cheeks flushed in the fading light. "Welcome back to Wilmington!"

She reached for their packs, and Spry handed them to her. "You're in time for supper. I've hot water at the ready." Her nose wrinkled. "You both picked up good bit of grime from the road. Better wash up out back before you eat." She pivoted with their gear and made brisk tracks for the house. "Turnips and rice, and I found a lovely beef roast at Market yesterday."

Spry gasped like a pirate who'd just been handed a treasure map and paced her in three strides. Michael caught up with them seconds later, as they entered the side yard. He said, "You read a man's mind so well, Enid."

"Hah! Is it so hard to figure what men want after weeks on the trail? Got your uniforms brushed out, too. Before I forget, Mrs. Farrell the tobacconist's wife said to tell you that the Wilmington ladies would reschedule the party, coordinate the affair more closely with Major Craig's office to make certain that the guest of honor and his lady weren't out of town." Her .72 caliber gossip smirk took aim on him. "Would the lady be the Widow Duncan, sir?"

Michael never blinked. Best to snatch the wind from that rumor's sails before it ever left port. "Your guess is as good as mine. By the bye, how did you manage to prepare such a sumptuous supper for us, heat bath water, *and* brush out our uniforms with less than an hour's notice?"

She never blinked, either. "Wee folk, sir. I packed them in my valise when I left Aberystwyth." Head high, she marched before them to the house.

***

Standing in his office before a window the next day, Craig perused Michael's report, daylight drenching the page. The major's gaze whipped across each line of script like a goodwife's broom on a dirty floor. At the end of the account, Craig's lips smashed together, and a ripple surged over his cheek muscles, suggestive of a clamped jaw.

Michael, ordered to stand at ease before the table, found he'd automatically resumed the rigid posture of attention.

Without looking at his junior officer, Craig strode two steps to his table and cast the paper among the clutter of missives and maps congesting the surface. His hand hesitated on the neck of the brandy decanter, then diverted to the tea service. He poured himself a cup of steaming tea, delivered five minutes earlier by the adjutant.

His back to Michael, he contemplated Wilmington beyond the window. A minute or so of tea sipping passed. Craig cleared his throat. "Spry is to be commended for the astute and professional manner in which he conducted himself during this business."

Michael worked his tongue over a parchment-dry mouth. "Sir."

"Mr. Stoddard, why did you bring Horatio Bowater back to Wilmington?"

"Sir. As I noted in my report—"

"I read your bloody report. Detached. Emotionless. Every piece of the affair accounted for neatly. The sort of thoroughness that delights a senior officer." Craig pivoted to face him without sloshing a drop of tea into the saucer. "After you returned yesterday, did you tally how many *more* prisoners to whom we're delivering meals in jail and in the pen?"

Michael's throat shrank. He opened his mouth. No sound came out.

"Surely by now, the Eighty-Second is feeding every stinking rebel and cutpurse in coastal North Carolina." Craig transferred his teacup and saucer to one hand. His free hand made a single, flinging motion over his shoulder, toward jail. "I've little room for more prisoners, no extra food to feed them. I didn't order Spry to bring Mr. Bowater back to Wilmington. I ordered him to ensure that Mr. Bowater didn't interfere with your mission, assist you in its completion. So you tell me. Why *did* you bring Mr. Bowater back?"

Beads of sweat stormed the skin on Michael's brow and froze. He forced through the blockade in his throat, his words blurted. "Sir, are we not to provide the King's justice?"

"The *King's* justice, or *your* justice?" The major stabbed his forefinger toward the floor. "You and I conversed here, in this office, on the sixth of February. You were obsessed with capturing Mr. Bowater yourself, distressed when I removed you from the investigation." Craig waved in a vague, northwest direction. "In Hillsborough, you performed the very act I told you not to do. Explain yourself."

"In Hillsborough, sir—" Michael paused, short of breath, as if a giant fist punched his ribs. More words spewed out. "The Griggs, Sewell, and White families, they had no justice!"

"Why did you not turn Mr. Bowater over to Mr. Schmidt's deputies for justice?"

Michael shook his head. "They'd have let him go. Or their incompetence would have allowed him to escape." He saw Craig's eyebrows batting the bridge of his nose. The obstruction in his throat burned away in a surge of fury. "Sir, two ladies in the White family and Miss Sewell knew the Committee of Safety and deputies wouldn't deliver justice! These women pleaded for the King's justice. Mr. Griggs was unable to request it, as were the families affected in New York years ago, before Bowater was packed off to North Carolina."

Craig set down the teacup and rested his fingertips on the tabletop. His stare became twin nails of iron that pounded into Michael's head. He said softly, "Surely some of the time you were in Hillsborough, your thoughts lingered on capturing the land agent, rather than seeing that dispatch to Lord Cornwallis. Is it not so?"

Michael imagined his return stare just as metallic. Did Craig question his loyalty?

No. His commander demanded that he justify the value of his actions.

A cord of tension stitched his lips together before he released them. "Sir, you'd ordered me on a specific mission. When I first arrived in Hillsborough, my life depended upon devoting all my concentration on that mission. I could spare no time to think of Mr. Bowater.

"But toward the end, I realized I also had a moral obligation to prevent Mr. Tierney from being falsely accused of murder, and to be the medium of justice for the White, Sewell, and Griggs families. Mr. Bowater had to be apprehended. Thus there was more to my assignment than the mission on which you'd originally sent me."

The major glanced at the report. "A mission that some commanders would determine you personally failed to complete. Hmm, Seventeenth Light Dragoons rescuing you and Spry from the rebels." Craig jutted his chin and skidded his gaze down his nose at Michael. "Had you made the acquaintance of this Lieutenant Dunstan Fairfax before the incident?"

The question tripped Michael's concentration. His jaw bounced.

"Ah hah! Where? When?" Craig scowled and leaned toward Michael.

"Alton, Georgia, last summer, sir."

The scowl transcended to a frown. "That business with St. James and the Spaniards, eh?"

"Sir." However did the major remember so much detail from reports he'd read?

"Well, then." Craig straightened, allowed one hand to rest upon his hip. "Thank you for clarifying your judgment in that matter, why you trusted Mr. Fairfax to deliver my message to Lord Cornwallis. I'd been meaning to write your former commander in Alton and inquire after his health anyway. I suppose there's no harm in my asking his impression of Mr. Fairfax, is there?"

Damn. "No, sir." He knew his previous commander was still covering his arse with subterfuge, depicting the devil in a less-than-evil light. Subterfuge snapped closed in Michael's larynx, and pain lanced his throat. With this report to Craig, he was now covering his own arse over Fairfax. He'd leapt in bed with those he disdained, men who kept mute about the monster in their midst.

And it had been the monster, of all those in Hillsborough, who had driven home hardest the point of Michael's moral obligation. Michael hoped to God that Fairfax had delivered Craig's message to Cornwallis. Another chunk of self-respect hollowed from his soul.

Craig retrieved his teacup, half-turned for the window, and presented a profile of chiseled marble. "Very well. I hereby consider the matter closed." His curt nod conveyed the grudging of a hungry man who had no choice but to gnash his way through stale bread. "That will be all, Mr. Stoddard."

Finis

Historical Afterword

HISTORY TEXTS AND fiction minimize the importance of the Southern colonies during the American War of Independence. Many scholars now believe that more Revolutionary War battles were fought in South Carolina than in any other colony, even New York. Of the wars North Americans have fought, the death toll from this war exceeds all except the Civil War in terms of percentage of the population. And yet our "revolution" was but one conflict in a ravenous world war.

By the spring of 1771, farmers and small landowners throughout the North Carolina Piedmont had had their fill of crooked tax collectors and land agents. Hostilities in the Regulator Rebellion climaxed with the Battle of Alamance in May 1771. Royal Governor Tryon and his militia quickly put down the insurrection and spent the next few weeks rounding up leaders of the rebellion. Tryon, scheduled to become the governor of New York, was eager to wrap up the conflict in North Carolina. Fourteen Regulator leaders were hastily tried. Two were acquitted. The other twelve were condemned to hang the next day. At the last moment, Tryon pardoned six of the condemned men to demonstrate the mercy of the Crown. The other six were executed. The location of their burial remains unknown, which I've used to my advantage in this story.

From late January to mid-November 1781, Crown forces occupied the city of Wilmington, North Carolina. The daunting presence of the Eighty-Second Regiment nearly paralyzed movements of the Continental Army in North Carolina and prolonged the war in the Southern theater. Short on resources the entire occupation, Major James Henry Craig, the regiment's commander, resorted to unconventional strategies that bordered on insubordination, won the devotion of area loyalists and many neutrals (a feat Lord Cornwallis was never able to achieve), and enhanced his garrison's effectiveness.

Almost never do we hear of Craig's accomplishments. True, history is written by the victors. But also, the Eighty-Second's triumphs were bracketed and overshadowed by disasters that same year for Crown forces at Cowpens, South Carolina in January and Yorktown, Virginia in October. Had more British commanders adopted Craig's creative, fluid style of thinking, the outcome of the war might have been vastly different.

In early 1781, the army of General Charles Lord Cornwallis chased General Nathanael Greene's army across North Carolina into Virginia without catching the Continentals. Cornwallis returned to North Carolina and occupied Hillsborough 19 February. The British general had expected loyalists to flock to the Crown's banner. Instead, he found the residents of Hillsborough apathetic, uninterested. He and his army departed town less than a week later.

In Wilmington, Major Craig had been ordered to strategize fortification of a supply depot in Cross Creek (now Fayetteville, North Carolina), to assist Lord Cornwallis's military initiatives in the backcountry. Early on, Craig realized the vulnerability of a supply train to Cross Creek, and thus the unsuitability of using the location as originally planned. Fearing that Cornwallis would enact a strategy that depended on replenishing his army's supplies in Cross Creek, Craig sent three messengers to the general to warn him about lack of supplies in Cross Creek. None of the messages reached Cornwallis. Suffering severe losses amidst his "victory" at the Battle of Guilford Courthouse 15 March 1781, Cornwallis's army limped on to Cross Creek, expecting supplies. Instead, the army was forced to march several days more to the only safe haven in North Carolina, Wilmington, and Major Craig.

Due to wartime instability, records haven't survived to tell us who was Sheriff of Orange County, North Carolina in February 1781. According to Dr. Carole W. Troxler, the sheriff in 1780 was named John Hawkins. In 1782, the sheriff was a different man. Thus I have again taken advantage of a historical unknown for the purpose of crafting entertainment.

Dramatis Personae

In order of appearance:

Michael Stoddard—officer of the King stationed in Wilmington, North Carolina. Lead criminal investigator for the Eighty-Second Regiment

Henshaw—King's man

Ferguson—King's man

James Henry Craig—officer of the King, commander of the Eighty-Second Regiment

Nick Spry—King's man, assistant investigator to Michael Stoddard

Kevin Marsh—manager of White's Tavern

Enid Jones—housekeeper for Helen Chiswell

Ezra Griggs—loyalist courier in Hillsborough, North Carolina

Georg Schmidt—sheriff in Hillsborough

O'Toole—deputy in Hillsborough

Henry—deputy in Hillsborough

Kate Duncan (neé Marsh)—owner of White's Tavern

Rachel White (aka Aunt Rachel)—widowed aunt of Kate Duncan and Kevin Marsh, mother of Aaron White

Martha—Rachel White's housekeeper

Philip—son of Martha

Blake Carroll—Ezra Griggs's neighbor

Noah Carroll—nephew of Blake Carroll, beau of Janet Sewell

Matthew Tierney—naturalist, dandy, and drunkard

Janet Sewell—sweetheart of Noah Carroll, best friend of Ezra Griggs's daughter, Violet Griggs

Gurney—a logger

Froggy—a logger

Dismal—a logger

Fanny—blonde friend of Matthew Tierney

Dunstan Fairfax—officer of the King, dragoon of the Seventeenth Light

Horatio Bowater—patriot land agent, business based in Wilmington

Selected Bibliography

Dozens of websites, interviews with subject-matter experts, the following books and more:

Balderston, Marion and David Syrett, eds. *The Lost War: Letters from British Officers During the American Revolution*. New York: Horizon Press, 1975.

Barefoot, Daniel W. *Touring South Carolina's Revolutionary War Sites*. Winston-Salem, North Carolina: John F. Blair Publisher, 1999.

Bass, Robert D. *The Green Dragoon*. Columbia, South Carolina: Sandlapper Press, Inc., 1973.

Boatner, Mark M. III. *Encyclopedia of the American Revolution*. Mechanicsburg, Pennsylvania: Stackpole Books, 1994.

Butler, Lindley S. *North Carolina and the Coming of the Revolution, 1763–1776*. Zebulon, North Carolina: Theo. Davis Sons, Inc., 1976.

Butler, Lindley S. and Alan D. Watson, eds. *The North Carolina Experience*. Chapel Hill, North Carolina: The University of North Carolina Press, 1984.

Gilgun, Beth. *Tidings from the Eighteenth Century*. Texarkana, Texas: Scurlock Publishing Co., Inc., 1993.

Hagist, Don N., ed. *A British Soldier's Story: Roger Lamb's Narrative of the American Revolution*. Baraboo, Wisconsin: Ballindalloch Press, 2004.

Kars, Marjoleine. *Breaking Loose Together: The Regulator Rebellion in Pre-Revolutionary North Carolina*. Chapel Hill, North Carolina: The University of North Carolina Press, 2002.

Lee, Wayne E. *Crowds and Soldiers in Revolutionary North Carolina: The Culture of Violence in Riot and War*. Gainesville, Florida: University Press of Florida, 2001.

Massey, Gregory De Van. "The British Expedition to Wilmington, North Carolina, January–November 1781." Master's thesis, East Carolina University, 1987.

Mayer, Holly A. *Belonging to the Army: Camp Followers and Community During the American Revolution*. Columbia, South Carolina: University of South Carolina Press, 1996.

Morrill, Dan L. *Southern Campaigns of the American Revolution*. Mount Pleasant, South Carolina: The Nautical & Aviation Publishing Company of America, Inc., 1993.

Peckham, Howard H. *The Toll of Independence: Engagements and Battle Casualties of the American Revolution*. Chicago: The University of Chicago Press, 1974.

Scotti, Anthony J. *Brutal Virtue: The Myth and Reality of Banastre Tarleton*. Bowie, Maryland: Heritage Books, Inc., 2002.

Schaw, Janet. *Journal of a Lady of Quality: Being the Narrative of a Journey from Scotland to the West Indies, North Carolina, and Portugal in the Years 1774 to 1776*. eds. Evangeline W. Andrews and Charles M. Andrews. New Haven: Yale University Press, 1921.

Tunis, Edwin. *Colonial Craftsmen and the Beginnings of American Industry*. Baltimore: The Johns Hopkins University Press, 1999.

Watson, Alan D. *Society in Colonial North Carolina*. Raleigh, North Carolina: North Carolina Division of Archives and History, 1996.

Watson, Alan D. *Wilmington, North Carolina, to 1861*. Jefferson, North Carolina: McFarland & Company, Inc., Publishers, 2003.

Watson, Alan D. *Wilmington: Port of North Carolina*. Columbia, South Carolina: University of South Carolina Press, 1992.

Discussion Questions for Book Clubs

1. What does author Suzanne Adair do to project an image of the Southern theater of the American Revolution in *Regulated for Murder*?

2. What did you learn about Revolutionary-era life that you didn't know before you read the novel?

3. What role does the historical setting play in *Regulated for Murder*? How does Suzanne Adair evoke a sense of place? What role does nature play?

4. In a thriller, the characters should be put in danger. What makes you worry about the fate of characters in *Regulated for Murder*?

5. For you, what is the most memorable scene in *Regulated for Murder*? Who is the most interesting character in the book? Why?

6. What is your reaction to the inclusion of real historical figures (book example: Major James Henry Craig) as characters in a work of fiction?

7. How would the use of modern forensics have changed the plot and outcome of *Regulated for Murder*?

8. Michael Stoddard leaves Wilmington to accomplish something. Is he successful in achieving it?

9. What do you think would have been Noah Carroll's personal and professional fate had Michael not informed townsfolk of the young man's talent? Why?

10. How successful do you think handicapped people in historical times were at living full lives? What influenced the degree of success?

11. How does Michael differ from your ideas of what redcoats were like during the Revolution? In what ways does having a redcoat as a hero challenge

your beliefs or teachings? Why do you feel that way?

12. In Revolutionary War America, do you think someone could heal emotionally from the kind of experience Janet Sewell and Violet Griggs had as children? Explain.

13. What was your reaction to the "deal" struck between Michael and Lieutenant Fairfax? If you'd been Michael, how would you have responded to Fairfax's terms? Why?

14. Is justice served at the end of the story? Explain.

15. What do you think happens to the characters after the story ends?

Follow Michael Stoddard's journey as an investigator
in Book 3 of his exciting series

A Hostage

to

Heritage

A Michael Stoddard
American Revolution Mystery

by Suzanne Adair

**A boy kidnapped for ransom. And a madman who didn't
bargain on Michael Stoddard's tenacity.**

Spring 1781. The American Revolution enters its seventh grueling
year. In Wilmington, North Carolina, redcoat investigator
Lieutenant Michael Stoddard expects to round up two miscreants
before Lord Cornwallis's army arrives for supplies. But his quarries'
trail crosses with that of a criminal who has abducted a high-
profile English heir. Michael's efforts to track down the boy plunge
him into a twilight of terror from radical insurrectionists, whiskey
smugglers, and snarled secrets out of his own past in Yorkshire.

A Hostage to Heritage, winner of the Indie Book of the Day Award

Please turn the page to read the first chapter.

Few men have virtue to withstand the highest bidder.
~ George Washington

Chapter One

BY THE TIME the road to Cabbage Inlet had straightened out to a sand-and-shell ribbon south of Wilmington, patriot "Devil Bill" Jones and his accomplice, Captain James Love, had widened their lead over the five mounted men from the Eighty-Second Regiment. Lieutenant Michael Stoddard cantered his mare around the final crook in the road, spotted his quarry picking up speed one-eighth mile ahead, and twisted in the saddle. "We have 'em, lads!"

A brisk March breeze briny with Atlantic Ocean whipped the words from his mouth. He waved his patrol of four redcoats onward and kicked Cleopatra into a gallop, two loaded pistols in the saddle holster before him.

Cleopatra gained on the rebels' horses while the thunder of support behind Michael diminished. Low on the mare's neck, his breath paced to hers, he saw Love swivel in the saddle for a look behind. The rebel's gaze snagged on him, and his eyes bugged. In the whistle of wind, Michael heard his shout of warning to Jones. The fugitives' horses put on a burst of speed.

Michael steered Cleopatra around a perilous section of loose sand on the road. Somewhere behind, he heard a soldier curse as his mount stumbled in the sand, what Love and his cohorts called "sand shuffling." Michael grimaced but maintained his mare's gallop. For several weeks, Jones and Love had made it their sport to ride pell-mell through the streets of Wilmington and discharge their carbines at soldiers and sentries of the Eighty-Second Regiment—even at civilians who got in their way. Michael closed the distance between himself and the outlaws.

Pistol in hand, Jones contorted in his saddle to fire toward Michael. The ball went wide, into salt marsh studded with longleaf pines, but Cleopatra flinched at the noise. Michael steadied her and pressed her to keep galloping, despite the fact that he no longer heard the thunder of his team's support.

On their raids through town, Jones and Love had moved so quickly that no one had been able to pursue them. This time, Michael and his four men had been returning from a trip when Jones and Love paid their respects. The regiment might never have another opportunity to chase the rascals on horseback, so Michael stayed on the criminals, less than fifty feet ahead. He could taste their apprehension, flung back to him on the salty afternoon air.

When he was but thirty feet behind his quarry, their horses jumped a small patch of treacherous sand. Cleopatra followed suit. Jones squirmed around for a second pistol shot. Michael heard the ball whine through air near his right ear and thwack off the trunk of a pine tree. Cleopatra's stride faltered. Michael put his heel to her to encourage her forward, cocked one of his pistols, sighted, and, despite the odds, squeezed the trigger.

Jones cried out and clutched his upper right arm, fouling the rhythm of his gallop. His horse startled, almost stumbled. At a command from Love, the men veered off south into a sea of wind-beaten marsh grass, where a man could lose his life and that of his mount in a moment to the suck of sand. Michael galloped past their departure point by more than sixty feet. When he'd brought the heaving Cleopatra about, the criminals had split up. Jones was riding due south, and Love was headed southeast, both on terrain they knew as well as their own palms.

God damn it. Although the rebels were probably out of range, Michael snatched the other pistol from its holster, took aim, and fired at Love. Both rebels rode on. Michael seized his breath and bellowed into the pistol's report, "Whoresons!" He jammed the pistol, stinking of sulfur, back in the holster. Then he yanked off his hat, raked a sweaty sprawl of dark hair off his brow, and shoved the hat back on his head.

While he paced Cleopatra back and forth on the road and glowered after the escaped rebels, one of his soldiers trotted into view, he and his horse winded. A quarter minute later, another private caught up with them and shook his head at the fugitives, mere specks amidst pines and wavy marsh grass. "Sorry, sir. They were just too fast for us. And their horses know how to run in the sand."

The other man said, "Jackson's and Stallings's mounts went down back there, sir. I sure hope we don't have to shoot the beasts."

The Eighty-Second had few horses. Another grimace pulled at Michael's face before he composed his expression. "I gave Mr. Jones a kiss of the pistol ball. Maybe those scoundrels will think twice about resuming their sport in Wilmington."

Tension eased from the privates' faces. "Yes, sir," they said in unison.

"We've done what we can this afternoon, lads. Let's see to those horses." After a final glare southward, Michael patted Cleopatra's neck and headed her toward town, his shoulders straight to project confidence he didn't feel.

Two escaped rebels. Two injured horses. Major James Henry Craig wasn't going to like the news his lead investigator brought back to Wilmington.

***

Twenty minutes later a sentry bumped out on a broad-backed workhorse in search of Michael. Major Craig had demanded Lieutenant Stoddard's presence at his headquarters. Immediately.

Leaving the two mounted infantrymen and two unhorsed soldiers walking their lamed geldings, Michael trotted on ahead, the sentry clomping along after. He didn't push Cleopatra after her run, allowing her instead to enjoy one of the most temperate spring afternoons North Carolina offered. From the sound of it, ill humor had already found his commanding officer over the business of Jones and Love, so he saw no point in hastening to the inevitable ear blistering.

He dismounted before the house on Market Street where Major Craig's headquarters was located, secured Cleopatra at the post, and checked a watch drawn from his waistcoat pocket. Ten minutes to four. Craig had said, "Immediately." Michael replaced the watch, straightened his scarlet coat, and swatted road dust from sleeves and breeches. Not much he could do about three days' stubble on his face that moment.

Twelve men, two runner boys, and a gossipy goodwife named Alice Farrell had queued up the walkway and front steps, waiting their turn to speak with the Eighty-Second's commander. As Michael strode for the steps, they spotted him. Jabber silenced. Most expressions adopted the guise of a neutral mask. The crowd of supplicants parted for Michael as if he were Moses at the shore of the Red Sea. At the top of the steps, the provost marshal's guard shoved the door open with a squeak of hinges.

Had Major Craig somehow already received word about the escape of Jones and Love and the incapacitation of the horses? Michael's parched tongue skidded over his lips. Grit crunched beneath the soles of his riding boots during his trudge up the steps to the porch. He wiped his boot soles at the threshold.

The guard jerked his head toward the dark maw of the house interior. "Private Spry arrived just before you did, sir."

Michael frowned at the guard, then at the inside of the house. Why had his assistant investigator also been summoned? This didn't bode well. Muscles in his stomach twisted.

After removing his hat, he entered the house and eased out a pent-up breath. One of the study's double wooden doors was open. Inside, his commander stood at the north window, one hand on his hip, gazing out toward a pen packed with rebel prisoners. At a small table near where Craig usually sat, his adjutant scratched out a letter to the major's dictation, the quill-to-ink motion a blur.

Creaky floorboards announced Michael's entrance. His tall eighteen-year-old assistant from Nova Scotia, Nick Spry, stood at ease, away from the doors. Spry nodded once to Michael before resuming his attention on Craig. Michael stepped one pace toward him and held a salute for Major Craig, hat in his left hand.

Mid-sentence, Craig glanced over his shoulder. He squashed his lips together at the sight of Michael. Then the short, stocky commander of the Eighty-Second snatched the top paper off a pile on the table and, while traversing the study to Michael, completed his sentence about a desperate need for bandages. Michael's salute acknowledged, Craig thrust the paper at him, and motioned Spry to join Michael. Then he resumed his stance at the window.

His next sentence of dictation was a request for willow bark and other medicines to reduce fever and inflammation in hundreds of wounded soldiers. Paper in hand, Michael blinked at his commander in puzzlement. From the context, he presumed the recipient of Craig's dictated letter to be Lieutenant Colonel Nisbet Balfour, in Charles Town. Balfour had been generous with such supplies before. But the season for malaria and yellow fever wasn't yet upon them. When he'd left Wilmington three days earlier, only two men were lodged in the infirmary. How did two multiply to hundreds?

Aware of Spry at his elbow, he righted the paper. It was a letter dated exactly one month earlier, 21 February 1781, from the town of Hillsborough, North Carolina. The salutation was to Major Craig. The correspondent was Lord Cornwallis. And despite the clement temperature of the room, a glacier slid down Michael's spine to his feet and froze them to his stockings inside his boots.

In the letter, the Commander in Chief of the Crown's Southern army urgently requested provisions that Major Craig had agreed to provide in January and send on to Cross Creek, eighty miles to the northwest of Wilmington. Cornwallis was still following a plan from January, still dependent on having stores available in Cross Creek for his army. But Cornwallis would never get those supplies.

Rebel interference had prevented Major Craig from establishing the requisite supply depot in Cross Creek. Thus he'd sent Michael to the Hillsborough area as a dispatch runner to find Cornwallis and tell him so. And in the life-threatening peril that had ensued for Michael in Hillsborough, he'd been unable to deliver Craig's warning directly to Cornwallis.

That was, he hadn't delivered it *personally*. He'd transferred the message.

The glacier vaporized. Michael crushed the letter in his fist.

Fairfax, that son of a dog! He'd shirked his duty. He hadn't delivered the message!

If it was the last thing that Michael did, he determined to find the dragoon and kill him. Oh, he'd already tried to kill that monster, but he hadn't planned it well. *Next* time—

"Mr. Stoddard, I received Lord Cornwallis's letter in this afternoon's post."

Michael jerked his attention back to Major Craig. Shock rolled over him. He'd been so absorbed in the letter's implications that he hadn't noticed the exit of Craig's adjutant. He, Spry, and Craig were alone, the study doors shut.

"And I find it as disturbing as you do, judging from your expression." Craig sat behind his table and gestured Michael to a chair opposite him. "Sit. We've much to discuss and, as usual, little time."

Michael rolled his shoulders back, smoothed out the letter, and passed it to Spry. As he seated himself, the major shifted his torso to present a profile like that of a Roman senator. With one hand, Craig massaged his jaw, as if he'd been dealt a blow. Then he clasped both hands in his lap. "The letter is a duplicate. Communications have been intercepted prolifically. I presume that his lordship never received the message you relayed in Hillsborough through Lieutenant Fairfax."

Damn Fairfax to hell. Michael unclenched his jaw but kept his voice even. "Reasonable presumption, sir." Instinct had warned him that Fairfax might be arrogant and self-serving enough to not bother with delivering the warning to Cornwallis. Even Spry had expressed doubts that Fairfax would convey the message. But at the time Michael had had no choice but to trust the other officer.

Failure scoured the inside of his gut, gripped the muscles of his abdomen. When he tried to settle against the chair's ladder-back, each vertebra of his spine scraped wood. He should have employed greater effort to make contact with Cornwallis last month.

Craig glanced his way. "Relax, Mr. Stoddard. Several senior officers have assured me of Mr. Fairfax's competence, courage, and dedication. Considering the intensity of combat action endured by the Seventeenth Light Dragoons, I must conclude that Mr. Fairfax was killed in action before he could deliver your message."

Michael started. Behind him, a soft sort of cough-choke sound issued from Spry.

Killed in action? Why, Michael had never considered that. Fairfax had emerged unscathed from so many battles and skirmishes that the cynic in Michael presumed him immortal.

Killed in action. Realizing that his jaw had dropped open, Michael shut his mouth. Knots in his stomach loosened. Surely this was too good to be true. He struggled to keep hope from his face. His cheek twitched with restraint.

Craig processed his expression before resuming his contemplation of the west wall of the study. "You were acquainted with him personally. My condolences."

Michael bowed his head and said what Craig expected to hear. "Thank you, sir."

Killed in action. A shudder of liberation wended through him. The Fates had smiled upon him. And upon Spry, too. His assistant must be squirming to contain his elation. The monster was dead.

But perhaps he'd jumped to conclusions. Craig did have more to tell him. Michael looked up.

The major pushed out a sigh. "Unless I hear otherwise, I shall operate on the assumption that Lord Cornwallis has no knowledge of the infeasibility of Cross Creek as a depot. Should he retreat there for provisions, he will find none. Thus the only refuge he currently has in North Carolina is here, in Wilmington. We must be prepared to accommodate his army for such a turn of events."

"Sir." Michael found his voice at last. And he understood the entreaty to Charles Town for medical supplies.

Craig must want him to courier that letter directly to Balfour. He detested running dispatches, one of the most dangerous jobs in the army. But this would be his penance for failing the mission in Hillsborough. He sat forward and awaited the order.

"The nautical supply line to Charles Town won't adequately provision his lordship's army, should he march here. Therefore, on the morrow, I shall head north with fifty men to supervise the drive of a herd of cattle to Wilmington. I expect to be gone no longer than three weeks."

Michael wiggled a finger in one ear, certain he'd misunderstood. "Cattle, sir?"

Craig assumed his original position facing his subordinate, the corners of his mouth pinched. He steepled fingers on the table and lowered his voice. "Cattle. *And* at least one rebel leader. Word has reached me of where I might find Cornelius Harnett."

"Ah." Muscles in Michael's shoulders relaxed. Harnett had been an aggravation to the Crown as chairman of Wilmington's Sons of Liberty and a member of the Continental Congress. Should circumstances require that Lord Cornwallis retreat to Wilmington, Harnett as Craig's prisoner would mitigate the testiness of his lordship.

"I shall take Captain Gordon and his dragoons with me." The major pressed the palms of his hands on the table. "I heard that you and your patrol gave chase to Captain James Love and William Jones an hour ago." He leaned forward. "How did you fare?"

Thank the gods Craig didn't appear to have heard about the lamed horses. Nine years in the Army had taught Michael to emphasize victories first, no matter how small. "I shot Jones in the right arm."

The major's head drew back, and a smile twisted his lips. "Did you, now? Good show, Mr. Stoddard. Where is Jones? In the pen?"

"No, sir. He and Love escaped into the marsh south of the Cabbage Inlet Road."

Craig's smile dissolved, and he slapped the surface of the table with his palm. "Blast!" He pushed back in his chair. "Jones and Love are a menace to the community, galloping through town, shooting at people. They planned to assassinate me several evenings ago, when I rode out with dragoons.

"Therefore, while I'm gone, Mr. Stoddard, I expect you and Spry to rid Wilmington of the pestilence of 'Devil Bill' Jones and Captain Love. Surely you comprehend how eager I am to see this matter resolved satisfactorily." Craig's gaze upon Michael sharpened like a hot spear of sunlight through a hand lens. His voice lowered. "Are my intentions clear?"

The commander of the Eighty-Second hadn't mentioned the overcrowded jail or pen for the two rebels, or even the belly of a prison ship. He'd used the word "rid." To Craig, Jones and Love were barely worth a noose or a musket ball. He wanted them exterminated like the varmints they were. Spring cleaning, in preparation for Cornwallis's visit.

Michael tracked a momentary drumming, a whisper almost, of Craig's fingertips among papers. What turmoil Jones and Love could inflict upon a Wilmington four times as crowded, its population bloated by Cornwallis's army. Craig wouldn't tolerate Michael's failure to neutralize the rebels. "I understand, sir."

Major Craig drew a breath. "Very good. I'm placing the resources of the Eighty-Second at your disposal for this task. Questions?"

Michael was fully aware that not only did Craig expect him to exterminate Jones and Love, but he also expected a halcyon Wilmington upon his return. All burglars, thieves, drunkards, murderers, and malefactors tidily contained in the pen. Michael's military career was indeed on the line with this assignment. Spry's, too. "None, sir."

"Excellent. You and Spry are dismissed."

***

On the front porch, out of the way of Major Craig's visitors and the marshal's guard, Michael checked his watch again. Only a quarter hour had elapsed since his arrival. He squinted in the westering sunlight. After his assistant had taken up a position beside him, he said softly, "So, Spry, what do you think of Major Craig's opinion that our good friend was killed in action?"

In his peripheral vision, he marked the way Spry drew himself to his full six-foot height, the motion swift and taut, his blond hair a splash of sunlight. Michael's gaze swept across the front yard and out into the street. Five weeks had passed since they'd escaped becoming Fairfax's sport, but neither he nor Spry had completely dropped his guard. A man's bones never forgot a monster's promise.

Spry's tone emerged low, even. "Shakespeare has words for every occasion, sir. For example, "Tis a consummation devoutly to be wished.' That's from Hamlet's soliloquy."

Michael eyed his assistant and restrained black humor from informing his lips. In five weeks, Spry had learned about tactful communication without overt insubordination. "Act three, scene one."

Spry's gaze met his. "A bit of official confirmation would surely be balm for the soul, sir."

"Agreed, but don't hold your breath for it. Remember, this is the Army." Michael swept his hand outward, to encompass Wilmington. "And we've two cockroaches to corral and squash. Let's have at it."

End of Chapter One

Thank you for purchasing this book. Word-of-mouth is crucial to the success of any author. If you enjoyed the book, please post a review wherever your social media allow (Amazon, Goodreads, etc.). Even a brief review is appreciated.

Made in the USA
Coppell, TX
11 July 2021